Women
of the
Century

Thirty Modern Short Stories

WOMEN

of the

CENTURY

Thirty Modern Short Stories

EDITED BY

Regina Barreca

University of Connecticut

St. Martin's Press   New York

This book is dedicated to my friends, who have listened eagerly—or at least patiently—to my stories, and who have told dazzling stories of their own. With thanks especially to Bonnie, Nancy, Pam, Mary Anne, Rose, and Brenda.

Senior editor: Catherine Pusateri
Managing editor: Patricia Mansfield-Phelan
Project editor: Talvi Laev
Production supervisor: Alan Fischer
Art director: Sheree Goodman
Text design: Eileen Burke
Cover design: Jeannette Jacobs Design
Cover art: Isabel Bishop, *Two Girls with a Book,* 1938, Private Collection. Courtesy Midtown-Payson Galleries, NYC.

Library of Congress Catalog Card Number: 92-50040
76543
fedcba

For information, write:
St. Martin's Press, Inc.
175 Fifth Avenue
New York, NY 10010

ISBN: 0-312-07523-5

Acknowledgments

Tina McElroy Ansa, "Sarah." From *Baby in the Family.* Copyright © 1989 by Tina McElroy Ansa, reprinted by permission of Harcourt Brace Jovanovich, Inc.

Margaret Atwood, "True Trash." From *Wilderness Tips* by Margaret Atwood. Copyright © 1991 by O.W. Toad Limited. Used by permission of Doubleday, a division of Bantam Doubleday Dell Publishing Group, Inc. Used by permission of the Canadian Publishers, McClelland & Stewart, Toronto.

Dorothy Baker, "Romance." From *It's a Woman's World: A Collection of Stories from Harper's Bazaar.* First published in 1944.

Marita Bonner, "Reap It As You Sow It." From *Frye Street and Environs* by Marita Bonner. Copyright © 1987 by Joyce Flynn and Joyce Occomy Stricklin. Reprinted by permission of Beacon Press.

Acknowledgments and copyrights are continued at the back of the book on pages 375–376, which constitute an extension of the copyright page.

Acknowledgments

I want to thank Susan Prenata for her excellent work on this volume. Without her, the collection would have been a poor shadow of what it is now. My thanks also go to Kendra Hansis, Allison Hild, and Kim Schleicher, as well as to the Research Foundation at the University of Connecticut, for their support. Cathy Pusateri, Melissa Candela, and Talvi Laev at St. Martin's Press were terrifically helpful, and, along with my husband, Michael Meyer, showed me just how well such a book can work.

CONTENTS

Acknowledgments   v

Introduction   1

Edith Wharton, The Other Two   17

Charlotte Perkins Gilman, If I Were a Man   36

Zora Neale Hurston, Sweat   43

Virginia Woolf, Lappin and Lapinova   55

Marita Bonner, Reap It As You Sow It   63

Carson McCullers, A Tree, a Rock, a Cloud   74

Dorothy Baker, Romance   83

Dorothy Parker, A Telephone Call   99

Elizabeth Bowen, Pink May   105

Flannery O'Connor, The River   113

Alice Childress, Men in Your Life   130

Grace Paley, An Interest in Life   136

Doris Lessing, A Man and Two Women   151

Muriel Spark, The House of the Famous Poet   169

Wakako Yamauchi, And the Soul Shall Dance   178

Leslie Marmon Silko, Lullaby   186

Anita Desai, A Devoted Son   196

Angela Carter, The Company of Wolves   206

Alice Walker, Coming Apart   216

Ellen Gilchrist, There's a Garden of Eden   226

Fay Weldon, Angel, All Innocence   236

Anne Tyler, Teenage Wasteland   252

Ruth Rendell, The Convolvulus Clock   263

Sandra Cisneros, Geraldo No Last Name   275

Helena Maria Viramontes, Snapshots   277

Nicholasa Mohr, A Time with a Future (Carmela)   285

Louise Erdrich, Fleur   301

Gish Jen, In the American Society   314

Tina McElroy Ansa, Sarah   329

Margaret Atwood, True Trash   351

Introduction

Why Consider Women Writers?

Why anthologize stories by modern women writers? Isn't a good short story simply a good short story, regardless of who wrote it? This collection grew from a belief that women have different stories to tell than do their male counterparts. Although these stories offer insights and pleasures to both male and female readers, they reflect a vision of the world that is particular to the woman writer. Both men and women know that there are gender-specific ways of telling stories as well as gender-specific topics. For example, you might be enraged by a story that amuses your brother, just as your brother might be bored by details that you consider crucial. Men and women hear and respond to different methods and topics of storytelling, but somehow the distinction gets smudged over in the study of literature. We have been misled into believing that we all hear the same story when we read the same words.

Many of us are introduced to short stories as a literary form during our school years. We learn that the short story is a modern form, one that evolved during the past 150 years. The perimeters of the conventional definitions come from ideas set forth by Edgar Allen Poe: that the narrative should be short enough to be read in one sitting and should have a unified effect. We are told that the "fathers" of the short story were Edgar Allen Poe, Nathaniel Hawthorne, Washington Irving, Anton Chekhov, and Guy de Maupassant, to name a few. Their "sons," the descendants whose work most closely

1

approximates these values, were Ernest Hemingway, Joseph Conrad, William Faulkner, D. H. Lawrence, O. Henry, and James Joyce. Of course, no one would argue that these men were not great writers. But I want to suggest that women writers have developed and made use of a different pattern for the short story. Although the names of the "mothers" of the short story might not be familiar to us, women writers have their own rich and important tradition. A shared fund of secrets, silences, surprises, and truths belongs to those who have experienced growing up female in a world where the experience is erased, written over, or devalued. This collection brings those secrets to light and gives voice to the silences.

Even though we might have first been introduced to the short story as a form of literature created exclusively by men, for many of us the stories we heard as children were told to us by women. We heard those words in a female voice; thus, we associate our earliest stories with women. Margaret Atwood, whose story "True Trash" is included in this anthology, points out that "the kinds of stories that are told to children have been called nursery tales or old wives' tales." Atwood explains this idea more fully when she argues that since we all listen before we can read,

> our listening is more like listening in, to the calamitous or seductive voices of the adult world, on the radio or the television or in our daily lives. Often it's an overhearing of things we aren't supposed to hear, eavesdropping on scandalous gossip or family secrets. From all these scraps of voices, from the whispers and shouts that surround us, even from the ominous silences, the unfilled gaps in meaning, we patch together for ourselves an order of events, a plot or plots; these, then, are the things that happen, these are the people they happen to, this is the forbidden knowledge.

What Makes a Short Story a Short Story?

Obviously, the tales we heard or overheard as children were not the finished works that we would label a "short story," but they nevertheless shaped the way we received and constructed our versions of the world. What is the difference between the stories we hear, or overhear, and the short stories we read? Perhaps the most significant difference is the way in which every word in the written work is chosen carefully, polished like a jewel by the author before it can be placed in the setting of the work. "One must be careful with words," cautions a narrator in one of Fay Weldon's works (Weldon's story "Angel, All Innocence" appears in this anthology): "Words turn probability into fact and by sheer force of definition, translate tendencies into habits." Every one of the thirty women whose stories fill these pages writes from a commitment to the idea that words, as much as actions, have consequences. For every writer in this collection, one thing is clear: Naming—defining the world through words—has power over the universe and draws the universe into every life. Women have a particular and complex relationship to language; because they have for so long been barred from acting on their ambitions or rebellions, they have turned to language as a way of dealing with and influencing the world.

Another important difference between the stories we hear and the stories we read is in the path of the plot. A finely written short story will generally focus on a single action or idea that profoundly changes the life of a character. Flannery O'Connor, author of "The River," tells us, "I often ask myself what makes a story work, and what makes it hold up as a story, and I have decided that it is probably some action, some gesture of a character that is unlike any other in the story, one which indicates where the real heart of the story lies." She argues that "all good stories are about conversion, about a character's changing." In nearly every story in this collection, you will be able to identify the point at which the world changes for one of the characters. This change might be caused by a small incident or an apparently ordinary thought, but it nevertheless causes the world to shift slightly on its axis. For example, the young couple in Virginia Woolf's story "Lappin and Lapinova" comes to depend increasingly on a fantasy-world inhabited by woodland creatures representing their inner selves. When one of the partners, tired after a long day at work, refuses to participate in this emotional game, their entire world collapses. Nothing actually changes in the "real world" insofar as the couple's circumstances remain unaltered. Nevertheless, nothing looks the same anymore. One or two words can change a relationship irrevocably. Picture a ten-ton freighter on the ocean, and picture the small rudder that need only move a fraction of an inch for the ten tons of steel to change direction. The moment of awareness or change in these stories acts like the movement of that rudder, changing the course of these lives irrevocably. The smallest motion has an enormous effect.

The Importance and Effects of Language

Few of us make such conscious and thoughtful word choices when we are speaking, and few of us experience conversions on a daily basis, but the short-story writer employs these elements every time she begins her work. As we read these stories, our own consciousness becomes revitalized. Language is pushed to the forefront of our perceptions; the language of the text becomes thick or opaque in that it deliberately draws attention to itself. The authors are aware of the way in which economies of language affect the reader. In most cases, they write in such a way that language concentrates time; there is less time for the reader to go back to earlier portions of the text in order to derive full meaning. The phenomenon is often synthesized most elegantly at the climax of the story, the turning point or moment of conversion at which, in one or two lines, the short-story writer makes her point with blinding intensity. Even names take on extraordinary meaning in a short story, where the writer has to make her point in the space of a very few pages.

How Do These Elements Appear in Particular Stories?

When, for example, Fay Weldon puts a young woman called "Angel" into a ghost story ("Angel, All Innocence"), the author makes no obvious commentary on the name but instead leaves it to the reader to recognize the significance of the name. As a character, Angel is at first insubstantial, naive, and (most significant) in awe of her artist husband. At night, however, she becomes increasingly disturbed by sounds coming from the supposedly empty floor overhead, the sounds of a woman crying and of someone packing up to leave. Angel's husband begins to abuse her physically when she becomes pregnant, and she finds out from her attending doctor that years ago a young woman lived in the space above whose husband used to beat her. But Angel, who doesn't want to admit that anything is wrong in her marriage, says she doesn't believe in ghosts. She falsely reassures herself by insisting that "the universe is not magic," despite the fact that she is contradicting her own experience when she denies that something uncanny is indeed happening.

By the end of the story, however, she learns to think differently. Angel ultimately confronts the ghost, a shabby thing, a "small, tired woman in a nightie, slippers silent on the stairs." Angel goes back to her own apartment and begins to pack, making noises like those she heard from above. The implication is that Angel and the woman above have acted as catalysts for each other. The supernatural experience affects both women profoundly: Angel and the ghost frighten each other, but not in the usual "horror story" way. Each frightens the other into recognizing that the violent relationships with their husbands should not be tolerated. In a way, then, the women act as guardian angels for each other, and Angel's name takes on a new meaning. We are, in Weldon's story, inhabiting a world of angels and ghosts, but we are also very much in the world of real women making real choices and facing difficult decisions. Angel finally gains the courage to leave her hell, to begin to live in the world. Angel's name is a flag to the reader, a shortcut to Weldon's meaning.

Another example of the importance of word choice in a short story appears in Muriel Spark's "The House of the Famous Poet." The unnamed narrator, who is living in London during World War II, becomes concerned with the adoption of the word "siren" for the purposes of war. "I was thinking of the word 'siren.' The sound [of the warning siren] became comical, for I imagined some maniac sea nymph from centuries past belching into the year 1944." "Warning siren" seems to be an oxymoron. In ancient mythology, the Sirens lured people to their deaths, their feminine voices seducing sailors away from reason. In contrast, the sirens set up during war were meant to drive people from danger, like an almost maternal "voice" calling all to safety. Certainly the meanings overlap and reflect back on one another: Is the safety offered by sirens, in fact, safe? "Actually," admits the narrator, "the sirens frightened me." It is important to consider the narrator's concern with words in light of the fact that the story takes place, in part, at the house of a poet whom the narrator greatly admires. The narrator is as concerned with the precise use of language as any poet might be, but in part her concern with language derives from her fear. It is interesting, too, to see Spark switch from an intellectual consideration of the use of language—thinking about mythology and etymology—to the bottom-line emotional anxiety felt by the narrator.

The writers here all acknowledge the importance of language in the structuring of reality. They write from the knowledge that words themselves matter and that language is a vital force, often the catalyst for far-reaching actions. The acknowledgment of the central role of language is linked, by these authors, to the acknowledgment of the validity of female experience. The boundaries of what has been considered the feminine world are systematically revised and refigured. Actions themselves do not offer definitions; the words describing the actions become the central factor. The manner in which language frames a situation determines that situation. In defining a situation by naming it, tagging it, limiting it, and categorizing it, the words themselves are clearly both manipulative and powerful. In Grace Paley's story "An Interest in Life," the narrator is told by her male companion that her life as an abandoned wife with small children is not the stuff of tragedy but is instead an ordinary life, simply filled with "the little disturbances of man." She depends upon an articulated definition of her life in order to understand it, even if she then chooses to revise the received definition. The words themselves give shape to experience and reality. It is a return to an almost primitive and superstitious belief in the magical powers associated with naming. Nothing is arbitrary. Everything, and every word, in these stories has a purpose.

How Do These Stories Differ from Traditional Short Stories?

Modern women writers challenge even the most traditional patterns for the short story, subverting the basic prescriptions: an unwavering unity of effect, and an inevitable movement toward closure. In other words, everything in the story should be swept along by one current toward a clear destination. But often in women's stories competing voices and alternatives present themselves even within a few pages; like the past, these offer alternative voices that force their way into definition and prominence. Even though one character usually occupies the center of the narrative without competition, we still sense that these stories refuse to offer a single interpretation of the world. In Charlotte Perkins Gilman's fantasy story "If I Were a Man," we are thrust into the mind of a turn-of-the-century woman who suddenly sees the world from her husband's perspective. There are no easy answers; the woman understands the world more fully, but Gilman does not answer the question of how women and men should behave toward one another. When Sandra Cisneros gives us a life in one brief page ("Geraldo No Last Name"), she tears apart the formal guidelines for a story; the story is effective because it takes the economy of the ordinary story and whittles it into a stiletto: sharp, pointed, and efficient.

It has been said of the traditional short story that its characters are often outcasts or socially unacceptable people living on the margins of conventional life. But the paradigm must be altered to accommodate women's stories. The stories presented here often depict the lives of women who would be considered perfectly ordinary because they have gone through much of their lives not calling attention to themselves; however, they are actually extraordinary women whose dreams, ambitions, desires, and rages have been suppressed. These women are not unusual—we might well recognize our own passions in them—but the fact that their emotions are depicted seriously makes them unusual representations of women. Many women in many stories by the writers we think of as canonical (writers who are seen as shaping the conventional literary tradition) are presented as two-dimensional characters—as either the bad-girl seductress or the good-girl wife-and-mom. A female character who is a whole human being, with inherent qualities of good and evil, insight and stubbornness, or desire and reluctance, seems out of place next to these standardized images of women. This might be one reason why the women in these stories seem more like outlaws than outcasts when they take some definitive action. A female character who breaks rank with the stereotype threatens society by refusing to do what society expects.

These stories regard society itself from a variety of perspectives. Society is reshaped, however minutely, every time one of these characters makes a change in her life. Some of the changes are ephemeral in that the character might choose to ignore what she has learned in the moment of crisis, but in most cases one cannot overlook the knowledge gained by the character. The character will be unable, for better or worse, to resume life as it has been. Most of the stories concern the individual, but ramifications extend far beyond the scope of that one life. Alongside women's growing self-assertion and social victory remains a consistent distrust of reality. If it is not true that women need male protection, as they have always been told, if it is not true that men should be educated but that women must remain ignorant to be attractive, if it is not true that destiny doles out individual punishment to any woman who rejects the role of wife and mother, women ask themselves in these stories, then what other false assumptions do we allow to control our destinies? What can we believe?

These writers come to the conclusion that shaping language itself can shape reality: Whoever speaks, writes, or thinks, *acts*. Facing the disruption of everything they considered indestructible, these writers argue for and illustrate the need to learn to restructure and revise the world by rethinking women's roles and expectations. In this way, the personal and the political become inextricably entwined: The different ways in which men and women face the world are shaped by frameworks that position them in terms of gender, class, and race. Even the most isolated and traditionally domestic lives are shaped by such politics.

Yet a breakdown of personal guardedness also characterizes these stories; women, especially, begin to feel connected to other women by links they would not have admitted, let alone explained, to their fathers, husbands, brothers, male co-workers, or male friends. This particularly feminine framing of relationships places integration above separation. Thus, the currency of official, masculine authority is devalued. In many of these works, women learn to look to themselves or to other women for validation or affirmation instead of relying on the judgments of men, who might not understand their goals or survival needs. By placing women at the center of their stories, these writers acknowledge the importance of recording all aspects of the world as perceived by women, offering without apology or explanation experience viewed through a feminine frame. One of the great strengths of these stories is their ability to juxtapose the small and the certain with the great and the uncertain, indicating through the lens of violence (Zora Neale Hurston's "Sweat" or Ruth Rendell's "The Convolvulus Clock") or romance (Dorothy Parker's "A Telephone Call" or Alice Childress's "Men in Your Life") the scope of the changes taking place. By investing the apparently trivial with significance, these writers establish that the gritty details of events and relationships are, in fact, their essence.

Because these writers present the world from a female perspective, it is not surprising that female characters dominate the texts. However, it is interesting to note those stories in which male characters control the story, such as Anita Desai's "A Devoted Son," Carson McCullers's "A Tree, a Rock, a Cloud," Anne Tyler's "Teenage Wasteland," and Edith Wharton's "The Other Two." Creating a male protagonist offers the writer important possibilities. Wharton herself cautioned editors and critics to avoid making generalizations about the creation of a short story since "general rules in art are useful chiefly as a lamp in a mine, or a handrail down a black stairway; they are necessary for the sake of the guidance they give, but it is a mistake, once they are formulated, to be too much in awe of them."

What Are the Concerns of the Woman Writer?

What are the particular concerns of the woman writer? Alice Walker ("Coming Apart"), who, like many of the writers in this collection, treats issues of race as well as issues of gender, asks the question: "Outwardly, what obstacles are there for a woman rather than for a man?" Walker then explains that in the very process of facing the blank page, women writers have to overcome objections they have internalized. Before beginning, women writers have to overcome the fear of the loss of femininity and the fear of failure. Walker says that the creative process is not the same for women as it is for men. "Inwardly," she writes, "the case is very different; [a woman] has still many ghosts to fight, many prejudices to overcome. Indeed it will be a long time still, I think, before a woman can sit down to write a book without finding a phantom to be slain, a rock to be dashed against." Writing fifty years before Alice Walker, British author Virginia Woolf came to many of the same conclusions. These conclusions, then, transcend issues of race, class, and national origin; they emerge from the experience of being a woman who writes.

Woolf ("Lappin and Lapinova") offers insight into this question. She writes that it has always been "obvious that the values of women differ very often from the values which have been made by the other sex; naturally, this is so. Yet it is the masculine values that prevail. Speaking crudely, football and sport are 'important'; the worship of fashion, the buying of clothes 'trivial.' " It is a rare woman who has not heard, at some point in her life, that what concerns her is not really important. Girls used to be told that a good education was not important because they would only "go off and get married anyway," as if a woman had to choose between having ideas and having a husband. Women's books, plays, and works of art were denied critical attention because they dealt with "unimportant" issues such as birth, death, marriage, sex, and friendship as opposed to "important" issues such as hunting, travel, war, finance, and sports. Woolf emphasizes this point when she writes that "these values are inevitably transferred from life to fiction. This is an important book, the critic assumes, because it deals with war. This is an insignificant book because it deals with the feelings of women in a drawing-room. A scene in a battlefield is more important than a scene in a shop—everywhere and much more subtly the difference of value persists."

That short stories by women have generally been overlooked or devalued by critics can be attributed at least in part to a "blind spot" where women writers are concerned. Because stories by women reject many of the conventions associated with traditional narratives not by way of attack but by subtle subversion, women's stories have been misread by critics who perceive good writing only when it is encased within inherited literary structures. Women's stories undo existing boundaries and stereotypes; they do not merely test them. These writers affirm the multiplicity of non-closure. In other words, they write against the restrictions of convention insofar as they do not shove women into prefabricated narrative structures. Few of these stories end with the stereotypical happy ending. For example, a work that ends with the dissolution of marriage and the abandonment of children does not invalidate its claim to be read as a complete and satisfactory story, even as one with a happy ending. So, while undeniably we want to celebrate when the narrator in Alice Childress's "Men in Your Life" decides to marry, we also rejoice when Angel leaves home in Fay Weldon's story. One happy ending involves marriage and another ending can only be happy if the marriage is over.

Why Do Writers Choose to Write Short Stories?

Why do writers write short stories? "However plain or lively or unpretentious be the manner of the story," writes Elizabeth Bowen, author of "Pink May," "the central emotion—emotion however remotely involved or hinted at—should be austere, major. The subject must have implicit dignity." Bowen insists on the importance of both emotion and thought behind the story when she says that "the first necessity for the short story, at the set out, is necessariness. The story, that is to say, must spring from an impression or perception pressing enough, acute enough, to have made the writer write."

What Bowen calls necessariness has been conventionally described as inspiration, that process whereby an idea is breathed into the mind and heart of the artist by the muse. The artist in this traditional picture is inevitably male and the muse with the heavy breathing is inevitably female. When the artist is a woman, what happens to the idea of the muse? Often, the traditional idea of the scantily clad muse is either ignored or turned into a more ordinary figure: The woman writer is inspired by her neighbors, family, friends, teachers, enemies, and lovers. The woman writer does not often claim to wait for inspiration itself. Instead, she writes out of a need, a demand made by the story to be told and by the silence inside her that demands articulation. Novelist Nora Ephron ends her novel *Heart-*

burn with a list of reasons why it is absolutely essential to "turn everything into a story." When a friend asks her why she has to give a funny answer to even the most serious questions, the heroine announces that it is important "because if I tell the story, I control the version. Because if I tell the story, I can make you laugh, and I would rather have you laugh than feel sorry for me. Because if I tell the story, it doesn't hurt as much. Because if I tell the story, I can get on with it." Many of the stories here are about "getting on with it" and about the importance of being able to tell your own story in your own way. The short stories collected here are about the importance of making yourself heard.

What Are Some of the Particular Issues Facing the Woman Writer?

The reasons why writers decide to publish their stories are important, especially for women. Women have a different relationship to ambition and success than do men, and they also have a different sense of themselves as artists. Girls, for the most part, are still not brought up to think of themselves as successes-in-the-making. They rarely admit their ambitions aloud. This is not only for fear of failure, which they share with their male counterparts, but because to want to succeed might make them seem less feminine. In a letter to a young aspiring woman writer, Flannery O'Connor insists on the importance of striving for success: "Success means being heard and don't stand there and tell me that you are indifferent to being heard. You may write for the joy of it, but the act of writing is not complete in itself. It has to end in its audience." Facing the idea of making their thoughts, emotions, and skills available to an audience who will judge them on their artistry rather than on the sincerity of their effort, girls are often encouraged to retreat. The reasons should drive women to achieve greatness in the public eye.

Girls are usually, but certainly not always, brought up not to take risks and not to call attention to themselves. A girl who shines in the classroom may feel she has to apologize for it. She may make self-deprecating remarks ("Oh, I just got lucky in answering that question") even when her achievement is a reflection of genuine ability. Some girls are not exposed to images of women whose work has changed the world or, on a more modest and personal basis, women who are both successful and happy. Girls read books written by men and study criticism that offers a masculine perspective, perhaps without identifying it as such. Young women take course after course on the "masterworks" written exclusively by white men who lived at least fifty years ago, and they are told that they study these works because they are "great" works of literature. Such mechanisms work on the female student's mind like a syllogism: "Great works of art are written by men; I am not a man; I cannot write a great work of art." It is crucial for women to recognize the tradition of women's work and women's art so that they will not feel like the first to set up camp on a territory that in fact is already richly explored.

When the women represented in this volume sat down to write, they often did it for reasons that would be alien to a male writer. Elizabeth Bowen candidly admits that she "did not so much envisage glory as cry out for affirmation. Publication would be the sign that I was not mad." Alice Walker seems to expand on Bowen's point when she says that she writes to gather up the "historical and psychological threads of the life my ancestors lived" and that she has "that wonderful feeling writers get sometimes, not very often, of being with a great many people, ancient spirits, all very happy to see me consulting and acknowledging them, and eager to let me know, through the joy of their presence, that indeed, I am not alone." Women, whose experience of life has rarely been presented publicly or taken seriously, look for affirmation from the women writers to whom they turn. "This happened to you too?" they often whisper. "You mean I'm not the only one who's ever felt this way?" A sense of community is built by sharing these stories that bridges generations, class, sexual preference, ethnicity, and race.

Emphasis on a community comprised of a diverse membership is not a new or trendy idea when it comes to women writers of the short story. In a book published over 100 years ago, *The Woman's Story As Told by Twenty American Women*, editor Laura Holloway declared in her introduction that "the differences in population; the varieties of classes, and the broad distinctions in local coloring are vividly exhibited in the annals of American fiction, the largest contributors to which are women." Apparently as far back as 1889, when Holloway's book first appeared, women realized that there was a need to present women's stories separately, as well as a need to highlight the way in which women writers bring their differences to bear as gifts rather than as threats to the larger community. Poet Adrienne Rich declares that "today women are talking to each other . . . reading aloud to one another the books that have moved and healed us, analyzing the language that has lied about us, reading our own words aloud to each other," but we can see that women have always had a story of their own.

How Do Women Writers Challenge Traditional Assumptions?

Women's stories subvert the traditional prerequisite for narrative: the assumption of a consensus of opinion, of shared values. It is standard practice in short stories for the author and reader to share a system of values into which a main character must be initiated. The traditional story often begins when the main character's uninitiated behavior sets him apart from his peers. But something else is at work in stories by women. Often the character learns to distrust and to refuse to participate in the system of dominant values. In other words, the triumphant values are the ones espoused by the uninitiated female protagonists. Refusal is at the heart of stories such as Wakako Yamauchi's "And the Soul Shall Dance" or Louise Erdrich's "Fleur." The story works not against the renegade woman-reader-heroine but against those who would confine her in the attic of "acceptable" behavior, who would write her out of her own text. Behind the humble curtsey to the ruling culture, the writer presents a wink to readers, an encoded signal to those who understand that the heroine's apparent submission does not negate her instinctive rebellion. The values shared by reader and heroine remain in ascendancy; the values of those in control are swept away.

These writers use their stories not to justify the ways of God to man, or to justify the ways of men to women, but rather to expose the problems inherent in such ways. Through intricate weavings of politics, aphoristic commentary, romance, and narrative, these short stories gain their profound power from small and large transgressions. The stories included in this collection delightedly and unrelentingly expose the myths that have helped keep women "in their place." By understanding the social and economic bases for women's exclusion from the power structure, women can begin to undo the system by refusing to play their assigned roles.

Indeed, few of these carefully constructed characters present themselves as role models. Here female characters are often no more "good" than male characters, although they are usually more complex, interesting, and important. No one wants to be like the woman waiting with crazed impatience for her boyfriend to call in Dorothy Parker's story "A Telephone Call" (although all too many of us will see ourselves in her, despite our best intentions), and we probably would not want to be like the older woman flirting with her carpenter in Ellen Gilchrist's "There's a Garden of Eden," but there is no reason to think that women writers have to show us only saints, good mothers, and selfless virgin spinsters. Writers like Grace Paley give us women whose lives we might not want to live ourselves, but whose strength of character and love of life we might well embrace. Angela Carter revises the fairy tale about Little Red Riding Hood in "The Company of Wolves" so that the innocent little girl no longer seems naive, but instead wily and in control. We see in Carter's fabular story the ways in which images of girls and women have changed over several hundred years, even though the life presented in the story bears little outward resemblance to our own.

Conclusions

You may feel a number of emotions when you recognize a situation, character, emotion, or idea in a short story. The way in which these stories hold a mirror up to your own life may shock you at first. It is often uncomfortable to have your secrets revealed, even or especially by a stranger. You may find your deepest responses called forth by a writer who died before you were born, or one who lived in an entirely different land. You may well be angered by the injustices explored in stories such as Tina McElroy Ansa's "Sarah" or unnerved by the choices made by a character, as in Nicholasa Mohr's "A Time with a Future," but you can judge these stories successful since they encourage you to rethink your way of viewing people as well as to alter the way you regard yourself. I hope, too, that you will laugh along with the writers of these stories, who, even when bringing to light their worst fears or exposing moments of great pain, manage to keep their sense of humor and sense of perspective. Ruth Rendell's murder mystery is wildly funny even at its most gruesome moments, and Gish Jen's exploration of racial prejudice in "In the American Society" is told within a triumphantly comic frame. To share the sense of community offered by the writer in a short story is, for a moment, to transcend all difference and even erase all fear of difference.

Fay Weldon believes that it is "wonderful to find out that there is a view of the world, not just the world: a pattern to experience, not just experience—and whether you agree with the view offered, or like the pattern, is neither here nor there. Views are possible, patterns discernible—it is exciting and exhilarating and enriching to know it. And it is why, I think, increasingly, any seminar on Women and Writing, or Women Writers, or the New Female Culture, or whatever, is instantly booked up—by men as well as by women." Finally, when Weldon says that in reading such stories we are relieved to see that "we are not alone in the oddity of our beliefs. Our neighbour, whom we never thought would laugh when we laughed, actually does," we hear in Weldon's remarks echoes of Atwood, Bowen, O'Connor, Walker, Woolf, and the other writers whose work is collected in *Women of the Century*.

These stories are successful attempts by the writers to broaden the sense of self, to reach an unrecorded past, to extend the limits of the possible, and to escape the bonds imposed by the routine allotted to women in society. With their blessing, and informed by their paradoxically wise wickedness and reassuring distrust of the world, we are permitted to review, revise, and renew our own lives.

NOTES

". . . the kinds of stories . . .": Margaret Atwood, "Reading Blind," in *Best American Short Stories,* ed. Margaret Atwood and Shannon Ravenel (Boston: Houghton Mifflin, 1989).

". . . our listening is . . .": ibid.

"One must be careful . . .": Fay Weldon, *The Fat Woman's Joke* (London: Coronet, 1982).

"I often ask myself . . .": Flannery O'Connor, *Mystery and Manners,* ed. Sally and Robert Fitzgerald (London: Faber & Faber, 1972).

". . . all good stories are about . . .": Flannery O'Connor, *The Habit of Being,* ed. Sally Fitzgerald (New York: Farrar, Straus & Giroux, 1979).

". . . general rules in art are useful chiefly . . .": Edith Wharton, "Telling a Short Story," in *Writing in Fiction* (New York: C. Scribner's Sons, 1925).

"Outwardly, what obstacles are there . . .": Alice Walker, "Saving the Life That Is Your Own," in *In Search of Our Mothers' Gardens* (San Diego: Harcourt Brace Jovanovich, 1983).

". . . obvious that the values of women differ . . .": Virginia Woolf, *A Room of One's Own* (New York: Harcourt, Brace, 1957).

". . . these values are inevitably transferred . . .": ibid.

"However plain or lively or unpretentious . . .": Elizabeth Bowen, *Early Stories* (New York: Knopf, 1951).

". . . because if I tell the story . . .": Nora Ephron, *Heartburn* (New York: Pocket Books, 1983).

"Success means being heard . . .": Flannery O'Connor, *The Habit of Being.*

". . . did not so much envisage glory as . . .": Elizabeth Bowen, *Early Stories.*

". . . historical and psychological threads of the life . . .": Alice Walker, "Saving the Life That Is Your Own."

"The differences in population; the varieties of classes . . .": Laura Holloway, *The Woman's Story as Told by Twenty American Women,* ed. Laura Holloway (New York: John B. Alden, 1889).

"Today women are talking to each other . . .": Adrienne Rich, *On Lies, Secrets and Silence: Selected Prose, 1966–1978* (New York: Norton, 1979).

". . . wonderful to find out that . . .": Fay Weldon, *Letters to Alice on First Reading Jane Austen* (London: Hodder and Stoughton, 1977).

". . . we are not alone . . .": ibid.

Edith Wharton
(1862–1937)

The Other Two

Educated by governesses and restricted to reading the classics, Edith Jones led an intellectually isolated childhood. In 1878, however, she published *Verses*, and in 1885 she married Edward Wharton, who launched her into Old New York society. Ten years later, after having a nervous breakdown and entering a sanatorium, Edith Wharton began her writing career. The early novels for which she is best known depict high society's philistinism; the paragon of these is her 1905 best-seller, *House of Mirth*.

After the success of *House of Mirth*, Wharton moved to France and wrote *Ethan Frome* (1911), *The Reef* (1912), and *Summer* (1917), all of which depict the conflict between society's dictates and individual desires. War-relief experiences then inspired her final phase of writing: She wrote *Fighting France: From Dunkerque to Belfort* (1915), *The Age of Innocence*, for which she won a Pulitzer Prize in 1921, and *A Son at the Front* (1923).

Henry James, "perhaps the most intimate friend [she] ever had," inspired her propensity for disengaging, as Wharton herself described, "crucial moments from the welter of existence"—such as the final scene of "The Other Two"—in order to ascertain that moment's true significance and how that moment affects each character.

I.

Waythorn, on the drawing-room hearth, waited for his wife to come down to dinner.

It was their first night under his own roof, and he was surprised at his thrill of boyish agitation. He was not so old, to be sure—his glass gave him little more than the five-and-thirty years to which his wife confessed—but he had fancied himself already in the temperate zone; yet here he was listening for her step with a tender sense of all it symbolised, with some old trail of verse about the garlanded nuptial door-posts floating through his enjoyment of the pleasant room and the good dinner just beyond it.

They had been hastily recalled from their honeymoon by the illness of Lily Haskett, the child of Mrs. Waythorn's first marriage. The little girl, at Waythorn's desire, had been transferred to his house on the day of her mother's wedding, and the doctor, on their arrival, broke the news that she was ill with typhoid, but declared that all the symptoms were favourable. Lily could show twelve years of unblemished health, and the case promised to be a light one. The nurse spoke as reassuringly, and after a moment of alarm Mrs. Waythorn had adjusted herself to the situation. She was very fond of Lily—her affection for the child had perhaps been her decisive charm in Waythorn's eyes—but she had the perfectly balanced nerves which her little girl had inherited, and no woman ever wasted less tissue in unproductive worry. Waythorn was therefore quite prepared to see her come in presently, a little late because of a last look at Lily, but as serene and well-appointed as if her goodnight kiss had been laid on the brow of health. Her composure was restful to him; it acted as ballast to his somewhat unstable sensibilities. As he pictured her bending over the child's bed he thought how soothing her presence must be in illness: her very step would prognosticate recovery.

His own life had been a gray one, from temperament rather than circumstance, and he had been drawn to her by the unperturbed gaiety which kept her fresh and elastic at an age when most women's activities are growing either slack or febrile. He knew what was said about her; for, popular as she was, there had always been a faint undercurrent of detraction. When she had appeared in New York, nine or ten years earlier, as the pretty Mrs. Haskett whom Gus Varick had unearthed somewhere—was it in Pittsburgh or Utica?—society, while promptly accepting her, had reserved the right to cast a doubt on its own indiscrimination. Enquiry, however, established her undoubted connection with a socially reigning family, and explained her recent divorce as the natural result of a runaway match at seventeen; and as nothing was known of Mr. Haskett it was easy to believe the worst of him.

Alice Haskett's remarriage with Gus Varick was a passport to the set whose recognition she coveted, and for a few years the Varicks were the most popular couple in town. Unfortunately, the alliance was brief and stormy, and this time the husband had his champions. Still, even Varick's staunchest supporters admitted that he was not meant for matrimony, and Mrs. Varick's grievances were of a nature to bear the inspection of the New York courts. A New York divorce is in itself a diploma of virtue, and in the semiwidowhood of this second separation Mrs. Varick took on an air of sanctity, and was allowed to confide her wrongs to some of the most scrupulous ears in town. But when it was known that she was to marry Waythorn there was a momentary reaction. Her best friends would have preferred to see her remain in the rôle of the injured wife, which was as becoming to her as crape to a rosy complexion. True, a decent time had elapsed, and it was not even suggested that Waythorn had supplanted his predecessor. People shook their heads over him, however, and one grudging friend, to whom he affirmed that he took the step with his eyes open, replied oracularly: "Yes—and with your ears shut."

Waythorn could afford to smile at these innuendoes. In the Wall Street phrase, he had "discounted" them. He knew that society has not yet adapted itself to the consequences of divorce, and that till the adaptation takes place every woman who uses the freedom the law accords her must be her own social justification. Waythorn had an amused confidence in his wife's ability to justify herself. His expectations were fulfilled, and before the wedding took place Alice Varick's group had rallied openly to her support. She took it all imperturbably: she had a way of surmounting obstacles without seeming to be aware of them, and Waythorn looked back with wonder at the trivialities over which he had worn his nerves thin. He had the sense of having found refuge in a richer, warmer nature than his own, and his satisfaction, at the moment, was humorously summed up in the thought that his wife, when she had done all she could for Lily, would not be ashamed to come down and enjoy a good dinner.

The anticipation of such enjoyment was not, however, the sentiment expressed by Mrs. Waythorn's charming face when she presently joined him. Though she had put on her most engaging tea-gown she had neglected to assume the smile that went with it, and Waythorn thought he had never seen her look so nearly worried.

"What is it?" he asked. "Is anything wrong with Lily?"

"No; I've just been in and she's still sleeping." Mrs. Waythorn hesitated. "But something tiresome has happened."

He had taken her two hands, and now perceived that he was crushing a paper between them.

"This letter?"

"Yes—Mr. Haskett has written—I mean his lawyer has written."

Waythorn felt himself flush uncomfortably. He dropped his wife's hands.

"What about?"

"About seeing Lily. You know the courts—"

"Yes, yes," he interrupted nervously.

Nothing was known about Haskett in New York. He was vaguely supposed to have remained in the outer darkness from which his wife had been rescued, and Waythorn was one of the few who were aware that he had given up his business in Utica and followed her to New York in order to be near his little girl. In the days of his wooing, Waythorn had often met Lily on the doorstep, rosy and smiling, on her way "to see papa."

"I am so sorry," Mrs. Waythorn murmured.

He roused himself. "What does he want?"

"He wants to see her. You know she goes to him once a week."

"Well—he doesn't expect her to go to him now, does he?"

"No—he has heard of her illness; but he expects to come here."

"Here?"

Mrs. Waythorn reddened under his gaze. They looked away from each other.

"I'm afraid he has the right. . . . You'll see. . . ." She made a proffer of the letter.

Waythorn moved away with a gesture of refusal. He stood staring about the softly lighted room, which a moment before had seemed so full of bridal intimacy.

"I'm so sorry," she repeated. "If Lily could have been moved—"

"That's out of the question," he returned impatiently.

"I suppose so."

Her lip was beginning to tremble, and he felt himself a brute.

"He must come, of course," he said. "When is—his day?"

"I'm afraid—to-morrow."

"Very well. Send a note in the morning."

The butler entered to announce dinner.

Waythorn turned to his wife. "Come—you must be tired. It's beastly, but try to forget about it," he said, drawing her hand through his arm.

"You're so good, dear. I'll try," she whispered back.

Her face cleared at once, and as she looked at him across the flowers, between the rosy candle-shades, he saw her lips waver back into a smile.

"How pretty everything is!" she sighed luxuriously.

He turned to the butler. "The champagne at once, please. Mrs. Waythorn is tired."

In a moment or two their eyes met above the sparkling glasses. Her own were quite clear and untroubled: he saw that she had obeyed his injunction and forgotten.

II.

Waythorn, the next morning, went down town earlier than usual. Haskett was not likely to come till the afternoon, but the instinct of flight drove him forth. He meant to stay away all day—he had thoughts of dining at his club. As his door closed behind him he reflected that before he opened it again it would have admitted another man who had as much right to enter it as himself, and the thought filled him with a physical repugnance.

He caught the "elevated" at the employees' hour, and found himself crushed between two layers of pendulous humanity. At Eighth Street the man facing him wriggled out, and another took his place. Waythorn glanced up and saw that it was Gus Varick. The men were so close together that it was impossible to ignore the smile of recognition on Varick's handsome overblown face. And after all—why not? They had always been on good terms, and Varick had been divorced before Waythorn's attentions to his wife began. The two exchanged a word on the perennial grievance of the congested trains, and when a seat at their side was miraculously left empty the instinct of self-preservation made Waythorn slip into it after Varick.

The latter drew the stout man's breath of relief. "Lord—I was beginning to feel like a pressed flower." He leaned back, looking unconcernedly at Waythorn. "Sorry to hear that Sellers is knocked out again."

"Sellers?" echoed Waythorn, starting at his partner's name.

Varick looked surprised. "You didn't know he was laid up with the gout?"

"No. I've been away—I only got back last night." Waythorn felt himself reddening in anticipation of the other's smile.

"Ah—yes; to be sure. And Sellers's attack came on two days ago. I'm afraid he's pretty bad. Very awkward for me, as it happens, because he was just putting through a rather important thing for me."

"Ah?" Waythorn wondered vaguely since when Varick had been dealing in "important things." Hitherto he had dabbled only in the shallow pools of speculation, with which Waythorn's office did not usually concern itself.

It occurred to him that Varick might be talking at random, to relieve the strain of their propinquity. That strain was becoming momentarily more apparent to Waythorn, and when, at Cortlandt Street, he caught sight of an acquaintance and had a sudden vision of the picture he and Varick must present to an initiated eye, he jumped up with a muttered excuse.

"I hope you'll find Sellers better," said Varick civilly, and he stammered back: "If I can be of any use to you—" and let the departing crowd sweep him to the platform.

At his office he heard that Sellers was in fact ill with the gout, and would probably not be able to leave the house for some weeks.

"I'm sorry it should have happened so, Mr. Waythorn," the senior clerk said with affable significance. "Mr. Sellers was very much upset at the idea of giving you such a lot of extra work just now."

"Oh, that's no matter," said Waythorn hastily. He secretly welcomed the pressure of additional business, and was glad to think that, when the day's work was over, he would have to call at his partner's on the way home.

He was late for luncheon, and turned in at the nearest restaurant instead of going to his club. The place was full, and the waiter hurried him to the back of the room to capture the only vacant table. In the cloud of cigar-smoke Waythorn did not at once distinguish his neighbours; but presently, looking about him, he saw Varick seated a few feet off. This time, luckily, they were too far apart for conversation, and Varick, who faced another way, had probably not even seen him; but there was an irony in their renewed nearness.

Varick was said to be fond of good living, and as Waythorn sat despatching his hurried luncheon he looked across half enviously at the other's leisurely degustation of his meal. When Waythorn first saw him he had been helping himself with critical deliberation to a bit of

Camembert at the ideal point of liquefaction, and now, the cheese removed, he was just pouring his *café double* from its little two-storied earthen pot. He poured slowly, his ruddy profile bent above the task, and one beringed white hand steadying the lid of the coffee-pot; then he stretched his other hand to the decanter of cognac at his elbow, filled a liqueur-glass, took a tentative sip, and poured the brandy into his coffee-cup.

Waythorn watched him in a kind of fascination. What was he thinking of—only of the flavour of the coffee and the liqueur? Had the morning's meeting left no more trace in his thoughts than on his face? Had his wife so completely passed out of his life that even this odd encounter with her present husband, within a week after her remarriage, was no more than an incident in his day? And as Waythorn mused, another idea struck him: had Haskett ever met Varick as Varick and he had just met? The recollection of Haskett perturbed him, and he rose and left the restaurant, taking a circuitous way out to escape the placid irony of Varick's nod.

It was after seven when Waythorn reached home. He thought the footman who opened the door looked at him oddly.

"How is Miss Lily?" he asked in haste.

"Doing very well, sir. A gentleman—"

"Tell Barlow to put off dinner for half an hour," Waythorn cut him off, hurrying upstairs.

He went straight to his room and dressed without seeing his wife. When he reached the drawing-room she was there, fresh and radiant. Lily's day had been good; the doctor was not coming back that evening.

At dinner Waythorn told her of Sellers's illness and of the resulting complications. She listened sympathetically, adjuring him not to let himself be overworked, and asking vague feminine questions about the routine of the office. Then she gave him the chronicle of Lily's day; quoted the nurse and doctor, and told him who had called to inquire. He had never seen her more serene and unruffled. It struck him, with a curious pang, that she was very happy in being with him, so happy that she found a childish pleasure in rehearsing the trivial incidents of her day.

After dinner they went to the library, and the servant put the coffee and liqueurs on a low table before her and left the room. She looked singularly soft and girlish in her rosy pale dress, against the dark leather of one of his bachelor armchairs. A day earlier the contrast would have charmed him.

He turned away now, choosing a cigar with affected deliberation. "Did Haskett come?" he asked, with his back to her.

"Oh, yes—he came."

"You didn't see him, of course?"

She hesitated a moment. "I let the nurse see him."

That was all. There was nothing more to ask. He swung round toward her, applying a match to his cigar. Well, the thing was over for a week, at any rate. He would try not to think of it. She looked up at him, a trifle rosier than usual, with a smile in her eyes.

"Ready for your coffee, dear?"

He leaned against the mantelpiece, watching her as she lifted the coffee-pot. The lamplight struck a gleam from her bracelets and tipped her soft hair with brightness. How light and slender she was, and how each gesture flowed into the next! She seemed a creature all compact of harmonies. As the thought of Haskett receded, Waythorn felt himself yielding again to the joy of possessorship. They were his, those white hands with their flitting motions, his the light haze of hair, the lips and eyes. . . .

She set down the coffee-pot, and reaching for the decanter of cognac, measured off a liqueur-glass and poured it into his cup.

Waythorn uttered a sudden exclamation.

"What is the matter?" she said, startled.

"Nothing; only—I don't take cognac in my coffee."

"Oh, how stupid of me," she cried.

Their eyes met, and she blushed a sudden agonised red.

III.

Ten days later, Mr. Sellers, still house-bound, asked Waythorn to call on his way down town.

The senior partner, with his swaddled foot propped up by the fire, greeted his associate with an air of embarrassment.

"I'm sorry, my dear fellow; I've got to ask you to do an awkward thing for me."

Waythorn waited, and the other went on, after a pause apparently given to the arrangement of his phrases: "The fact is, when I was knocked out I had just gone into a rather complicated piece of business for—Gus Varick."

"Well?" said Waythorn, with an attempt to put him at his ease.

"Well—it's this way: Varick came to me the day before my attack. He had evidently had an inside tip from somebody, and had made about a hundred thousand. He came to me for advice, and I suggested his going in with Vanderlyn."

"Oh, the deuce!" Waythorn exclaimed. He saw in a flash what had happened. The investment was an alluring one, but required negotiation. He listened quietly while Sellers put the case before him, and, the statement ended, he said: "You think I ought to see Varick?"

"I'm afraid I can't as yet. The doctor is obdurate. And this thing can't wait. I hate to ask you, but no one else in the office knows the ins and outs of it."

Waythorn stood silent. He did not care a farthing for the success of Varick's venture, but the honour of the office was to be considered, and he could hardly refuse to oblige his partner.

"Very well," he said, "I'll do it."

That afternoon, apprised by telephone, Varick called at the office. Waythorn, waiting in his private room, wondered what the others thought of it. The newspapers, at the time of Mrs. Waythorn's marriage, had acquainted their readers with every detail of her previous matrimonial ventures, and Waythorn could fancy the clerks smiling behind Varick's back as he was ushered in.

Varick bore himself admirably. He was easy without being undignified, and Waythorn was conscious of cutting a much less impressive figure. Varick had no experience of business, and the talk prolonged itself for nearly an hour while Waythorn set forth with scrupulous precision the details of the proposed transaction.

"I'm awfully obliged to you," Varick said as he rose. "The fact is I'm not used to having much money to look after, and I don't want to make an ass of myself—" He smiled, and Waythorn could not help noticing that there was something pleasant about his smile. "It feels uncommonly queer to have enough cash to pay one's bills. I'd have sold my soul for it a few years ago!"

Waythorn winced at the allusion. He had heard it rumoured that a lack of funds had been one of the determining causes of the Varick separation, but it did not occur to him that Varick's words were intentional. It seemed more likely that the desire to keep clear of embarrassing topics had fatally drawn him into one. Waythorn did not wish to be outdone in civility.

"We'll do the best we can for you," he said. "I think this is a good thing you're in."

"Oh, I'm sure it's immense. It's awfully good of you—" Varick broke off, embarrassed. "I suppose the thing's settled now—but if—"

"If anything happens before Sellers is about, I'll see you again," said Waythorn quietly. He was glad, in the end, to appear the more self-possessed of the two.

The course of Lily's illness ran smooth, and as the days passed Waythorn grew used to the idea of Haskett's weekly visit. The first time the day came round, he stayed out late, and questioned his wife as to the visit on his return. She replied at once that Haskett had merely seen the nurse downstairs, as the doctor did not wish any one in the child's sick-room till after the crisis.

The following week Waythorn was again conscious of the recurrence of the day, but had forgotten it by the time he came home to dinner. The crisis of the disease came a few days later, with a rapid decline of fever, and the little girl was pronounced out of danger. In the rejoicing which ensued the thought of Haskett passed out of Waythorn's mind, and one afternoon, letting himself into the house with a latchkey, he went straight to his library without noticing a shabby hat and umbrella in the hall.

In the library he found a small effaced-looking man with a thinnish gray beard sitting on the edge of a chair. The stranger might have been a piano-tuner, or one of those mysteriously efficient persons who are summoned in emergencies to adjust some detail of the domestic machinery. He blinked at Waythorn through a pair of gold-rimmed spectacles and said mildly: "Mr. Waythorn, I presume? I am Lily's father."

Waythorn flushed. "Oh—" he stammered uncomfortably. He broke off, disliking to appear rude. Inwardly he was trying to adjust the actual Haskett to the image of him projected by his wife's reminiscences. Waythorn had been allowed to infer that Alice's first husband was a brute.

"I am sorry to intrude," said Haskett, with his over-the-counter politeness.

"Don't mention it," returned Waythorn, collecting himself. "I suppose the nurse has been told?"

"I presume so. I can wait," said Haskett. He had a resigned way of speaking, as though life had worn down his natural powers of resistance.

Waythorn stood on the threshold, nervously pulling off his gloves.

"I'm sorry you've been detained. I will send for the nurse," he said; and as he opened the door he added with an effort: "I'm glad we can give you a good report of Lily." He winced as the *we* slipped out, but Haskett seemed not to notice it.

"Thank you, Mr. Waythorn. It's been an anxious time for me."

"Ah, well, that's past. Soon she'll be able to go to you." Waythorn nodded and passed out.

In his own room he flung himself down with a groan. He hated the womanish sensibility which made him suffer so acutely from the grotesque chances of life. He had known when he married that his wife's former husbands were both living, and that amid the multiplied contacts of modern existence there were a thousand chances to one that he would run against one or the other, yet he found himself as much disturbed by his brief encounter with Haskett as though the law had not obligingly removed all difficulties in the way of their meeting.

Waythorn sprang up and began to pace the room nervously. He had not suffered half as much from his two meetings with Varick. It was Haskett's presence in his own house that made the situation so intolerable. He stood still, hearing steps in the passage.

"This way, please," he heard the nurse say. Haskett was being taken upstairs, then: not a corner of the house but was open to him. Waythorn dropped into another chair, staring vaguely ahead of him. On his dressing-table stood a photograph of Alice, taken when he had first known her. She was Alice Varick then—how fine and exquisite he had thought her! Those were Varick's pearls about her neck. At Waythorn's instance they had been returned before her marriage. Had Haskett ever given her any trinkets—and what had become of them, Waythorn wondered? He realised suddenly that he knew very little of Haskett's past or present situation; but from the man's appearance and manner of speech he could reconstruct with curious precision the surroundings of Alice's first marriage. And it startled him to think that she had, in the background of her life, a phase of existence so different from anything with which he had connected her. Varick, whatever his faults, was a gentleman, in the conventional, traditional sense of the term: the sense which at that moment seemed, oddly enough, to have most meaning to Waythorn. He and Varick had the same social habits, spoke the same language, understood the same allusions. But this other man . . . it was grotesquely uppermost in Waythorn's mind that Haskett had worn a made-up tie attached with an elastic. Why should that ridiculous detail symbolise the whole man? Waythorn was exasperated by his own paltriness, but the fact of the tie expanded, forced itself on him, became as it were the key to Alice's past. He could see her, as Mrs. Haskett, sitting in a "front parlour" furnished in plush, with a pianola, and a copy of "Ben Hur" on the centre-table. He could see her going to the theatre with Haskett—or perhaps even to a "Church Sociable"—she in a "picture hat" and Haskett in a black frock-coat, a little creased, with the made-up tie on an elastic. On the way home they would stop and look at the illuminated shop-windows, lingering over the photographs of New York actresses. On Sunday afternoons Haskett would take her for a walk, pushing Lily ahead of them in a white enamelled perambulator, and Waythorn had a vision of the people they would stop and talk to. He could fancy how pretty Alice must have looked, in a dress adroitly constructed from the hints of a New York fashion-paper, and how she must have looked down on the other women, chafing at her life, and secretly feeling that she belonged in a bigger place.

For the moment his foremost thought was one of wonder at the way in which she had shed the phase of existence which her marriage with Haskett implied. It was as if her whole aspect, every gesture, every inflection, every allusion, were a studied negation of that period of her life. If she had denied being married to Haskett she could hardly have stood more convicted of duplicity than in this obliteration of the self which had been his wife.

Waythorn started up, checking himself in the analysis of her motives. What right had he to create a fantastic effigy of her and then pass judgment on it? She had spoken vaguely of her first marriage as unhappy, had hinted, with becoming reticence, that Haskett had wrought havoc among her young illusions. . . . It was a pity for Waythorn's peace of mind that Haskett's very inoffensiveness shed a new light on the nature of those illusions. A man would rather think that his wife has been brutalised by her first husband than that the process has been reversed.

IV.

"Mr. Waythorn, I don't like that French governess of Lily's."

Haskett, subdued and apologetic, stood before Waythorn in the library, revolving his shabby hat in his hand.

Waythorn, surprised in his armchair over the evening paper, stared back perplexedly at his visitor.

"You'll excuse my asking to see you," Haskett continued. "But this is my last visit, and I thought if I could have a word with you it would be a better way than writing to Mrs. Waythorn's lawyer."

Waythorn rose uneasily. He did not like the French governess either; but that was irrelevant.

"I am not so sure of that," he returned stiffly; "but since you wish it I will give your message to—my wife." He always hesitated over the possessive pronoun in addressing Haskett.

The latter sighed. "I don't know as that will help much. She didn't like it when I spoke to her."

Waythorn turned red. "When did you see her?" he asked.

"Not since the first day I came to see Lily—right after she was taken sick. I remarked to her then that I didn't like the governess."

Waythorn made no answer. He remembered distinctly that, after that first visit, he had asked his wife if she had seen Haskett. She had lied to him then, but she had respected his wishes since; and the incident cast a curious light on her character. He was sure she would not have seen Haskett that first day if she had divined that Waythorn would object, and the fact that she did not divine it was almost as disagreeable to the latter as the discovery that she had lied to him.

"I don't like the woman," Haskett was repeating with mild persistency. "She ain't straight, Mr. Waythorn—she'll teach the child to be underhand. I've noticed a change in Lily—she's too anxious to please—and she don't always tell the truth. She used to be the straightest child, Mr. Waythorn—" He broke off, his voice a little thick. "Not but what I want her to have a stylish education," he ended.

Waythorn was touched. "I'm sorry, Mr. Haskett; but frankly, I don't quite see what I can do."

Haskett hesitated. Then he laid his hat on the table, and advanced to the hearth-rug, on which Waythorn was standing. There was nothing aggressive in his manner, but he had the solemnity of a timid man resolved on a decisive measure.

"There's just one thing you can do, Mr. Waythorn," he said. "You can remind Mrs. Waythorn that, by the decree of the courts, I am entitled to have a voice in Lily's bringing up." He paused, and went on more deprecatingly: "I'm not the kind to talk about enforcing my rights, Mr. Waythorn. I don't know as I think a man is entitled to rights he hasn't known how to hold on to; but this business of the child is different. I've never let go there—and I never mean to."

The scene left Waythorn deeply shaken. Shamefacedly, in indirect ways, he had been finding out about Haskett; and all that he had learned was favourable. The little man, in order to be near his daughter, had sold out his share in a profitable business in Utica, and accepted a modest clerkship in a New York manufacturing house. He boarded in a shabby street and had few acquaintances. His passion for Lily filled his life. Waythorn felt that this exploration of Haskett was like groping about with a dark-lantern in his wife's past; but he saw now that there were recesses his lantern had not explored. He had never enquired into the exact circumstances of his wife's first matrimonial rupture. On the surface all had been fair. It was she who had obtained the divorce, and the court had given her the child. But Waythorn knew how many ambiguities such a verdict might cover. The mere fact that Haskett retained a right over his daughter implied an unsuspected compromise. Waythorn was an idealist. He always refused to recognise unpleasant contingencies till he found himself confronted with them, and then he saw them followed by a spectral train of consequences. His next days were thus haunted, and he determined to try to lay the ghosts by conjuring them up in his wife's presence.

When he repeated Haskett's request a flame of anger passed over her face; but she subdued it instantly and spoke with a slight quiver of outraged motherhood.

"It is very ungentlemanly of him," she said.

The word grated on Waythorn. "That is neither here nor there. It's a bare question of rights."

She murmured: "It's not as if he could ever be a help to Lily—"

Waythorn flushed. This was even less to his taste. "The question is," he repeated, "what authority has he over her?"

She looked downward, twisting herself a little in her seat. "I am willing to see him—I thought you objected," she faltered.

In a flash he understood that she knew the extent of Haskett's claims. Perhaps it was not the first time she had resisted them.

"My objecting has nothing to do with it," he said coldly; "if Haskett has a right to be consulted you must consult him."

She burst into tears, and he saw that she expected him to regard her as a victim.

Haskett did not abuse his rights. Waythorn had felt miserably sure that he would not. But the governess was dismissed, and from time to time the little man demanded an interview with Alice. After the first outburst she accepted the situation with her usual adaptability. Haskett had once reminded Waythorn of the piano-tuner, and Mrs. Waythorn, after a month or two, appeared to class him with that domestic familiar. Waythorn could not but respect the father's tenacity. At first he had tried to cultivate the suspicion that Haskett might be "up to" something, that he had an object in securing a foothold in the house. But in his heart Waythorn was sure of Haskett's single-mindedness; he even guessed in the latter a mild contempt for such advantages as his relation with the Waythorns might offer. Haskett's sincerity of purpose made him invulnerable, and his successor had to accept him as a lien on the property.

Mr. Sellers was sent to Europe to recover from his gout, and Varick's affairs hung on Waythorn's hands. The negotiations were prolonged and complicated; they necessitated frequent conferences between the two men, and the interests of the firm forbade Waythorn's suggesting that his client should transfer his business to another office.

Varick appeared well in the transaction. In moments of relaxation his coarse streak appeared, and Waythorn dreaded his geniality; but in the office he was concise and clear-headed, with a flattering deference to Waythorn's judgment. Their business relations being so affably established, it would have been absurd for the two men to ignore each other in society. The first time they met in a drawing-room, Varick took up their intercourse in the same easy key, and his hostess's grateful glance obliged Waythorn to respond to it. After that they ran across each other frequently, and one evening at a ball Waythorn, wandering through the remoter rooms, came upon Varick seated beside his wife. She coloured a little, and faltered in what she was saying; but Varick nodded to Waythorn without rising, and the latter strolled on.

In the carriage, on the way home, he broke out nervously: "I didn't know you spoke to Varick."

Her voice trembled a little. "It's the first time—he happened to be standing near me; I didn't know what to do. It's so awkward, meeting everywhere—and he said you had been very kind about some business."

"That's different," said Waythorn.

She paused a moment. "I'll do just as you wish," she returned pliantly. "I thought it would be less awkward to speak to him when we meet."

Her pliancy was beginning to sicken him. Had she really no will of her own—no theory about her relation to these men? She had accepted Haskett—did she mean to accept Varick? It was "less awkward," as she had said, and her instinct was to evade difficulties or to circumvent them. With sudden vividness Waythorn saw how the instinct had developed. She was "as easy as an old shoe"—a shoe that too many feet had worn. Her elasticity was the result of tension in too many different directions. Alice Haskett—Alice Varick—Alice Waythorn—she had been each in turn, and had left hanging to each name a little of her privacy, a little of her personality, a little of the inmost self where the unknown god abides.

"Yes—it's better to speak to Varick," said Waythorn wearily.

V.

The winter wore on, and society took advantage of the Waythorns' acceptance of Varick. Harassed hostesses were grateful to them for bridging over a social difficulty, and Mrs. Waythorn was held up as a miracle of good taste. Some experimental spirits could not resist the diversion of throwing Varick and his former wife together, and there were those who thought he found a zest in the propinquity. But Mrs. Waythorn's conduct remained irreproachable. She neither avoided Varick nor sought him out. Even Waythorn could not but admit that she had discovered the solution of the newest social problem.

He had married her without giving much thought to that problem. He had fancied that a woman can shed her past like a man. But now he saw that Alice was bound to hers both by the circumstances which forced her into continued relation with it, and by the traces it had left on her nature. With grim irony Waythorn compared himself to a member of a syndicate. He held so many shares in his wife's personality and his predecessors were his partners in the business. If there had been any element of passion in the transaction he would have felt less deteriorated by it. The fact that Alice took her change of husbands like a change of weather reduced the situation to mediocrity. He could have forgiven her for blunders, for excesses; for resisting Haskett, for yielding to Varick; for anything but her acquiescence and her tact. She reminded him of a juggler tossing knives; but the knives were blunt and she knew they would never cut her.

And then, gradually, habit formed a protecting surface for his sensibilities. If he paid for each day's comfort with the small change of his illusions, he grew daily to value the comfort more and set less store upon the coin. He had drifted into a lulling propinquity with Haskett and Varick and he took refuge in the cheap revenge of satirising the situation. He even began to reckon up the advantages which accrued from it, to ask himself if it were not better to own a third of a wife who knew how to make a man happy than a whole one who had lacked opportunity to acquire the art. For it *was* an art, and made up, like all others, of concessions, eliminations and embellishments; of lights judiciously thrown and shadows skilfully softened. His wife knew exactly how to manage the lights, and he knew exactly to what training she owed her skill. He even tried to trace the source of his obligations, to discriminate between the influences which had combined to produce his domestic happiness: he perceived that Haskett's commonness had made Alice worship good breeding, while Varick's liberal construction of the marriage bond had taught her to value the conjugal virtues; so that he was directly indebted to his predecessors for the devotion which made his life easy if not inspiring.

From this phase he passed into that of complete acceptance. He ceased to satirise himself because time dulled the irony of the situation and the joke lost its humour with its sting. Even the sight of Haskett's hat on the hall table had ceased to touch the springs of epigram. The hat was often seen there now, for it had been decided that it was better for Lily's father to visit her than for the little girl to go to his boarding-house. Waythorn, having acquiesced in this arrangement, had been surprised to find how little difference it made. Haskett was never obtrusive, and the few visitors who met him on the stairs were unaware of his identity. Waythorn did not know how often he saw Alice, but with himself Haskett was seldom in contact.

One afternoon, however, he learned on entering that Lily's father was waiting to see him. In the library he found Haskett occupying a chair in his usual provisional way. Waythorn always felt grateful to him for not leaning back.

"I hope you'll excuse me, Mr. Waythorn," he said rising. "I wanted to see Mrs. Waythorn about Lily, and your man asked me to wait here till she came in."

"Of course," said Waythorn, remembering that a sudden leak had that morning given over the drawing-room to the plumbers.

He opened his cigar-case and held it out to his visitor, and Haskett's acceptance seemed to mark a fresh stage in their intercourse. The spring evening was chilly, and Waythorn invited his guest to draw up his chair to the fire. He meant to find an excuse to leave Haskett in a moment; but he was tired and cold, and after all the little man no longer jarred on him.

The two were enclosed in the intimacy of their blended cigar-smoke when the door opened and Varick walked into the room. Waythorn rose abruptly. It was the first time that Varick had come to the house, and the surprise of seeing him, combined with the singular inopportuneness of his arrival, gave a new edge to Waythorn's blunted sensibilities. He stared at his visitor without speaking.

Varick seemed too preoccupied to notice his host's embarrassment.

"My dear fellow," he exclaimed in his most expansive tone, "I must apologise for tumbling in on you in this way, but I was too late to catch you down town, and so I thought—"

He stopped short, catching sight of Haskett, and his sanguine colour deepened to a flush which spread vividly under his scant blond hair. But in a moment he recovered himself and nodded slightly. Haskett returned the bow in silence, and Waythorn was still groping for speech when the footman came in carrying a tea-table.

The intrusion offered a welcome vent to Waythorn's nerves. "What the deuce are you bringing this here for?" he said sharply.

"I beg your pardon, sir, but the plumbers are still in the drawing-room, and Mrs. Waythorn said she would have tea in the library." The footman's perfectly respectful tone implied a reflection on Waythorn's reasonableness.

"Oh, very well," said the latter resignedly, and the footman proceeded to open the folding tea-table and set out its complicated appointments. While this interminable process continued the three men stood motionless, watching it with a fascinated stare, till Waythorn, to break the silence, said to Varick: "Won't you have a cigar?"

He held out the case he had just tendered to Haskett, and Varick helped himself with a smile. Waythorn looked about for a match, and finding none, proffered a light from his own cigar. Haskett, in the background, held his ground mildly, examining his cigar-tip now and then, and stepping forward at the right moment to knock its ashes into the fire.

The footman at last withdrew, and Varick immediately began: "If I could just say half a word to you about this business—"

"Certainly," stammered Waythorn; "in the dining-room—"

But as he placed his hand on the door it opened from without, and his wife appeared on the threshold.

She came in fresh and smiling, in her street dress and hat, shedding a fragrance from the boa which she loosened in advancing.

"Shall we have tea in here, dear?" she began; and then she caught sight of Varick. Her smile deepened, veiling a slight tremor of surprise.

"Why, how do you do?" she said with a distinct note of pleasure.

As she shook hands with Varick she saw Haskett standing behind him. Her smile faded for a moment, but she recalled it quickly, with a scarcely perceptible side-glance at Waythorn.

"How do you do, Mr. Haskett?" she said, and shook hands with him a shade less cordially.

The three men stood awkwardly before her, till Varick, always the most self-possessed, dashed into an explanatory phrase.

"We—I had to see Waythorn a moment on business," he stammered, brick-red from chin to nape.

Haskett stepped forward with his air of mild obstinacy. "I am sorry to intrude; but you appointed five o'clock"—he directed his resigned glance to the timepiece on the mantel.

She swept aside their embarrassment with a charming gesture of hospitality.

"I'm so sorry—I'm always late; but the afternoon was so lovely." She stood drawing off her gloves, propitiatory and graceful, diffusing about her a sense of ease and familiarity in which the situation lost its grotesqueness. "But before talking business," she added brightly, "I'm sure every one wants a cup of tea."

She dropped into her low chair by the tea-table, and the two visitors, as if drawn by her smile, advanced to receive the cups she held out.

She glanced about for Waythorn, and he took the third cup with a laugh.

[1911]

Charlotte Perkins Gilman
(1860–1935)

If I Were a Man

Educated primarily by her father with emphasis on sciences and history, Charlotte Perkins Gilman was a progressive reformer. The greatniece of Harriet Beecher Stowe, she recognized at an early age the plight of her mother and other New England housewives, particularly their economic servitude.

As a teenager, she worked as an art teacher, governess, and commercial artist; she had a spirited and intellectually lively personal style. Very much like the teenage heroine of her novel *Benigna Machiavelli* (1914), Gilman wanted "to be big—Big—BIG!/I want to know everything . . . I want to be strong, skillful." She married and, after the death of her daughter, had a nervous breakdown. Her doctor diagnosed her as having "inappropriate ambition" and prescribed that she spend the summer in isolation, forbidding her from writing; this inspired *The Yellow Wallpaper* (1892), a partly autobiographical story of a woman artist's nervous breakdown.

In 1894 Gilman moved to California. There she lectured extensively on labor and the woman's place and wrote feminist political poetry and novels. Her feminist utopian masterpiece, *Herland* (1915), celebrates the vigor and strength of an all-women community. Just as Mollie Mathewson in "If I Were a Man" recognizes the possible freedom and potential of being in a man's place, Gilman recognizes the gross lack of balance between the sexes that is fostered by concepts of women's "appropriate" behavior.

"If I were a man, . . ." that was what pretty little Mollie Mathewson always said when Gerald would not do what she wanted him to—which was seldom.

That was what she said this bright morning, with a stamp of her little high-heeled slipper, just because he had made a fuss about that bill, the long one with the "account rendered," which she had forgotten to give him the first time and been afraid to the second—and now he had taken it from the postman himself.

Mollie was "true to type." She was a beautiful instance of what is reverentially called "a true woman." Little, of course—no true woman may be big. Pretty, of course—no true woman could possibly be plain. Whimsical, capricious, charming, changeable, devoted to pretty clothes and always "wearing them well," as the esoteric phrase has it. (This does not refer to the clothes—they do not wear well in the least—but to some special grace of putting them on and carrying them about, granted to but few, it appears.)

She was also a loving wife and a devoted mother possessed of "the social gift" and the love of "society" that goes with it, and, with all these was fond and proud of her home and managed it as capably as—well, as most women do.

If ever there was a true woman it was Mollie Mathewson, yet she was wishing heart and soul she was a man.

And all of a sudden she was!

She was Gerald, walking down the path so erect and square-shouldered, in a hurry for his morning train, as usual, and, it must be confessed, in something of a temper.

Her own words were ringing in her ears—not only the "last word," but several that had gone before, and she was holding her lips tight shut, not to say something she would be sorry for. But instead of acquiescence in the position taken by that angry little figure on the veranda, what she felt was a sort of superior pride, a sympathy as with weakness, a feeling that "I must be gentle with her," in spite of the temper.

A man! Really a man—with only enough subconscious memory of herself remaining to make her recognize the differences.

At first there was a funny sense of size and weight and extra thickness, the feet and hands seemed strangely large, and her long, straight, free legs swung forward at a gait that made her feel as if on stilts.

This presently passed, and in its place, growing all day, wherever she went, came a new and delightful feeling of being *the right size.*

Everything fitted now. Her back snugly against the seat-back, her feet comfortably on the floor. Her feet? . . . His feet! She studied them carefully. Never before, since her early school days, had she felt such freedom and comfort as to feet—they were firm and solid on the ground when she walked; quick, springy, safe—as when, moved by an unrecognizable impulse, she had run after, caught, and swung aboard the car.

Another impulse fished in a convenient pocket for change—instantly, automatically, bringing forth a nickel for the conductor and a penny for the newsboy.

These pockets came as a revelation. Of course she had known they were there, had counted them, made fun of them, mended them, even envied them; but she never had dreamed of how it *felt* to have pockets.

Behind her newspaper she let her consciousness, that odd mingled consciousness, rove from pocket to pocket, realizing the armored assurance of having all those things at hand, instantly get-at-able, ready to meet emergencies. The cigar case gave her a warm feeling of comfort—it was full; the firmly held fountain pen, safe unless she stood on her head; the keys, pencils, letters, documents, notebook, checkbook, bill folder—all at once, with a deep rushing sense of power and pride, she felt what she had never felt before in all her life—the possession of money, of her own earned money—hers to give or to withhold, not to beg for, tease for, wheedle for—hers.

That bill—why, if it had come to her—to him, that is—he would have paid it as a matter of course, and never mentioned it—to her.

Then, being he, sitting there so easily and firmly with his money in his pockets, she wakened to his life-long consciousness about money. Boyhood—its desires and dreams, ambitions. Young manhood—working tremendously for the wherewithal to make a home—for her. The present years with all their net of cares and hopes and dangers; the present moment, when he needed every cent for special plans of great importance, and this bill, long overdue and demanding payment, meant an amount of inconvenience wholly unnecessary if it had been given him when it first came; also, the man's keen dislike of that "account rendered."

"Women have no business sense!" she found herself saying. "And all that money just for hats—idiotic, useless, ugly things!"

With that she began to see the hats of the women in the car as she had never seen hats before. The men's seemed normal, dignified, becoming, with enough variety for personal taste, and with distinction in style and in age, such as she had never noticed before. But the women's—

With the eyes of a man and the brain of a man; with the memory of a whole lifetime of free action wherein the hat, close-fitting on cropped hair, had been no handicap; she now perceived the hats of women.

The massed fluffed hair was at once attractive and foolish, and on that hair, at every angle, in all colors, tipped, twisted, tortured into every crooked shape, made of any substance chance might offer, perched these formless objects. Then, on their formlessness the trimmings—these squirts of stiff feathers, these violent outstanding bows of glistening ribbon, these swaying, projecting masses of plumage which tormented the faces of bystanders.

Never in all her life had she imagined that this idolized millinery could look, to those who paid for it, like the decorations of an insane monkey.

And yet, when there came into the car a little woman, as foolish as any, but pretty and sweet-looking, up rose Gerald Mathewson and gave her his seat. And, later, when there came in a handsome red-cheeked girl, whose hat was wilder, more violent in color and eccentric in shape than any other—when she stood nearby and her soft curling plumes swept his cheek once and again—he felt a sense of sudden pleasure at the intimate tickling touch—and she, deep down within, felt such a wave of shame as might well drown a thousand hats forever.

When he took his train, his seat in the smoking car, she had a new surprise. All about him were the other men, commuters too, and many of them friends of his.

To her, they would have been distinguished as "Mary Wade's husband," "the man Belle Grant is engaged to," "that rich Mr. Shopworth," or "that pleasant Mr. Beale." And they would all have lifted their hats to her, bowed, made polite conversation if near enough—especially Mr. Beale.

Now came the feeling of open-eyed acquaintance, of knowing men—as they were. The mere amount of this knowledge was a surprise to her—the whole background of talk from boyhood up, the gossip of barber-shop and club, the conversation of morning and evening hours on trains, the knowledge of political affiliation, of business standing and prospects, of character—in a light she had never known before.

They came and talked to Gerald, one and another. He seemed quite popular. And as they talked, with this new memory and new understanding, an understanding which seemed to include all these men's minds, there poured in on the submerged consciousness beneath a new, a startling knowledge—what men really think of women.

Good, average, American men were there; married men for the most part, and happy—as happiness goes in general. In the minds of each and all there seemed to be a two-story department, quite apart from the rest of their ideas, a separate place where they kept their thoughts and feelings about women.

In the upper half were the tenderest emotions, the most exquisite ideals, the sweetest memories, all lovely sentiments as to "home" and "mother," all delicate admiring adjectives, a sort of sanctuary, where a veiled statue, blindly adored, shared place with beloved yet commonplace experiences.

In the lower half—here that buried consciousness woke to keen distress—they kept quite another assortment of ideas. Here, even in this clean-minded husband of hers, was the memory of stories told at men's dinners, of worse ones overheard in street or car, of base traditions, coarse epithets, gross experiences—known, though not shared.

And all these in the department "woman," while in the rest of the mind—here was new knowledge indeed.

The world opened before her. Not the world she had been reared in—where Home had covered all the map, almost, and the rest had been "foreign," or "unexplored country," but the world as it was—man's world, as made, lived in, and seen, by men.

It was dizzying. To see the houses that fled so fast across the car window, in terms of builders' bills, or of some technical insight into materials and methods; to see a passing village with lamentable knowledge of who "owned it" and of how its Boss was rapidly aspiring in state power, or of how that kind of paving was a failure; to see shops, not as mere exhibitions of desirable objects, but as business ventures, many mere sinking ships, some promising a profitable voyage—this new world bewildered her.

She—as Gerald—had already forgotten about that bill, over which she—as Mollie—was still crying at home. Gerald was "talking business" with this man, "talking politics" with that, and now sympathizing with the carefully withheld troubles of a neighbor.

Mollie had always sympathized with the neighbor's wife before.

She began to struggle violently with this large dominant masculine consciousness. She remembered with sudden clearness things she had read, lectures she had heard, and resented with increasing intensity this serene masculine preoccupation with the male point of view.

Mr. Miles, the little fussy man who lived on the other side of the street, was talking now. He had a large complacent wife; Mollie had never liked her much, but had always thought him rather nice—he was so punctilious in small courtesies.

And here he was talking to Gerald—such talk!

"Had to come in here," he said. "Gave my seat to a dame who was bound to have it. There's nothing they won't get when they make up their minds to it—eh?"

"No fear!" said the big man in the next seat. "They haven't much mind to make up, you know—and if they do, they'll change it."

"The real danger," began the Rev. Alfred Smythe, the new Episcopal clergyman, a thin, nervous, tall man with a face several centuries behind the times, "is that they will overstep the limits of their God-appointed sphere."

"Their natural limits ought to hold 'em, I think," said cheerful Dr. Jones. "You can't get around physiology, I tell you."

"I've never seen any limits, myself, not to what they want, anyhow," said Mr. Miles. "Merely a rich husband and a fine house and no end of bonnets and dresses, and the latest thing in motors, and a few diamonds—and so on. Keeps us pretty busy."

There was a tired gray man across the aisle. He had a very nice wife, always beautifully dressed, and three unmarried daughters, also beautifully dressed—Mollie knew them. She knew he worked hard, too, and she looked at him now a little anxiously.

But he smiled cheerfully.

"Do you good, Miles," he said. "What else would a man work for? A good woman is about the best thing on earth."

"And a bad one's the worst, that's sure," responded Miles.

"She's a pretty weak sister, viewed professionally," Dr. Jones averred with solemnity, and the Rev. Alfred Smythe added, "She brought evil into the world."

Gerald Mathewson sat up straight. Something was stirring in him which he did not recognize—yet could not resist.

"Seems to me we all talk like Noah," he suggested drily. "Or the ancient Hindu scriptures. Women have their limitations, but so do we, God knows. Haven't we known girls in school and college just as smart as we were?"

"They cannot play our games," coldly replied the clergyman.

Gerald measured his meager proportions with a practiced eye.

"I never was particularly good at football myself," he modestly admitted, "but I've known women who could outlast a man in all-round endurance. Besides—life isn't spent in athletics!"

This was sadly true. They all looked down the aisle where a heavy ill-dressed man with a bad complexion sat alone. He had held the top of the columns once, with headlines and photographs. Now he earned less than any of them.

"It's time we woke up," pursued Gerald, still inwardly urged to unfamiliar speech. "Women are pretty much *people*, seems to me. I know they dress like fools—but who's to blame for that? We invent all those idiotic hats of theirs, and design their crazy fashions, and, what's more, if a woman is courageous enough to wear common-sense clothes—and shoes—which of us wants to dance with her?

"Yes, we blame them for grafting on us, but are we willing to let our wives work? We are not. It hurts our pride, that's all. We are always criticizing them for making mercenary marriages, but what do we call a girl who marries a chump with no money? Just a poor fool, that's all. And they know it.

"As for Mother Eve—I wasn't there and can't deny the story, but I will say this. If she brought evil into the world, we men have had the lion's share of keeping it going ever since—how about that?"

They drew into the city, and all day long in his business, Gerald was vaguely conscious of new views, strange feelings, and the submerged Mollie learned and learned.

[1914]

Zora Neale Hurston
(1901–1960)

Sweat

A fiercely independent child, Zora Neale Hurston was born in a self-governed, all-black Florida town and used this fact to the best of her advantage: She recognized the richness of her racial exposure and built her writing from it. Her first short fiction was written while she was a student at Howard University; she then moved to New York and earned an anthropology scholarship to Barnard College. Later, she went south on a fellowship to collect folklore. As a result of this expedition, she developed a style of her own in which black characters usually struggle with human, not racial, problems.

All of Hurston's female protagonists, like Delia in "Sweat," are independent, proud, and strong. Her fiction is laced with elements of the folklore and sermons of the black South, capturing for the reader the essence of Southern black culture while at the same time making universally human statements.

Her novels include *Jonah's Gourd Vine* (1934), *Their Eyes Were Watching God* (1937), *Moses, Man of the Mountain* (1939), and *Seraph on the Suwanee* (1948). Her reputation peaked in 1942 upon publication of her autobiography, *Dust Tracks on a Road*. Her withdrawal following a false morals charge in 1948 and increasing poverty contributed to the decline that preceded her death. However, she is admired for seeking and drawing strength from her African-American heritage.

It was eleven o'clock of a Spring night in Florida. It was Sunday. Any other night, Delia Jones would have been in bed for two hours by this time. But she was a washwoman, and Monday morning meant a great deal to her. So she collected the soiled clothes on Saturday when she returned the clean things. Sunday night after church, she sorted them and put the white things to soak. It saved her almost a half day's start. A great hamper in the bedroom held the clothes that she brought home. It was so much neater than a number of bundles lying around.

She squatted in the kitchen floor beside the great pile of clothes, sorting them into small heaps according to color, and humming a song in a mournful key, but wondering through it all where Sykes, her husband, had gone with her horse and buckboard.

Just then something long, round, limp and black fell upon her shoulders and slithered to the floor beside her. A great terror took hold of her. It softened her knees and dried her mouth so that it was a full minute before she could cry out or move. Then she saw that it was the big bull whip her husband liked to carry when he drove.

She lifted her eyes to the door and saw him standing there bent over with laughter at her fright. She screamed at him.

"Sykes, what you throw dat whip on me like dat? You know it would skeer me—looks like a snake, an' you knows how skeered Ah is of snakes."

"Course Ah knowed it! That's how come Ah done it." He slapped his leg with his hand and almost rolled on the ground in his mirth. "If you such a big fool dat you got to have a fit over a earth worm or a string, Ah don't keer how bad Ah skeer you."

"You aint got no business doing it. Gawd knows it's a sin. Some day Ah'm gointuh drop dead from some of yo' foolishness. 'Nother thing, where you been wid mah rig? Ah feeds dat pony. He aint fuh you to be drivin' wid no bull whip."

"You sho is one aggravatin' nigger woman!" he declared and stepped into the room. She resumed her work and did not answer him at once. "Ah done tole you time and again to keep them white folks' clothes outa dis house."

He picked up the whip and glared down at her. Delia went on with her work. She went out into the yard and returned with a galvanized tub and set it on the washbench. She saw that Sykes had kicked all of the clothes together again, and now stood in her way truculently, his whole manner hoping, *praying*, for an argument. But she walked calmly around him and commenced to re-sort the things.

"Next time, Ah'm gointer kick 'em outdoors," he threatened as he struck a match along the leg of his corduroy breeches.

Delia never looked up from her work, and her thin, stooped shoulders sagged further.

"Ah aint for no fuss t'night, Sykes. Ah just come from taking sacrament at the church house."

He snorted scornfully. "Yeah, you just come from de church house on a Sunday night, but heah you is gone to work on them clothes. You aint nothing but a hypocrite. One of them amen-corner Christians—sing, whoop, and shout, then come home and wash white folks' clothes on the Sabbath."

He stepped roughly upon the whitest pile of things, kicking them helter-skelter as he crossed the room. His wife gave a little scream of dismay, and quickly gathered them together again.

"Sykes, you quit grindin' dirt into these clothes! How can Ah git through by Sat'day if Ah don't start on Sunday?"

"Ah don't keer if you never git through. Anyhow, Ah done promised Gawd and a couple of other men, Ah aint gointer have it in mah house. Don't gimme no lip neither, else Ah'll throw 'em out and put mah fist up side yo' head to boot."

Delia's habitual meekness seemed to slip from her shoulders like a blown scarf. She was on her feet; her poor little body, her bare knuckly hands bravely defying the strapping hulk before her.

"Looka heah, Sykes, you done gone too fur. Ah been married to you fur fifteen years, and Ah been takin' in washin' fur fifteen years, Sweat, sweat, sweat! Work and sweat, cry and sweat, pray and sweat!"

"What's that got to do with me?" he asked brutally.

"What's it got to do with you, Sykes? Mah tub of suds is filled yo' belly with vittles more times than yo' hands is filled it. Mah sweat is done paid for this house and Ah reckon Ah kin keep on sweatin' in it."

She seized the iron skillet from the stove and struck a defensive pose, which act surprised him greatly, coming from her. It cowed him and he did not strike her as he usually did.

"Naw you won't," she panted, "that ole snaggle-toothed black woman you runnin' with aint comin' heah to pile up on *mah* sweat and blood. You aint paid for nothin' on this place, and Ah'm gointer stay right heah till Ah'm toted out foot foremost."

"Well, you better quit gittin' me riled up, else they'll be totin' you out sooner than you expect. Ah'm so tired of you Ah don't know whut to do. Gawd! how Ah hates skinny wimmen!"

A little awed by his new Delia, he sidled out of the door and slammed the back gate after him. He did not say where he had gone, but she knew too well. She knew very well that he would not return until nearly daybreak also. Her work over, she went on to bed but not to sleep at once. Things had come to a pretty pass!

She lay awake, gazing upon the debris that cluttered their matrimonial trail. Not an image left standing along the way. Anything like flowers had long ago been drowned in the salty stream that had been pressed from her heart. Her tears, her sweat, her blood. She had brought love to the union and he had brought a longing after the flesh. Two months after the wedding, he had given her the first brutal beating. She had the memory of his numerous trips to Orlando with all of his wages when he had returned to her penniless, even before the first year had passed. She was young and soft then, but now she thought of her knotty, muscled limbs, her harsh knuckly hands, and drew herself up into an unhappy little ball in the middle of the big feather bed. Too late now to hope for love, even if it were not Bertha it would be someone else. This case differed from the others only in that she was bolder than the others. Too late for everything except her little home. She had built it for her old days, and planted one by one the trees and flowers there. It was lovely to her, lovely.

Somehow, before sleep came, she found herself saying aloud: "Oh well, whatever goes over the Devil's back, is got to come under his belly. Sometime or ruther, Sykes, like everybody else, is gointer reap his sowing." After that she was able to build a spiritual earthworks against her husband. His shells could no longer reach her. *Amen.* She went to sleep and slept until he announced his presence by kicking her feet and rudely snatching the covers away.

"Gimme some kivah heah, an' git yo' damn foots over on yo' own side! Ah oughter mash you in yo' mouf fuh drawing dat skillet on me."

Delia went clear to the rail without answering him. A triumphant indifference to all that he was or did.

The week was full of work for Delia as all other weeks, and Saturday found her behind her little pony, collecting and delivering clothes.

It was a hot, hot day near the end of July. The village men on Joe Clarke's porch even chewed cane listlessly. They did not hurl the caneknots as usual. They let them dribble over the edge of the porch. Even conversation had collapsed under the heat.

"Heah come Delia Jones," Jim Merchant said, as the shaggy

pony came 'round the bend of the road toward them. The rusty buckboard was heaped with baskets of crisp, clean laundry.

"Yep," Joe Lindsay agreed. "Hot or col', rain or shine, jes ez reg'lar ez de weeks roll roun' Delia carries 'em an' fetches 'em on Sat'day."

"She better if she wanter eat," said Moss. "Syke Jones aint wuth de shot an' powder hit would tek tuh kill 'em. Not to *huh* he aint."

"He sho' aint," Walter Thomas chimed in. "It's too bad, too, cause she wuz a right pritty lil trick when he got huh. Ah'd uh mah'ied huh mahseff if he hadnter beat me to it."

Delia nodded briefly at the men as she drove past.

"Too much knockin' will ruin *any* 'oman. He done beat huh 'nough tuh kill three women, let 'lone change they looks," said Elijah Moseley. "How Syke kin stommuck dat big black greasy Mogul he's layin' roun' wid, gits me. Ah swear dat eight-rock couldn't kiss a sardine can Ah done thowed out de back do' 'way las' yeah."

"Aw, she's fat, thass how come. He's allus been crazy 'bout fat women," put in Merchant. "He'd a' been tied up wid one long time ago if he could a' found one tuh have him. Did Ah tell yuh 'bout him come sidlin' in' roun' *mah* wife—bringin' her a basket uh peecans outa his yard fur a present? Yessir, mah wife! She tol' him tuh take em right straight back home, cause Delia works so hard ovah dat wash tub she reckon everything on de place taste lak sweat an' soapsuds. Ah jus' wisht Ah'd a caught 'im 'roun' dere! Ah'd a' made his hips ketch on fiah down dat shell road."

"Ah know he done it, too. Ah sees 'im grinnin' at every 'oman dat passes," Walter Thomas said. "But even so, he useter eat some mighty big hunks uh humble pie tuh git dat lil' 'oman he got. She wuz ez pritty ez a speckled pup! Dat wuz fifteen yeahs ago. He useter be so skeered uh losin' huh, she could make him do some parts of a husband's duty. Dey never wuz de same in de mind."

"There oughter be a law about him," said Lindsay. "He aint fit tuh carry guts tuh a bear."

Clarke spoke for the first time. "Taint no law on earth dat kin make a man be decent if it aint in 'im. There's plenty men dat takes a wife lak dey do a joint uh sugar-cane. It's round, juicy an' sweet when dey gits it. But dey squeeze an' grind, squeeze an' grind an' wring tell dey wring every drop uh pleasure dat's in 'em out. When dey's satisfied dat dey is wrung dry, dey treats 'em jes lak dey do a cane-chew. Dey throws 'em away. Dey knows whut dey is doin' while dey is at it, an' hates theirselves fuh it but they keeps on hangin' after huh tell she's empty. Den dey hates huh fuh bein' a cane-chew an' in de way."

"We oughter take Syke an' dat stray 'oman uh his'n down in Lake Howell swamp an' lay on de rawhide till they cain't say 'Lawd a' mussy.' He allus wuz uh ovahbearin' niggah, but since dat white 'oman from up north done teached 'im how to run a automobile, he done got too biggety to live—an' we oughter kill 'im." Old man Anderson advised.

A grunt of approval went around the porch. But the heat was melting their civic virtue and Elijah Moseley began to bait Joe Clarke.

"Come on, Joe, git a melon outa dere an' slice it up for yo' customers. We'se all sufferin' wid de heat. De bear's done got *me!*"

"Thass right, Joe, a watermelon is jes' whut Ah needs tuh cure de eppizudicks," Walter Thomas joined forces with Moseley. "Come on dere, Joe. We all is steady customers an' you aint set us up in a long time. Ah chooses dat long, bowlegged Floridy favorite."

"A god, an' be dough. You all gimme twenty cents and slice way." Clarke retorted. "Ah needs a col' slice m'self. Heah, everybody chip in. Ah'll lend y'll mah meat knife."

The money was quickly subscribed and the huge melon brought forth. At that moment, Sykes and Bertha arrived. A determined silence fell on the porch and the melon was put away again.

Merchant snapped down the blade of his jackknife and moved toward the store door.

"Come on in, Joe, an' gimme a slab uh sow belly an' uh pound uh coffee—almost fuhgot 'twas Sat'day. Got to git on home." Most of the men left also.

Just then Delia drove past on her way home, as Sykes was ordering magnificently for Bertha. It pleased him for Delia to see.

"Git whutsoever yo' heart desires, Honey. Wait a minute, Joe. Give huh two bottles uh strawberry soda-water, uh quart uh parched ground-peas, an' a block uh chewin' gum."

With all this they left the store, with Sykes reminding Bertha that this was his town and she could have it if she wanted it.

The men returned soon after they left, and held their watermelon feast.

"Where did Syke Jones git da 'oman from nohow?" Lindsay asked.

"Ovah Apopka. Guess dey musta been cleanin' out de town when she lef'. She don't look lak a thing but a hunk uh liver wid hair on it."

"Well, she sho' kin squall," Dave Carter contributed. "When she gits ready tuh laff, she jes' opens huh mouf an' latches it back tuh de las' notch. No ole grandpa alligator down in Lake Bell aint got nothin' on huh."

Bertha had been in town three months now. Sykes was still paying her room rent at Della Lewis'—the only house in town that would have taken her in. Sykes took her frequently to Winter Park to "stomps." He still assured her that he was the swellest man in the state.

"Sho' you kin have dat lil' ole house soon's Ah kin git dat 'oman outa dere. Everything b'longs tuh me an' you sho' kin have it. Ah sho' 'bominates uh skinny 'oman. Lawdy, you sho' is got one portly shape on you! You kin git *anything* you wants. Dis is *mah* town an' you sho' kin have it."

Delia's work-worn knees crawled over the earth in Gethesemane and up the rocks of Calvary many, many times during these months. She avoided the villagers and meeting places in her efforts to be blind and deaf. But Bertha nullified this to a degree, by coming to Delia's house to call Sykes out to her at the gate.

Delia and Sykes fought all the time now with no peaceful interludes. They slept and ate in silence. Two or three times Delia had attempted a timid friendliness, but she was repulsed each time. It was plain that the breaches must remain agape.

The sun had burned July to August. The heat streamed down like a million hot arrows, smiting all things living upon the earth. Grass withered, leaves browned, snakes went blind in shedding and men and dogs went mad. Dog days!

Delia came home one day and found Sykes there before her. She wondered, but started to go on into the house without speaking, even though he was standing in the kitchen door and she must either stoop under his arm or ask him to move. He made no room for her. She noticed a soap box beside the steps, but paid no particular attention to it, knowing that he must have brought it there. As she was stooping to pass under his outstretched arm, he suddenly pushed her backward, laughingly.

"Look in de box dere Delia, Ah done brung yuh somethin'!"

She nearly fell upon the box in her stumbling, and when she saw what it held, she all but fainted outright.

"Syke! Syke, mah Gawd! You take dat rattlesnake 'way from heah! You *gottuh*. Oh, Jesus, have mussy!"

"Ah aint gut tuh do nuthin' uh de kin'—fact is Ah aint got tuh do nothin' but die. Taint no use uh you puttin' on airs makin' out lak you skeered uh dat snake—he's gointer stay right heah tell he die. He wouldn't bite me cause Ah knows how tuh handle 'im. Nohow he wouldn't risk breakin' out his fangs 'gin *yo'* skinny laigs."

"Naw, now Syke, don't keep dat thing 'roun' heah tuh skeer me tuh death. You knows Ah'm even feared uh earth worms. Thass de biggest snake Ah evah did see. Kill 'im Syke, please."

"Doan ast me tuh do nothin' fuh yuh. Goin' 'roun' tryin' tuh be so damn asterperious. Naw, Ah aint gonna kill it. Ah think uh damn sight mo' uh him dan you! Dat's a nice snake an' anybody doan lak 'im kin jes' hit de grit."

The village soon heard that Sykes had the snake, and came to see and ask questions.

"How de hen-fire did you ketch dat six-foot rattler, Syke?" Thomas asked.

"He's full uh frogs so he caint hardly move, thass how Ah eased up on 'm. But Ah'm a snake charmer an' knows how tuh handle 'em. Shux, dat aint nothin'. Ah could ketch one eve'y day if Ah so wanted tuh."

"Whut he needs is a heavy hick'ry club leaned real heavy on his head. Dat's de bes' way tuh charm a rattlesnake."

"Naw, Walt, y'll jes' don't understand dese diamon' backs lak Ah do," said Sykes in a superior tone of voice.

The village agreed with Walter, but the snake stayed on. His box remained by the kitchen door with its screen wire covering. Two or three days later it had digested its meal of frogs and literally came to life. It rattled at every movement in the kitchen or the yard. One day as Delia came down the kitchen steps she saw his chalky-white fangs curved like scimitars hung in the wire meshes. This time she did not run away with averted eyes as usual. She stood for a long time in the doorway in a red fury that grew bloodier for every second that she regarded the creature that was her torment.

That night she broached the subject as soon as Sykes sat down to the table.

"Syke, Ah wants you tuh take dat snake 'way fum heah. You done starved me an' Ah put up widcher, you done beat me an' Ah took dat, but you done kilt all mah insides bringin' dat varmint heah."

Sykes poured out a saucer full of coffee and drank it deliberately before he answered her.

"A whole lot Ah keer 'bout how you feels inside uh out. Dat snake aint goin' no damn wheah till Ah gits ready fuh 'im tuh go. So fur as beatin' is concerned, yuh aint took near all dat you gointer take ef yuh stay 'roun' *me*."

Delia pushed back her plate and got up from the table. "Ah hates you, Sykes," she said calmly. "Ah hates you tuh de same degree dat Ah useter love yuh. Ah done took an' took till mah belly is full up tuh mah neck. Dat's de reason Ah got mah letter fum de church an' moved mah membership tuh Woodbridge—so Ah don't haftuh take no sacrament wid yuh. Ah don't wantuh see yuh 'roun' me atall. Lay 'roun' wid dat 'oman all yuh wants tuh, but gwan 'way fum me an' mah house. Ah hates yuh lak uh suck-egg dog."

Sykes almost let the huge wad of corn bread and collard greens he was chewing fall out of his mouth in amazement. He had a hard time whipping himself up to the proper fury to try to answer Delia.

"Well, Ah'm glad you does hate me. Ah'm sho' tiahed uh you hangin' ontuh me. Ah don't want yuh. Look at yuh stringey old neck! Yo' rawbony laigs an' arms is enough tuh cut uh man tuh death. You looks jes' lak de devvul's doll-baby tuh *me*. You cain't hate me no worse dan Ah hates you. Ah been hatin' *you* fuh years."

"Yo' ole black hide don't look lak nothin' tuh me, but uh passle uh wrinkled up rubber, wid yo' big ole yeahs flappin' on each side lak uh paih uh buzzard wings. Don't think Ah'm gointuh be run 'way fum mah house neither. Ah'm goin' tuh de white folks bout *you*, mah young man, de very nex' time you lay yo' han's on me. Mah cup is done run ovah."

Delia said this with no signs of fear and Sykes departed from the house, threatening her, but made not the slightest move to carry out any of them.

That night he did not return at all, and the next day being Sunday, Delia was glad she did not have to quarrel before she hitched up her pony and drove the four miles to Woodbridge.

She stayed to the night service—"love feast"—which was very warm and full of spirit. In the emotional winds her domestic trials were borne far and wide so that she sang as she drove homeward,

> "Jurden water, black an' col'
> Chills de body, not de soul
> An' Ah wantah cross Jurden in uh calm time."

She came from the barn to the kitchen door and stopped.

"Whut's de mattah, ol' satan, you aint kickin' up yo' racket?" She addressed the snake's box. Complete silence. She went on into the house with a new hope in its birth struggles. Perhaps her threat to go to the white folks had frightened Sykes! Perhaps he was sorry! Fifteen years of misery and suppression had brought Delia to the place where she would hope *anything* that looked towards a way over or through her wall of inhibitions.

She felt in the match safe behind the stove at once for a match. There was only one there.

"Dat niggah wouldn't fetch nothin' heah tuh save his rotten neck, but he kin run thew whut Ah brings quick enough. Now he done toted off nigh on tuh haff uh box uh matches. He done had dat 'oman heah in mah house too."

Nobody but a woman could tell how she knew this even before she struck the match. But she did and it put her into a new fury.

Presently she brought in the tubs to put the white things to soak. This time she decided she need not bring the hamper out of the bedroom: she would go in there and do the sorting. She picked up the pot-bellied lamp and went in. The room was small and the hamper stood hard by the foot of the white iron bed. She could sit and reach through the bedposts—resting as she worked.

"Ah wantah cross Jurden in uh calm time." She was singing again. The mood of the "love feast" had returned. She threw back the lid of the basket almost gaily. Then, moved by both horror and terror, she sprang back toward the door. *There lay the snake in the basket!* He moved sluggishly at first, but even as she turned round and round, jumped up and down in an insanity of fear, he began to stir vigorously. She saw him pouring his awful beauty from the basket upon the bed, then she seized the lamp and ran as fast as she could to the kitchen. The wind from the open door blew out the light and the darkness added to her terror. She sped to the darkness of the yard, slamming the door after her before she thought to set down the lamp. She did not feel safe even on the ground, so she climbed up in the hay barn.

There for an hour or more she lay sprawled upon the hay a gibbering wreck.

Finally she grew quiet, and after that, coherent thought. With this, stalked through her a cold, bloody rage. Hours of this. A period of introspection, a space of retrospection, then a mixture of both. Out of this an awful calm.

"Well, Ah done de bes' Ah could. If things aint right, Gawd knows taint mah fault."

She went to sleep—a twitch sleep—and woke up to a faint gray sky. There was a loud hollow sound below. She peered out. Sykes was at the wood-pile, demolishing a wire-covered box.

He hurried to the kitchen door, but hung outside there some minutes before he entered, and stood some minutes more inside before he closed it after him.

The gray in the sky was spreading. Delia descended without fear now, and crouched beneath the low bedroom window. The drawn shade shut out the dawn, shut in the night. But the thin walls held back no sound.

"Dat ol' scratch is woke up now!" She mused at the tremendous whirr inside, which every woodsman knows, is one of the sound illusions. The rattler is a ventriloquist. His whirr sounds to the right, to the left, straight ahead, behind, close under foot—everywhere but where it is. Woe to him who guesses wrong unless he is prepared to hold up his end of the argument! Sometimes he strikes without rattling at all.

Inside, Sykes heard nothing until he knocked a pot lid off the stove while trying to reach the match safe in the dark. He had emptied his pockets at Bertha's.

The snake seemed to wake up under the stove and Sykes made a quick leap into the bedroom. In spite of the gin he had had, his head was clearing now.

"Mah Gawd!" he chattered, "ef Ah could on'y strack uh light!"

The rattling ceased for a moment as he stood paralyzed. He waited. It seemed that the snake waited also.

"Oh, fuh de light! Ah thought he'd be too sick"—Sykes was muttering to himself when the whirr began again, closer, right underfoot this time. Long before this, Sykes' ability to think had been flattened down to primitive instinct and he leaped—onto the bed.

Outside Delia heard a cry that might have come from a maddened chimpanzee, a stricken gorilla. All the terror, all the horror, all the rage that man possibly could express, without a recognizable human sound.

A tremendous stir inside there, another series of animal screams, the intermittent whirr of the reptile. The shade torn violently down from the window, letting in the red dawn, a huge brown hand seizing the window stick, great dull blows upon the wooden floor punctuating the gibberish of sound long after the rattle of the snake had abruptly subsided. All this Delia could see and hear from her place beneath the window, and it made her ill. She crept over to the four-o'clocks and stretched herself on the cool earth to recover.

She lay there. "Delia, Delia!" She could hear Sykes calling in a most despairing tone as one who expected no answer. The sun crept on up, and he called. Delia could not move—her legs were gone flabby. She never moved, he called, and the sun kept rising.

"Mah Gawd!" She heard him moan, "Mah Gawd fum Heben!" She heard him stumbling about and got up from her flower-bed. The sun was growing warm. As she approached the door she heard him call out hopefully, "Delia, is dat you Ah heah?"

She saw him on his hands and knees as soon as she reached the door. He crept an inch or two toward her—all that he was able, and she saw his horribly swollen neck and his one open eye shining with hope. A surge of pity too strong to support bore her away from that eye that must, could not, fail to see the tubs. He would see the lamp. Orlando with its doctors was too far. She could scarcely reach the Chinaberry tree, where she waited in the growing heat while inside she knew the cold river was creeping up and up to extinguish that eye which must know by now that she knew.

[1926]

Virginia Woolf
(1882–1941)

Lappin and Lapinova

The daughter of a Victorian scholar, editor, and critic, Virginia Ste-
phen read incessantly and was educated by her parents, but envied her
brothers' school and university careers. As an early modernist and a
member of the Bloomsbury group, she violated the conventions of
traditional fiction and sought to awaken the reader to the intensity she
recognized in both life and art. She married Leonard Woolf in 1912.
Amid several suicide attempts and severe breakdowns, she wrote such
celebrated novels as *The Voyage Out* (1915), *To the Lighthouse*
(1927), *Orlando* (1928), and *Mrs. Dalloway* (1928). Her definitive
essay on women and writing, *A Room of One's Own* (1929), which
was based on lectures she gave at a women's college at Cambridge,
asserts that a woman must have £500 a year and her own private room
in order to write to her full capacity. In 1941 Woolf drowned herself.

They were married. The wedding march pealed out. The pigeons
fluttered. Small boys in Eton jackets threw rice; a fox terrier sauntered
across the path; and Ernest Thorburn led his bride to the car through
that small inquisitive crowd of complete strangers which always
collects in London to enjoy other people's happiness or unhappiness.
Certainly he looked handsome and she looked shy. More rice was
thrown, and the car moved off.

That was on Tuesday. Now it was Saturday. Rosalind had still to
get used to the fact that she was Mrs. Ernest Thorburn. Perhaps she

never would get used to the fact that she was Mrs. Ernest Anybody, she thought, as she sat in the bow window of the hotel looking over the lake to the mountains, and waited for her husband to come down to breakfast. Ernest was a difficult name to get used to. It was not the name she would have chosen. She would have preferred Timothy, Antony, or Peter. He did not look like Ernest either. The name suggested the Albert Memorial, mahogany sideboards, steel engravings of the Prince Consort with his family—her mother-in-law's dining-room in Porchester Terrace in short.

But here he was. Thank goodness he did not look like Ernest—no. But what did he look like? She glanced at him sideways. Well, when he was eating toast he looked like a rabbit. Not that anyone else would have seen a likeness to a creature so diminutive and timid in this spruce, muscular young man with the straight nose, the blue eyes, and the very firm mouth. But that made it all the more amusing. His nose twitched very slightly when he ate. So did her pet rabbit's. She kept watching his nose twitch; and then she had to explain, when he caught her looking at him, why she laughed.

"It's because you're like a rabbit, Ernest," she said. "Like a wild rabbit," she added, looking at him. "A hunting rabbit; a King Rabbit; a rabbit that makes laws for all the other rabbits."

Ernest had no objection to being that kind of rabbit, and since it amused her to see him twitch his nose—he had never known that his nose twitched—he twitched it on purpose. And she laughed and laughed; and he laughed too, so that the maiden ladies and the fishing man and the Swiss waiter in his greasy black jacket all guessed right; they were very happy. But how long does such happiness last? they asked themselves; and each answered according to his own circumstances.

At lunch time, seated on a clump of heather beside the lake, "Lettuce, rabbit?" said Rosalind, holding out the lettuce that had been provided to eat with the hard-boiled eggs. "Come and take it out of my hand," she added, and he stretched out and nibbled the lettuce and twitched his nose.

"Good rabbit, nice rabbit," she said, patting him, as she used to pat her tame rabbit at home. But that was absurd. He was not a tame rabbit, whatever he was. She turned it into French. "Lapin," she called him. But whatever he was, he was not a French rabbit. He was simply and solely English—born at Porchester Terrace, educated at Rugby; now a clerk in His Majesty's Civil Service. So she tried "Bunny" next; but that was worse. "Bunny" was someone plump and soft and comic; he was thin and hard and serious. Still, his nose twitched. "Lappin," she exclaimed suddenly; and gave a little cry as if she had found the very word she looked for.

"Lappin, Lappin, King Lappin," she repeated. It seemed to suit him exactly; he was not Ernest, he was King Lappin. Why? She did not know.

When there was nothing new to talk about on their long solitary walks—and it rained, as everyone had warned them that it would rain; or when they were sitting over the fire in the evening, for it was cold, and the maiden ladies had gone and the fishing man, and the waiter only came if you rang the bell for him, she let her fancy play with the story of the Lappin tribe. Under her hands—she was sewing; he was reading—they became very real, very vivid, very amusing. Ernest put down the paper and helped her. There were the black rabbits and the red; there were the enemy rabbits and the friendly. There were the wood in which they lived and the outlying prairies and the swamp. Above all there was King Lappin, who, far from having only the one trick—that he twitched his nose—became as the days passed an animal of the greatest character; Rosalind was always finding new qualities in him. But above all he was a great hunter.

"And what," said Rosalind, on the last day of the honeymoon, "did the King do today?"

In fact they had been climbing all day; and she had worn a blister on her heel; but she did not mean that.

"Today," said Ernest, twitching his nose as he bit the end off his cigar, "he chased a hare." He paused; struck a match, and twitched again.

"A woman hare," he added.

"A white hare!" Rosalind exclaimed, as if she had been expecting this. "Rather a small hare; silver grey; with big bright eyes?"

"Yes," said Ernest, looking at her as she had looked at him, "a smallish animal; with eyes popping out of her head, and two little front paws dangling." It was exactly how she sat, with her sewing dangling in her hands; and her eyes, that were so big and bright, were certainly a little prominent.

"Ah, Lapinova," Rosalind murmured.

"Is that what she's called?" said Ernest—"the real Rosalind?" He looked at her. He felt very much in love with her.

"Yes; that's what she's called," said Rosalind. "Lapinova." And before they went to bed that night it was all settled. He was King Lappin; she was Queen Lapinova. They were the opposite of each other; he was bold and determined; she wary and undependable. He ruled over the busy world of rabbits; her world was a desolate, mysterious place, which she ranged mostly by moonlight. All the same, their territories touched; they were King and Queen.

Thus when they came back from their honeymoon they possessed a private world, inhabited, save for the one white hare, entirely by rabbits. No one guessed that there was such a place, and that of course made it all the more amusing. It made them feel, more even than most young married couples, in league together against the rest of the world. Often they looked slyly at each other when people talked about rabbits and woods and traps and shooting. Or they winked furtively across the table when Aunt Mary said that she could never bear to see a hare in a dish—it looked so like a baby: or when John, Ernest's sporting brother, told them what price rabbits were fetching that autumn in Wiltshire, skins and all. Sometimes when they wanted a gamekeeper, or a poacher or a Lord of the Manor, they amused themselves by distributing the parts among their friends. Ernest's mother, Mrs. Reginald Thorburn, for example, fitted the part of the Squire to perfection. But it was all secret—that was the point of it; nobody save themselves knew that such a world existed.

Without that world, how, Rosalind wondered that winter, could she have lived at all? For instance, there was the golden-wedding party, when all the Thorburns assembled at Porchester Terrace to celebrate the fiftieth anniversary of that union which had been so blessed—had it not produced Ernest Thorburn?—and so fruitful—had it not produced nine other sons and daughters into the bargain, many themselves married and also fruitful? She dreaded that party. But it was inevitable. As she walked upstairs she felt bitterly that she was an only child and an orphan at that; a mere drop among all those Thorburns assembled in the great drawing-room with the shiny satin wallpaper and the lustrous family portraits. The living Thorburns much resembled the painted; save that instead of painted lips they had real lips; out of which came jokes; jokes about schoolrooms, and how they had pulled the chair from under the governess; jokes about frogs and how they had put them between the virgin sheets of maiden ladies. As for herself, she had never even made an apple-pie bed. Holding her present in her hand she advanced toward her mother-in-law sumptuous in yellow satin; and toward her father-in-law decorated with a rich yellow carnation. All round them on tables and chairs there were golden tributes, some nestling in cotton wool; others branching resplendent—candlesticks; cigar boxes; chains; each stamped with the goldsmith's proof that it was solid gold, hall-marked, authentic. But her present was only a little pinchbeck box pierced with holes; an old sand caster, an eighteenth-century relic, once used to sprinkle sand over wet ink. Rather a senseless present she felt—in an age of blotting paper; and as she proffered it, she saw in front of her the stubby black handwriting in which her mother-in-law when they were engaged had expressed the hope that "My son will make you happy." No, she was not happy. Not at all happy. She looked at Ernest, straight as a ramrod with a nose like all the noses in the family portraits; a nose that never twitched at all.

Then they went down to dinner. She was half hidden by the great chrysanthemums that curled their red and gold petals into large tight balls. Everything was gold. A gold-edged card with gold initials intertwined recited the list of all the dishes that would be set one after another before them. She dipped her spoon in a plate of clear golden fluid. The raw white fog outside had been turned by the lamps into a golden mesh that blurred the edges of the plates and gave the pineapples a rough golden skin. Only she herself in her white wedding dress peering ahead of her with her prominent eyes seemed insoluble as an icicle.

As the dinner wore on, however, the room grew steamy with heat. Beads of perspiration stood out on the men's foreheads. She felt that her icicle was being turned to water. She was being melted; dispersed; dissolved into nothingness; and would soon faint. Then through the surge in her head and the din in her ears she heard a woman's voice exclaim, "But they breed so!"

The Thorburns—yes; they breed so, she echoed; looking at all the round red faces that seemed doubled in the giddiness that overcame her; and magnified in the gold mist that enhaloed them. "They breed so." Then John bawled:

"Little devils! . . . Shoot 'em! Jump on 'em with big boots! That's the only way to deal with 'em . . . rabbits!"

At that word, that magic word, she revived. Peeping between the chrysanthemums she saw Ernest's nose twitch. It rippled, it ran with successive twitches. And at that a mysterious catastrophe befell the Thorburns. The golden table became a moor with the gorse in full bloom; the din of voices turned to one peal of lark's laughter ringing down from the sky. It was a blue sky—clouds passed slowly. And they had all been changed—the Thorburns. She looked at her father-in-law, a furtive little man with dyed moustaches. His foible was collecting things—seals, enamel boxes, trifles from eighteenth-century dressing tables which he hid in the drawers of his study from his wife. Now she saw him as he was—a poacher, stealing off with his coat bulging with pheasants and partridges to drop them stealthily into a three-legged pot in his smoky little cottage. That was her real father-in-law—a poacher. And Celia, the unmarried daughter, who always nosed out other people's secrets, the little things they wished to hide—she was a white ferret with pink eyes, and a nose clotted with earth from her horrid underground nosings and pokings. Slung round men's shoulders, in a net, and thrust down a hole—it was a pitiable life—Celia's; it was none of her fault. So she saw Celia. And then she looked at her mother-in-law—whom they dubbed The Squire. Flushed, coarse, a bully—she was all that, as she stood returning thanks, but now that Rosalind—that is Lapinova—saw her, she saw behind her the decayed family mansion, the plaster peeling off the walls, and heard her, with a sob in her voice, giving thanks to her children (who hated her) for a world that had ceased to exist. There was a sudden silence. They all stood with their glasses raised; they all drank; then it was over.

"Oh, King Lappin!" she cried as they went home together in the fog, "if your nose hadn't twitched just at that moment, I should have been trapped!"

"But you're safe," said King Lappin, pressing her paw.

"Quite safe," she answered.

And they drove back through the Park, King and Queen of the marsh, of the mist, and of the gorse-scented moor.

Thus time passed; one year; two years of time. And on a winter's night, which happened by a coincidence to be the anniversary of the golden-wedding party—but Mrs. Reginald Thorburn was dead; the house was to let; and there was only a caretaker in residence—Ernest came home from the office. They had a nice little home; half a house above a saddler's shop in South Kensington, not far from the Tube station. It was cold, with fog in the air, and Rosalind was sitting over the fire, sewing.

"What d'you think happened to me today?" she began as soon as he had settled himself down with his legs stretched to the blaze. "I was crossing the stream when——"

"What stream?" Ernest interrupted her.

"The stream at the bottom, where our wood meets the black wood," she explained.

Ernest looked completely blank for a moment.

"What the deuce are you talking about?" he asked.

"My dear Ernest!" she cried in dismay. "King Lappin," she added, dangling her little front paws in the firelight. But his nose did not twitch. Her hands—they turned to hands—clutched the stuff she was holding; her eyes popped half out of her head. It took him five minutes at least to change from Ernest Thorburn to King Lappin; and while she waited she felt a load on the back of her neck, as if somebody were about to wring it. At last he changed to King Lappin; his nose twitched; and they spent the evening roaming the woods much as usual.

But she slept badly. In the middle of the night she woke, feeling as if something strange had happened to her. She was stiff and cold. At last she turned on the light and looked at Ernest lying beside her. He was sound asleep. He snored. But even though he snored, his nose remained perfectly still. It looked as if it had never twitched at all. Was it possible that he was really Ernest; and that she was really married to Ernest? A vision of her mother-in-law's dining-room came before her; and there they sat, she and Ernest, grown old, under the engravings, in front of the sideboard. . . . It was their golden-wedding day. She could not bear it.

"Lappin, King Lappin!" she whispered, and for a moment his nose seemed to twitch of its own accord. But he still slept. "Wake up, Lappin, wake up!" she cried.

Ernest woke; and seeing her sitting bolt upright beside him he asked:

"What's the matter?"

"I thought my rabbit was dead!" she whimpered. Ernest was angry.

"Don't talk such rubbish, Rosalind," he said. "Lie down and go to sleep."

He turned over. In another moment he was sound asleep and snoring.

But she could not sleep. She lay curled up on her side of the bed, like a hare in its form. She had turned out the light, but the street lamp lit the ceiling faintly, and the trees outside made a lacy network over it as if there were a shadowy grove on the ceiling in which she wandered, turning, twisting, in and out, round and round, hunting, being hunted, hearing the bay of hounds and horns; flying, escaping . . . until the maid drew the blinds and brought their early tea.

Next day she could settle to nothing. She seemed to have lost something. She felt as if her body had shrunk; it had grown small, and black and hard. Her joints seemed stiff too, and when she looked in the glass, which she did several times as she wandered about the flat, her eyes seemed to burst out of her head, like currants in a bun. The rooms also seemed to have shrunk. Large pieces of furniture jutted out at odd angles and she found herself knocking against them. At last she put on her hat and went out. She walked along the Cromwell Road; and every room she passed and peered into seemed to be a dining-room where people sat eating under steel engravings, with thick yellow lace curtains, and mahogany sideboards. At last she reached the Natural History Museum; she used to like it when she was a child. But the first thing she saw when she went in was a stuffed hare standing on sham snow with pink glass eyes. Somehow it made her shiver all over. Perhaps it would be better when dusk fell. She went home and sat over the fire, without a light, and tried to imagine that she was out alone on a moor; and there was a stream rushing; and beyond the stream a dark wood. But she could get no further than the stream. At last she squatted down on the bank on the wet grass, and sat crouched in her chair, with her hands dangling empty, and her eyes glazed, like glass eyes, in the firelight. Then there was the crack of a gun. . . . She started as if she had been shot. It was only Ernest, turning his key in the door. She waited, trembling. He came in and switched on the light. There he stood tall, handsome, rubbing his hands that were red with cold.

"Sitting in the dark?" he said.

"Oh, Ernest, Ernest!" she cried, starting up in her chair.

"Well, what's up, now?" he asked briskly, warming his hands at the fire.

"It's Lapinova . . ." she faltered, glancing wildly at him out of her great startled eyes. "She's gone, Ernest. I've lost her!"

Ernest frowned. He pressed his lips tight together. "Oh, that's what's up, is it?" he said, smiling rather grimly at his wife. For ten seconds he stood there, silent; and she waited, feeling hands tightening at the back of her neck.

"Yes," he said at length. "Poor Lapinova . . ." He straightened his tie at the looking-glass over the mantelpiece.

"Caught in a trap," he said, "killed," and sat down and read the newspaper.

So that was the end of that marriage.

[1938]

Marita Bonner
(1898–1971)

Reap It As You Sow It

Marita Bonner, who became an influential contributor to the Harlem Renaissance, began writing in high school and went on to study writing at Radcliffe. There, well-known professor Charles Townsend Copeland recognized Bonner's literary talent but urged her not to be so "bitter," in Bonner's words, a "cliché to colored people who write." Instead, Bonner dared to write about the racist society in which she lived; her determination to voice protest was only strengthened by such admonitions.

Her short stories, plays, and teaching all reflect her perception of racism, sexism, and class consciousness. Her characters, particularly her women, are perpetually locked into social conflict and seek self-realization but are often unable—spiritually, physically, and psychologically—to surmount the odds against them.

Like much of Bonner's writing, "Reap It As You Sow It" takes place in the fictional setting of Frye Street in Chicago, which represents a microcosm of American society. Her plays include *The Pot Maker* (1927), *The Purple Flower* (1928), and *Exit an Illusion* (1929), all of which respond to the dynamics of sex, class, and, most of all, race.

Much of Bonner's work went unpublished before her death.

Now Nola was one of those people who blind their eyes with their desires—seal their hearts with their sins—then consider the Scriptures.

It happens to state clearly in the twentieth chapter of Exodus that you must not lie—cheat—kill—steal—or commit adultery.

It says just plain do *not* do these things.

Nola, though, thought it said: "Go ahead! Do what you want to do! You won't have to pay! Never! No one keeps the books that balance your account of living."

And it is written on every page, "God alone is the chief *accountant.*"

He posts and spreads and checks.

His final sheet is never a penny off. And it balances—somewhere—to the last mite—to the last damnable trick you have played.

Perhaps because Frye Street was so little and insignificant in such a big city, Nola thought God had forgotten her and everyone around her.

Nola was one of those colored girls who seem to come from nowhere bringing nothing with them and who are hell-bent on going nowhere as fast as they can live it.

She was tawny, easy-limbed, with enough fundamental good looks to draw the eye when she wanted to. She was twenty-four and there was not a tavern on Frye Street or Grand Avenue that she did not go into whenever she wanted a drink or a man.

Frye Street is that crooked little tumbled red brick place that joins the river to the edge of the city.

Some part of every race from everywhere lives there.

And from Number 11 to Number 49 on both sides of the street, colored people lived.

In Number 12 lived Nola.

At Number 14 lived Mollie and James.

James and his wife Mollie had only been in the city three months when Nola saw them. Some of the dreamy distances of the South they had just left cut them off from the rest of Frye Street.

Mollie was brown and stout wide-eyed and clean country nice looking. Some people would have called her stout and plump. To colored folks on Frye Street she was just plain "blockety." That meant she was fat in odd spots.

James was grey-eyed and ivory colored with brownish hair. Even the Frye Streeters called him handsome.

It happened that James and Mollie took a walk one night. They walked slowly hand in hand, the way they used to follow country lanes—up Frye Street to Grand Avenue, where the El rushed by.

They never went further. They always stopped at the windows of Lowinsky's department store to pick out the clothes they meant to buy if ever James got a job that was steady.

This night they walked and stood—and Nola swung by on her way to one of her taverns.

She cast a casual eye at Lowinsky's—saw Mollie and James—looked again—saw James—and walked up to him.

"Good evenin'!" Nola put just the right amount of down-homey-ness in her voice. "How y'all this evenin'?"

James and Mollie both answered. "Evenin'! We well, thank you."

"My—er—church is givin' a little party at this here number," Nola began hastily. She dug in her purse and produced a blank card. "I clean forgot the tickets but I'll just put the number of the house on here! We want y'all to come. You strangers in the city, aren't you?"

James nodded dumbly. So did Mollie.

Nola wrote the number fifteen. "Right across the street." She pointed down Frye Street.

"That's right 'cross from where we live!" Mollie exclaimed.

"We might walk by there! Thanks!" James told Nola.

"We want y'all to come!" Nola insisted. "Bye!"

And she swung off up Grand Avenue.

"You reckon it be all right for us to go?" the woman in Mollie made her ask.

"Ought not to hurt! Church folks givin' it," James answered.

They were tired of sitting up in one room.

They spoke to no one but their landlady.

It would be nice to meet some church folks.

They walked along Grand Avenue a while, then they turned back and found themselves hurrying—they were so eager to talk to someone new.

Number 15 was really having a party.

A piano was tinkling a Negroid motley. In the center of the room a loose-hung Negro danced.

"These ain't no church folks!" Mollie told James at the front door. "Dancin'!"

"This ain't down home! Church folks dances if they want to in the city."

"I'm going home!" Mollie started back to the door.

"How 'bout some nice barbecue?" a man's voice asked behind her.

"Have some pop?" offered another voice.

Nola was standing beside them with a man who was grinning dreadfully.

"How much?" James began.

"Oh this my treat!" Nola laughed. "Help yourself, y'all!"

Mollie and James were dazed. They ate and drank in a quiet corner in the hall. Nola hovered near them.

Two girls came in the front door.

"Lawd! Look at all the paint on these women's faces!" Mollie started to whisper to James.

"Meet my friends Mr. and Mrs.—What is you all's name?" Nola asked loudly of Mollie and James.

"Smith," James told her.

"Aw what's your first name, big boy?" Nola persisted.

Mollie made an internal recoil at the close touch in Nola's voice.

"James and Mollie Smith!" James supplied meekly.

The girls muttered, "Pleese-ter-meet-cher!"

"Gimme something to drink!" one of the girls yelled loudly. "Ain't y'all got nothing to drink?"

"Have some pop?" Nola stuck a bottle of strawberry pop into the woman's hands.

"What I want with this stuff!" demanded the girl. "Gimme some beer!"

"You must a had too much already!" Nola told her.

"I'm going home," Mollie began sotto voce to James again.

"Have some more pop," Nola told Jim. She passed him a bottle already open.

James drew on it. "Whoo-ee!" he cried. "This stuff tastes like spirits of nitre."

Mollie took his bottle and drank too. "Sure do!" she agreed.

"Tain't no nitre! That's gin!" Nola said.

"I'm going home!" Mollie said it aloud this time. "Church folks don't drink!"

"Who said they did and who said they didn't?" Nola bristled.

"Aw come on! Let's dance!" James told Mollie. "No use to get mad!"

He was enjoying the excitement strange faces produced in him. He did not want to go back to his one room yet.

So they danced out into the front room. After that, James danced with Nola—then with Mollie once more.

Again he danced with Nola.

Pretty soon Mollie found herself standing in the doorway, while

Nola and James circled the room and James was laughing and talking to Nola as if he were having a good time.

At eleven o'clock, maybe, somebody put some more gin or whiskey into the pop.

Anyhow, Nola began dancing in the center of the floor by herself. Higher and wilder she stepped until she was trying to see if she could kick over James's head.

Everyone else *herded* along the walls to watch Nola.

Now there are some ladies who will giggle with the best of them from the sidelines where the tame herd gathers, while the life of the party sees if she can kick her pumps over somebody's husband's head.

There are some women who will stand herded up and giggle.

Mollie was not one of those to stand still.

She walked out blindly and followed a narrow hall. It led directly into the little smoked boxes that served as kitchens in Frye Street houses.

Mollie did not know why she had walked into someone else's kitchen at first. Then she saw a large black frying pan on the back of the stove.

Mollie grabbed it and started back up the narrow hall.

Nola's kicks were at superlative heights.

"Bring up some laundry, Nola!" a voice screamed from the sidelines.

And Nola obliged with a wider display of lingerie and tawny limbs.

And James, his face flooded with a shame-faced flush still stood where Mollie had last seen him—in the very center of the screaming women.

Mollie swung the frying pan.

Grease splattered from it across the faces of two women.

"What the hell you doing?" one woman out-screamed the laughing group.

She pushed the pan aside. It bounced off of Nola's shoulder.

The gin and the kicks had Nola entirely off balance.

She collapsed at once. James reached out his arms automatically and she fell into them.

Someone kicked the pan out of Mollie's hands. It fell on a man's toes and he filled the room with wide-mouthed cursing.

Nola lay stunned a second. Then she started to leap up like a cat and beat Mollie.

She could easily have done so.

But, glancing up, she saw into whose arms she had fallen.

So Nola—Nola who could fight anyone in any tavern—pretended to faint and lay heavier against James.

Fierce fighting exploded all over the room. Mollie ran out of the door and across Frye Street.

She could hear the clang of the bell on a patrol wagon before she reached her room.

Nola heard the clang too.

By the time the policemen were scraping the battlers into the wagon, Nola had showed James how to drop out of the kitchen window, cut across the back *alley* and saunter along Grand Avenue as if that were all they had been doing all night.

Upstairs in Number 14, Mollie watched panic-stricken as they loaded the patrol across the street.

"Lawd! Guess James'll go to the lock-up too! Wish I never went to that place! That dirty ole woman!"

Mollie fell across the bed and cried.

The door opened.

Mollie rolled over. "James! How come you ain't gone to the lock-up?"

"Oh Nola she done tole me how to git out the back way!"

Mollie sniffed. "Is that that thing's name? That was one low-down crowd of nigger women, wasn't they, James?"

James sat down on the side of the bed and took off his shoes. He said nothing.

"I don't never want to get mixed up no more with them kind of folks! No suh! Not me!" Mollie chattered nervously.

James shook out his trousers and hung them up.

Still he said nothing.

"I ain't never gone to speak to none of them ef ever I meet one of them on the street!" Mollie could not stop talking. "Fighting and cursing and kicking up like some—"

"Shut up!" James roared suddenly. "You done the fightin' yourself! You 'bout kill Nola! You lucky ef the patrol don't back up here and git you!"

Mollie began to scream loudly.

James had to agree that the people were rather low-down and evil: he had to promise that they would move away from Frye Street the next day.

But long after Mollie had quieted and was asleep, James lay awake beside her tingling with the excitement that their party had set in him.

It was all Mollie's fault that anything had gone wrong. She was too countryfied!

Church folks in the city did things country church folks would not think of doing. There was no need of anyone expecting it. He fell asleep promising himself that he would join the church that gave parties like the one he had left.

Mollie and James did not move next day.

They stayed at Number 14 Frye Street.

Soon it became apparent to all the world that Mollie was "expecting." And it became just as apparent to that same world that Nola was expecting to get James for her own. As Mollie blossomed and bloomed—Nola grew bolder and bolder.

It reached the point that James stayed out all night.

It was as easy as a knife through cheeses—a knife of evil through a cheesy nigger-man.

Yet—people do not break off at once from anything. Something hacks and hacks and hacks at the roots that they have sunk into some relationships.

Then they weaken.

They weaken. They totter. Finally they crash down—cut loose with no roots.

It got so that Jim took the money he was supposed to be paying in the hospital each week so Mollie might go in when her time came—he took the money and bought gifts for Nola. James bought gifts and went places—parties—taverns—everywhere—anywhere with Nola.

James acted as if he were indeed crazy about Nola.

One Saturday night, Mollie was hungry.

She had waited since six for James to come home from work. At nine o'clock she was still sitting at the window—too heavy to move, watching everyone who passed.

As she stared, Nola came down Frye Street on the other side.

Mollie threw up the window. "You Nola?" she called. "You Nola!"

Nola halted a second. "What you want?"

"You see James? Where's James at?"

"Now I ain't see him! How I know where he at?"

"You ought to know! You old dirty thing! Running after him all the time!"

"Shut your damn black mouth or I'll come up there and shut it!"

"You let James alone! Let him alone! I'm 'bout to have the child and he ain't paid the hospital nuthin'! Let him alone!"

Nola cursed long and loud. Then she swung away up the street. Mollie could only stare after her.

She closed the window and started to get up.

It was then that the pain began to knife deep within her. Her time had come.

Her scream brought the landlady running.

"Lawd! Git to the hospital! Let me help you!"

Mollie found enough breath to say, "Can't go! They won't take me! James ain't paid yet!"

"Now ain't that the devil!! Ain't men fools! Racin' and chasing 'round!"

The knife tore into Mollie again and she screamed once more.

"Let me run git Granny Gray! She used to catch babies down home." The landlady panted and ran off again.

Granny Gray came.

She was an old-time midwife. She never heard of sterilization or any particular hygiene. She did all the things she should never have done.

The baby was born at two o'clock.

Mollie died at three.

James came home at four.

The blood, the baby, and Mollie dead on the bed—knocked him sober.

He stayed sober for a while—even after the funeral. He stayed away from Nola, too.

Old lady Jones whose husband was a janitor way uptown in a wealthy white neighborhood, took the baby.

James shifted away from Number 14. He drifted until he found Nola once more.

Nola set about comforting James. She comforted him so well that they were married six months later.

Now after she married, Nola grew very very strange. It may be that she really loved James.

"Look like to me a married woman ought to b'long to some church," she told James one night.

"Yeah."

"I want you should take me to the Loving Lambs up on the corner some night."

James took her.

And Nola got happy and screamed and cried and plucked up her skirts and walked over the backs of the benches when the preaching was going on.

The reverend bellowed: "If only by keeping God's law of love—love your neighbor and all the rest of it—is the only way folks can make heaven—then there's going to be a mighty passel of niggers toasting in hell with the chaff and the goats after the wheat and the lambs get saved!"

Nola fell back against James. "Amen" she cried in agreement.

"Sperits on her," one old lady hollered.

"Dem sperits is *in* dat gal!" sneered another who knew Nola for what she really was.

James had to take Nola out for some air.

Soon after it became apparent to the world that Nola was "expecting."

She stayed at home and cooked and cleaned with that awful scrupulous cleanliness that only a dirty woman can give a place.

Odd, isn't it, how these women are usually so clean about externals!

James worked hard.

They moved from their one-room place to a little four-room house up on Grand Avenue.

Nola forgot about Mollie dying at home with no doctor to help her. She forgot about James Junior—Mollie's baby—knocked around somewhere uptown.

Nola forgot all the men she had dodged and slipped and danced around with.

She thought God had forgotten, too.

He had not forgotten. It only seemed so. It was merely time for the flourishing—the blossoming—the spreading of branches of rich plenty.

Nola's baby was a girl—beautifully bronzed and so lovable that Nola worshipped her.

No dress was too expensive, no hours too late to work for baby Nola.

One Saturday when baby Nola was two years old, her mother dressed her and let the little girl next door take her for a walk.

The two children stopped to play with some other youngsters in front of the door.

"Guess I'll comb my hair and change my dress 'fore I bring baby Nola in!" Nola thought.

She took a mirror and sat by her bedroom window. She combed her hair and smiled at herself as she listened to little Nola's laughing below her in the street.

"Ain't she too sweet! Listen to her!" Nola spoke aloud to herself.

She stood up and moved her chair nearer to the window so that she might the better watch the perky red hair bow dancing along the red gingham dress in Saturday's late afternoon sunshine.

Life was so good! Pretty soon James would be coming home from his job. No relief and stuff for them like most of the colored folks on Frye Street.

James had a good job sweeping sawdust at the Big Market. He would bring home a good roast for Sunday and maybe chops or a nice steak and a piece of ham.

Life was so good.

Nola yawned a "God-life-is-so-everlastingly-good-as-I-know-it" yawn.

As I know it in this body.

Then she stood up.

There was Jim already, turning the corner of Frye Street, his arms crowded with bundles.

She would go down and open the door for him.

She started to leave the room—remembered that little Nola might see her father across the street and run across to meet him.

She had better call out of the windows for the kids to watch her.

Nola lifted the window and saw baby Nola below her.

Little Nola looked across the street and saw James.

A trailer-truck swung around the corner.

Little Nola saw her father.

She did not see the truck. The driver did not see her.

Nola, up in the window, saw the truck coming—saw the baby run out into the street—and she started to climb out of the window, tearing out her clothes and her hair as she went.

The screams of the children as the truck dragged little Nola were all she heard.

As long as she lived Nola swore that she could not jump through that window to die in that moment little Nola was killed.

She could not move.

For a hand—a woman's hand—brown, stubby, plump—with cracked worn fingernails and an old gold wedding band like Mollie's old-fashioned ring—held her.

A woman's hand locked in a steel grasp in that window. The

other hand pointed past Nola to the street below. "See! See!! There!! That is the end of loveliness and hope! Right now your misery begins!"

Nola afterwards thought she heard these very words as she followed the pointing of that finger.

That is what Nola swore afterwards.

I do not know.

When you and your conscience are alone with God in some places and there is a reckoning going on—anything can happen.

You can only wonder which was worse: to go off to an unknown world, leaving your first-born newly come—behind you—drawing you ever back to this earth that hurt you most—or living on days and days and days after a dear little body has been put to sleep for the last time—in the ground—away from you.

How must it be to start up night after night, half awake, to go and tuck blankets around a crib that is empty.

Anyhow—the columns were balanced.

The chief accountant had put the last penny in its proper place.

Nola went back to wondering—seeing if the happy content that filled her one Saturday afternoon when she sat by her window—would ever come again.

Men—lots of men—liquor—lots of liquor—nothing filled her again.

Jim took to staying away from a neighborhood where sorrow had laid darkly on him.

Nola fought and cursed and sank lower and deeper.

One night they had to put her in the wagon to take her to the lock-up for breaking all the glasses in Tarry's tavern.

"Nola! Why don't you behave yourself!" the captain asked as he booked her.

Nola hung to the desk so she could look fully into the man's face: "Lawd don't want me to be no good! He won't let me! He ain't never give me no chance!" she answered.

And she believed that she had spoken the truth when she said it.

[1940–1941]

Carson McCullers
(1917–1967)

A Tree, a Rock, a Cloud

An imaginative introvert as a child, Carson McCullers grew up in Columbus, Georgia, which later became the setting for many of her novels. Her musical and literary talents bloomed early, and at age eighteen she moved to New York City and took small jobs so that she could study at Juilliard and Columbia. At age twenty-three she published her first novel, *The Heart Is a Lonely Hunter* (1940), for which she was remarkably acclaimed, and became one of the most controversial writers in America.

All of her writing concerns the spiritual isolation of the individual and the attempt to overcome loneliness by means of love. The tone is at once melancholy and sardonically humorous. "A Tree, a Rock, a Cloud," which was chosen for inclusion in *O. Henry Memorial Prize Stories of 1942,* is often compared to "The Rime of the Ancient Mariner."

The quality of McCullers's despair is unique. This may be because, for all of the personal loneliness that is reflected in her writing, McCullers is said to have had an enormous capacity for loyalty and affection to her friends. In the same way, the man in "A Tree, a Rock, a Cloud" is alone but has a nearly boundless capacity to love. As in the story, the theme of McCullers's work is that one's only defense against life's indifference is love, tragically flawed as it is.

It was raining that morning, and still very dark. When the boy reached the streetcar café he had almost finished his route and he went in for a cup of coffee. The place was an all-night café owned by a bitter and stingy man called Leo. After the raw, empty street the café seemed friendly and bright: along the counter there were a couple of soldiers, three spinners from the cotton mill, and in a corner a man who sat hunched over with his nose and half his face down in a beer mug. The boy wore a helmet such as aviators wear. When he went into the café he unbuckled the chin strap and raised the right flap up over his pink little ear; often as he drank his coffee someone would speak to him in a friendly way. But this morning Leo did not look into his face and none of the men were talking. He paid and was leaving the café when a voice called out to him:

"Son! Hey Son!"

He turned back and the man in the corner was crooking his finger and nodding to him. He had brought his face out of the beer mug and he seemed suddenly very happy. The man was long and pale, with a big nose and faded orange hair.

"Hey Son!"

The boy went toward him. He was an undersized boy of about twelve, with one shoulder drawn higher than the other because of the weight of the paper sack. His face was shallow, freckled, and his eyes were round child eyes.

"Yeah Mister?"

The man laid one hand on the paper boy's shoulders, then grasped the boy's chin and turned his face slowly from one side to the other. The boy shrank back uneasily.

"Say! What's the big idea?"

The boy's voice was shrill; inside the café it was suddenly very quiet.

The man said slowly: "I love you."

All along the counter the men laughed. The boy, who had scowled and sidled away, did not know what to do. He looked over the counter at Leo, and Leo watched him with a weary, brittle jeer. The boy tried to laugh also. But the man was serious and sad.

"I did not mean to tease you, Son," he said. "Sit down and have a beer with me. There is something I have to explain."

Cautiously, out of the corner of his eye, the paper boy questioned the men along the counter to see what he should do. But they had gone back to their beer or their breakfast and did not notice him. Leo put a cup of coffee on the counter and a little jug of cream.

"He is a minor," Leo said.

The paper boy slid himself up onto the stool. His ear beneath the upturned flap of the helmet was very small and red. The man was nodding at him soberly. "It is important," he said. Then he reached in his hip pocket and brought out something which he held up in the palm of his hand for the boy to see.

"Look very carefully," he said.

The boy stared, but there was nothing to look at very carefully. The man held in his big, grimy palm a photograph. It was the face of a woman, but blurred, so that only the hat and the dress she was wearing stood out clearly.

"See?" the man asked.

The boy nodded and the man placed another picture in his palm. The woman was standing on a beach in a bathing suit. The suit made her stomach very big, and that was the main thing you noticed.

"Got a good look?" He leaned over closer and finally asked: "You ever seen her before?"

The boy sat motionless, staring slantwise at the man. "Not so I know of."

"Very well." The man blew on the photographs and put them back into his pocket. "That was my wife."

"Dead?" the boy asked.

Slowly the man shook his head. He pursed his lips as though about to whistle and answered in a long-drawn way: "Nuuu—" he said. "I will explain."

The beer on the counter before the man was in a large brown mug. He did not pick it up to drink. Instead he bent down and, putting his face over the rim, he rested there for a moment. Then with both hands he tilted the mug and sipped.

"Some night you'll go to sleep with your big nose in a mug and drown," said Leo. "Prominent transient drowns in beer. That would be a cute death."

The paper boy tried to signal to Leo. While the man was not looking he screwed up his face and worked his mouth to question soundlessly: "Drunk?" But Leo only raised his eyebrows and turned away to put some pink strips of bacon on the grill. The man pushed the mug away from him, straightened himself, and folded his loose crooked hands on the counter. His face was sad as he looked at the paper boy. He did not blink, but from time to time the lids closed down with delicate gravity over his pale green eyes. It was nearing dawn and the boy shifted the weight of the paper sack.

"I am talking about love," the man said. "With me it is a science."

The boy half slid down from the stool. But the man raised his forefinger, and there was something about him that held the boy and would not let him go away.

"Twelve years ago I married the woman in the photograph. She was my wife for one year, nine months, three days, and two nights. I loved her. Yes . . ." He tightened his blurred, rambling voice and said again: "I loved her. I thought also that she loved me. I was a railroad engineer. She had all home comforts and luxuries. It never crept into my brain that she was not satisfied. But do you know what happened?"

"Mgneeow!" said Leo.

The man did not take his eyes from the boy's face. "She left me. I came in one night and the house was empty and she was gone. She left me."

"With a fellow?" the boy asked.

Gently the man placed his palm down on the counter. "Why naturally, Son. A woman does not run off like that alone."

The café was quiet, the soft rain black and endless in the street outside. Leo pressed down the frying bacon with the prongs of his long fork. "So you have been chasing the floozie for eleven years. You frazzled old rascal!"

For the first time the man glanced at Leo. "Please don't be vulgar. Besides, I was not speaking to you." He turned back to the boy and said in a trusting and secretive undertone: "Let's not pay any attention to him. O.K.?"

The paper boy nodded doubtfully.

"It was like this," the man continued. "I am a person who feels many things. All my life one thing after another has impressed me. Moonlight. The leg of a pretty girl. One thing after another. But the point is that when I had enjoyed anything there was a peculiar sensation as though it was laying around loose in me. Nothing seemed to finish itself up or fit in with the other things. Women? I had my portion of them. The same. Afterwards laying around loose in me. I was a man who had never loved."

Very slowly he closed his eyelids, and the gesture was like a curtain drawn at the end of a scene in a play. When he spoke again his voice was excited and the words came fast—the lobes of his large, loose ears seemed to tremble.

"Then I met this woman. I was fifty-one years old and she always said she was thirty. I met her at a filling station and we were married within three days. And do you know what it was like? I just can't tell you. All I had ever felt was gathered together around this woman. Nothing lay around loose in me any more but was finished up by her."

The man stopped suddenly and stroked his long nose. His voice sank down to a steady and reproachful undertone: "I'm not explaining this right. What happened was this. There were these beautiful feelings and loose little pleasures inside me. And this woman was something like an assembly line for my soul. I run these little pieces of myself through her and I come out complete. Now do you follow me?"

"What was her name?" the boy asked.

"Oh," he said. "I called her Dodo. But that is immaterial."

"Did you try to make her come back?"

The man did not seem to hear. "Under the circumstances you can imagine how I felt when she left me."

Leo took the bacon from the grill and folded two strips of it between a bun. He had a gray face, with slitted eyes, and a pinched nose saddled by faint blue shadows. One of the mill workers signaled for more coffee and Leo poured it. He did not give refills on coffee free. The spinner ate breakfast there every morning, but the better Leo knew his customers the stingier he treated them. He nibbled his own bun as though he grudged it to himself.

"And you never got hold of her again?"

The boy did not know what to think of the man, and his child's face was uncertain with mingled curiosity and doubt. He was new on the paper route; it was still strange to him to be out in the town in the black, queer early morning.

"Yes," the man said. "I took a number of steps to get her back. I went around trying to locate her. I went to Tulsa where she had folks. And to Mobile. I went to every town she had ever mentioned to me, and I hunted down every man she had formerly been connected with. Tulsa, Atlanta, Chicago, Cheehaw, Memphis. . . . For the better part of two years I chased around the country trying to lay hold of her."

"But the pair of them had vanished from the face of the earth!" said Leo.

"Don't listen to him," the man said confidentially. "And also just forget those two years. They are not important. What matters is that around the third year a curious thing begun to happen to me."

"What?" the boy asked.

The man leaned down and tilted his mug to take a sip of beer. But as he hovered over the mug his nostrils fluttered slightly; he sniffed the staleness of the beer and did not drink. "Love is a curious thing to begin with. At first I thought only of getting her back. It was a kind of mania. But then as time went on I tried to remember her. But do you know what happened?"

"No," the boy said.

"When I laid myself down on a bed and tried to think about her my mind became a blank. I couldn't see her. I would take out her pictures and look. No good. Nothing doing. A blank. Can you imagine it?"

"Say Mac!" Leo called down the counter. "Can you imagine this bozo's mind a blank!"

Slowly, as though fanning away flies, the man waved his hand. His green eyes were concentrated and fixed on the shallow little face of the paper boy.

"But a sudden piece of glass on a sidewalk. Or a nickel tune in a music box. A shadow on a wall at night. And I would remember. It might happen in a street and I would cry or bang my head against a lamppost. You follow me?"

"A piece of glass . . ." the boy said.

"Anything. I would walk around and I had no power of how and when to remember her. You think you can put up a kind of shield. But remembering don't come to a man face forward—it corners around sideways. I was at the mercy of everything I saw and heard. Suddenly instead of me combing the countryside to find her she begun to chase me around in my very soul. *She* chasing *me*, mind you! And in my soul."

The boy asked finally: "What part of the country were you in then?"

"Ooh," the man groaned. "I was a sick mortal. It was like smallpox. I confess, Son, that I boozed. I fornicated. I committed any sin that suddenly appealed to me. I am loath to confess it but I will do so. When I recall that period it is all curdled in my mind, it was so terrible."

The man leaned his head down and tapped his forehead on the counter. For a few seconds he stayed bowed over in this position, the back of his stringy neck covered with orange furze, his hands with their long warped fingers held palm to palm in an attitude of prayer. Then the man straightened himself; he was smiling and suddenly his face was bright and tremulous and old.

"It was in the fifth year that it happened," he said. "And with it I started my science."

Leo's mouth jerked with a pale, quick grin. "Well none of we boys are getting any younger," he said. Then with sudden anger he balled up a dishcloth he was holding and threw it down hard on the floor. "You draggle-tailed old Romeo!"

"What happened?" the boy asked.

The old man's voice was high and clear: "Peace," he answered.

"Huh?"

"It is hard to explain scientifically, Son," he said. "I guess the logical explanation is that she and I had fleed around from each other for so long that finally we just got tangled up together and lay down and quit. Peace. A queer and beautiful blankness. It was spring in Portland and the rain came every afternoon. All evening I just stayed there on my bed in the dark. And that is how the science come to me."

The windows in the streetcar were pale blue with light. The two soldiers paid for their beers and opened the door—one of the soldiers combed his hair and wiped off his muddy puttees before they went outside. The three mill workers bent silently over their breakfasts. Leo's clock was ticking on the wall.

"It is this. And listen carefully. I meditated on love and reasoned it out. I realized what is wrong with us. Men fall in love for the first time. And what do they fall in love with?"

The boy's soft mouth was partly open and he did not answer.

"A woman," the old man said. "Without science, with nothing to go by, they undertake the most dangerous and sacred experience in God's earth. They fall in love with a woman. Is that correct, Son?"

"Yeah," the boy said faintly.

"They start at the wrong end of love. They begin at the climax. Can you wonder it is so miserable? Do you know how men should love?"

The old man reached over and grasped the boy by the collar of his leather jacket. He gave him a gentle little shake and his green eyes gazed down unblinking and grave.

"Son, do you know how love should be begun?"

The boy sat small and listening and still. Slowly he shook his head. The old man leaned closer and whispered:

"A tree. A rock. A cloud."

It was still raining outside in the street: a mild, gray, endless rain. The mill whistle blew for the six o'clock shift and the three spinners paid and went away. There was no one in the café but Leo, the old man, and the little paper boy.

"The weather was like this in Portland," he said. "At the time my science was begun. I meditated and I started very cautious. I would pick up something from the street and take it home with me. I bought a goldfish and I concentrated on the goldfish and I loved it. I graduated from one thing to another. Day by day I was getting this technique. On the road from Portland to San Diego—"

"Aw shut up!" screamed Leo suddenly. "Shut up! Shut up!"

The old man still held the collar of the boy's jacket; he was trembling and his face was earnest and bright and wild. "For six years now I have gone around by myself and built up my science. And now I am a master, Son. I can love anything. No longer do I have to think about it even. I see a street full of people and a beautiful light comes in me. I watch a bird in the sky. Or I meet a traveler on the road. Everything, Son. And anybody. All stranger and all loved! Do you realize what a science like mine can mean?"

The boy held himself stiffly, his hands curled tight around the counter edge. Finally he asked: "Did you ever really find that lady?"

"What? What say, Son?"

"I mean," the boy asked timidly. "Have you fallen in love with a woman again?"

The old man loosened his grasp on the boy's collar. He turned away and for the first time his green eyes had a vague and scattered look. He lifted the mug from the counter, drank down the yellow beer. His head was shaking slowly from side to side. Then finally he answered: "No, Son. You see that is the last step in my science. I go cautious. And I am not quite ready yet."

"Well!" said Leo. "Well well well!"

The old man stood in the open doorway. "Remember," he said. Framed there in the gray damp light of the early morning he looked shrunken and seedy and frail. But his smile was bright. "Remember I love you," he said with a last nod. And the door closed quietly behind him.

The boy did not speak for a long time. He pulled down the bangs on his forehead and slid his grimy little forefinger around the rim of his empty cup. Then without looking at Leo he finally asked:

"Was he drunk?"

"No," said Leo shortly.

The boy raised his clear voice higher. "Then was he a dope fiend?"

"No."

The boy looked up at Leo, and his flat little face was desperate, his voice urgent and shrill. "Was he crazy? Do you think he was a lunatic?" The paper boy's voice dropped suddenly with doubt. "Leo? Or not?"

But Leo would not answer him. Leo had run a night café for fourteen years, and he held himself to be a critic of craziness. There were the town characters and also the transients who roamed in from the night. He knew the manias of all of them. But he did not want to satisfy the questions of the waiting child. He tightened his pale face and was silent.

So the boy pulled down the right flap of his helmet and as he turned to leave he made the only comment that seemed safe to him, the only remark that could not be laughed down and despised:

"He sure has done a lot of traveling."

[1942]

Dorothy Baker
(1907–1968)

Romance

After studying music at UCLA, Dorothy Baker attempted a writing career in France but was not successful. She married a poet, endured what she describes as "constant chastening criticism" from him for her writing, and returned to UCLA to earn her M.A. degree and to teach Latin. The acceptance of a short story about teaching motivated her to try a career in writing once again, and she wrote *Young Man with a Horn* (1938), a best-seller about the life of a jazz musician.

As she continued to write, Baker's knack for capturing human expression (as seen in "Romance") and the struggle of characters to communicate with each other became her hallmark. Her characters, like Danny and Janet, often have a single concern. Baker's psychological insight into the concerns of others renders her fiction deeply human and perceptive.

The apartment where Danny Blake lived was an above-and-below sort of place; from the floor to the windows it was basement, but the bottoms of the windows were on a level with the sidewalk outside, so that anybody looking out the window could just stand there and look at the feet that walked by. It was a good enough pastime, but it ended by making Danny very conscious of the seams in women's stockings. He'd sit at his desk, studying, and when he'd hear footsteps on the sidewalk outside, he'd look; and if it was a woman and her seams were crooked, he always felt bad about it. He was doing a thesis in the department of philosophy on "The Concept of Property in the Roman Empire," and this worry about seams took up too much of his time.

At night he always had to keep the blinds pulled, so that people walking by couldn't look down on him. It was one of the drawbacks to the apartment. Another one was that the ceiling was all crossed up with a lot of asbestos-bound pipes. But there were good things about it, too. It was private, a no-neighbor apartment, like a house, almost; and it had a kitchen with an electric refrigerator in it, and a bathroom with a shower in it. And he didn't pay any rent, because he had the job of watching the heating plant and seeing to it that there was heat in the pipes when there should be, and none when there didn't absolutely have to be. He did that and some other little duties of a menial nature and that took care of his rent.

So he had a place to work in and sleep in and eat in and bathe in, and the fact that he could live, rent free, in the basement of another man's apartment had no connection with his choosing property as the subject of his thesis. It wasn't a doctoral dissertation, either, it was only a master's thesis, and all he had to do was get all the information he could handily come by, and then draw some sort of conclusion.

For all the tender care he gave the heating system, his own apartment was cold all winter. The pipes on the ceiling were warm but not enough to do any real good. The builders had omitted to put a radiator into the basement apartment, and the only thing to do when it got too cold was to light the oven in the kitchen. And this ran into money, the way comforts do.

This night he was sitting at his desk in front of a typewriter. He sat there with his chin in his hand and thought and thought. Once in a while he would type out two or three words and then cross them out with x's right away, and then wait again. It was cold, and he got up and went into the kitchen and took a look at the oven, and then went into the bathroom and got a bath towel and looped it around his neck, like a scarf, and stuck the ends inside his robe. When he came out, he stood for a while in the middle of his living room and looked up thoughtfully at the pipes, as if he might be intending to jump up and chin himself on one of them, but nothing came of it, and he sat down again in front of the typewriter and sighed a great many times. It took him a long time to get started, but after a while he began to write and the typewriter clicked along nicely and kept him from hearing a couple of taps at his window.

There were two taps, quite timid, and the typewriter made hay of both of them. But no man can write for very long without stopping to think, and so there came a pause and in the pause there was another tap, and this one made itself felt. The boy jumped at the window, got the blind up, and took a look. There was a girl outside, crouched down beside the window and all huddled up in her coat.

Danny Blake unlocked the window and shoved it up and said hello.

"I forgot where the door was," the girl said.

"It's clear around the other side of the building. Go around that way and I'll be there to meet you."

"What about the window?"

"All right."

The girl sat down on the sidewalk and stuck both legs in the window, and then ducked her head in, squirmed around a little, and let herself slide. There was a little tearing sound, and as soon as she landed she straightened her coat and then felt the back of it.

"What did you do, tear it?"

"There must have been a nail somewhere."

She looked at the window sill, and the nail was there, guilty as sin, with a tuft of camel's hair on its head. The boy was very sorry. He'd put the nail there himself, because the blind wouldn't stay down unless he wrapped the cord around something to hold it. The spring caught at the wrong places, and he needed some way to keep the blind down, so he drove the nail in, and it seemed like a good idea when he thought of it, but he had never supposed anyone would ever come in the window. "Especially you," he said.

"If anyone had told me," he said, "that I could ever hope to have you climb in my window and tear your coat on my window sill . . ." He stopped, holding out for a logical conclusion, and then said, "I never would have believed it, that's all."

"Why don't you put down the window?" the girl said. She was feeling the back of her coat. There was a little jag in it. Nothing that couldn't be fixed, but it was a very good coat, soft and tan with pearl buttons down the front and big pockets with flaps. Even the way she stood now, somewhat dejected and with one hand reaching low behind her, she looked almost cavalier in it.

Danny closed the window and locked it and then pulled down the blind and held it down.

"See," he said, "it won't stay down by itself." He relaxed and let the blind go up, to prove it, and then pulled it down again and twisted the cord around the nail.

"It's got to have something to hold it down," he said, "but it's a damned shame about your coat."

"It doesn't matter," the girl said. "I can get an invisible mender to invisibly mend it. I'll ask him invisibly to mend it."

"I never heard of an invisible mender."

"Oh, they're all over. Everywhere you look."

The thing of standing here and talking like strangers about such indifferent subjects as nails and blinds and coats and tailors was fine, because these two were not strangers; they were intimates, only they didn't know each other very well. They would have to say things like this for a while until one or the other of them broke down, or until they let themselves look at each other, and that would be any minute now. The girl was looking down at the floor, getting ready to say something else, laying it out straight in her mind, and while she watched the floor Danny watched her.

"I didn't have much time," the girl said finally, "but I had to see you."

"Don't get the idea I didn't have to see *you*," Danny said. "You know what I've done today? I spent the morning at Liggett's in a phone booth. Put in my nickel and ring your boarding house, and in ten minutes or so somebody'd answer, and I'd ask for you, and whoever it was would go try to find you and then come back and say you weren't there. So I'd hang up and walk around the block, and come back and try it again, and next time go around the block twice, and then finally they got so they wouldn't answer the phone, so I went over and rang the doorbell, and you know what they said?"

"I wasn't there?" the girl said.

Danny nodded. "You might say I combed the town," he said. "Where were you?"

"I was in the French office correcting a set of papers."

"Not any of the times I was in there."

He didn't say this in any spirit of checking up, but the girl answered it fast, as if he had. "I don't always work in the French office," she said. "When there's a lot to do, I work in Renée's apartment, where it's quiet."

"Is that where you were?"

The girl nodded. "I've been there since eleven o'clock this morning. It's been an awful day."

"Where'd you have lunch?"

"Renée's."

"Do you call her Renée?"

"What should I call her?"

Danny thought a minute and said, "I sat in on a course of hers last year." He sounded embarrassed, as if he were saying, "I spent last year in a sanitarium, but I'm all right now."

The girl waited, and then he said the rest of it. "I didn't know any French, I just wanted to look at her three days a week."

"So did you?"

Danny nodded. "Three days a week, all year," he said. "And here you can go right into her house and call her Renée and stay for lunch."

The girl felt the back of her coat and looked annoyed.

"I've known her for four years," she said. "She taught at St. Catherine's when I was there and then when I came here she gave me a job reading for her."

She looked down a minute, and then said, "She's not very easy to work for. Not today anyhow."

"Where'd you have to go? Where's she live?"

"Up Amherst, clear to the end."

"That crazy-looking glass place with the round front, way up there?"

The girl nodded. "It's called The Piedmont, I don't know why."

"It's a mess," Danny said. "All it needs is some neon."

The girl raised her shoulders as if to say it was no fault of hers, and then she said, "It's nice inside."

Danny was tired of talking about French teachers and architecture and coats and nails. He looked at the girl now the way he wanted to look at her and said very quietly, "I'll tell you what. If it's really nice inside, we'll go there and live." He said it to see how it would sound to say it. They knew they couldn't go and live anywhere, all that could happen would be that the girl could come here and spend parts of some nights with him.

The girl didn't look up or give any sign of hearing him, and so he said what he really wanted to say.

"I'm glad you came. I was afraid maybe you'd got lost and I wouldn't be able to find you again."

That got through to her. She jerked her head up, almost as if he'd scared her, and then looked away again.

"What's the matter?" he said.

"What with?"

This wasn't going right. They ought to have been thinking the same thing, but maybe they weren't. Then the girl said it.

"I haven't got any time," she said. "I only wanted to see you."

"I've got all night," Danny said. "I had all night last night and I've got all night tonight."

It was a tender speech nicely said and deeply felt, but the girl moved away and pulled her coat higher around her shoulders and spoke in the other direction, away from him, but clearly enough. He heard the words.

"I can't come here again, and I hope you won't be. . . . I hope it will be all right, that's all."

"Sit down. Take off your coat."

The girl only looked at him, puzzled. Why should anyone want to take off a coat in a room as cold as this one, and why, since she had just said she couldn't stay, should she sit down?

She should sit down, Danny said, because he had some things to tell her, and it was very important to tell her, and to make her understand all about it. She shouldn't get herself worked up and make any funny decisions not to see him any more. He was afraid of that, and that's one reason why he'd spent the day trying to find her and tell her how it was. "*Look, Janet, this is how it is. Don't look that way. Listen to me. This is how it is:* Two people meet each other, that's the way it starts out, and that much is all clear. Somebody comes along and introduces them very correctly: Miss So-and-So, let me present Mr. So-and-So. People get themselves introduced to other people every day, and it doesn't matter at all. But anyhow they shake hands, these two, and then somebody asks them to go someplace, and then they're in a room with a lot of people they don't like much, and that makes a bond, so they clear out together, just the two of them, freshly introduced, and they go to a place called Bert's. And there they get sort of tight, just pleasantly hallucinated."

"You don't call what *I* was 'pleasantly hallucinated,' do you?"

"Wait a minute," he said, "hear me out, and then if you want to you can have a turn.

"They're at a place called Bert's, pleasantly hallucinated, and the first thing you know Danny Blake is out of money, as it so frequently happens, and Janet what's-her-name——"

"Black," the girl said. "The name's Janet Black."

"I know," Danny said. "I didn't think of it last night, but wouldn't we sound good hyphenated?"

She thought it over and liked it.

"But Daniel Blake is out of money, and Janet Black has left her purse at home, like a dope, so they come back here to Danny's to see about making some coffee, and they go in the basement door, and weave around through the furnace room, and Danny checks the thermostat and puts coal in the stoker, and Janet tells him about purgatory.

"Up to there it was all right, wasn't it?" Danny said, and the girl didn't say whether it was or wasn't.

Up to there it was fine. And if the rest of the night was a mess or a disappointment, if she got scared and everything went wrong, it wasn't anything to blow their brains out about. Give them time. Give them a little forbearance.

"I thought you were very beautifully inexperienced," he said.

"What do you say we don't talk about it?" the girl said.

"Sit down, please. Don't stand there with one foot up, like a stork."

"Oh, my God," the girl said. "I don't look like a stork, do I? I'd better get out of here."

She started fast for the door, and Danny ran and got between her and it like a villain in a play and said, "Now listen."

"Don't you see," he said, "that this is just the way it ought to be?" And when he said that, she went to pieces a little. All the stiffening went out of her legs and she went to the couch in the corner and sat down on the edge of it and put her hands over her face.

"I'm sick," she said between her hands. "I think I'm just about sick enough to die, but I don't seem to be able to."

Danny started to sit down beside her, and she jumped; so he stood up again and let her have it to herself. He went to his desk and turned the chair around and sat down all the way across the room from her and watched her. She took her hands away from her face, pushed up a coat sleeve, and took a look at her watch. When she saw it, she drew a sharp breath.

"I've got to go."

"Where to?"

She didn't answer him directly, but she began to talk in a voice that she pushed out just enough for him to hear. She didn't say anything but that she was tired, she'd had a horrible day, one of the worst, and she felt somehow as if she had just finished being flogged through the fleet, the whole damned entire fleet and a couple of tugboats to grow on, and what she'd like best would be to go to sleep, only it wouldn't do much good, because sooner or later she would have to wake up again.

She looked across at him, first time she'd looked him in the face since she came in, and she said: "If I could only go to sleep and stay where it's dark, and never hear any more talk, and never look at any more faces." She stopped short, and then added one thing more: "And never answer another question."

She reached into her pocket and brought out a flat leather cigarette case, and snapped it open. Danny started to jump for a match, but then he sat back again. It could be that having people jump to light cigarettes for you is the same as having to look at faces and hear talk and answer questions, and perhaps if a man could get to know what's wanted and what isn't, he might be better thought of.

She felt in both coat pockets, and then found a card of matches in the pocket of her sweater, lighted her cigarette, and held onto the burnt match. She was very nice to see, slumped there on the couch, with her coat collar turned up around her neck, and a cigarette in her mouth and the dead match between her fingers.

"You do look sort of shot," Danny said. "Did you *have* to work? Couldn't you have told her you were sick, and gone home and got some sleep?"

"No, that's something I couldn't have told her."

"You're too conscientious. You'll never get anywhere."

"I'm not conscientious, I'm just healthy, and . . ."

"And what?"

"And everybody knows I'm healthy. So it wouldn't do to play sick, that's all."

"Healthy people get sick. You just told me you felt sick. Doesn't your friend Renée ever get sick?"

The girl answered this with a little heat. "She's always sick."

"She doesn't look it," Danny said. "Something I used to wonder about her," he said. "Is she all French? Where's she get that color?"

"Sun lamp," the girl said. "She works very hard on herself."

She felt the end of the match and then put it into her pocket. The ash tray was on the desk, and Danny didn't bring it to her, and she didn't go get it, and so they both seemed calm. They sat silent for a while, and the girl began to look as if she wouldn't bolt. She looked as if she would stay right where she was and think whatever her thoughts were for a long time, and maybe in the end stay even longer. Right now she was lost, submerged, thinking whatever it was. Her face was gray and her eyelids were blue, and her hair hung in a full light sweep across her cheek; and Danny sat across the room from her and watched her without making any point of it. After a while he went into the kitchen and lighted the oven and put the coffee on top of the stove.

"I'm going to heat the coffee," he said. "Same coffee we didn't drink last night."

"It ought to be aged by now," the girl said. She said it dully, but it was a sign she'd stay and drink it.

"Do you want sugar?" he said. "There isn't any cream."

"Neither," she said, and that brought him to the door to say some of the things he'd been thinking.

"What I like about this," he said, "is that I don't know anything about you—when your birthday is, or what your middle name is, or what size shoes you wear, or whether you're rich or poor. Most people find out all those things, and dawdle along and if everything checks up then they go ahead."

He was getting cups and saucers out of the cupboard, and he dropped a saucer and kicked the pieces under the sink.

"All right, then, break," he said to the saucer, and to the girl he said, "but us, we go ahead first, and then go back over the rest of the stuff at our leisure."

He looked around the door to see how she was taking it, and she had her hands over her face again.

"Today's the best day I ever had in my life," he said, so quietly that she could hear it or not, just as she pleased. "Hear me or not. I've felt good today, like chinning myself on the damned pipes."

It got through to her. "That's because you're not me," she said. She looked up and smiled about half and then looked down again and said, "And don't ever get yourself in a spot where you have to feel like this, because it's the hell, I'm telling you. Keep yourself out in the open, stay free, and—" Her voice wobbled, and then she pulled it together and looked across at Danny and said, "Go chin yourself."

The whole thing was good news and Danny snatched at it.

"You mean," he said, "that's all it is that's got you down? Nothing but that?"

"Nothing but what? I didn't say anything had me down. I'm sick, that's all." She said it all fast, with her guard up.

"Why didn't you say all this before, and not keep me wondering how I stand?"

He left the coffeepot where it was and came toward the couch. "Look, you," he said. "This way it's easy. If some other bastard thinks you're his girl, and you don't want to tell him about me, that's all right, take it very easy. I'll tell him myself."

The girl stared at him and licked her lips the way people do when there isn't anything to say.

Danny didn't see how scared she was; he was too happy.

"Then it will all be done, and it will all be straight, and it won't bother him for long. That's a fact. It won't. Figure it out for yourself, how would you feel yourself?"

"Forget it," she said. "Please let's forget it. I've got to go."

"No, you don't. I've poured your coffee."

He went back to the kitchen and brought one cup in a saucer and carried the other cup, saucerless, by the handle.

"Here you are."

She took it and laid her cigarette on the edge of the saucer, and her hand shook so that the cup clicked like a train on a track.

"Drink it."

She raised the cup, and the cigarette rolled down to the center of the saucer, and when she set the cup down it tipped, and a little coffee spilled over and put out the cigarette.

"God," she said, "what a mess. What can I do?"

"Here," Danny said, "give it to me," and he took the cup and saucer to the kitchen, threw away the cigarette and washed and dried the saucer, and set the cup back in it and filled it up and brought it back and handed it to her. Then he lighted a cigarette, laid it on the edge of the ash tray, and set the ash tray down on the couch beside her.

"See?" Danny said. "I'm very crazy about you, only I don't want to tell you now. Here's what we'll do. You drink that, and I'll go put on some pants and a shirt, and you tell me what the name of this guy is, and I'll go tell him how it was, and you wait here for me, and then I'll come back, and we'll go to sleep. And tomorrow when we wake up, if we ever do, it will all be fixed and you won't be jumpy and we'll get up and have breakfast and walk around the lake."

He looked down at her. "Is it somebody I already know?"

She waited a moment with the cup up to her lips, and then set it down on the couch and picked up the cigarette and stood up.

"No," she said. "It isn't anybody at all. It isn't anyone."

Danny was between her and the door. She saw how it was, and then put the cigarette in her mouth and pulled a pair of gloves out of her pocket and put them on. It was to say she was leaving, she was getting out, she was not stopping to drink any more coffee or say any more words. She would have to walk around Danny and go to the door and open it, and then get through all those furnaces in the basement and find the door to the outside. It could be done. It could be done as easily as jumping four feet from the roof of one building to the roof of another building. Four feet is no distance, one way you think about it.

"Good-by." She said it flatly, without looking, and Danny came up to her and said, "Huh uh, no, you don't just go out of here without saying anything. You don't do that, not to me. Whoever this is we can tell him how it is."

"No, we can't," the girl said.

"Why can't we?"

"Because we can't. This can't be fixed. Could you maybe take my word for it and let me alone?"

"You said it wasn't anybody."

"It isn't anybody."

"Then what is it?"

Janet Black was out on a limb, and there wasn't any safe way to solid ground, so she tried to stay where she was.

"I came here tonight," she said, "because I wanted to see you, this one time. That's all. It was the wrong thing to do, of course. But I thought maybe I could come in and tell you how it was and you'd be willing to let it go at that, and not set up a holler and shove me around."

She pushed her hair back from her cheek, and she looked as tired as anyone ever looked.

"I thought maybe we could just be quiet for a while, without questions and answers, and then I'd go."

She stepped back, not steady, and Danny caught her; and then she slumped and he held her and she let him.

"Hell, I didn't know I was asking questions," Danny said to her. "I'm thick-headed, that's all. I won't ask you anything, don't even think about it. No questions, no questions."

He looked down at her and said it. "No questions from me to you, did you hear me?"

"I heard you."

"Will it be all right, if I keep my silly trap shut and don't ever ask anything?"

She didn't answer, and he went on. "See, I don't give a damn. All I wanted to do was to fix it for you so we could be together and you could stay. But look, if you'd rather fix it yourself and not have me pushing in, well, go ahead and fix it. That's all I want. Only get it straight about me, I'm with you. It doesn't matter whether I know what I'm with you on or not, but I'm with you. As long as you live, whatever you do, you're my girl and I'm with you. Is that all clear? Is that nice?"

"Yes, that's right."

"Would you rather get married, or not get married?"

She started to cry then, and she didn't like to cry. She pushed herself away from him and kicked down at the floor.

"What's the matter?"

She didn't say, because she was trying to quit crying.

"Don't burn your glove." The cigarette was down to a half inch, and Danny took hold of the girl's hand and turned it over and took the cigarette out from between her fingers and put it into the ash tray.

"Thank you."

"You're welcome."

"Why don't I just go out the window, the way I came in?"

"Do you have to go?"

"Yes." She looked at her watch. "It's a quarter past twelve."

"Does it matter?"

"Yes."

She went toward the window, and took a look at the nail. Danny went with her and untwisted the cord and started pushing the nail back and forth.

"I can get it out," he said. "It's not in very deep."

He wiggled the nail back and forth and made his voice sound casual. "You coming back?"

"I can't," the girl said.

"Where you going?"

"Now? I'm going back to my room and go to sleep."

"Stay here then."

"You said you'd let me alone."

"All right, all right. O.K., I will. Look, why don't I walk over with you?"

"It's only a block. Why should you?"

"Because I want to. I'll get dressed."

"No. I want to go right now."

"I'll just put on some shoes and a coat."

"I don't want you to go with me." It was a flat statement: I do not want you to go with me, I do not want you, and it quieted Danny Blake the way a knife in the heart can quiet.

It was a shut-out and he didn't try again. He got the nail out, and let the blind go up, and then put up the window.

"There you are," he said. "Take it away."

She didn't try anything either. She took hold of the window sill with both hands, and jumped up and got one knee on it, like a swimmer coming out of a tank, and then ducked her head and got out. She sat on the sidewalk and Danny looked out at her. One side of her face was lighted from the street light on the corner. Her coat collar and her face looked the same color, and her hair looked white. Danny put the window down and they looked at each other through the glass. There was no expression on either of their faces, not love or hate. When the girl started to get up, Danny drew the blind. He must have stood there and held it down. There wasn't any nail.

Janet Black started to walk. Her coat collar was turned up and she kept her hands in her pockets and moved slowly down the street. It was only a block to the boarding house where she had a room, but when she got to the house she didn't go in. She stood in front of it a minute, and looked up at it, like a sight-seer taking a look at a public building, and then she turned away and moved again in another direction. There were some things she had to do, and now she moved again, slowly and smoothly, almost as if she were standing on an endless belt, just standing there and letting herself be pulled along with it. And all the time words kept coming at her, pushing up to her and making themselves heard. They were all words that had been put into her mind at one time or another, and now they were all on their own, and they shot up at her in little spurts, all unconnected. It didn't make much difference whose they were, her own or other people's old words. All she did was move along on the endless belt and hear direct quotations unconnected. She didn't resist; she let them come as they would.

" 'Choices,' I said, 'simple choices, that's all. Nothing but simple choices.' Look here, don't mix yourself up about it, because it's this way. This is the way it is, and has to be, and I'm with you. You know that. I'm with you. I don't even know what I'm with you on, but my country right or wrong. 'You don't know this,' I said, 'and I trust it won't come as a shock to you, oh, I do trust. But the thing about it is that I have decided to marry a man named Daniel, in fact, no, no, nothing. If you really want to know where I've been, I'll tell you. I've been to the public library, and that's God's holy truth. Nothing. No, forget it, forget I mentioned it, it's only a piece of old American folk humor, and it has absolutely nothing to do with the famed French clarity, and still less with the bleary stone so dear to the heart of every loyal Irish. Very well, then, Blarney, I can be accurate. I can check my references with the best of them. No, I absolutely insist on correcting it. It was a stupid mistake. I was under the impression I'd said Blarney all along. And I'll never go near the public library again, never. I hate a scene as much as the next one, as I was remarking just now.' Oh, I do hate them, especially if I'm in them. A good fight, now, is something else. A good fight is better, only may the best man win, which to my knowledge is not in the cards. You talk like a rummy, all loose and freely associational, but it probably is just some sort of mental disorder; there are mental disorders, which will have to remain nameless because my memory for names seems to be slipping, but there are ones that take the victim like this exactly. The victim hears talk. A pertinent example is Jeanne d'Arc, *la vièrge d'Orléans,* of whom you think so highly. And anybody, I don't care who, can go this way and hear voices in the head if there's a reason for it, if enough pressure has been put on for a long enough time. That's why innocent men say all right, I did it, after they've been kept awake for sixty hours and put under a light every time they start to sleep. That's me, every time I nod my head you hit me with a scene, fast talk, fancy words, diatribe. But do you know something? Do you know I could stand up and say look, I've had enough of this. This isn't the way it started out to be. This affair was something else, now it's what shall I say? Is there a word bad enough to say what it has become? It has become an incest, a closeness, an airlessness. It's a tube, a rubber tube, and I'm inside it and both ends are sewed up, and there I am. No, it's worse than that; there we both are. Whew. Whew. But what *we* did, we got up and walked around the lake. No, first we had breakfast, and I looked at this man and I said to him, Daniel, I don't care if school keeps or not, it's so nice to know that we'll be out there walking around the lake, just kicking around loose in the open air, right or wrong. Keep in a cool dry place."

The university campus split the town into two parts. The book stores and clothing stores and restaurants and students' dormitories and boarding houses were on one side, on the level; and on the other side, up the hill, were the homes and gardens, and clubs, and two-car garages. At the edge of the campus, on the lower side, the girl ducked between the bars of a fence and took a little path through an open field. It was the shortest way to the main road that crossed the campus, and when she got to the main one she shuffled her feet along the gravel walk and got the mud off her shoes. Halfway across she came to a circle, heavily landscaped, with a fountain and a pool, drained now, and a ring of concrete benches around it. It was a bright

night with a late, misshapen moon riding high, and Janet Black
stopped a minute and put a knee on one of the benches and looked
over the back of it at the statue above the fountain. It was Pan, naked
and dull, playing a set of pipes, and below him the pool was full of
moldy leaves.

That was the last time she stopped. The words kept going all the
time: "I hope you may be able to understand this. Don't try to stop
me, or talk me away from it, because it's what I'm going to do. No,
I don't care what you say or who you tell. I'm not afraid. Scarcely at
all am I afraid. And words to that effect. I'll just take my things and
leave, and that will be done. Wouldn't you think, wouldn't you think
if I said it and took my things and left, that that would be all? Tonight,
even. Because that's what I'd most certainly think. If ever, this night."

She kept her head down and moved along the gravel walk past the
library, and past the administration building, and past the law
building, and then she was out in the open again. She took another
cut away from the walk and came out at the foot of Amherst Avenue.
The big apartment house was at the end of the street and it shone up
there on this bright night, all glass and metal with a round front. All
the way up there, a fine example of the future trend in modern
architecture, a most forward-looking edifice. And if one wanted to ask
the opinion of Daniel Blake, all it needed was some neon.

When the girl got to the door, she pulled a key ring out of her
pocket, found a key, and put it in the lock. Inside, the hall was bare
and immaculate. There were big black-and-white tiles on the floor, a
checkerboard of squares two feet across, and the walls were soft and
pinkish with side lights made of fan-shaped layers of frosted glass. The
girl walked across the squares and put her feet, by habit, only into the
black ones. The elevator was at the end of the hall, and she slid the
door back and stepped inside. It was a narrow little box with
aluminum walls and a checkered floor and a panel with a row of five
pearl buttons on it. She pushed the fourth one and the current came
on and the elevator got itself started. Four floors of it, and the girl
turned down her coat collar, and pushed her hair back and took off
her gloves, and then the elevator died, suddenly but smoothly, and
she hunched her shoulders under her coat, and slid the door back and
got out.

The hall was like the other one: checkered floor and pink walls
and frosted lights. She walked herself down the black squares to the
end of the hall and stood for a moment in front of a door. Then she
found another key and put it into the lock and opened the door.

It was dark inside, and very warm. The girl closed the door and put her back against it and stood quietly a moment, waiting. There was a light in an inner room, and the door was not quite closed, and the girl stood and waited, shivering.

Then the voice came. It was a clear cold voice, but rich, like the voice of an actress or a drinker. It made itself sound careless, and the words were:

"Ah, *tu es enfin de retour?*"

Nothing but that, and the girl stiffened up, there in the dark, and knew this was the time to say what she had to say. It had to be now, right now, and she tried to open her mouth and her teeth were clamped. She swallowed and pushed her hair back and tried again, but she knew she didn't have it, and that she never would be able to get it said. The question had come to her carelessly, and she sat down in the dark and answered it tonelessly:

"Yes, I'm back."

[1944]

Dorothy Parker
(1893–1967)

A Telephone Call

Dorothy Parker first expressed herself to the world in sharp and biting reviews for *The New Yorker* and *Vanity Fair*. Described by biographer Marion Meade as the "darling of the New York smart set [and] the most quotable, quoted, and misquoted person in America" (*Dorothy Parker: What Fresh Hell Is This?* Villard, 1988), Parker, a member of New York's "Algonquin Round Table," became known for her trademark clever comments.

In 1926 her first volume of poetry, *Enough Rope,* became a best-seller, and she went on to write more volumes of poetry and stories. Her book-review column, the "Constant Reader," was characterized by a relaxed, conversational tone, which can be seen also in the stream of consciousness of "A Telephone Call." In this particular story, a woman shifts between desperation and pain as she waits for her recalcitrant lover to phone. The accuracy of the biting humor suggests that this story may be a reflection of Parker's own unstable personal life.

Please, God, let him telephone me now. Dear God, let him call me now. I won't ask anything else of You, truly I won't. It isn't very much to ask. It would be so little to You, God, such a little, little thing. Only let him telephone now. Please, God. Please, please, please.

If I didn't think about it, maybe the telephone might ring.

Sometimes it does that. If I could think of something else. If I could think of something else. Maybe if I counted five hundred by fives, it might ring by that time. I'll count slowly. I won't cheat. And if it rings when I get to three hundred, I won't stop; I won't answer it until I get to five hundred. Five, ten, fifteen, twenty, twenty-five, thirty, thirty-five, forty, forty-five, fifty. . . . Oh, please ring. Please.

This is the last time I'll look at the clock. I will not look at it again. It's ten minutes past seven. He said he would telephone at five o'clock. "I'll call you at five, darling." I think that's where he said "darling." I'm almost sure he said it there. I know he called me "darling" twice, and the other time was when he said good-by. "Good-by, darling." He was busy, and he can't say much in the office, but he called me "darling" twice. He couldn't have minded my calling him up. I know you shouldn't keep telephoning them—I know they don't like that. When you do that, they know you are thinking about them and wanting them, and that makes them hate you. But I hadn't talked to him in three days—not in three days. And all I did was ask him how he was; it was just the way anybody might have called him up. He couldn't have minded that. He couldn't have thought I was bothering him. "No, of course you're not," he said. And he said he'd telephone me. He didn't have to say that. I didn't ask him to, truly I didn't. I'm sure I didn't. I don't think he would say he'd telephone me, and then just never do it. Please don't let him do that, God. Please don't.

"I'll call you at five, darling." "Good-by, darling." He was busy, and he was in a hurry, and there were people around him, but he called me "darling" twice. That's mine, that's mine. I have that, even if I never see him again. Oh, but that's so little. That isn't enough. Nothing's enough, if I never see him again. Please let me see him again, God. Please, I want him so much. I want him so much. I'll be good, God. I will try to be better, I will, if You will let me see him again. If You let him telephone me. Oh, let him telephone me now.

Ah, don't let my prayer seem too little to You, God. You sit up there, so white and old, with all the angels about You and the stars slipping by. And I come to You with a prayer about a telephone call. Ah, don't laugh, God. You see, You don't know how it feels. You're so safe, there on Your throne, with the blue swirling under You. Nothing can touch You; no one can twist Your heart in his hands. This is suffering, God, this is bad, bad suffering. Won't You help me? For Your Son's sake, help me. You said You would do whatever was asked of You in His name. Oh, God, in the name of Thine only beloved Son, Jesus Christ, our Lord, let him telephone me now.

I must stop this. I mustn't be this way. Look. Suppose a young man says he'll call a girl up, and then something happens, and he doesn't. That isn't so terrible, is it? Why, it's going on all over the world, right this minute. Oh, what do I care what's going on all over the world? Why can't that telephone ring? Why can't it, why can't it? Couldn't you ring? Ah, please, couldn't you? You damned, ugly, shiny thing. It would hurt you to ring, wouldn't it? Oh, that would hurt you. Damn you, I'll pull your filthy roots out of the wall, I'll smash your smug black face in little bits. Damn you to hell.

No, no, no. I must stop. I must think about something else. This is what I'll do. I'll put the clock in the other room. Then I can't look at it. If I do have to look at it, then I'll have to walk into the bedroom, and that will be something to do. Maybe, before I look at it again, he will call me. I'll be so sweet to him, if he calls me. If he says he can't see me tonight, I'll say, "Why, that's all right, dear. Why, of course it's all right." I'll be the way I was when I first met him. Then maybe he'll like me again. I was always sweet, at first. Oh, it's so easy to be sweet to people before you love them.

I think he must still like me a little. He couldn't have called me "darling" twice today, if he didn't still like me a little. It isn't all gone, if he still likes me a little; even if it's only a little, little bit. You see, God, if You would just let him telephone me, I wouldn't have to ask You anything more. I would be sweet to him, I would be gay, I would be just the way I used to be, and then he would love me again. And then I would never have to ask You for anything more. Don't You see, God? So won't You please let him telephone me? Won't You please, please, please?

Are You punishing me, God, because I've been bad? Are You angry with me because I did that? Oh, but, God, there are so many bad people—You could not be hard only to me. And it wasn't very bad; it couldn't have been bad. We didn't hurt anybody, God. Things are only bad when they hurt people. We didn't hurt one single soul; You know that. You know it wasn't bad, don't You, God? So won't You let him telephone me now?

If he doesn't telephone me, I'll know God is angry with me. I'll count five hundred by fives, and if he hasn't called me then, I will know God isn't going to help me, ever again. That will be the sign. Five, ten, fifteen, twenty, twenty-five, thirty, thirty-five, forty, forty-five, fifty, fifty-five. . . . It was bad. I knew it was bad. All right,

God, send me to hell. You think You're frightening me with Your hell, don't You? You think Your hell is worse than mine.

I mustn't. I mustn't do this. Suppose he's a little late calling me up—that's nothing to get hysterical about. Maybe he isn't going to call—maybe he's coming straight up here without telephoning. He'll be cross if he sees I have been crying. They don't like you to cry. He doesn't cry. I wish to God I could make him cry. I wish I could make him cry and tread the floor and feel his heart heavy and big and festering in him. I wish I could hurt him like hell.

He doesn't wish that about me. I don't think he even knows how he makes me feel. I wish he could know, without my telling him. They don't like you to tell them they've made you cry. They don't like you to tell them you're unhappy because of them. If you do, they think you're possessive and exacting. And then they hate you. They hate you whenever you say anything you really think. You always have to keep playing little games. Oh, I thought we didn't have to; I thought this was so big I could say whatever I meant. I guess you can't, ever. I guess there isn't ever anything big enough for that. Oh, if he would just telephone, I wouldn't tell him I had been sad about him. They hate sad people. I would be so sweet and so gay, he couldn't help but like me. If he would only telephone. If he would only telephone.

Maybe that's what he is doing. Maybe he is coming on here without calling me up. Maybe he's on his way now. Something might have happened to him. No, nothing could ever happen to him. I can't picture anything happening to him. I never picture him run over. I never see him lying still and long and dead. I wish he were dead. That's a terrible wish. That's a lovely wish. If he were dead, he would be mine. If he were dead, I would never think of now and the last few weeks. I would remember only the lovely times. It would be all beautiful. I wish he were dead. I wish he were dead, dead, dead.

This is silly. It's silly to go wishing people were dead just because they don't call you up the very minute they said they would. Maybe the clock's fast; I don't know whether it's right. Maybe he's hardly late at all. Anything could have made him a little late. Maybe he had to stay at his office. Maybe he went home, to call me up from there, and somebody came in. He doesn't like to telephone me in front of people. Maybe he's worried, just a little, little bit, about keeping me waiting. He might even hope that I would call him up. I could do that. I could telephone him.

I mustn't. I mustn't, I mustn't. Oh, God, please don't let me telephone him. Please keep me from doing that. I know, God, just as well as You do, that if he were worried about me, he'd telephone no matter where he was or how many people there were around him. Please make me know that, God. I don't ask You to make it easy for me—You can't do that, for all that You could make a world. Only let me know it, God. Don't let me go on hoping. Don't let me say comforting things to myself. Please don't let me hope, dear God. Please don't.

I won't telephone him. I'll never telephone him again as long as I live. He'll rot in hell, before I'll call him up. You don't have to give me strength, God; I have it myself. If he wanted me, he could get me. He knows where I am. He knows I'm waiting here. He's so sure of me, so sure. I wonder why they hate you, as soon as they are sure of you. I should think it would be so sweet to be sure.

It would be so easy to telephone him. Then I'd know. Maybe it wouldn't be a foolish thing to do. Maybe he wouldn't mind. Maybe he'd like it. Maybe he has been trying to get me. Sometimes people try and try to get you on the telephone, and they say the number doesn't answer. I'm not just saying that to help myself; that really happens. You know that really happens, God. Oh, God, keep me away from that telephone. Keep me away. Let me still have just a little bit of pride. I think I'm going to need it, God. I think it will be all I'll have.

Oh, what does pride matter, when I can't stand it if I don't talk to him? Pride like that is such a silly, shabby little thing. The real pride, the big pride, is in having no pride. I'm not saying that just because I want to call him. I am not. That's true, I know that's true. I will be big. I will be beyond little prides.

Please, God, keep me from telephoning him. Please, God.

I don't see what pride has to do with it. This is such a little thing, for me to be bringing in pride, for me to be making such a fuss about. I may have misunderstood him. Maybe he said for me to call him up, at five. "Call me at five, darling." He could have said that, perfectly well. It's so possible that I didn't hear him right. "Call me at five, darling." I'm almost sure that's what he said. God, don't let me talk this way to myself. Make me know, please make me know.

I'll think about something else. I'll just sit quietly. If I could sit still. If I could sit still. Maybe I could read. Oh, all the books are about people who love each other, truly and sweetly. What do they want to write about that for? Don't they know it isn't true? Don't they know it's a lie, it's a God damned lie? What do they have to tell about that for, when they know how it hurts? Damn them, damn them, damn them.

I won't. I'll be quiet. This is nothing to get excited about. Look. Suppose he were someone I didn't know very well. Suppose he were another girl. Then I'd just telephone and say, "Well, for goodness' sake, what happened to you?" That's what I'd do, and I'd never even think about it. Why can't I be casual and natural, just because I love him? I can be. Honestly, I can be. I'll call him up, and be so easy and pleasant. You see if I won't, God. Oh, don't let me call him. Don't, don't, don't.

God, aren't You really going to let him call me? Are You sure, God? Couldn't You please relent? Couldn't You? I don't even ask You to let him telephone me this minute, God: only let him do it in a little while. I'll count five hundred by fives. I'll do it so slowly and so fairly. If he hasn't telephoned then, I'll call him. I will. Oh, please, dear God, dear kind God, my blessed Father in Heaven, let him call before then. Please, God. Please.

Five, ten, fifteen, twenty, twenty-five, thirty, thirty-five . . .

[1944]

Elizabeth Bowen
(1899–1973)

Pink May

Elizabeth Bowen, born in Dublin, Ireland, was in her own words "a writer for whom places loom large." She wrote of the places of her youth in both *Seven Winters* (1943) and *Bowen's Court* (1942). After nursing wounded soldiers in Dublin and then studying art in London, she published her first book of stories, *Encounters* (1923).

Bowen's masterpiece, *The Death of the Heart* (1938), is prototypical of her work. One line of the novel reveals the central conviction of all of Bowen's fiction: "Illusions are art, for the feeling person, and it is by art that we live, if we do." Bowen's writing deals with the human need for support in an impersonal world. Her other work includes *The Last September* (1929), set in her native Ireland; *The House of Pain* (1935); *The Heat of the Day* (1949); and *To the North* (1932).

Although they are polished and restrained, Bowen's novels and stories reveal intense passions such as selfless love, jealousy, hatred, and most often, loneliness. Her relation to Ireland is undeniable and her poignancy as a woman writer is obvious, but Bowen's work transcends both national and gender boundaries. Her stories are frequently mentioned in discussions of her novels, because they are often sketches in character, setting, or technique, or studies of a theme.

"Yes, it was funny," she said, "about the ghost. It used to come into my bedroom when I was dressing for dinner—when I was dressing to go out."

"*You were frightened?*"

"I was in such a hurry; there never was any time. When you have to get dressed in such a hell of a hurry any extra thing is just one thing more. And the room at the times I'm talking about used to be full of daylight—sunset. It had two french windows, and they were on a level with the tops of may trees out in the square. Then may was in flower that month, and it was pink. In that sticky sunshine you have in the evenings the may looked sort of theatrical. It used to be part of my feeling of going out." She paused, then said, "That was the month of my life."

"*What month?*"

"The month we were in that house. I told you, it was a furnished house that we took. With rents the way they are now, it cost less than a flat. They say a house is more trouble, but this was no trouble, because we treated it like a flat, you see. I mean, we were practically never in. I didn't try for a servant because I know there aren't any. When Neville got up in the mornings he percolated the coffee; a char came in to do the cleaning when I'd left for the depot, and we fixed with the caretaker next door to look after the boiler, so the baths were hot. And the beds were comfortable, too. The people who really lived there did themselves well."

"*You never met them?*"

"No, never—why should we? We'd fixed everything through an agent, the way one does. I've an idea the man was soldiering somewhere, and she'd gone off to be near him somewhere in the country. They can't have had any children, any more than we have—it was one of those small houses, just for two."

"*Pretty?*"

"Y-yes," she said. "It was chintzy. It was one of those oldish houses made over new inside. But you know how it is about other people's belongings—you can't ever quite use them, and they seem to watch you the whole time. Not that there was any question of settling down—how could we, when we were both out all day? And at the beginning of June we moved out again."

"*Because of the . . . ?*"

"Oh no," she said quickly. "Not that reason, at all." She lighted a cigarette, took two puffs and appeared to deliberate. "But what I'm telling you *now* is about the ghost."

"*Go on.*"

"I was going on. As I say, it used to be funny, dressing away at top speed at the top of an empty house, with the sunset blazing away outside. It seems to me that all those evenings were fine. I used to take taxis back from the depot: you must pay money these days if you want time, and a bath and a change from the skin up was essential—you don't know how one feels after packing parcels all day! I couldn't do like some of the girls I worked with and go straight from the depot on to a date. I can't go and meet someone unless I'm feeling special. So I used to hare home. Neville was never in."

"I'd been going to say . . ."

"No, Neville worked till all hours, or at least he had to hang round in case something else should come in. So he used to dine at his club on the way back. Most of the food would be off by the time he got there. It was partly that made him nervy, I dare say."

"But you weren't nervy?"

"I tell you," she said, "I was happy. Madly happy—perhaps in rather a nervy way. Whatever you are these days, you are rather more so. That's one thing I've discovered about this war."

"You were happy . . ."

"I had my reasons—which don't come into the story."

After two or three minutes of rapid smoking she leaned forward to stub out her cigarette. "Where was I?" she said, in a different tone.

"Dressing . . ."

"Well, first thing when I got in I always went across and opened my bedroom windows, because it seemed to me the room smelled of the char. So I always did that before I turned on my bath. The glare on the trees used to make me blink, and the thick sort of throaty smell of the may came in. I was never certain if I liked it or not, but it somehow made me feel like after a drink. Whatever happens tomorrow, I've got tonight. You know the feeling? Then I turned on my bath. The bathroom was the other room on that floor, and a door led through to it from one side of the bed. I used to have my bath with that door ajar, to let light in. The bathroom black-out took so long to undo.

"While the bath ran in I used to potter about and begin to put out what I meant to wear, and cold-cream off my old make-up, and so on. I say 'potter' because you cannot hurry a bath. I also don't mind telling you that I whistled. Well, what's the harm in *somebody's* being happy? Simply thinking things over won't win this war. Looking back at that month, I whistled most of the time. The way they used to look at me, at the depot! The queer thing is, though, I remember whistling but I can't remember when I happened to stop. But I must *have* stopped, because it was then I heard."

"*Heard?*"

She lit up again, with a slight frown. "What was it I heard first, that first time? I suppose, the silence. So I must have stopped whistling, mustn't I? I was lying there in my bath, with the door open behind me, when the silence suddenly made me sit right up. Then I said to myself, 'My girl, there's nothing queer about *that*. What else would you expect to hear, in an empty house?' All the same, it made me heave the other way round in my bath, in order to keep one eye on the door. After a minute I heard what wasn't a silence—which immediately made me think that Neville had come in early, and I don't mind telling you I said 'Damn'."

"*Oh?*"

"It's a bore being asked where one is going, though it's no bother to say where one has been. If Neville *was* in he'd be certain to search the house, so I put a good face on things and yelled 'Hoi'. But he didn't answer, because it wasn't him."

"*?*"

"No, it wasn't. And whatever was in my bedroom must have been in my bedroom for some time. I thought, 'A wind has come up and got into that damned chintz!' Any draught always fidgets me; somehow it gets me down. So I got out of my bath and wrapped the big towel round me and went through to shut the windows in my room. But I was surprised when I caught sight of the may trees—all their branches were standing perfectly still. That seemed queer. At the same time, the door I'd come through from the bathroom blew shut, and the lid fell off one of my jars of face cream on to the dressing-table, which had a glass top.

"No, I didn't see what it was. The point was, whatever it was saw me.

"That first time, the whole thing was so slight. If it had been only that one evening, I dare say I shouldn't have thought of it again. Things only get a hold on you when they go on happening. But I always have been funny in one way—I especially don't like being watched. You might not think so from my demeanour, but I don't really like being criticized. I don't think I get my knife into other people: why should they get their knife into me? I don't like it when my ear begins to burn.

"I went to put the lid back on the jar of cream and switch the lights on into the mirror, which being between the two windows never got the sort of light you would want. I thought I looked odd in the mirror—rattled. I said to myself, 'Now what have I done to *someone?*' but except for Neville I literally couldn't think. Anyway, there was no time—when I picked up my wristwatch I said, 'God!' So I flew round, dressing. Or rather, I flew round as much as one could with something or somebody getting in the way. That's all I remember about that *first* time, I think. Oh yes, I did notice that the veil on my white hat wasn't all that it ought to be. When I had put that hat out before my bath the whole affair had looked as crisp as a marguerite—a marguerite that has only opened today.

"You know how it is when a good deal hangs on an eve-ning—you simply can't afford to be not in form. So I gave myself a good shake on the way downstairs. 'Snap out of that!' I said. 'You've got personality. You can carry a speck or two on the veil.'

"Once I got to the restaurant—once I'd met him—the whole thing went out of my mind. I was in twice as good form as I'd ever been. And the turn events took . . .

"It was about a week later that I had to face it. I was up against something. The more the rest of my life got better and better, the more that one time of each evening got worse and worse. Or rather, it wanted to. But I wasn't going to let it. With everything else quite perfect—well, would *you* have? There's something exciting, I mean, some sort of a challenge about knowing someone's *trying* to get you down. And when that someone's another woman you soon get a line on her technique. She was jealous, that was what was the matter with her.

"Because, at all other times the room was simply a room. There wasn't any objection to me and Neville. When I used to slip home he was always asleep. I could switch all the lights on and kick my shoes off and open and shut the cupboards—he lay like the dead. He *was* abnormally done in, I suppose. And the room was simply a room in somebody else's house. And the mornings, when he used to roll out of bed and slip-slop down to make the coffee, without speaking, exactly like someone walking in his sleep, the room was no more than a room in which you've just woken up. The may outside looked pink-pearl in the early sunshine, and there were some regular birds who sang. Nice. While I waited for Neville to bring the coffee I used to like to lie there and think my thoughts.

"If he was awake at all before he had left the house, he and I exchanged a few perfectly friendly words. I had *no* feeling of anything blowing up. If I let him form the impression that I'd been spending the evenings at movies with girl friends I'd begun to make at the depot, then going back to their flats to mix Ovaltine—well, that seemed to me the considerate thing to do. If he'd even been more *interested* in my life—but he wasn't interested in anything but his work. I never picked on him about that—I must say, I do know when a war's a war. Only men are so different. You see, this other man worked just as hard but *was* interested in me. He said he found me so restful. Neville never said that. In fact, all the month we were in that house, I can't remember anything Neville said at all.

"No, what *she* couldn't bear was my going out, like I did. She was either a puritan, with some chip on her shoulder, or else she'd once taken a knock. I incline to that last idea—though I can't say why.

"No, I can't say why. I have never at all been a subtle person. I don't know whether that's a pity or not. I must say I don't care for subtle people—my instinct would be to give a person like that a miss. And on the whole I should say I'd succeeded in doing so. But that, you see, was where her advantage came in. You can't give a . . . well, I couldn't give *her* a miss. She was there. And she aimed at encircling me.

"I think maybe she had a poltergeist that she brought along with her. The little things that happened to my belongings . . . Each evening I dressed in that room I lost five minutes—I mean, each evening it took me five minutes longer to dress. But all that was really below her plane. That was just one start at getting me down before she opened up with her real technique. The really subtle thing was the way her attitude changed. That first time (as I've told you) I felt her disliking me—well, really 'dislike' was to put it mildly. But after an evening or two she was through with that. She conveyed the impression that she had got me taped and was simply so damned sorry for me. She was sorry about every garment I put on, and my hats were more than she was able to bear. She was sorry about the way I did up my face—she used to be right at my elbow when I got out my make-up, absolutely silent with despair. She was sorry I should never again see thirty, and sorry I should kid myself about that . . . I mean to say, she started pitying me.

"Do you see what I mean when I say her attitude could have been quite infectious?

"And that wasn't all she was sorry for me about. I mean, there are certain things that a woman who's being happy keeps putting out of her mind. (I mean, when she's being happy about a man.) And other things you keep putting out of your mind if your husband is *not* the man you are being happy about. There's a certain amount you don't ask yourself, and a certain amount that you might as well not remember. Now those were exactly the things she kept bringing up. She liked to bring those up better than anything.

"What I don't know is, and what I still don't know—*why* do all that to a person who's being happy? To a person who's living the top month of her life, with the may in flower and everything? What had I ever done to her? She was dead—I suppose? . . . Yes, I see now, she must have taken a knock."

"What makes you think that?"

"I know now how a knock feels."

"Oh . . .?"

"Don't look at me such a funny way. I haven't changed, have I? You wouldn't have noticed anything? . . . I expect it's simply this time of year: August's rather a tiring month. And things end without warning, before you know where you are. I hope the war will be over by next spring; I do want to be abroad, if I'm able to. Somewhere where there's nothing but pines or palms. I don't want to see London pink may in flower again—*ever.*"

"Won't Neville . . .?"

"Neville? Oh, didn't you really realize? Didn't I . . .? He, I, we've—I mean, we're living apart." She rose and took the full, fuming ash-tray across to another table, and hesitated, then brought an empty tray back. "Since we left that house," she said. "I told you we left that house. That was why. We broke up.

"It was the *other* thing that went wrong," she said. "If I'd still kept my head with Neville, he and I needn't ever—I mean, one's marriage *is* something . . . I'd thought I'd always be married, whatever else happened. I ought to have realized Neville was in a nervy state. Like a fool I spilled over to Neville; I lost my head. But by that time I hadn't any control left. When the one thing you've lived for has crashed to bits . . .

"Crashed was the word. And yet I see now, really, that things had been weakening for some time. At the time I didn't see, any more than I noticed the may was fading out in the square—till one morning the weather changed and I noticed the may was brown. All the happiness stopped like my stopping whistling—but at what particular moment I'm never sure.

"The beginnings of the end of it were so small. Like my being a bit more unpunctual every evening we met. That made us keep losing our table at restaurants—you know how the restaurants are these days. Then I somehow got the idea that none of my clothes were becoming; I began to think he was eyeing my hats unkindly, and that made me fidget and look my worst. Then I got an idiot thing about any girl that he spoke of—I didn't like anyone being younger than me. Then, at what had once been our most perfect moments, I began to ask myself if I *was* really happy, till I said to him—which was fatal—'Is there so much in this?' . . . I should have seen more red lights—when, for instance, he said, 'You know, *you're* getting nervy.' And he quite often used to say 'Tired?' in rather a tired way. I used to say, it was just getting dressed in a rush. But the fact is, a man hates the idea of a woman rushing. One night I know I did crack: I said, 'Hell, I've got a ghost in my room!' He put me straight into a taxi and sent me—not took me—home.

"I did see him several times after that. So his letter—his letter was a complete surprise . . . The joke was, I really had been out with a girl that evening I came in, late, to find his letter.

"If Neville had not been there when I got the letter, Neville and I might still—I suppose—be married. On the other hand—there are always two ways to see things—if Neville had *not* been there I should have gone mad . . . So now," she said, with a change of tone, "I'm living in an hotel. Till I see how things turn out. Till the war is over, or something. It isn't really so bad, and I'm out all day. Look, I'll give you my address and telephone number. It's been wonderful seeing you, darling. You promise we'll meet again? I do really need to keep in touch with my friends. And *you* don't so often meet someone who's seen a ghost!"

"But look, did you ever see it?"

"Well, not exactly. No, I can't say I *saw* it."

"You mean, you simply heard it?"

"Well, not exactly that . . ."

"You saw things move?"

"Well, I never turned around in time. I . . .

"If you don't understand—I'm sorry I ever told you the story! Not a ghost—when it ruined my whole life! Don't you see, can't you see there must have been *something*? Left to oneself, one doesn't ruin one's life!"

[1946]

Flannery O'Connor
(1925–1964)

The River

Born in Savannah, Georgia, Flannery O'Connor was raised in a strict Roman Catholic tradition. Her religious faith deepened when she contracted lupus erythematosus at age twenty-five. As a reaction to her illness, O'Connor often wrote of religious individuals, people financially, emotionally, and physically damaged who confront issues of faith and grace.

O'Connor published two novels, *Wise Blood* (1952) and *The Violent Bear It Away* (1960), and two volumes of stories, *A Good Man Is Hard to Find* (1955) and *Everything That Rises Must Converge* (1965). *Collected Stories* (1971), of which "The River" is a part, includes both published and previously unpublished work.

According to Carol Achloss (*Flannery O'Connor's Dark Comedies: The Limits of Inference,* Louisiana State University Press, 1980, p. 128), O'Connor's work is "valuable to readers of any persuasion because its haunting truth rests on sharable experience rather than prohibitive religious allusion."

The child stood glum and limp in the middle of the dark living room while his father pulled him into a plaid coat. His right arm was hung in the sleeve but the father buttoned the coat anyway and pushed him forward toward a pale spotted hand that stuck through the half-open door.

"He ain't fixed right," a loud voice said from the hall.

"Well then for Christ's sake fix him," the father muttered. "It's six o'clock in the morning." He was in his bathrobe and barefooted. When he got the child to the door and tried to shut it, he found her looming in it, a speckled skeleton in a long pea-green coat and felt helmet.

"And his and my carfare," she said. "It'll be twict we have to ride the car."

He went in the bedroom again to get the money and when he came back, she and the boy were both standing in the middle of the room. She was taking stock. "I couldn't smell those dead cigarette butts long if I was ever to come sit with you," she said, shaking him down in his coat.

"Here's the change," the father said. He went to the door and opened it wide and waited.

After she had counted the money she slipped it somewhere inside her coat and walked over to a watercolor hanging near the phonograph. "I know what time it is," she said, peering closely at the black lines crossing into broken planes of violent color. "I ought to. My shift goes on at 10 P.M. and don't get off till 5 and it takes me one hour to ride the Vine Street car."

"Oh, I see," he said. "Well, we'll expect him back tonight, about eight or nine?"

"Maybe later," she said. "We're going to the river to a healing. This particular preacher don't get around this way often. I wouldn't have paid for that," she said, nodding at the painting, "I would have drew it myself."

"All right, Mrs. Connin, we'll see you then," he said drumming on the door.

A toneless voice called from the bedroom, "Bring me an ice-pack."

"Too bad his mamma's sick," Mrs. Connin said. "What's her trouble?"

"We don't know," he muttered.

"We'll ask the preacher to pray for her. He's healed a lot of folks. The Reverend Bevel Summers. Maybe she ought to see him sometime."

"Maybe so," he said. "We'll see you tonight," and he disappeared into the bedroom and left them to go.

The little boy stared at her silently, his nose and eyes running. He was four or five. He had a long face and bulging chin and half-shut eyes set far apart. He seemed mute and patient, like an old sheep waiting to be let out.

"You'll like this preacher," she said. "The Reverend Bevel Summers. You ought to hear him sing."

The bedroom door opened suddenly and the father stuck his head out and said, "Good-by, old man. Have a good time."

"Good-by," the little boy said and jumped as if he had been shot.

Mrs. Connin gave the watercolor another look. Then they went out into the hall and rang for the elevator. "I wouldn't have drew it," she said.

Outside the gray morning was blocked off on either side by the unlit empty buildings. "It's going to fair up later," she said, "but this is the last time we'll be able to have any preaching at the river this year. Wipe your nose, Sugar Boy."

He began rubbing his sleeve across it but she stopped him. "That ain't nice," she said. "Where's your handkerchief?"

He put his hands in his pockets and pretended to look for it while she waited. "Some people don't care how they send one off," she murmured to her reflection in the coffee shop window. "You pervide." She took a red and blue flowered handkerchief out of her pocket and stooped down and began to work on his nose. "Now blow," she said and he blew. "You can borry it. Put it in your pocket."

He folded it up and put it in his pocket carefully and they walked on to the corner and leaned against the side of a closed drugstore to wait for the car. Mrs. Connin turned up her coat collar so that it met her hat in the back. Her eyelids began to droop and she looked as if she might go to sleep against the wall. The little boy put a slight pressure on her hand.

"What's your name?" she asked in a drowsy voice. "I don't know but only your last name. I should have found out your first name."

His name was Harry Ashfield and he had never thought at any time before of changing it. "Bevel," he said.

Mrs. Connin raised herself from the wall. "Why ain't that a coincident!" she said. "I told you that's the name of this preacher!"

"Bevel," he repeated.

She stood looking down at him as if he had become a marvel to her. "I'll have to see you meet him today," she said. "He's no ordinary preacher. He's a healer. He couldn't do nothing for Mr. Connin though. Mr. Connin didn't have the faith but he said he would try anything once. He had this griping in his gut."

The trolley appeared as a yellow spot at the end of the deserted street.

"He's gone to the government hospital now," she said, "and they taken one-third of his stomach. I tell him he better thank Jesus for what he's got left but he says he ain't thanking nobody. Well I declare," she murmured, "Bevel!"

They walked out to the tracks to wait. "Will he heal me?" Bevel asked.

"What you got?"

"I'm hungry," he decided finally.

"Didn't you have your breakfast?"

"I didn't have time to be hungry yet then," he said.

"Well when we get home we'll both have us something," she said. "I'm ready myself."

They got in the car and sat down a few seats behind the driver and Mrs. Connin took Bevel on her knees. "Now you be a good boy," she said, "and let me get some sleep. Just don't get off my lap." She lay her head back and as he watched, gradually her eyes closed and her mouth fell open to show a few long scattered teeth, some gold and some darker than her face; she began to whistle and blow like a musical skeleton. There was no one in the car but themselves and the driver and when he saw she was asleep, he took out the flowered handkerchief and unfolded it and examined it carefully. Then he folded it up again and unzipped a place in the innerlining of his coat and hid it in there and shortly he went to sleep himself.

Her house was a half-mile from the end of the car line, set back a little from the road. It was tan paper brick with a porch across the front of it and a tin top. On the porch there were three little boys of different sizes with identical speckled faces and one tall girl who had her hair up in so many aluminum curlers that it glared like the roof. The three boys followed them inside and closed in on Bevel. They looked at him silently, not smiling.

"That's Bevel," Mrs. Connin said, taking off her coat. "It's a coincident he's named the same as the preacher. These boys are J. C., Spivey, and Sinclair, and that's Sarah Mildred on the porch. Take off that coat and hang it on the bed post, Bevel."

The three boys watched him while he unbuttoned the coat and took it off. Then they watched him hang it on the bed post and then they stood, watching the coat. They turned abruptly and went out the door and had a conference on the porch.

Bevel stood looking around him at the room. It was part kitchen and part bedroom. The entire house was two rooms and two porches. Close to his foot the tail of a light-colored dog moved up and down between two floor boards as he scratched his back on the underside of the house. Bevel jumped on it but the hound was experienced and had already withdrawn when his feet hit the spot.

The walls were filled with pictures and calendars. There were two round photographs of an old man and woman with collapsed mouths and another picture of a man whose eyebrows dashed out of two bushes of hair and clashed in a heap on the bridge of his nose; the rest of his face stuck out like a bare cliff to fall from. "That's Mr. Connin," Mrs. Connin said, standing back from the stove for a second to admire the face with him, "but it don't favor him any more." Bevel turned from Mr. Connin to a colored picture over the bed of a man wearing a white sheet. He had long hair and a gold circle around his head and he was sawing on a board while some children stood watching him. He was going to ask who that was when the three boys came in again and motioned for him to follow them. He thought of crawling under the bed and hanging onto one of the legs but the three boys only stood there, speckled and silent, waiting, and after a second he followed them at a little distance out on the porch and around the corner of the house. They started off through a field of rough yellow weeds to the hog pen, a five-foot boarded square full of shoats, which they intended to ease him over into. When they reached it, they turned and waited silently, leaning against the side.

He was coming very slowly, deliberately bumping his feet together as if he had trouble walking. Once he had been beaten up in the park by some strange boys when his sitter forgot him, but he hadn't known anything was going to happen that time until it was over. He began to smell a strong odor of garbage and to hear the noises of a wild animal. He stopped a few feet from the pen and waited, pale but dogged.

The three boys didn't move. Something seemed to have happened to them. They stared over his head as if they saw something coming behind him but he was afraid to turn his own head and look. Their speckles were pale and their eyes were still and gray as glass. Only their ears twitched slightly. Nothing happened. Finally, the one in the middle said, "She'd kill us," and turned, dejected and hacked, and climbed up on the pen and hung over, staring in.

Bevel sat down on the ground, dazed with relief, and grinned up at them.

The one sitting on the pen glanced at him severely. "Hey you," he said after a second, "if you can't climb up and see these pigs you can lift that bottom board off and look in thataway." He appeared to offer this as a kindness.

Bevel had never seen a real pig but he had seen a pig in a book and knew they were small fat pink animals with curly tails and round grinning faces and bow ties. He leaned forward and pulled eagerly at the board.

"Pull harder," the littlest boy said. "It's nice and rotten. Just lift out thet nail."

He eased a long reddish nail out of the soft wood.

"Now you can lift up the board and put your face to the . . ." a quiet voice began.

He had already done it and another face, gray, wet and sour, was pushing into his, knocking him down and back as it scraped out under the plank. Something snorted over him and charged back again, rolling him over and pushing him up from behind and then sending him forward, screaming through the yellow field, while it bounded behind.

The three Connins watched from where they were. The one sitting on the pen held the loose board back with his gangling foot. Their stern faces didn't brighten any but they seemed to become less taut, as if some great need had been partly satisfied. "Maw ain't going to like him lettin' out thet hawg," the smallest one said.

Mrs. Connin was on the back porch and caught Bevel up as he reached the steps. The hog ran under the house and subsided, panting, but the child screamed for five minutes. When she had finally calmed him down, she gave him his breakfast and let him sit on her lap while he ate it. The shoat climbed the two steps onto the back porch and stood outside the screen door, looking in with his head lowered sullenly. He was long-legged and humpbacked and part of one of his ears had been bitten off.

"Git away!" Mrs. Connin shouted. "That one yonder favors Mr. Paradise that has the gas station," she said. "You'll see him today at the healing. He's got the cancer over his ear. He always comes to show he ain't been healed."

The shoat stood squinting a few seconds longer and then moved off slowly. "I don't want to see him," Bevel said.

They walked to the river, Mrs. Connin in front with him and the three boys strung out behind and Sarah Mildred, the tall girl, at the end to holler if one of them ran out on the road. They looked like the skeleton of an old boat with two pointed ends, sailing slowly on the edge of the highway. The white Sunday sun followed at a little distance, climbing fast through a scum of gray cloud as if it meant to overtake them. Bevel walked on the outside edge, holding Mrs. Connin's hand and looking down into the orange and purple gulley that dropped off from the concrete.

It occurred to him that he was lucky this time that they had found Mrs. Connin who would take you away for the day instead of an ordinary sitter who only sat where you lived or went to the park. You found out more when you left where you lived. He had found out already this morning that he had been made by a carpenter named Jesus Christ. Before he had thought it had been a doctor named Sladewall, a fat man with a yellow mustache who gave him shots and thought his name was Herbert, but this must have been a joke. They joked a lot where he lived. If he had thought about it before, he would have thought Jesus Christ was a word like "oh" or "damn" or "God," or maybe somebody who had cheated them out of something sometime. When he had asked Mrs. Connin who the man in the sheet in the picture over her bed was, she had looked at him a while with her mouth open. Then she had said, "That's Jesus," and she had kept on looking at him.

In a few minutes she had got up and got a book out of the other room. "See here," she said, turning over the cover, "this belonged to my great grandmamma. I wouldn't part with it for nothing on earth." She ran her finger under some brown writing on a spotted page. "Emma Stevens Oakley, 1832," she said. "Ain't that something to have? And every word of it the gospel truth." She turned the next page and read him the name: "The Life of Jesus Christ for Readers Under Twelve." Then she read him the book.

It was a small book, pale brown on the outside with gold edges and a smell like old putty. It was full of pictures, one of the carpenter driving a crowd of pigs out of a man. They were real pigs, gray and sour-looking, and Mrs. Connin said Jesus had driven them all out of this one man. When she finished reading, she let him sit on the floor and look at the pictures again.

Just before they left for the healing, he had managed to get the book inside his innerlining without her seeing him. Now it made his coat hang down a little farther on one side than the other. His mind was dreamy and serene as they walked along and when they turned off the highway onto a long red clay road winding between banks of honeysuckle, he began to make wild leaps and pull forward on her hand as if he wanted to dash off and snatch the sun which was rolling away ahead of them now.

They walked on the dirt road for a while and then they crossed a field stippled with purple weeds and entered the shadows of a wood where the ground was covered with thick pine needles. He had never been in woods before and he walked carefully, looking from side to side as if he were entering a strange country. They moved along a bridle path that twisted downhill through crackling red leaves, and once, catching at a branch to keep himself from slipping, he looked into two frozen green-gold eyes enclosed in the darkness of a tree hole. At the bottom of the hill, the woods opened suddenly onto a pasture dotted here and there with black and white cows and sloping down, tier after tier, to a broad orange stream where the reflection of the sun was set like a diamond.

There were people standing on the near bank in a group, singing. Long tables were set up behind them and a few cars and trucks were parked in a road that came up by the river. They crossed the pasture, hurrying, because Mrs. Connin, using her hand for a shed over her eyes, saw the preacher already standing out in the water. She dropped her basket on one of the tables and pushed the three boys in front of her into the knot of people so that they wouldn't linger by the food. She kept Bevel by the hand and eased her way up to the front.

The preacher was standing about ten feet out in the stream where the water came up to his knees. He was a tall youth in khaki trousers that he had rolled up higher than the water. He had on a blue shirt and a red scarf around his neck but no hat and his light-colored hair was cut in sideburns that curved into the hollows of his cheeks. His face was all bone and red light reflected from the river. He looked as if he might have been nineteen years old. He was singing in a high twangy voice, above the singing on the bank, and he kept his hands behind him and his head tilted back.

He ended the hymn on a high note and stood silent, looking down at the water and shifting his feet in it. Then he looked up at the people on the bank. They stood close together, waiting; their faces were solemn but expectant and every eye was on him. He shifted his feet again.

"Maybe I know why you come," he said in the twangy voice, "maybe I don't.

"If you ain't come for Jesus, you ain't come for me. If you just come to see can you leave your pain in the river, you ain't come for

Jesus. You can't leave your pain in the river," he said. "I never told nobody that." He stopped and looked down at his knees.

"I seen you cure a woman oncet!" a sudden high voice shouted from the hump of people. "Seen that woman git up and walk out straight where she had limped in!"

The preacher lifted one foot and then the other. He seemed almost but not quite to smile. "You might as well go home if that's what you come for," he said.

Then he lifted his head and arms and shouted, "Listen to what I got to say, you people! There ain't but one river and that's the River of Life, made out of Jesus' Blood. That's the river you have to lay your pain in, in the River of Faith, in the River of Life, in the River of Love, in the rich red river of Jesus' Blood, you people!"

His voice grew soft and musical. "All the rivers come from that one River and go back to it like it was the ocean sea and if you believe, you can lay your pain in that River and get rid of it because that's the River that was made to carry sin. It's a River full of pain itself, pain itself, moving toward the Kingdom of Christ, to be washed away, slow, you people, slow as this here old red water river round my feet.

"Listen," he sang, "I read in Mark about an unclean man, I read in Luke about a blind man, I read in John about a dead man! Oh you people hear! The same blood that makes this River red, made that leper clean, made that blind man stare, made that dead man leap! You people with trouble," he cried, "lay it in that River of Blood, lay it in that River of Pain, and watch it move away toward the Kingdom of Christ."

While he preached, Bevel's eyes followed drowsily the slow circles of two silent birds revolving high in the air. Across the river there was a low red and gold grove of sassafras with hills of dark blue trees behind it and an occasional pine jutting over the skyline. Behind, in the distance, the city rose like a cluster of warts on the side of the mountain. The birds revolved downward and dropped lightly in the top of the highest pine and sat hunch-shouldered as if they were supporting the sky.

"If it's this River of Life you want to lay your pain in, then come up," the preacher said, "and lay your sorrow here. But don't be thinking this is the last of it because this old red river don't end here. This old red suffering stream goes on, you people, slow to the Kingdom of Christ. This old red river is good to Baptize in, good to lay your faith in, good to lay your pain in, but it ain't this muddy water here that saves you. I been all up and down this river this week," he said. "Tuesday I was in Fortune Lake, next day in Ideal, Friday me and my wife drove to Lulawillow to see a sick man there. Them people didn't see no healing," he said and his face burned redder for a second. "I never said they would."

While he was talking a fluttering figure had begun to move forward with a kind of butterfly movement—an old woman with flapping arms whose head wobbled as if it might fall off any second. She managed to lower herself at the edge of the bank and let her arms churn in the water. Then she bent farther and pushed her face down in it and raised herself up finally, streaming wet; and still flapping, she turned a time or two in a blind circle until someone reached out and pulled her back into the group.

"She's been that way for thirteen years," a rough voice shouted. "Pass the hat and give this kid his money. That's what he's here for." The shout, directed out to the boy in the river, came from a huge old man who sat like a humped stone on the bumper of a long ancient gray automobile. He had on a gray hat that was turned down over one ear and up over the other to expose a purple bulge on his left temple. He sat bent forward with his hands hanging between his knees and his small eyes half closed.

Bevel stared at him once and then moved into the folds of Mrs. Connin's coat and hid himself.

The boy in the river glanced at the old man quickly and raised his fist. "Believe Jesus or the devil!" he cried. "Testify to one or the other!"

"I know from my own self-experience," a woman's mysterious voice called from the knot of people, "I know from it that this preacher can heal. My eyes have been opened! I testify to Jesus!"

The preacher lifted his arms quickly and began to repeat all that he had said before about the River and the Kingdom of Christ and the old man sat on the bumper, fixing him with a narrow squint. From time to time Bevel stared at him again from around Mrs. Connin.

A man in overalls and a brown coat leaned forward and dipped his hand in the water quickly and shook it and leaned back, and a woman held a baby over the edge of the bank and splashed its feet with water. One man moved a little distance away and sat down on the bank and took off his shoes and waded out into the stream; he stood there for a few minutes with his face tilted as far back as it would go, then he waded back and put on his shoes. All this time, the preacher sang and did not appear to watch what went on.

As soon as he stopped singing, Mrs. Connin lifted Bevel up and said, "Listen here, preacher, I got a boy from town today that I'm keeping. His mamma's sick and he wants you to pray for her. And this is a coincident—his name is Bevel! Bevel," she said, turning to look at the people behind her, "same as his. Ain't that a coincident, though?"

There were some murmurs and Bevel turned and grinned over her shoulder at the faces looking at him. "Bevel," he said in a loud jaunty voice.

"Listen," Mrs. Connin said, "have you ever been Baptized, Bevel?"

He only grinned.

"I suspect he ain't ever been Baptized," Mrs. Connin said, raising her eyebrows at the preacher.

"Swang him over here," the preacher said and took a stride forward and caught him.

He held him in the crook of his arm and looked at the grinning face. Bevel rolled his eyes in a comical way and thrust his face forward, close to the preacher's. "My name is Bevvvuuuuul," he said in a loud deep voice and let the tip of his tongue slide across his mouth.

The preacher didn't smile. His bony face was rigid and his narrow gray eyes reflected the almost colorless sky. There was a loud laugh from the old man sitting on the car bumper and Bevel grasped the back of the preacher's collar and held it tightly. The grin had already disappeared from his face. He had the sudden feeling that this was not a joke. Where he lived everything was a joke. From the preacher's face, he knew immediately that nothing the preacher said or did was a joke. "My mother named me that," he said quickly.

"Have you ever been Baptized?" the preacher asked.

"What's that?" he murmured.

"If I Baptize you," the preacher said, "you'll be able to go to the Kingdom of Christ. You'll be washed in the River of Suffering, son, and you'll go by the deep River of Life. Do you want that?"

"Yes," the child said, and thought, I won't go back to the apartment then, I'll go under the river.

"You won't be the same again," the preacher said. "You'll count." Then he turned his face to the people and began to preach and Bevel looked over his shoulder at the pieces of the white sun scattered in the river. Suddenly the preacher said, "All right, I'm going to Baptize you now," and without more warning, he tightened his hold and swung him upside down and plunged his head into the water. He held him under while he said the words of Baptism and then he jerked him up again and looked sternly at the gasping child. Bevel's eyes were dark and dilated. "You count now," the preacher said. "You didn't even count before."

The little boy was too shocked to cry. He spit out the muddy water and rubbed his wet sleeve into his eyes and over his face.

"Don't forget his mamma," Mrs. Connin called. "He wants you to pray for his mamma. She's sick."

"Lord," the preacher said, "we pray for somebody in affliction who isn't here to testify. Is your mother sick in the hospital?" he asked. "Is she in pain?"

The child stared at him. "She hasn't got up yet," he said in a high dazed voice. "She has a hangover." The air was so quiet he could hear the broken pieces of the sun knocking the water.

The preacher looked angry and startled. The red drained out of his face and the sky appeared to darken in his eyes. There was a loud guffaw from the bank and Mr. Paradise shouted, "Haw! Cure the afflicted woman with the hangover!" and began to beat his knee with his fist.

"He's had a long day," Mrs. Connin said, standing with him in the door of the apartment and looking sharply into the room where the party was going on. "I reckon it's past his regular bedtime." One of Bevel's eyes was closed and the other half closed; his nose was running and he kept his mouth open and breathed through it. The damp plain coat dragged down on one side.

That would be her, Mrs. Connin decided, in the black britches—long black satin britches and barefoot sandals and red toenails. She was lying on half the sofa, with her knees crossed in the air and her head propped on the arm. She didn't get up.

"Hello Harry," she said. "Did you have a big day?" She had a long pale face, smooth and blank, and straight sweet-potato-colored hair, pulled back.

The father went off to get the money. There were two other couples. One of the men, blond with little violet-blue eyes, leaned out of his chair and said, "Well Harry, old man, have a big day?"

"His name ain't Harry. It's Bevel," Mrs. Connin said.

"His name is Harry," *she* said from the sofa. "Whoever heard of anybody named Bevel?"

The little boy had seemed to be going to sleep on his feet, his head drooping farther and farther forward; he pulled it back suddenly and opened one eye; the other was stuck.

"He told me this morning his name was Bevel," Mrs. Connin said in a shocked voice. "The same as our preacher. We been all day at a preaching and healing at the river. He said his name was Bevel, the same as the preacher's. That's what he told me."

"Bevel!" his mother said. "My God! what a name."

"This preacher is name Bevel and there's no better preacher around," Mrs. Connin said. "And furthermore," she added in a defiant tone, "he Baptized this child this morning!"

His mother sat straight up. "Well the nerve!" she muttered.

"Furthermore," Mrs. Connin said, "he's a healer and he prayed for you to be healed."

"Healed!" she almost shouted. "Healed of what for Christ's sake?"

"Of your affliction," Mrs. Connin said icily.

The father had returned with the money and was standing near Mrs. Connin waiting to give it to her. His eyes were lined with red threads. "Go on, go on," he said, "I want to hear more about her affliction. The exact nature of it has escaped . . ." He waved the bill and his voice trailed off. "Healing by prayer is mighty inexpensive," he murmured.

Mrs. Connin stood a second, staring into the room, with a skeleton's appearance of seeing everything. Then, without taking the money, she turned and shut the door behind her. The father swung around, smiling vaguely, and shrugged. The rest of them were looking at Harry. The little boy began to shamble toward the bedroom.

"Come here, Harry," his mother said. He automatically shifted his direction toward her without opening his eyes any farther. "Tell me what happened today," she said when he reached her. She began to pull off his coat.

"I don't know," he muttered.

"Yes you do know," she said, feeling the coat heavier on one side. She unzipped the innerlining and caught the book and a dirty handkerchief as they fell out. "Where did you get these?"

"I don't know," he said and grabbed for them. "They're mine. She gave them to me."

She threw the handkerchief down and held the book too high for him to reach and began to read it, her face after a second assuming an exaggerated comical expression. The others moved around and looked at it over her shoulder. "My God," somebody said.

One of the men peered at it sharply from behind a thick pair of glasses. "That's valuable," he said. "That's a collector's item," and he took it away from the rest of them and retired to another chair.

"Don't let George go off with that," his girl said.

"I tell you it's valuable," George said. "1832."

Bevel shifted his direction again toward the room where he slept. He shut the door behind him and moved slowly in the darkness to the bed and sat down and took off his shoes and got under the cover. After a minute a shaft of light let in the tall silhouette of his mother. She tiptoed lightly cross the room and sat down on the edge of his bed. "What did that dolt of a preacher say about me?" she whispered. "What lies have you been telling today, honey?"

He shut his eye and heard her voice from a long way away, as if he were under the river and she on top of it. She shook his shoulder. "Harry," she said, leaning down and putting her mouth to his ear, "tell me what he said." She pulled him into a sitting position and he felt as if he had been drawn up from under the river. "Tell me," she whispered and her bitter breath covered his face.

He saw the pale oval close to him in the dark. "He said I'm not the same now," he muttered. "I count."

After a second, she lowered him by his shirt front onto the pillow. She hung over him an instant and brushed her lips against his forehead. Then she got up and moved away, swaying her hips lightly through the shaft of light.

He didn't wake up early but the apartment was still dark and close when he did. For a while he lay there, picking his nose and eyes. Then he sat up in bed and looked out the window. The sun came in palely, stained gray by the glass. Across the street at the Empire Hotel, a colored cleaning woman was looking down from an upper window, resting her face on her folded arms. He got up and put on his shoes and went to the bathroom and then into the front room. He ate two crackers spread with anchovy paste, that he found on the coffee table, and drank some ginger ale left in a bottle and looked around for his book but it was not there.

The apartment was silent except for the faint humming of the refrigerator. He went into the kitchen and found some raisin bread heels and spread a half jar of peanut butter between them and climbed up on the tall kitchen stool and sat chewing the sandwich slowly, wiping his nose every now and then on his shoulder. When he finished he found some chocolate milk and drank that. He would rather have had the ginger ale he saw but they left the bottle openers where he couldn't reach them. He studied what was left in the refrigerator for a while—some shriveled vegetables that she had forgot were there and a lot of brown oranges that she bought and didn't squeeze; there were three or four kinds of cheese and something fishy in a paper bag; the rest was a pork bone. He left the refrigerator door open and wandered back into the dark living room and sat down on the sofa.

He decided they would be out cold until one o'clock and that they would all have to go to a restaurant for lunch. He wasn't high enough for the table yet and the waiter would bring a highchair and he was too big for a highchair. He sat in the middle of the sofa, kicking it with his heels. Then he got up and wandered around the room, looking into the ashtrays at the butts as if this might be a habit. In his own room he had picture books and blocks but they were for the most part torn up; he found the way to get new ones was to tear up the ones he had. There was very little to do at any time but eat; however, he was not a fat boy.

He decided he would empty a few of the ashtrays on the floor. If he only emptied a few, she would think they had fallen. He emptied two, rubbing the ashes carefully into the rug with his finger. Then he lay on the floor for a while, studying his feet which he held up in the air. His shoes were still damp and he began to think about the river.

Very slowly, his expression changed as if he were gradually seeing appear what he didn't know he'd been looking for. Then all of a sudden he knew what he wanted to do.

He got up and tiptoed into their bedroom and stood in the dim light there, looking for her pocketbook. His glance passed her long pale arm hanging off the edge of the bed down to the floor, and across the white mound his father made, and past the crowded bureau, until it rested on the pocketbook hung on the back of a chair. He took a car-token out of it and half a package of Life Savers. Then he left the apartment and caught the car at the corner. He hadn't taken a suitcase because there was nothing from there he wanted to keep.

He got off the car at the end of the line and started down the road he and Mrs. Connin had taken the day before. He knew there wouldn't be anybody at her house because the three boys and the girl went to school and Mrs. Connin had told him she went out to clean. He passed her yard and walked on the way they had gone to the river. The paper brick houses were far apart and after a while the dirt place to walk on ended and he had to walk on the edge of the highway. The sun was pale yellow and high and hot.

He passed a shack with an orange gas pump in front of it but he didn't see the old man looking out at nothing in particular from the doorway. Mr. Paradise was having an orange drink. He finished it slowly, squinting over the bottle at the small plaid-coated figure disappearing down the road. Then he set the empty bottle on a bench and, still squinting, wiped his sleeve over his mouth. He went in the shack and picked out a peppermint stick, a foot long and two inches thick, from the candy shelf, and stuck it in his hip pocket. Then he got in his car and drove slowly down the highway after the boy.

By the time Bevel came to the field speckled with purple weeds, he was dusty and sweating and he crossed it at a trot to get into the woods as fast as he could. Once inside, he wandered from tree to tree, trying to find the path they had taken yesterday. Finally he found a line worn in the pine needles and followed it until he saw the steep trail twisting down through the trees.

Mr. Paradise had left his automobile back some way on the road and had walked to the place where he was accustomed to sit almost every day, holding an unbaited fishline in the water while he stared at the river passing in front of him. Anyone looking at him from a distance would have seen an old boulder half hidden in the bushes.

Bevel didn't see him at all. He only saw the river, shimmering reddish yellow, and bounded into it with his shoes and his coat on and took a gulp. He swallowed some and spit the rest out and then he stood there in water up to his chest and looked around him. The sky was a clear pale blue, all in one piece—except for the hole the sun made—and fringed around the bottom with treetops. His coat floated to the surface and surrounded him like a strange gay lily pad and he stood grinning in the sun. He intended not to fool with preachers any more but to Baptize himself and to keep on going this time until he found the Kingdom of Christ in the river. He didn't mean to waste any more time. He put his head under the water at once and pushed forward.

In a second he began to gasp and sputter and his head reappeared on the surface; he started under again and the same thing happened. The river wouldn't have him. He tried again and came up, choking. This was the way it had been when the preacher held him under—he had had to fight with something that pushed him back in the face. He stopped and thought suddenly: it's another joke, it's just another joke! He thought how far he had come for nothing and he began to hit and splash and kick the filthy river. His feet were already treading on nothing. He gave one low cry of pain and indignation. Then he heard a shout and turned his head and saw something like a giant pig bounding after him, shaking a red and white club and shouting. He plunged under once and this time, the waiting current caught him like a long gentle hand and pulled him swiftly forward and down. For an instant he was overcome with surprise: then since he was moving quickly and knew that he was getting somewhere, all his fury and fear left him.

Mr. Paradise's head appeared from time to time on the surface of the water. Finally, far downstream, the old man rose like some ancient water monster and stood empty-handed, staring with his dull eyes as far down the river line as he could see.

[1953]

Alice Childress
(1920–present)

Men in Your Life

A high school drop-out, Alice Childress taught herself various literary and dramatic forms, learning "to break rules and follow [her] own thought and structure." While Childress was a child in Harlem, her grandmother urged her to "write that thought down on a piece of paper"; Childress went on to write and speak out for accurate portrayals of black life, offending many and yet never compromising her dignity.

An actor, director, and writer with the American Negro Theatre, Childress was the first black woman to write a play that would be professionally produced. She became a playwright and scholar at the Radcliffe Institute for Independent Study, and she studied art and culture in the Soviet Union and theater arts in China.

Childress's writing treats subjects ranging from adolescent drug abuse to the life of Harriet Tubman. Her novels include *A Hero Ain't Nothin' But a Sandwich* (1973), which was made into an award-winning film in 1977; *Rainbow Jordan* (1983); and *Those Other People* (1989). Her plays include *When the Rattlesnake Sounds* (1975) and *Let's Hear It for the Queen* (1976). All of her work, according to Childress, has a common purpose: "The Black writer explains pain to those who inflict it."

No, Marge, I don't think you have any more hard luck with men than anybody else. Neither do I go in for this downin' of men all the time like they are so many strange bein's or enemies. I think men are people the same as women and you will run into some bad characters in this life be they men or women!

. . . Well, I'm in perfect agreement with that! A lot of men *do* think that they are just the cock o' the walk and oughta have the last word about everything! There are also a lot of them that look down on women and make fun of everything we say and do. I'm tellin' you they really can rile me when they end up sayin' something like, "Women! can't live with 'em or without, bless their souls!" Of course, rilin' is what they usually got in mind when they say those things.

But, Marge, we women are also the first ones that get a crack at these men. . . . Well, I mean, ain't we the ones that get to raise them from the time they are babies? While it's true that a heap of women have drawn some sad pick of husbands, it is also true that they raise their sons to make somebody else a mighty poor kinda spouse!

It is not a easy thing to raise a boy so's that he'll be as close to right as you can make him! It takes more than a bit of commonsense and a whole lot of tryin'. If I had a son, I would want him to be fair and square and good and worthwhile and at the same time not let anybody walk over him. Well, you know how Marie can hang-dog her husband around! . . . No, that is not at all necessary, and he shouldn't allow it! I would raise a son of mine to think for himself and get a good feelin' for the right and wrong of things! And I think a little application of the golden rule toward everybody oughta get him off to a good start! . . . Sure, everybody *says* they live by the golden rule, but how many people really and truly treat other folks like they'd like to be treated themselves? Not too many, you can be sure, 'cause everybody wants the tip-top best for themselves and then a *little bit more!*

I stopped off to see Tessie the other day in order to go over her club minutes. You know, I would never have gone if I thought Clarence was gonna be home from work that day! He can make me so mad 'til it ain't funny!

That man can say and do some of the worst kinda things! In the first place, he is *grumpy.* Yes, always frownin' up and mumblin' under his breath about nothin' in particular! . . . That alone would get me in a fistfight or a strait-jacket or both! I couldn't stand somebody goin', "mumble-mumble-make me sick-mumble-mumble-my dinner-mumble mumble-tired of this. . . ." Yes, that's the way he goes on all the time! And don't let her have a visitor 'cause that's when he'll do it most!

It gets real embarrassin' to sit around pretendin' that you don't notice it. Lots of times when I've been there he would come walkin' in and say, "Where's my dinner?" before he would say good evenin' to anybody! And no matter how I try to recollect I can never remember a time when I could say I saw him laughin'!

The other day she went in the kitchen when he called her, and I could hear him sayin' "Where's that ten dollars I gave you last week?" And Tessie was whisperin' soft-like so's I couldn't hear what she was sayin', but it was plain to see that he was mad 'cause she wanted to pay out two dollars for club dues. When I left, I said, "Good night folks!" and he says, "mumble-mumble-night." Like it was killin' him to even do that much. He acts that way with everybody but mostly with Tessie!

I'll never forget the time when I went out with his brother Wallace! He was supposed to be takin' me out on this bang-up dinner date! Honey, as soon as we got in the restaurant he says, "The hash is real good in this place, they make it better than any other restaurant."

. . . No, dear, I wasn't payin' him no mind! I hadn't asked him to take me out to dinner! Neither had I told him to pick out a expensive restaurant, so I went ahead and ordered me some spring lamb chops with a salad on the side! I can stand a *broke* man but I dearly detest a *cheap* man! And he was just pure *cheap*!

Next thing he started lookin' in his newspaper for a good movie and the way he told it everything that was playin' at the high-priced picture houses was *no good*, but there was a couple of fine things showin' in the neighborhood places! So, since he'd asked me what *I* wanted to see, I picked out the exact one I had in mind. However, I didn't pick it out 'til I had ordered me a cocktail!

Then you should have heard him twistin' and turnin'! Started talkin' 'bout how long he'd been alone since his wife died and how he really *needed* somebody and things like that. I just sat there sippin' and noddin' in a understandin' way, but every once in a while I'd take a peek at my watch 'cause it was gettin' mighty close to bein' too late to catch a movie.

Next thing you know, he starts talkin' about *wastin'* our time. He says, "We're both grown and there ain't no need of us wastin' each other's time if we're not gonna get anywhere!" . . . Honey, I caught on real fast! He was lettin' me know that he didn't *want* to go to the movies unless I would come on out and declare how obligin' I was gonna be in the love-makin' department! . . . So I says, "It's gettin' late Wallace, I have a splittin' headache and I think I'd better get on back home before we waste any more time *or* money!" And that was that! . . . Yes, he took me home and when we got to my door he says, "Do you want to give me a little kiss?" I just looked at him real calm-like and says, "Get off of that act, Wallace. You can tell whether somebody wants to kiss you or not, you don't have to ask! Now look at me and tell me whether I want to kiss you or not!" He didn't say another word, all he did was turn around and go on home!

I hate any man to be creepin' and pinchin' along tryin' all kinds of tricks and foolishness with me. . . . Of course, he had money, Marge! He has been workin' on a good steady job for the last fifteen years and ain't never missed a day's work in all that time. . . . Tessie was the one who really talked me into goin' out with him 'cause she told me I ought to go out with a "good steady fellow who has a reliable job."

I guess she was takin' a dig at Eddie 'cause he is a salesman and don't seem to be doin' so hot at sellin' them race-records and books. But I'll take Eddie any day and you can *have* Wallace! Eddie is the kind of man I like. He doesn't play any games or try no four-flushin'!

Whenever Eddie's in town I have a grand time and even a letter from him is worth more than a whole evenin' with somebody else. Sometimes he will say, "Well, honey, there ain't but five dollars in the cash register so let's try and stretch it into a good time!" And he can figure out a lot of swell things to do. We will go dancin' and then have a few beers and take the subway home or sometimes walk even! But the whole time we're laughin' and talkin' and enjoyin' ourselves so much 'til you couldn't believe how happy I feel!

Some Sunday afternoons Eddie is *broke* and then we go walkin' and he will take me up to a pawnshop window and turn it into a regular movin' picture show. . . . Well, I mean he will make up stories about the things that he sees in the window and try to figure out who they belonged to in the first place and how they happen to be in the pawnshop window now. . . . Oh, foolishness stories like, "I see where some cat had to pawn his saxophone, now why do you think he did that?" And I'll say, "To pay his room-rent!" And he'll say, "No, he got a letter tellin' him that if he came to East Jalappi, there would be a fine old steady job waitin' for him, so he hocked his horn in order to buy a ticket, only when he got off the boat he didn't have no horn to play so the poor old guy is hangin' 'round Jalappi tryin' to save up enough money to buy him a second-hand horn, and this horn is hangin' here in the window tryin' to tempt some youngster into takin' up music so that he can get to Jalappi some day himself!"

I like him to tell me them pawnshop stories. He can tell electric-iron stories, radio stories, ring stories, suitcase stories, silverware stories, and all manner of tales about cocktail shakers, toasters, suits and overcoats, cameras and all such things as that!

Eddie will do me favors, too. Like goin' downtown to buy things that I don't have time to pick up, washin' dishes for me, mindin' my cousin's kids so's she can go to church and a whole lot of other things like that. But what I really like about him is that sometimes when I ask him to do a lot of things, one comin' right after the other, he will say, "You runnin' a good thing in the ground, and furthermore I don't feel like it, what do you take me for?" I'm glad when he does that, too, 'cause just like I don't want nobody walkin' all over me, I sure wouldn't have any use for a man that's gonna let people trample him!

Marge, you know Eddie has loaned me money, too. But the first time he tried to borrow some from me, I got real scared 'cause you do hear so many stories 'bout how men try to take advantage of women sometimes by gettin' their money away from them. . . . Yes, I loaned it to him, but I worried him to death until I got it back. When he returned it, he said, "Whew! I don't *never* want to borrow *nothin'* from you no more 'cause it's too much of a strain!"

I felt a little bit shamed about that, but now we don't never have that kind of trouble no more 'cause all the time we know we can depend on each other no matter what happens! . . . Yes, we have been talkin' 'bout gettin' married, but neither one of us got enough change to start up family life in the way we'd want it to be, and you know how you can start puttin' things off 'til everything is shaped up just right.

But I get to thinkin' awful deep sometimes. And when Eddie is away, I start picturin' his easy-goin', happy ways, how he likes children, how he looks at me so that I don't have to wonder how he feels, how he never had to ask for a "little kiss" but knew when was the right time to kiss me, how he loves people, how he hates meanness and ugliness—how he wants me to get out of other folks' kitchens, when I think on all of that and stand him up side of those steady, reliable guys like Clarence and Wallace, it seems like Wallace and Clarence don't look so hot!

Yes, I think I will marry Eddie 'cause the only, single thing we will have to worry about is bein' poor. . . . Yes, that is a pretty big thing to have to worry about all the time, but if a man gives you all of the very best that he has to offer, all the time, what more could a woman want? . . .

[1956]

Grace Paley
(1922–present)

An Interest in Life

Grace Paley was born in New York City and "always knew I would write and I did," despite poor high school grades and unfinished studies at both Hunter College and New York University. She was active in many nonviolent anti–Vietnam war organizations but always wrote of the "irremediableness of modern life."

Often writing through ethnic, first-person narrators who unconsciously reveal the pathos of their lives to the reader, Paley is known for her insight into the emotional nature of women. Lovers are depicted as transient, as are Ginny's in "An Interest in Life"; children comfort and inspire. Paley's three collections of short stories, *The Little Disturbances of Man* (1959), *Enormous Changes at the Last Minute* (1974), and *Later the Same Day* (1985), link, as do their titles, lofty abstractions with colloquial normality. Similarly, Paley's characters battle overwhelming odds with humor, acceptance, and love.

Paley has taught at Columbia and Syracuse universities and now teaches at Sarah Lawrence College.

My husband gave me a broom one Christmas. This wasn't right. No one can tell me it was meant kindly.

"I don't want you not to have anything for Christmas while I'm away in the Army," he said. "Virginia, please look at it. It comes with this fancy dustpan. It hangs off a stick. Look at it, will you? Are you blind or cross-eyed?"

"Thanks, chum," I said. I had always wanted a dustpan hooked up that way. It was a good one. My husband doesn't shop in bargain basements or January sales.

Still and all, in spite of the quality, it was a mean present to give a woman you planned on never seeing again, a person you had children with and got onto all the time, drunk or sober, even when everybody had to get up early in the morning.

I asked him if he could wait and join the Army in a half hour, as I had to get the groceries. I don't like to leave kids alone in a three-room apartment full of gas and electricity. Fire may break out from a nasty remark. Or the oldest decides to get even with the youngest.

"Just this once," he said. "But you better figure out how to get along without me."

"You're a handicapped person mentally," I said. "You should've been institutionalized years ago." I slammed the door. I didn't want to see him pack his underwear and ironed shirts.

I never got further than the front stoop, though, because there was Mrs. Raftery, wringing her hands, tears in her eyes as though she had a monopoly on all the good news.

"Mrs. Raftery!" I said, putting my arm around her. "Don't cry." She leaned on me because I am such a horsy build. "Don't cry, Mrs Raftery, please!" I said.

"That's like you, Virginia. Always looking at the ugly side of things. 'Take in the wash. It's rainin'!' That's you. You're the first one knows it when the dumb-waiter breaks."

"Oh, come on now, that's not so. It just isn't so," I said. "I'm the exact opposite."

"Did you see Mrs. Cullen yet?" she asked, paying no attention.

"Where?"

"Virginia!" she said, shocked. "She's passed away. The whole house knows it. They've got her in white like a bride and you never saw a beautiful creature like that. She must be eighty. Her husband's proud."

"She was never more than an acquaintance; she didn't have any children," I said.

"Well, I don't care about that. Now, Virginia, you do what I say now, you go downstairs and you say like this—listen to me—say, 'I hear, Mr. Cullen, your wife's passed away. I'm sorry.' Then ask him how he is. Then you ought to go around the corner and see her. She's in Witson & Wayde. Then you ought to go over to the church when they carry her over."

"It's not my church," I said.

"That's no reason, Virginia. You go up like this," she said, parting from me to do a prancy dance. "Up the big front steps, into the church you go. It's beautiful in there. You can't help kneeling only for a minute. Then round to the right. Then up the other stairway. Then you come to a great oak door that's arched above you, then," she said, seizing a deep, deep breath, for all the good it would do her, "and then turn the knob slo-owly and open the door and see for yourself: Our Blessed Mother is in charge. Beautiful. Beautiful. Beautiful."

I sighed in and I groaned out, so as to melt a certain pain around my heart. A steel ring like arthritis, at my age.

"You are a groaner," Mrs. Raftery said, gawking into my mouth.

"I am not," I said. I got a whiff of her, a terrible cheap wine lush.

My husband threw a penny at the door from the inside to take my notice from Mrs. Raftery. He rattled the glass door to make sure I looked at him. He had a fat duffel bag on each shoulder. Where did he acquire so much worldly possession? What was in them? My grandma's goose feathers from across the ocean? Or all the diaper-service diapers? To this day the truth is shrouded in mystery.

"What the hell are you doing, Virginia?" he said, dumping them at my feet. "Standing out here on your hind legs telling everybody your business? The Army gives you a certain time, for God's sakes, they're not kidding." Then he said, "I beg your pardon," to Mrs. Raftery. He took hold of me with his two arms as though in love and pressed his body hard against mine so that I could feel him for the last time and suffer my loss. Then he kissed me in a mean way to nearly split my lip. Then he winked and said, "That's all for now," and skipped off into the future, duffel bags full of rags.

He left me in an embarrassing situation, nearly fainting, in front of that old widow, who can't even remember the half of it. "He's a crock," said Mrs. Raftery. "Is he leaving for good or just temporarily, Virginia?"

"Oh, he's probably deserting me," I said, and sat down on the stoop, pulling my big knees up to my chin.

"If that's the case, tell the Welfare right away," she said. "He's a bum, leaving you just before Christmas. Tell the cops," she said. "They'll provide the toys for the little kids gladly. And don't forget to let the grocer in on it. He won't be so hard on you expecting payment."

She saw that sadness was stretched world-wide across my face. Mrs. Raftery isn't the worst person. She said, "Look around for comfort, dear." With a nervous finger she pointed to the truckers eating lunch on their haunches across the street, leaning on the loading platforms. She waved her hand to include in all the men marching up and down in search of a decent luncheonette. She didn't leave out the six longshoremen loafing under the fish-market marquee. "If their lungs and stomachs ain't crushed by overwork, they disappear somewhere in the world. Don't be disappointed, Virginia. I don't know a man living'd last you a lifetime."

Ten days later Girard asked, "Where's Daddy?"

"Ask me no questions, I'll tell you no lies." I didn't want the children to know the facts. Present or past, a child should have a father.

"Where *is* Daddy?" Girard asked the week after that.

"He joined the Army," I said.

"He made my bunk bed," said Phillip.

"The truth shall make ye free," I said.

Then I sat down with pencil and pad to get in control of my resources. The facts, when I added and subtracted them, were that my husband had left me with fourteen dollars, and the rent unpaid, in an emergency state. He'd claimed he was sorry to do this, but my opinion is, out of sight, out of mind. "The city won't let you starve," he'd said. "After all, you're half the population. You're keeping up the good work. Without you the race would die out. Who'd pay the taxes? Who'd keep the streets clean? There wouldn't be no Army. A man like me wouldn't have no place to go."

I sent Girard right down to Mrs. Raftery with a request about the whereabouts of Welfare. She responded RSVP with an extra comment in left-handed script: "Poor Girard . . . he's never the boy my John was!"

Who asked her?

I called on Welfare right after the new year. In no time I discovered that they're rigged up to deal with liars, and if you're truthful it's disappointing to them. They may even refuse to handle your case if you're too truthful.

They asked sensible questions at first. They asked where my husband had enlisted. I didn't know. They put some letter writers and agents after him. "He's not in the United States Army," they said. "Try the Brazilian Army," I suggested.

They have no sense of kidding around. They're not the least bit lighthearted and they tried. "Oh no," they said. "That was incorrect. He is not in the Brazilian Army."

"No?" I said. "How strange! He must be in the Mexican Navy."

By law, they had to hound his brothers. They wrote to his brother who has a first-class card in the Teamsters and owns an apartment house in California. They asked his two brothers in Jersey to help me. They have large families. Rightfully they laughed. Then they wrote to Thomas, the oldest, the smart one (the one they all worked so hard for years to keep him in college until his brains could pay off). He was the one who sent ten dollars immediately, saying, "What a bastard! I'll send something time to time, Ginny, but whatever you do, don't tell the authorities." Of course I never did. Soon they began to guess they were better people than me, that I was in trouble because I deserved it, and then they liked me better.

But they never fixed my refrigerator. Every time I called I said patiently, "The milk is sour . . ." I said, "Corn beef went bad." Sitting in that beer-stinking phone booth in Felan's for the sixth time (sixty cents) with the baby on my lap and Barbie tapping at the glass door with an American flag, I cried into the secretary's hardhearted ear, "I bought real butter for the holiday, and it's rancid . . ." They said, "You'll have to get a better bid on the repair job."

While I waited indoors for a man to bid, Girard took to swinging back and forth on top of the bathroom door, just to soothe himself, giving me the laugh, dreamy, nibbling calcimine off the ceiling. On first sight Mrs. Raftery said, "Whack the monkey, he'd be better off on arsenic."

But Girard is my son and I'm the judge. It means a terrible thing for the future, though I don't know what to call it.

It was from constantly thinking of my foreknowledge on this and other subjects, it was from observing when I put my lipstick on daily, how my face was just curling up to die, that John Raftery came from Jersey to rescue me.

On Thursdays, anyway, John Raftery took the tubes in to visit his mother. The whole house knew it. She was cheerful even before breakfast. She sang out loud in a girlish brogue that only came to tongue for grand occasions. Hanging out the wash, she blushed to recall what a remarkable boy her John had been. "Ask the sisters around the corner," she said to the open kitchen windows. "They'll never forget John."

That particular night after supper Mrs. Raftery said to her son, "John, how come you don't say hello to your old friend Virginia? She's had hard luck and she's gloomy."

"Is that so, Mother?" he said, and immediately climbed two flights to knock at my door.

"Oh, John," I said at the sight of him, hat in hand in a white shirt and blue-striped tie, spick-and-span, a Sunday-school man. "Hello!"

"Welcome, John!" I said. "Sit down. Come right in. How are you? You look awfully good. You do. Tell me, how've you been all this time, John?"

"How've I been?" he asked thoughtfully. To answer within reason, he described his life with Margaret, marriage, work, and children up to the present day.

I had nothing good to report. Now that he had put the subject around before my very eyes, every burnt-up day of my life smoked in shame, and I couldn't even get a clear view of the good half hours.

"Of course," he said, "you do have lovely children. Noticeable-looking, Virginia. Good looks is always something to be thankful for."

"Thankful?" I said. "I don't have to thank anything but my own foolishness for four children when I'm twenty-six years old, deserted, and poverty-struck, regardless of looks. A man can't help it, but I could have behaved better."

"Don't be so cruel on yourself, Ginny," he said. "Children come from God."

"You're still great on holy subjects, aren't you? You know damn well where children come from."

He did know. His red face reddened further. John Raftery has had that color coming out on him boy and man from keeping his rages so inward.

Still he made more sense in his conversation after that, and I poured fresh tea to tell him how my husband used to like me because I was a passionate person. That was until he took a look around and saw how in the long run this life only meant more of the same thing. He tried to turn away from me once he came to this understanding, and make me hate him. His face changed. He gave up his brand of cigarettes, which we had in common. He threw out the two pairs of socks I knitted by hand. "If there's anything I hate in this world, it's navy blue," he said. Oh, I could have dyed them. I would have done anything for him, if he were only not too sorry to ask me.

"You were a nice kid in those days," said John, referring to certain Saturday nights. "A wild, nice kid."

"Aaah," I said, disgusted. Whatever I was then, was on the way to where I am now. "I was fresh. If I had a kid like me, I'd slap her cross-eyed."

The very next Thursday John gave me a beautiful radio with a record player. "Enjoy yourself," he said. That really made Welfare speechless. We didn't own any records, but the investigator saw my burden was lightened and he scribbled a dozen pages about it in his notebook.

On the third Thursday he brought a walking doll (twenty-four inches) for Linda and Barbie with a card inscribed, "A baby doll for a couple of dolls." He had also had a couple of drinks at his mother's, and this made him want to dance. "La-la-la," he sang, a ramrod swaying in my kitchen chair. "La-la-la, let yourself go . . ."

"You gotta give a little," he sang, "live a little . . ." He said, "Virginia, may I have this dance?"

"Sssh, we finally got them asleep. Please, turn the radio down. Quiet. Deathly silence, John Raftery."

"Let me do your dishes, Virginia."

"Don't be silly, you're a guest in my house," I said. "I still regard you as a guest."

"I want to do something for you, Virginia."

"Tell me I'm the most gorgeous thing," I said, dipping my arm to the funny bone in dish soup.

He didn't answer. "I'm having a lot of trouble at work," was all he said. Then I heard him push the chair back. He came up behind me, put his arms around my waistline, and kissed my cheek. He whirled me around and took my hands. He said, "An old friend is better than rubies." He looked me in the eye. He held my attention by trying to be honest. And he kissed me a short sweet kiss on my mouth.

"Please sit down, Virginia," he said. He kneeled before me and put his head in my lap. I was stirred by so much activity. Then he looked up at me and, as though proposing marriage for life, he offered—because he was drunk—to place his immortal soul in peril to comfort me.

First I said, "Thank you." Then I said, "No."

I was sorry for him, but he's devout, a leader of the Fathers' Club at his church, active in all the lay groups for charities, orphans, etc. I knew that if he stayed late to love with me, he would not do it lightly but would in the end pay terrible penance and ruin his long life. The responsibility would be on me.

So I said no.

And Barbie is such a light sleeper. All she has to do, I thought, is wake up and wander in and see her mother and her new friend John with his pants around his knees, wrestling on the kitchen table. A vision like that could affect a kid for life.

I said no.

Everyone in this building is so goddamn nosy. That evening I had to say no.

But John came to visit, anyway, on the fourth Thursday. This time he brought the discarded dresses of Margaret's daughters, organdy party dresses and glazed cotton for every day. He gently admired Barbara and Linda, his blue eyes rolling to back up a couple of dozen oohs and ahs.

Even Phillip, who thinks God gave him just a certain number of hellos and he better save them for the final judgment, Phillip leaned on John and said, "Why don't you bring your boy to play with me? I don't have nobody who to play with." (Phillip's a liar. There must be at least seventy-one children in this house, pale pink to medium brown, English-talking and gibbering in Spanish, rough-and-tough boys, the Lone Ranger's bloody pals, or the exact picture of Supermouse. If a boy wanted a friend, he could pick the very one out of his neighbors.)

Also, Girard is a cold fish. He was in a lonesome despair. Sometimes he looked in the mirror and said, "How come I have such an ugly face? My nose is funny. Mostly people don't like me." He was a liar too. Girard has a face like his father's. His eyes are the color of those little blue plums in August. He looks like an advertisement in a magazine. He could be a child model and make a lot of money. He is my first child, and if he thinks he is ugly, I think I am ugly.

John said, "I can't stand to see a boy mope like that. . . . What do the sisters say in school?"

"He doesn't pay attention is all they say. You can't get much out of them."

"My middle boy was like that," said John. "Couldn't take an interest. Aaah, I wish I didn't have all that headache on the job. I'd grab Girard by the collar and make him take notice of the world. I wish I could ask him out to Jersey to play in all that space."

"Why not?" I said.

"Why, Virginia, I'm surprised you don't know why not. You know I can't take your children out to meet my children."

I felt a lot of strong arthritis in my ribs.

"My mother's the funny one, Virginia." He felt he had to continue with the subject matter. "I don't know. I guess she likes the idea of bugging Margaret. She says, 'You goin' up, John?' 'Yes, Mother,' I say. 'Behave yourself, John,' she says. 'That husband might come home and hack-saw you into hell. You're a Catholic man, John,' she says. But I figured it out. She likes to know I'm in the building. I swear, Virginia, she wishes me the best of luck."

"I do too, John," I said. We drank a last glass of beer to make sure of a peaceful sleep. "Good night, Virginia," he said, looping his muffler neatly under his chin. "Don't worry. I'll be thinking of what to do about Girard."

I got into the big bed that I share with the girls in the little room. For once I had no trouble falling asleep. I only had to worry about Linda and Barbara and Phillip. It was a great relief to me that John had taken over the thinking about Girard.

John was sincere. That's true. He paid a lot of attention to Girard, smoking out all his sneaky sorrows. He registered him into a wild pack of cub scouts that went up to the Bronx once a week to let off steam. He gave him a Junior Erector Set. And sometimes when his family wasn't listening he prayed at great length for him.

One Sunday, Sister Veronica said in her sweet voice from another life, "He's not worse. He might even be a little better. How are *you*, Virginia?" putting her hand on mine. Everybody around here acts like they know everything.

"Just fine," I said.

"We ought to start on Phillip," John said, "if it's true Girard's improving."

"You should've been a social worker, John."

"A lot of people have noticed that about me," said John.

"Your mother was always acting so crazy about you, how come she didn't knock herself out a little to see you in college? Like we did for Thomas?"

"Now, Virginia, be fair. She's a poor old woman. My father was a weak earner. She had to have my wages, and I'll tell you, Virginia, I'm not sorry. Look at Thomas. He's still in school. Drop him in this jungle and he'd be devoured. He hasn't had a touch of real life. And here I am with a good chunk of a family, a home of my own, a name in the building trades. One thing I have to tell you, the poor old woman is sorry. I said one day (oh, in passing—years ago) that I might marry you. She stuck a knife in herself. It's a fact. Not more than an eighth of an inch. You never saw such a gory Sunday. One thing—you would have been a better daughter-in-law to her than Margaret."

"Marry me?" I said.

"Well, yes. . . . Aaah—I always liked you, then . . . Why do you think I'd sit in the shade of this kitchen every Thursday night? For God's sakes, the only warm thing around here is this teacup. Yes, sir, I did want to marry you, Virginia."

"No kidding, John? Really?" It was nice to know. Better late than never, to learn you were desired in youth.

I didn't tell John, but the truth is, I would never have married him. Once I met my husband with his winking looks, he was my only interest. Wild as I had been with John and others, I turned all my wildness over to him and then there was no question in my mind.

Still, face facts, if my husband didn't budge on in life, it was my fault. On me, as they say, be it. I greeted the morn with a song. I had a hello for everyone but the landlord. Ask the people on the block, come or go—even the Spanish ones, with their sad dark faces—they have to smile when they see me.

But for his own comfort, he should have done better lifewise and moneywise. I was happy, but I am now in possession of knowledge that this is wrong. Happiness isn't so bad for a woman. She gets fatter, she gets older, she could lie down, nuzzling a regiment of men and little kids, she could just die of the pleasure. But men are different, they have to own money, or they have to be famous, or everybody on the block has to look up to them from the cellar stairs.

A woman counts her children and acts snotty, like she invented life, but men *must* do well in the world. I know that men are not fooled by being happy.

"A funny guy," said John, guessing where my thoughts had gone. "What stopped him up? He was nobody's fool. He had a funny thing about him, Virginia, if you don't mind my saying so. He wasn't much distance up, but he was all set and ready to be looking down on us all."

"He was very smart, John. You don't realize that. His hobby was crossword puzzles, and I said to him real often, as did others around here, that he ought to go out on the '$64 Question.' Why not? But he laughed. You know what he said? He said, 'That proves how dumb you are if you think I'm smart.' "

"A funny guy," said John. "Get it all off your chest," he said. "Talk it out, Virginia; it's the only way to kill the pain."

By and large, I was happy to oblige. Still I could not carry through about certain cruel remarks. It was like trying to move back into the dry mouth of a nightmare to remember that the last day I was happy was the middle of a week in March, when I told my husband I was going to have Linda. Barbara was five months old to the hour. The boys were three and four. I had to tell him. It was the last day with anything happy about it.

Later on he said, "Oh, you make me so sick, you're so goddamn big and fat, you look like a goddamn brownstone, the way you're squared off in front."

"Well, where are you going tonight?" I asked.

"How should I know?" he said. "Your big ass takes up the whole goddamn bed," he said. "There's no room for me." He bought a sleeping bag and slept on the floor.

I couldn't believe it. I would start every morning fresh. I couldn't believe that he would turn against me so, while I was still young and even his friends still liked me.

But he did, he turned absolutely against me and became no friend of mine. "All you ever think about is making babies. This place stinks like the men's room in the BMT. It's a fucking *pissoir*." He was strong on truth all through the year. "That kid eats more than the five of us put together," he said. "Stop stuffing your face, you fat dumbbell," he said to Phillip.

Then he worked on the neighbors. "Get that nosy old bag out of here," he said. "If she comes on once more with 'my son in the building trades' I'll squash her for the cat."

Then he turned on Spielvogel, the checker, his oldest friend, who only visited on holidays and never spoke to me (shy, the way some bachelors are). "That sonofabitch, don't hand me that friendship crap, all he's after is your ass. That's what I need—a little shitmaker of his using up the air in this flat."

And then there was no one else to dispose of. We were left alone fair and square, facing each other.

"Now, Virginia," he said, "I come to the end of my rope. I see a black wall ahead of me. What the hell am I supposed to do? I only got one life. Should I lie down and die? I don't know what to do any more. I'll give it to you straight, Virginia, if I stick around, you can't help it, you'll hate me . . ."

"I hate you right now," I said. "So do whatever you like."

"This place drives me nuts," he mumbled. "I don't know what to do around here. I want to get you a present. Something."

"I told you, do whatever you like. Buy me a rattrap for rats."

That's when he went down to the House Appliance Store, and he brought back a new broom and a classy dustpan.

"A new broom sweeps clean," he said. "I got to get out of here," he said. "I'm going nuts." Then he began to stuff the duffel bags, and I went to the grocery store but was stopped by Mrs. Raftery, who had to tell me what she considered so beautiful—death—then he kissed and went to join some army somewhere.

I didn't tell John any of this, because I think it makes a woman look too bad to tell on how another man has treated her. He begins to see her through the other man's eyes, a sitting duck, a skinful of flaws. After all, I had come to depend on John. All my husband's friends were strangers now, though I had always said to them, "Feel welcome."

And the family men in the building looked too cunning, as though they had all personally deserted me. If they met me on the stairs, they carried the heaviest groceries up and helped bring Linda's stroller down, but they never asked me a question worth answering at all.

Besides that, Girard and Phillip taught the girls the days of the week: Monday, Tuesday, Wednesday, Johnday, Friday. They waited for him once a week, under the hallway lamp, half asleep like bugs in the sun, sitting in their little chairs with their names on in gold, a birth present from my mother-in-law. At fifteen after eight he punctually came, to read a story, pass out some kisses, and tuck them into bed.

But one night, after a long Johnday of them squealing my eardrum split, after a rainy afternoon with brother constantly raising up his hand against brother, with the girls near ready to go to court over the proper ownership of Melinda Lee, the twenty-four-inch walking doll, the doorbell rang three times. Not any of those times did John's face greet me.

I was too ashamed to call down to Mrs. Raftery, and she was too mean to knock on my door and explain.

He didn't come the following Thursday either. Girard said sadly, "He must've run away, John."

I had to give him up after two weeks' absence and no word. I didn't know how to tell the children: something about right and wrong, goodness and meanness, men and women. I had it all at my fingertips, ready to hand over. But I didn't think I ought to take mistakes and truth away from them. Who knows? They might make a truer friend in this world somewhere than I have ever made. So I just put them to bed and sat in the kitchen and cried.

In the middle of my third beer, searching in my mind for the next step, I found the decision to go on "Strike It Rich." I scrounged some paper and pencil from the toy box and I listed all my troubles, which must be done in order to qualify. The list when complete could have brought tears to the eye of God if He had a minute. At the sight of it my bitterness began to improve. All that is really necessary for survival of the fittest, it seems, is an interest in life, good, bad, or peculiar.

As always happens in these cases where you have begun to help yourself with plans, news comes from an opposite direction. The doorbell rang, two short and two long—meaning John.

My first thought was to wake the children and make them happy. "No! No!" he said. "Please don't put yourself to that trouble. Virginia, I'm dog-tired," he said. "Dog-tired. My job is a damn headache. It's too much. It's all day and it scuttles my mind at night, and in the end who does the credit go to?

"Virginia," he said, "I don't know if I can come any more. I've been wanting to tell you. I just don't know. What's it all about? Could you answer me if I asked you? I can't figure this whole thing out at all."

I started the tea steeping because his fingers when I touched them were cold. I didn't speak. I tried looking at it from his man point of view, and I thought he had to take a bus, the tubes, and a subway to see me; and then the subway, the tubes, and a bus to go back home at 1 A.M. It wouldn't be any trouble at all for him to part with us forever. I thought about my life, and I gave strongest consideration to my children. If given the choice, I decided to choose not to live without him.

"What's that?" he asked, pointing to my careful list of troubles. "Writing a letter?"

"Oh no," I said, "it's for 'Strike It Rich.' I hope to go on the program."

"Virginia, for goodness' sake," he said, giving it a glance, "you don't have a ghost. They'd laugh you out of the studio. Those people really suffer."

"Are you sure, John?" I asked.

"No question in my mind at all," said John. "Have you ever seen the program? I mean, in addition to all of this—the little disturbances of man"—he waved a scornful hand at my list—"they *suffer*. They live in the forefront of tornadoes, their lives are washed off by floods—catastrophes of God. Oh, Virginia."

"Are you sure, John?"

"For goodness' sake . . ."

Sadly I put my list away. Still, if things got worse, I could always make use of it.

Once that was settled, I acted on an earlier decision. I pushed his cup of scalding tea aside. I wedged myself onto his lap between his hard belt buckle and the table. I put my arms around his neck and said, "How come you're so cold, John?" He has a kind face and he knew how to look astonished. He said, "Why, Virginia, I'm getting warmer." We laughed.

John became a lover to me that night.

Mrs. Raftery is sometimes silly and sick from her private source of cheap wine. She expects John often. "Honor your mother, what's the matter with you, John?" she complains. "Honor. Honor."

"Virginia dear," she says. "You never would've taken John away to Jersey like Margaret. I wish he'd've married you."

"You didn't like me much in those days."

"That's a lie," she says. I know she's a hypocrite, but no more than the rest of the world.

What is remarkable to me is that it doesn't seem to conscience John as I thought it might. It is still hard to believe that a man who sends out the Ten Commandments every year for a Christmas card can be so easy buttoning and unbuttoning.

Of course we must be very careful not to wake the children or disturb the neighbors who will enjoy another person's excitement just so far, and then the pleasure enrages them. We must be very careful for ourselves too, for when my husband comes back, realizing the babies are in school and everything easier, he won't forgive me if I've started it all up again—noisy signs of life that are so much trouble to a man.

We haven't seen him in two and a half years. Although people have suggested it, I do not want the police or Intelligence or a private eye or anyone to go after him to bring him back. I know that if he expected to stay away forever he would have written and said so. As it is, I just don't know what evening, any time, he may appear. Sometimes, stumbling over a blockbuster of a dream at midnight, I wake up to vision his soft arrival.

He comes in the door with his old key. He gives me a strict look and says, "Well, you look older, Virginia." "So do you," I say, although he hasn't changed a bit.

He settles in the kitchen because the children are asleep all over the rest of the house. I unknot his tie and offer him a cold sandwich. He raps my backside, paying attention to the bounce. I walk around him as though he were a Maypole, kissing as I go.

"I didn't like the Army much," he says. "Next time I think I might go join the Merchant Marine."

"What army?" I say.

"It's pretty much the same everywhere," he says.

"I wouldn't be a bit surprised," I say.

"I lost my cuff link, goddamnit," he says, and drops to the floor to look for it. I go down too on my knees, but I know he never had a cuff link in his life. Still I would do a lot for him.

"Got you off your feet that time," he says, laughing. "Oh yes, I did." And before I can even make myself half comfortable on that polka-dotted linoleum, he got onto me right where we were, and the truth is, we were so happy, we forgot the precautions.

[1956]

Doris Lessing
(1919–present)

A Man and Two Women

Born in Iran but brought to Rhodesia (now Zimbabwe) at age five, Doris Lessing began writing when she was nine. She educated herself by reading, and soon perceived racial inequality and came to resent her mother's English middle-class values. She wrote two unpublished novels before turning nineteen, and became politically active, working first for the Rhodesian government and then for a small Marxist group seeking black liberation. Her political views continued to change and evolve throughout her life.

Lessing made her name with *The Grass Is Singing* (1949), a novel about a white farmer's wife who crumbles in the isolation of the African veld. Her short-story volumes include *This Was the Old Chief's Country* (1951), *Five Short Novels* (1953), and the five-volume series *Children of Violence* (1952–1969). Her stories are set in England and Africa; they address issues both political and personal.

As more and more of Lessing's books, especially *The Golden Notebook* (1962), are translated into other languages, she attracts new devoted audiences and critical acclaim. Her stature as a major novelist, short-story writer, and dramatist is secure.

Stella's friends the Bradfords had taken a cheap cottage in Essex for the summer, and she was going down to visit them. She wanted to see them, but there was no doubt there was something of a letdown (and for them too) in the English cottage. Last summer Stella had been wandering with her husband around Italy; had seen the English couple at a cafe table, and found them sympathetic. They all liked each other, and the four went about for some weeks, sharing meals, hotels, trips. Back in London the friendship had not, as might have been expected, fallen off. Then Stella's husband departed abroad, as he often did, and Stella saw Jack and Dorothy by herself. There were a great many people she might have seen, but it was the Bradfords she saw most often, two or three times a week, at their flat or hers. They were at ease with each other. Why were they? Well, for one thing they were all artists—in different ways. Stella designed wallpapers and materials; she had a name for it.

The Bradfords were real artists. He painted, she drew. They had lived mostly out of England in cheap places around the Mediterranean. Both from the North of England, they had met at art school, married at twenty, had taken flight from England, then returned to it, needing it, then off again: and so on, for years, in the rhythm of so many of their kind, needing, hating, loving England. There had been seasons of real poverty, while they lived on pasta or bread or rice, and wine and fruit and sunshine, in Majorca, southern Spain, Italy, North Africa.

A French critic had seen Jack's work, and suddenly he was successful. His show in Paris, then one in London, made money; and now he charged in the hundreds where a year or so ago he charged ten or twenty guineas. This had deepened his contempt for the values of the markets. For a while Stella thought that this was the bond between the Bradfords and herself. They were so very much, as she was, of the new generation of artists (and poets and playwrights and novelists) who had one thing in common, a cool derision about the racket. They were so very unlike (they felt) the older generation with their Societies and their Lunches and their salons and their cliques: their atmosphere of connivance with the snobberies of success. Stella, too, had been successful by a fluke. Not that she did not consider herself talented; it was that others as talented were unfêted, and unbought. When she was with the Bradfords and other fellow spirits, they would talk about the racket, using each other as yardsticks or fellow consciences about how much to give in, what to give, how to use without being used, how to enjoy without becoming dependent on enjoyment.

Of course Dorothy Bradford was not able to talk in quite the same way, since she had not yet been "discovered"; she had not "broken through." A few people with discrimination bought her unusual delicate drawings, which had a strength that was hard to understand unless one knew Dorothy herself. But she was not at all, as Jack was, a great success. There was a strain here, in the marriage, nothing much; it was kept in check by their scorn for their arbitrary rewards of "the racket." But it was there, nevertheless.

Stella's husband had said: "Well, I can understand that, it's like me and you—you're creative, whatever that may mean, I'm just a bloody TV journalist." There was no bitterness in this. He was a good journalist, and besides he sometimes got the chance to make a good small film. All the same, there was that between him and Stella, just as there was between Jack and his wife.

After a time Stella saw something else in her kinship with the couple. It was that the Bradfords had a close bond, bred of having spent so many years together in foreign places, dependent on each other because of their poverty. It had been a real love marriage; one could see it by looking at them. It was now. And Stella's marriage was a real marriage. She understood she enjoyed being with the Bradfords because the two couples were equal in this. Both marriages were those of strong, passionate, talented individuals; they shared a battling quality that strengthened them, not weakened them.

The reason why it had taken Stella so long to understand this was that the Bradfords had made her think about her own marriage, which she was beginning to take for granted, sometimes even found exhausting. She had understood, through them, how lucky she was in her husband; how lucky they all were. No marital miseries; nothing of (what they saw so often in friends) one partner in a marriage victim to the other, resenting the other; no claiming of outsiders as sympathisers or allies in an unequal battle.

There had been a plan for these four people to go off again to Italy or Spain, but then Stella's husband departed, and Dorothy got pregnant. So there was the cottage in Essex instead, a bad second choice, but better, they all felt, to deal with a new baby on home ground, at least for the first year. Stella, telephoned by Jack (on Dorothy's particular insistence, he said), offered and received commiserations on its being only Essex and not Majorca or Italy. She also received sympathy because her husband had been expected back this weekend, but had wired to say he wouldn't be back for another month, probably—there was trouble in Venezuela. Stella wasn't really forlorn; she didn't mind living alone, since she was always supported by knowing her man would be back. Besides, if she herself were offered the chance of a month's "trouble" in Venezuela, she wouldn't hesitate, so it wasn't fair . . . fairness characterised their relationship. All the same, it was nice that she could drop down (or up) to the Bradfords, people with whom she could always be herself, neither more nor less.

She left London at midday by train, armed with food unobtainable in Essex: salamis, cheeses, spices, wine. The sun shone, but it wasn't particularly warm. She hoped there would be heating in the cottage, July or not.

The train was empty. The little station seemed stranded in a green nowhere. She got out, cumbered by bags full of food. A porter and a stationmaster examined, then came to succour her. She was a tallish, fair woman, rather ample; her soft hair, drawn back, escaped in tendrils, and she had great helpless-looking blue eyes. She wore a dress made in one of the materials she had designed. Enormous green leaves laid hands all over her body, and fluttered about her knees. She stood smiling, accustomed to men running to wait on her, enjoying them enjoying her. She walked with them to the barrier where Jack waited, appreciating the scene. He was a smallish man, compact, dark. He wore a blue-green summer shirt, and smoked a pipe and smiled, watching. The two men delivered her into the hands of the third, and departed, whistling, to their duties.

Jack and Stella kissed, then pressed their cheeks together.

"Food," he said, "food," relieving her of the parcels.

"What's it like here, shopping?"

"Vegetables all right, I suppose."

Jack was still northern in this: he seemed brusque, to strangers; he wasn't shy, he simply hadn't been brought up to enjoy words. Now he put his arms briefly around Stella's waist, and said: "Marvellous, Stell, marvellous." They walked on, pleased with each other. Stella had with Jack, her husband had with Dorothy, these moments, when they said to each other wordlessly: If I were not married to my husband, if you were not married to your wife, how delightful it would be to be married to you. These moments were not the least of the pleasures of this four-sided friendship.

"Are you liking it down here?"

"It's what we bargained for."

There was more than his usual shortness in this, and she glanced at him to find him frowning. They were walking to the car, parked under a tree.

"How's the baby?"

"Little bleeder never sleeps; he's wearing us out, but he's fine."

The baby was six weeks old. Having the baby was a definite achievement: getting it safely conceived and born had taken a couple of years. Dorothy, like most independent women, had had divided thoughts about a baby. Besides, she was over thirty and complained she was set in her ways. All this—the difficulties, Dorothy's hesitations—had added up to an atmosphere which Dorothy herself described as "like wondering if some damned horse is going to take the fence." Dorothy would talk, while she was pregnant, in a soft staccato voice: "Perhaps I don't really want a baby at all? Perhaps I'm not fitted to be a mother? Perhaps . . . and if so . . . and how . . . ?"

She said: "Until recently Jack and I were always with people who took it for granted that getting pregnant was a disaster, and now suddenly all the people we know have young children and baby-sitters and . . . perhaps . . . if . . ."

Jack said: "You'll feel better when it's born."

Once Stella had heard him say, after one of Dorothy's long troubled dialogues with herself: "Now that's enough, that's enough, Dorothy." He had silenced her, taking the responsibility.

They reached the car, got in. It was a secondhand job recently bought. "They" (being the Press, the enemy generally) "wait for us" (being artists or writers who have made money) "to buy flashy cars." They had discussed it, decided that *not* to buy an expensive car if they felt like it would be allowing themselves to be bullied; but bought a secondhand one after all. Jack wasn't going to give *them* so much satisfaction, apparently.

"Actually we could have walked," he said, as they shot down a narrow lane, "but with these groceries, it's just as well."

"If the baby's giving you a tough time, there can't be much time for cooking." Dorothy was a wonderful cook. But now again there was something in the air as he said: "Food's definitely not too good just now. You can cook supper, Stell, we could do with a good feed."

Now Dorothy hated anyone in her kitchen, except, for certain specified jobs, her husband; and this was surprising.

"The truth is, Dorothy's worn out," he went on, and now Stella understood he was warning her.

"Well, it is tiring," said Stella soothingly.

"You were like that?"

"Like that" was saying a good deal more than just worn out, or tired, and Stella understood that Jack was really uneasy. She said, plaintively humorous: "You two always expect me to remember things that happened a hundred years ago. Let me think. . . ."

She had been married when she was eighteen, got pregnant at once. Her husband had left her. Soon she had married Philip, who also had a small child from a former marriage. These two children, her daughter, seventeen, his son, twenty, had grown up together.

She remembered herself at nineteen, alone, with a small baby. "Well, I was alone," she said. "That makes a difference. I remember I was exhausted. Yes, I was definitely irritable and unreasonable."

"Yes," said Jack, with a brief reluctant look at her.

"All right, don't worry," she said, replying aloud as she often did to things that Jack had not said aloud.

"Good," he said.

Stella thought of how she had seen Dorothy, in the hospital room, with the new baby. She had sat up in bed, in a pretty bed-jacket, the baby beside her in a basket. He was restless. Jack stood between basket and bed, one large hand on his son's stomach. "Now, you just shut up, little bleeder," he had said, as he grumbled. Then he had picked him up, as if he'd been doing it always, held him against his shoulder, and, as Dorothy held her arms out, had put the baby into them. "Want your mother, then? Don't blame you."

That scene, the ease of it, the way the two parents were together, had, for Stella, made nonsense of all the months of Dorothy's self-questioning. As for Dorothy, she had said, parodying the expected words but meaning them: "He's the most beautiful baby ever born. I can't imagine why I didn't have him before."

"There's the cottage," said Jack. Ahead of them was a small labourer's cottage, among full green trees, surrounded by green grass. It was painted white, had four sparkling windows. Next to it a long shed or structure that turned out to be a greenhouse.

"The man grew tomatoes," said Jack. "Fine studio now."

The car came to rest under another tree.

"Can I just drop in to the studio?"

"Help yourself." Stella walked into the long, glass-roofed shed. In London Jack and Dorothy shared a studio. They had shared huts, sheds, any suitable building, all around the Mediterranean. They always worked side by side. Dorothy's end was tidy, exquisite, Jack's lumbered with great canvases, and he worked in a clutter. Now Stella looked to see if this friendly arrangement continued, but as Jack came in behind her he said: "Dorothy's not set herself up yet. I miss her, I can tell you."

The greenhouse was still partly one: trestles with plants stood along the ends. It was lush and warm.

"As hot as hell when the sun's really going, it makes up. And Dorothy brings Paul in sometimes, so he can get used to a decent climate young."

Dorothy came in, at the far end, without the baby. She had recovered her figure. She was a small dark woman, with neat, delicate limbs. Her face was white, with scarlet rather irregular lips, and black glossy brows, a little crooked. So while she was not pretty, she was lively and dramatic-looking. She and Stella had their moments together, when they got pleasure from contrasting their differences, one woman so big and soft and blond, the other so dark and vivacious.

Dorothy came forward through shafts of sunlight, stopped, and said: "Stella, I'm glad you've come." Then forward again, to a few steps off, where she stood looking at them. "You two look good together," she said, frowning. There was something heavy and over-emphasised about both statements, and Stella said: "I was wondering what Jack had been up to."

"Very good, I think," said Dorothy, coming to look at the new canvas on the easel. It was of sunlit rocks, brown and smooth, with blue sky, blue water, and people swimming in spangles of light. When Jack was in the south, he painted pictures that his wife described as "dirt and grime and misery"—which was how they both described their joint childhood background. When he was in England he painted scenes like these.

"Like it? It's good, isn't it?" said Dorothy.

"Very much," said Stella. She always took pleasure from the contrast between Jack's outward self—the small, self-contained little man who could have vanished in a moment into a crowd of factory workers in, perhaps Manchester, and the sensuous bright pictures like these.

"And you?" asked Stella.

"Having a baby's killed everything creative in me—quite different from being pregnant," said Dorothy, but not complaining of it. She had worked like a demon while she was pregnant.

"Have a heart," said Jack, "he's only just got himself born."

"Well, I don't care," said Dorothy. "That's the funny thing, I *don't* care." She said this flat, indifferent. She seemed to be looking at them both again from a small troubled distance. "You two look good together," she said, and again there was the small jar.

"Well, how about some tea?" said Jack, and Dorothy said at once: "I made it when I heard the car. I thought better inside, it's not really hot in the sun." She led the way out of the greenhouse, her white linen dress dissolving in lozenges of yellow light from the glass panes above, so that Stella was reminded of the white limbs of Jack's swimmers disintegrating under sunlight in his new picture. The work of these two people was always reminding one of each other, or each other's work, and in all kinds of ways: they were so much married, so close.

The time it took to cross the space of rough grass to the door of the little house was enough to show Dorothy was right: it was really chilly in the sun. Inside two electric heaters made up for it. There had been two little rooms downstairs, but they had been knocked into one fine lowceilinged room, stone-floored, whitewashed. A tea table, covered with a purple checked cloth, stood waiting near a window where flowering bushes and trees showed through clean panes. Charming. They adjusted the heaters and arranged themselves so they could admire the English countryside through glass. Stella looked for the baby; Dorothy said: "In the pram at the back." Then she asked: "Did yours cry a lot?"

Stella laughed and said again: "I'll try to remember."

"We expect you to guide and direct, with all your experience," said Jack.

"As far as I can remember, she was a little demon for about three months, for no reason I could see, then suddenly she became civilised."

"Roll on the three months," said Jack.

"Six weeks to go," said Dorothy, handling teacups in a languid indifferent manner Stella found new in her.

"Finding it tough going?"

"I've never felt better in my life," said Dorothy at once, as if being accused.

"You look fine."

She looked a bit tired, nothing much; Stella couldn't see what reason there was for Jack to warn her. Unless he meant the languor, a look of self-absorption? Her vivacity, a friendly aggressiveness that was the expression of her lively intelligence, was dimmed. She sat leaning back in a deep airchair, letting Jack manage things, smiling vaguely.

"I'll bring him in in a minute," she remarked, listening to the silence from the sunlit garden at the back.

"Leave him," said Jack. "He's quiet seldom enough. Relax, woman, and have a cigarette."

He lit a cigarette for her, and she took it in the same vague way, and sat breathing out smoke, her eyes half-closed.

"Have you heard from Philip?" she asked, not from politeness, but with sudden insistence.

"Of course she has, she got a wire," said Jack.

"I want to know how she feels," said Dorothy. "How do you feel, Stell?" She was listening for the baby all the time.

"Feel about what?"

"About his not coming back."

"But he is coming back, it's only a month," said Stella, and heard, with surprise, that her voice sounded edgy.

"You see?" said Dorothy to Jack, meaning the words, not the edge on them.

At this evidence that she and Philip had been discussed, Stella felt, first, pleasure: because it was pleasurable to be understood by two such good friends; then she felt discomfort, remembering Jack's warning.

"See what?" she asked Dorothy, smiling.

"That's enough now," said Jack to his wife in a flash of stubborn anger, which continued the conversation that had taken place.

Dorothy took direction from her husband, and kept quiet a moment, then seemed impelled to continue: "I've been thinking it must be nice, having your husband go off, then come back. Do you realise Jack and I haven't been separated since we married? That's over ten years. Don't you think there's something awful in two grown people stuck together all the time like Siamese twins?" This ended in a wail of genuine appeal to Stella.

"No, I think it's marvellous."

"But you don't mind being alone so much?"

"It's not *so* much; it's two or three months in a year. Well of course I mind. But I enjoy being alone, really. But I'd enjoy it too if we were together all the time. I envy you two." Stella was surprised to find her eyes wet with self-pity because she had to be without her husband another month.

"And what does he think?" demanded Dorothy. "What does Philip think?"

Stella said: "Well, I think he likes getting away from time to time—yes. He likes intimacy, he enjoys it, but it doesn't come as easily to him as it does to me." She had never said this before because she had never thought about it. She was annoyed with herself that she had had to wait for Dorothy to prompt her. Yet she knew that getting annoyed was what she must not do, with the state Dorothy was in, whatever it was. She glanced at Jack for guidance, but he was determinedly busy on his pipe.

"Well, I'm like Philip," announced Dorothy. "Yes, I'd love it if Jack went off sometimes. I think I'm being stifled being shut up with Jack day and night, year in year out."

"Thanks," said Jack, short but good-humoured.

"No, but I mean it. There's something humiliating about two adult people never for one second out of each other's sight."

"Well," said Jack, "when Paul's a bit bigger, you buzz off for a month or so and you'll appreciate me when you get back."

"It's not that I don't appreciate you, it's not that at all," said Dorothy, insistent, almost strident, apparently fevered with restlessness. Her languor had quite gone, and her limbs jerked and moved. And now the baby, as if he had been prompted by his father's mentioning him, let out a cry. Jack got up, forestalling his wife, saying: "I'll get him."

Dorothy sat, listening for her husband's movements with the baby, until he came back, which he did, supporting the infant sprawled against his shoulder with a competent hand. He sat down, let his son slide on to his chest, and said: "There now, you shut up and leave us in peace a bit longer." The baby was looking up into his face with the astonished expression of the newly born, and Dorothy sat smiling at both of them. Stella understood that her restlessness, her repeated curtailed movements, meant that she longed—more, needed—to have the child in her arms, have its body against hers. And Jack seemed to feel this, because Stella could have sworn it was not a conscious decision that made him rise and slide the infant into his wife's arms. Her flesh, her needs, had spoken direct to him without words, and he had risen at once to give her what she wanted. This silent instinctive conversation between husband and wife made Stella miss her own husband violently, and with resentment against fate that kept them apart so often. She ached for Philip.

Meanwhile Dorothy, now the baby was sprawled softly against her chest, the small feet in her hand, seemed to have lapsed into good humour. And Stella, watching, remembered something she really had forgotten: the close, fierce physical tie between herself and her daughter when she had been a tiny baby. She saw this bond in the way Dorothy stroked the small head that trembled on its neck as the baby looked up into his mother's face. Why, she remembered it was like being in love, having a new baby. All kinds of forgotten or unused instincts woke in Stella. She lit a cigarette, took herself in hand; set herself to enjoy the other woman's love affair with her baby instead of envying her.

The sun, dropping into the trees, struck the windowpanes; and there was a dazzle and a flashing of yellow and white light into the room, particularly over Dorothy in her white dress and the baby. Again Stella was reminded of Jack's picture of the white-limbed swimmers in sun-dissolving water. Dorothy shielded the baby's eyes with her hand and remarked dreamily: "This is better than any man, isn't it, Stell? Isn't it better than any man?"

"Well—no," said Stella laughing. "No, not for long."

"If you say so, you should know . . . but I can't imagine ever . . . Tell me, Stell, does your Philip have affairs when he's away?"

"For God's sake!" said Jack, angry. But he checked himself.

"Yes, I am sure he does."

"Do you mind?" asked Dorothy, loving the baby's feet with her enclosing palm.

And now Stella was forced to remember, to think about having minded, minding, coming to terms, and the ways in which she now did not mind.

"I don't think about it," she said.

"Well, I don't think I'd mind," said Dorothy.

"Thanks for letting me know," said Jack, short despite himself. Then he made himself laugh.

"And you, do you have affairs while Philip's away?"

"Sometimes. Not really."

"Do you know, Jack was unfaithful to me this week," remarked Dorothy, smiling at the baby.

"That's *enough*," said Jack, really angry.

"No it isn't enough, it isn't. Because what's awful is, I don't care."

"Well why should you care, in the circumstances?" Jack turned to Stella. "There's a silly bitch Lady Edith lives across that field. She got all excited, real live artists living down her lane. Well Dorothy was lucky, she had an excuse in the baby, but I had to go to her silly party. Booze flowing in rivers, and the most incredible people—you know. If you read about them in a novel, you'd never believe . . . but I can't remember much after about twelve."

"Do you know what happened?" said Dorothy. "I was feeding

the baby, it was terribly early. Jack sat straight up in bed and said: 'Jesus, Dorothy, I've just remembered, I screwed that silly bitch Lady Edith on her brocade sofa.' "

Stella laughed. Jack let out a snort of laughter. Dorothy laughed, an unscrupulous chuckle of appreciation. Then she said seriously: "But that's the point, Stella—the thing is, I don't care a tuppenny damn."

"But why should you?" asked Stella.

"But it's the first time he ever has, and surely I should have minded?"

"Don't you be too sure of that," said Jack, energetically puffing his pipe. "Don't be too sure." But it was only for form's sake, and Dorothy knew it, and said: "Surely I should have cared, Stell?"

"No. You'd have cared if you and Jack weren't so marvellous together. Just as I'd care if Philip and I weren't. . . ." Tears came running down her face. She let them. These were her good friends; and besides, instinct told her tears weren't a bad thing, with Dorothy in this mood. She said, sniffing: "When Philip gets home, we always have a flaming bloody row in the first day or two, about something unimportant, but what it's really about, and we know it, is that I'm jealous of any affair he's had and vice versa. Then we go to bed and make up." She wept, bitterly, thinking of this happiness, postponed for a month, to be succeeded by the delightful battle of their day-to-day living.

"Oh Stella," said Jack. "Stell . . ." He got up, fished out a handkerchief, dabbed her eyes for her. "There, love, he'll be back soon."

"Yes, I know. It's just that you two are so good together and whenever I'm with you I miss Philip."

"Well, I suppose we're good together?" said Dorothy, sounding surprised. Jack, bending over Stella with his back to his wife, made a warning grimace, then stood up and turned, commanding the situation. "It's nearly six. You'd better feed Paul. Stella's going to cook supper."

"Is she? How nice," said Dorothy. "There's everything in the kitchen, Stella. How lovely to be looked after."

"I'll show you our mansion," said Jack.

Upstairs were two small white rooms. One was the bedroom, with their things and the baby's in it. The other was an overflow room jammed with stuff. Jack picked up a large leather folder off the spare bed and said: "Look at these, Stell." He stood at the window, back to her, his thumb at work in his pipe bowl, looking into the garden. Stella sat on the bed, opened the folder and at once exclaimed: "When did she do these?"

"The last three months she was pregnant. Never seen anything like it, she just turned them out one after the other."

There were a couple of hundred pencil drawings, all of two bodies in every kind of balance, tension, relationship. The two bodies were Jack's and Dorothy's, mostly unclothed, but not all. The drawings startled, not only because they marked a real jump forward in Dorothy's achievement, but because of their bold sensuousness. They were a kind of chant, or exaltation about the marriage. The instinctive closeness, the harmony of Jack and Dorothy, visible in every movement they made towards or away from each other, visible even when they were not together, was celebrated here with a frank, calm triumph.

"Some of them are pretty strong," said Jack, the northern workingclass boy reviving in him for a moment's puritanism.

But Stella laughed, because the prudishness masked pride: some of the drawings were indecent.

In the last few of the series the woman's body was swollen in pregnancy. They showed her trust in her husband, whose body, commanding hers, stood or lay in positions of strength and confidence. In the very last Dorothy stood turned away from her husband, her two hands supporting her big belly, and Jack's hands were protective on her shoulders.

"They are marvellous," said Stella.

"They are, aren't they."

Stella looked, laughing, and with love, towards Jack: for she saw that his showing her the drawings was not only pride in his wife's talent, but that he was using this way of telling Stella not to take Dorothy's mood too seriously. And to cheer himself up. She said impulsively: "Well that's all right then, isn't it?"

"What? Oh yes, I see what you mean, yes, I think it's all right."

"Do you know what?" said Stella, lowering her voice. "I think Dorothy's guilty because she feels unfaithful to you."

"What?"

"No, I mean, with the baby, and that's what it's all about."

He turned to face her, troubled, then slowly smiling. There was the same rich unscrupulous quality of appreciation in that smile as there had been in Dorothy's laugh over her husband and Lady Edith. "You think so?" They laughed together, irrepressibly and loudly.

"What's the joke?" shouted Dorothy.

"I'm laughing because your drawings are so good," shouted Stella.

"Yes, they are, aren't they?" But Dorothy's voice changed to flat incredulity: "The trouble is, I can't imagine how I ever did them, I can't imagine ever being able to do it again."

"Downstairs," said Jack to Stella, and they went down to find Dorothy nursing the baby. He nursed with his whole being, all of him in movement. He was wrestling with the breast, thumping Dorothy's plump pretty breast with his fists. Jack stood looking down at the two of them, grinning. Dorothy reminded Stella of a cat, half-closing her yellow eyes to stare over her kittens at work on her side, while she stretched out a paw where claws sheathed and unsheathed themselves, making a small rip-rip-rip on the carpet she lay on.

"You're a savage creature," said Stella, laughing.

Dorothy raised her small vivid face and smiled. "Yes, I am," she said, and looked at the two of them calm, and from a distance, over the head of her energetic baby.

Stella cooked supper in a stone kitchen, with a heater brought by Jack to make it tolerable. She used the good food she had brought with her, taking trouble. It took some time, then the three ate slowly over a big wooden table. The baby was not asleep. He grumbled for some minutes on a cushion on the floor, then his father held him briefly, before passing him over, as he had done earlier, in response to his mother's need to have him close.

"I'm supposed to let him cry," remarked Dorothy. "But why should he? If he were an Arab or an African baby he'd be plastered to my back."

"And very nice too," said Jack. "I think they come out too soon into the light of day; they should just stay inside for about eighteen months, much better all around."

"Have a heart," said Dorothy and Stella together, and they all laughed; but Dorothy added, quite serious: "Yes, I've been thinking so too."

This good nature lasted through the long meal. The light went cool and thin outside; and inside they let the summer dusk deepen, without lamps.

"I've got to go quite soon," said Stella, with regret.

"Oh, no, you've got to stay!" said Dorothy, strident. It was sudden, the return of the woman who made Jack and Dorothy tense themselves to take strain.

"We all thought Philip was coming. The children will be back tomorrow night, they've been on holiday."

"Then stay till tomorrow, I *want* you," said Dorothy, petulant.

"But I can't," said Stella.

"I never thought I'd want another woman around, cooking in my kitchen, looking after me, but I do," said Dorothy, apparently about to cry.

"Well, love, you'll have to put up with me," said Jack.

"Would you mind, Stell?"

"Mind *what?*" asked Stella, cautious.

"Do you find Jack attractive?"

"Very."

"Well I know you do. Jack, do you find Stella attractive?"

"Try me," said Jack, grinning; but at the same time signalling warnings to Stella.

"Well, then!" said Dorothy.

"A *ménage à trois?*" asked Stella, laughing. "And how about my Philip? Where does he fit in?"

"Well, if it comes to that, I wouldn't mind Philip myself," said Dorothy, knitting her sharp black brows and frowning.

"I don't blame you," said Stella, thinking of her handsome husband.

"Just for a month, till he comes back," said Dorothy. "I tell you what, we'll abandon this silly cottage, we must have been mad to stick ourselves away in England in the first place. The three of us'll just pack up and go off to Spain or Italy with the baby."

"And what else?" enquired Jack, good-natured at all costs, using his pipe as a safety valve.

"Yes, I've decided I approve of polygamy," announced Dorothy. She had opened her dress and the baby was nursing again, quietly this time, relaxed against her. She stroked his head, softly, softly, while her voice rose and insisted at the other two people: "I never understood it before, but I do now. I'll be the senior wife, and you two can look after me."

"Any other plans?" enquired Jack, angry now. "You just drop in from time to time to watch Stella and me have a go, is that it? Or are you going to tell us when we can go off and do it, give us your gracious permission?"

"Oh I don't care what you do, that's the point," said Dorothy, sighing, sounding forlorn, however.

Jack and Stella, careful not to look at each other, sat waiting.

"I read something in the newspaper yesterday, it struck me," said Dorothy, conversational. "A man and two women living to-gether—here, in England. They are both his wives, they consider themselves his wives. The senior wife has a baby, and the younger wife sleeps with him—well, that's what it looked like, reading between the lines."

"You'd better stop reading between lines," said Jack. "It's not doing you any good."

"No, I'd like it," insisted Dorothy. "I think our marriages are silly. Africans and people like that, they know better, they've got some sense."

"I can just see you if I did make love to Stella," said Jack.

"Yes!" said Stella, with a short laugh, which, against her will, was resentful.

"But I wouldn't mind," said Dorothy, and burst into tears.

"Now, Dorothy, that's enough," said Jack. He got up, took the baby, whose sucking was mechanical now, and said: "Now listen, you're going right upstairs and you're going to sleep. This little stinker's full as a tick, he'll be asleep for hours, that's my bet."

"I don't feel sleepy," said Dorothy, sobbing.

"I'll give you a sleeping pill, then."

Then started a search for sleeping pills. None to be found.

"That's just like us," wailed Dorothy, "we don't even have a sleeping pill in the place. . . . Stella, I wish you'd stay, I really do. Why can't you?"

"Stella's going in just a minute, I'm taking her to the station," said Jack. He poured some Scotch into a glass, handed it to his wife and said: "Now drink that, love, and let's have an end of it. I'm getting fed-up." He sounded fed-up.

Dorothy obediently drank the Scotch, got unsteadily from her chair and went slowly upstairs. "Don't let him cry," she demanded, as she disappeared.

"Oh you silly bitch!" he shouted after her. "When have I let him cry? Here, you hold on a minute," he said to Stella, handing her the baby. He ran upstairs.

Stella held the baby. This was almost for the first time, since she sensed how much another woman's holding her child made Dorothy's fierce new possessiveness uneasy. She looked down at the small, sleepy, red face and said softly: "Well, you're causing a lot of trouble, aren't you?"

Jack shouted from upstairs: "Come up a minute, Stell." She went up, with the baby. Dorothy was tucked up in bed, drowsy from the Scotch, the bedside light turned away from her. She looked at the baby, but Jack took it from Stella.

"Jack says I'm a silly bitch," said Dorothy, apologetic, to Stella.

"Well, never mind, you'll feel different soon."

"I suppose so, if you say so. All right. I *am* going to sleep," said Dorothy, in a stubborn, sad little voice. She turned over, away from them. In the last flare of her hysteria she said: "Why don't you two walk to the station together? It's a lovely night."

"We're going to," said Jack, "don't worry."

She let out a weak giggle, but did not turn. Jack carefully deposited the now sleeping baby in the bed, about a foot from Dorothy. Who suddenly wriggled over until her small, defiant white back was in contact with the blanketed bundle that was her son.

Jack raised his eyebrows at Stella: but Stella was looking at mother and baby, the nerves of her memory filling her with sweet warmth. What right had this woman, who was in possession of such delight, to torment her husband, to torment her friend, as she had been doing—what right had she to rely on their decency as she did?

Surprised by these thoughts, she walked away downstairs, and stood at the door into the garden, her eyes shut, holding herself rigid against tears.

She felt a warmth on her bare arm—Jack's hand. She opened her eyes to see him bending towards her, concerned.

"It'd serve Dorothy right if I did drag you off into the bushes. . . ."

"Wouldn't have to drag me," he said; and while the words had the measure of facetiousness the situation demanded, she felt his seriousness envelop them both in danger.

The warmth of his hand slid across her back, and she turned towards him under its pressure. They stood together, cheeks touching, scents of skin and hair mixing with the smells of warmed grass and leaves.

She thought: What is going to happen now will blow Dorothy and Jack and that baby sky-high; it's the end of my marriage; I'm going to blow everything to bits. There was almost uncontrollable pleasure in it.

She saw Dorothy, Jack, the baby, her husband, and two half-grown children, all dispersed, all spinning downwards through the sky like bits of debris after an explosion.

Jack's mouth was moving along her cheek towards her mouth,

dissolving her whole self in delight. She saw, against closed lids, the bundled baby upstairs, and pulled back from the situation, exclaiming energetically: "Damn Dorothy, damn her, damn her, I'd like to kill her. . . ."

And he, exploding into reaction, said in a low furious rage: "Damn you both! I'd like to wring both your bloody necks. . . ."

Their faces were at a foot's distance from each other, their eyes staring hostility. She thought that if she had not the vision of the helpless baby they would now be in each other's arms—generating tenderness and desire like a couple of dynamos, she said to herself, trembling with dry anger.

"I'm going to miss my train if I don't go," she said.

"I'll get your coat," he said, and went in, leaving her defenceless against the emptiness of the garden.

When he came out, he slid the coat around her without touching her, and said: "Come on, I'll take you by car." He walked away in front of her to the car, and she followed meekly over rough lawn. It really was a lovely night.

[1958]

Muriel Spark
(1918–present)

The House of the Famous Poet

Born and educated in Edinburgh, Scotland, Muriel Spark moved to southern Africa and worked in the Political Intelligence Department of the British Foreign Office. She then held various editorial posts in London, published works on Mary Wollstonecraft Shelley and Emily Brontë, and converted from Judaism to Catholicism. Her fiction reflects her experiences and the various phases of her life.

Her work includes *The Go-Away Bird* (1958), *The Mandelbaum Gate* (1965), *The Hothouse by the East River* (1973), *The Only Problem* (1984), and *A Far Cry from Kensington* (1988). *Loitering with Intent* (1981), Spark's autobiographical novel, presents a character who says, "How wonderful it feels to be an artist and a woman in the twentieth century." *Bang-Bang You're Dead and Other Stories* (1960) is Spark's major collection of short stories, of which "The House of the Famous Poet" is a part.

In the summer of 1944, when it was nothing for trains from the provinces to be five or six hours late, I travelled to London on the night train from Edinburgh, which, at York, was already three hours late. There were ten people in the compartment, only two of whom I remember well, and for good reason.

I have the impression, looking back on it, of a row of people opposite me, dozing untidily with heads askew, and, as it often seems when we look at sleeping strangers, their features had assumed extra emphasis and individuality, sometimes disturbing to watch. It was as if they had rendered up their daytime talent for obliterating the outward traces of themselves in exchange for mental obliteration. In this way they resembled a twelfth-century fresco; there was a look of medieval unselfconsciousness about these people, all except one.

This was a private soldier who was awake to a greater degree than most people are when they are not sleeping. He was smoking cigarettes one after the other with long, calm puffs. I thought he looked excessively evil—an atavistic type. His forehead must have been less than two inches high above dark, thick eyebrows, which met. His jaw was not large, but it was apelike; so was his small nose and so were his deep, close-set eyes. I thought there must have been some consanguinity in the parents. He was quite a throwback.

As it turned out, he was extremely gentle and kind. When I ran out of cigarettes, he fished about in his haversack and produced a packet for me and one for a girl sitting next to me. We both tried, with a flutter of small change, to pay him. Nothing would please him at all but that we should accept his cigarettes, whereupon he returned to his silent, reflective smoking.

I felt a sort of pity for him then, rather as we feel towards animals we know to be harmless, such as monkeys. But I realized that, like the pity we expend on monkeys merely because they are not human beings, this pity was not needed.

Receiving the cigarettes gave the girl and myself common ground, and we conversed quietly for the rest of the journey. She told me she had a job in London as a domestic helper and nursemaid. She looked as if she had come from a country district—her very blonde hair, red face and large bones gave the impression of power, as if she was used to carrying heavy things, perhaps great scuttles of coal, or two children at a time. But what made me curious about her was her voice, which was cultivated, melodious and restrained.

Towards the end of the journey, when the people were beginning to jerk themselves straight and the rushing to and fro in the corridor had started, this girl, Elise, asked me to come with her to the house where she worked. The master, who was something in a university, was away with his wife and family.

I agreed to this, because at that time I was in the way of thinking that the discovery of an educated servant girl was valuable and something to be gone deeper into. It had the element of experience—perhaps, even of truth—and I believed, in those days, that truth is stranger than fiction. Besides, I wanted to spend that

Sunday in London. I was due back next day at my job in a branch of the civil service, which had been evacuated to the country and for a reason that is another story, I didn't want to return too soon. I had some telephoning to do, I wanted to wash and change. I wanted to know more about the girl. So I thanked Elise and accepted her invitation.

I regretted it as soon as we got out of the train at King's Cross, some minutes after ten. Standing up tall on the platform, Elise looked unbearably tired, as if not only the last night's journey but every fragment of her unknown life was suddenly heaping up on top of her. The power I had noticed in the train was no longer there. As she called, in her beautiful voice, for a porter, I saw that on the side of her head that had been away from me in the train, her hair was parted in a dark streak, which, by contrast with the yellow, looked navy blue. I had thought, when I first saw her, that possibly her hair was bleached, but now, seeing it so badly done, seeing this navy blue parting pointing like an arrow to the weighted weariness of her face, I, too, got the sensation of great tiredness. And it was not only the strain of the journey that I felt, but the foreknowledge of boredom that comes upon us unaccountably at the beginning of a quest, and that checks, perhaps mercifully, our curiosity.

And, as it happened, there really wasn't much to learn about Elise. The explanation of her that I had been prompted to seek, I got in the taxi between King's Cross and the house at Swiss Cottage. She came of a good family, who thought her a pity, and she them. Having no training for anything else, she had taken a domestic job on leaving home. She was engaged to an Australian soldier billeted also at Swiss Cottage.

Perhaps it was the anticipation of a day's boredom, maybe it was the effect of no sleep or the fact that the V-1 sirens were sounding, but I felt some sourness when I saw the house. The garden was growing all over the place. Elise opened the front door, and we entered a darkish room almost wholly taken up with a long, plain wooden work-table. On this, were a half-empty marmalade jar, a pile of papers, and a dried-up ink bottle. There was a steel-canopied bed, known as a Morrison shelter, in one corner and some photographs on the mantelpiece, one of a schoolboy wearing glasses. Everything was tainted with Elise's weariness and my own distaste. But Elise didn't seem to be aware of the exhaustion so plainly revealed on her face. She did not even bother to take her coat off, and as it was too tight for her I wondered how she could move about so quickly with this restriction added to the weight of her tiredness. But, with her coat still buttoned tight Elise phoned her boy-friend and made breakfast, while I washed in a dim, blue, cracked bathroom upstairs.

When I found that she had opened my hold-all without asking me and had taken out my rations, I was a little pleased. It seemed a friendly action, with some measure of reality about it, and I felt better. But I was still irritated by the house. I felt there was no justification for the positive lack of consequence which was lying about here and there. I asked no questions about the owner who was something in a university, for fear of getting the answer I expected—that he was away visiting his grandchildren, at some family gathering in the home counties. The owners of the house had no reality for me, and I looked upon the place as belonging to, and permeated with, Elise.

I went with her to a nearby public house, where she met her boy-friend and one or two other Australian soldiers. They had with them a thin Cockney girl with bad teeth. Elise was very happy, and insisted in her lovely voice that they should all come along to a party at the house that evening. In a fine aristocratic tone, she demanded that each should bring a bottle of beer.

During the afternoon Elise said she was going to have a bath, and she showed me a room where I could use the telephone and sleep if I wanted. This was a large, light room with several windows, much more orderly than the rest of the house, and lined with books. There was only one unusual thing about it: beside one of the windows was a bed, but this bed was only a fairly thick mattress made up neatly on the floor. It was obviously a bed on the floor with some purpose, and again I was angered to think of the futile crankiness of the elderly professor who had thought of it.

I did my telephoning, and decided to rest. But first I wanted to find something to read. The books puzzled me. None of them seemed to be automatically part of a scholar's library. An inscription in one book was signed by the author, a well-known novelist. I found another inscribed copy, and this had the name of the recipient. On a sudden idea, I went to the desk, where while I had been telephoning I had noticed a pile of unopened letters. For the first time, I looked at the name of the owner of the house.

I ran to the bathroom and shouted through the door to Elise, "Is this the house of the famous poet?"

"Yes," she called. "I *told* you."

She had told me nothing of the kind. I felt I had no right at all to be there, for it wasn't, now, the house of Elise acting by proxy for some unknown couple. It was the house of a famous modern poet. The thought that at any moment he and his family might walk in and find me there terrified me. I insisted that Elise should open the bathroom door and tell me to my face that there was no possible chance of their returning for many days to come.

Then I began to think about the house itself, which Elise was no longer accountable for. Its new definition, as the house of a poet whose work I knew well, many of whose poems I knew by heart, gave it altogether a new appearance.

To confirm this, I went outside and stood exactly where I had been when I first saw the garden from the door of the taxi. I wanted to get my first impression for a second time.

And this time I saw an absolute purpose in the overgrown garden, which, since then, I have come to believe existed in the eye of the beholder. But, at the time, the room we had first entered, and which had riled me, now began to give back a meaning, and whatever was, was right. The caked-up bottle of ink, which Elise had put on the mantelpiece, I replaced on the table to make sure. I saw a photograph I hadn't noticed before, and I recognized the famous poet.

It was the same with the upstairs room where Elise had put me, and I handled the books again, not so much with the sense that they belonged to the famous poet but with some curiosity about how they had been made. The sort of question that occurred to me was where the paper had come from and from what sort of vegetation was manufactured the black print, and these things have not troubled me since.

The Australians and the Cockney girl came around about seven. I had planned to catch an eight-thirty train to the country, but when I telephoned to confirm the time I found there were no Sunday trains running. Elise, in her friendly and exhausted way, begged me to stay without attempting to be too serious about it. The sirens were starting up again. I asked Elise once more to repeat that the poet and his family could by no means return that night. But I asked this question more abstractedly than before, as I was thinking of the sirens and of the exact proportions of the noise they made. I wondered, as well, what sinister genius of the Home Office could have invented so ominous a wail, and why. And I was thinking of the word "siren." The sound then became comical, for I imagined some maniac sea nymph from centuries past belching into the year 1944. Actually, the sirens frightened me.

Most of all, I wondered about Elise's party. Everyone roamed about the place as if it were nobody's house in particular, with Elise the best-behaved of the lot. The Cockney girl sat on the long table and gave of her best to the skies every time a bomb exploded. I had the feeling that the house had been requisitioned for an evening by the military. It was so hugely and everywhere occupied that it became not the house I had first entered, nor the house of the famous poet, but a third house—the one I had vaguely prefigured when I stood, bored, on the platform at King's Cross station. I saw a great amount of tiredness among these people, and heard, from the loud noise they made, that they were all lacking sleep. When the beer was finished and they were gone, some to their billets, some to pubs, and the Cockney girl to her Underground shelter where she had slept for weeks past, I asked Elise, "Don't you feel tired?"

"No," she said with agonizing weariness, "I never feel tired."

I fell asleep myself, as soon as I had got into the bed on the floor in the upstairs room, and overslept until Elise woke me at eight. I had wanted to get up early to catch a nine o'clock train, so I hadn't much time to speak to her. I did notice, though, that she had lost some of her tired look.

I was pushing my things into my hold-all while Elise went up the street to catch a taxi when I heard someone coming upstairs. I thought it was Elise come back, and I looked out of the open door. I saw a man in uniform carrying an enormous parcel in both hands. He looked down as he climbed, and had a cigarette in his mouth.

"Do you want Elise?" I called, thinking it was one of her friends.

He looked up, and I recognized the soldier, the throwback, who had given us cigarettes in the train.

"Well, anyone will do," he said. "The thing is, I've got to get back to camp and I'm stuck for the fare—eight and six."

I told him I could manage it, and was finding the money when he said, putting his parcel on the floor, "I don't want to borrow it. I wouldn't think of borrowing it. I've got something for sale."

"What's that?" I said.

"A funeral," said the soldier. "I've got it here."

This alarmed me, and I went to the window. No hearse, no coffin stood below. I saw only the avenue of trees.

The soldier smiled. "It's an abstract funeral," he explained, opening the parcel.

He took it out and I examined it carefully, greatly comforted. It was very much the sort of thing I had wanted—rather more purple in parts than I would have liked, for I was not in favour of this colour of mourning. Still, I thought I could tone it down a bit.

Delighted with the bargain, I handed over the eight shillings and sixpence. There was a great deal of this abstract funeral. Hastily, I packed some of it into the hold-all. Some I stuffed in my pockets, and there was still some left over. Elise had returned with a cab and I hadn't much time. So I ran for it, out of the door and out of the gate of the house of the famous poet, with the rest of my funeral trailing behind me.

You will complain that I am withholding evidence. Indeed, you may wonder if there is any evidence at all. "An abstract funeral," you will say, "is neither here nor there. It is only a notion. You cannot pack a notion into your bag. You cannot see the colour of a notion."

You will insinuate that what I have just told you is pure fiction.

Hear me to the end.

I caught the train. Imagine my surprise when I found, sitting opposite me, my friend the soldier, of whose existence you are so sceptical.

"As a matter of interest," I said, "how would you describe all this funeral you sold me?"

"Describe it?" he said. "Nobody describes an abstract funeral. You just conceive it."

"There is much in what you say," I replied. "Still, describe it I must, because it is not every day one comes by an abstract funeral."

"I am glad you appreciate that," said the soldier.

"And after the war," I continued, "when I am no longer a civil servant, I hope, in a few deftly turned phrases, to write of my experiences at the house of the famous poet, which has culminated like this. But of course," I added, "I will need to say what it looks like."

The soldier did not reply.

"If it were an okapi or a sea-cow," I said, "I would have to say what it looked like. No one would believe me otherwise."

"Do you want your money back?" asked the soldier. "Because if so, you can't have it. I spent it on my ticket."

"Don't misunderstand me," I hastened to say. "The funeral is a delightful abstraction. Only, I wish to put it down in writing."

I felt a great pity for the soldier on seeing his worried look. The apelike head seemed the saddest thing in the world.

"I make them by hand," he said, "these abstract funerals."

A siren sounded somewhere, far away.

"Elise bought one of them last month. She hadn't any complaints. I change at the next stop," he said, getting down his kit from the rack. "And what's more," he said, "your famous poet bought one."

"Oh, did he?" I said.

"Yes," he said. "No complaints. It was just what he wanted—the idea of a funeral."

The train pulled up. The soldier leaped down and waved. As the train started again, I unpacked my abstract funeral and looked at it for a few moments.

"To hell with the idea," I said. "It's a real funeral I want."

"All in good time," said a voice from the corridor.

"*You* again," I said. It was the soldier.

"No," he said, "I got off at the last station. I'm only a notion of myself."

"Look here," I said, "would you be offended if I throw all this away?"

"Of course not," said the soldier. "You can't offend a notion."

"I want a real funeral," I explained. "One of my own."

"That's right," said the soldier.

"And then I'll be able to write about it and go into all the details," I said.

"Your own funeral?" he said. "You want to write it up?"

"Yes," I said.

"But," said he, "you're only human. Nobody reports on their own funeral. It's got to be abstract."

"You see my predicament?" I said.

"I see it," he replied. "I get off at this stop."

This notion of a soldier alighted. Once more the train put on speed. Out of the window I chucked all my eight and sixpence worth of abstract funeral. I watched it fluttering over the fields and around the tops of camouflaged factories with the sun glittering richly upon it, until it was out of sight.

In the summer of 1944 a great many people were harshly and suddenly killed. The papers reported, in due course, those whose names were known to the public. One of these, the famous poet, had returned unexpectedly to his home at Swiss Cottage a few moments before it was hit direct by a flying bomb. Fortunately, he had left his wife and children in the country.

When I got to the place where my job was, I had some time to spare before going on duty. I decided to ring Elise and thank her properly, as I had left in such a hurry. But the lines were out of order, and the operator could not find words enough to express her annoyance with me. Behind this overworked, quarrelsome voice from the exchange I heard the high, long hoot which means that the telephone at the other end is not functioning, and the sound made me infinitely depressed and weary; it was more intolerable to me than the sirens, and I replaced the receiver; and, in fact, Elise had already perished under the house of the famous poet.

The blue cracked bathroom, the bed on the floor, the caked ink bottle, the neglected garden, and the neat rows of books—I try to gather them together in my mind whenever I am enraged by the thought that Elise and the poet were killed outright. The angels of the Resurrection will invoke the dead man and the dead woman, but who will care to restore the fallen house of the famous poet if not myself? Who else will tell its story?

When I reflect how Elise and the poet were taken in—how they calmly allowed a well-meaning soldier to sell them the notion of a funeral, I remind myself that one day I will accept, and so will you, an abstract funeral, and make no complaints.

[1960]

Wakako Yamauchi
(1924–present)

And the Soul Shall Dance

Born to a farming family in Westmorland, California, Wakako Yamauchi spent much of her childhood reading. During her family's internment in a concentration camp in Arizona in 1942, Yamauchi met and formed an enduring friendship with nisei writer Hisaye Yamamoto. Yamauchi did not begin writing herself until she was older. This was not due to lack of interest but because, in her words, "Opportunities were few for ethnic writers. Also, I thought you had to be brilliant to write. . . . No, I didn't get brilliant with age; I merely decided to write some stories about my people."

Yamauchi's stories deal with the Asian American's search for an ethnic identity in the United States. "And the Soul Shall Dance" explores the American-born Asian's contradictory feelings toward the older, immigrant generation. Herself the daughter of a Japanese immigrant, Yamauchi creates personal, vibrant representations of the struggle for self-definition within an atmosphere of white racism. Yamauchi's published works include "Songs My Mother Taught Me" (1977), "Boatmen on Toneh River" (1983), "Surviving the Wasteland Years" (1988), "Makapoo Bay" (1989), and "Maybe" (1990).

It's all right to talk about it now. Most of the principals are dead, except, of course, me and my younger brother, and possibly Kiyoko Oka, who might be near forty-five now, because, yes, I'm sure of it, she was fourteen then. I was nine, and my brother about four, so he hardly counts at all. Kiyoko's mother is dead, my father is dead, my mother is dead, and her father could not have lasted all these years with his tremendous appetite for alcohol and pickled chilies—those little yellow ones, so hot they could make your mouth hurt; he'd eat them like peanuts and tears would surge from his bulging thyroid eyes in great waves and stream down the dark coarse terrain of his face.

My father farmed then in the desert basin resolutely named Imperial Valley, in the township called Westmoreland; twenty acres of tomatoes, ten of summer squash, or vice versa, and the Okas lived maybe a mile, mile and a half, across an alkaline road, a stretch of greasewood, tumbleweed and white sand, to the south of us. We didn't hobnob much with them, because you see, they were a childless couple and we were a family: father, mother, daughter, and son, and we went to the Buddhist church on Sundays where my mother taught Japanese, and the Okas kept pretty much to themselves. I don't mean they were unfriendly; Mr. Oka would sometimes walk over (he rarely drove) on rainy days, all dripping wet, short and squat under a soggy newspaper, pretending to need a plow-blade or a file, and he would spend the afternoon in our kitchen drinking sake and eating chilies with my father. As he got progressively drunker, his large mouth would draw down and with the stream of tears, he looked like a kindly weeping bullfrog.

Not only were they childless, impractical in an area where large families were looked upon as labor potentials, but there was a certain strangeness about them. I became aware of it the summer our bathhouse burned down, and my father didn't get right down to building another, and a Japanese without a bathhouse . . . well, Mr. Oka offered us the use of his. So every night that summer we drove to the Okas for our bath, and we came in frequent contact with Mrs. Oka, and this is where I found the strangeness.

Mrs. Oka was small and spare. Her clothes hung on her like loose skin and when she walked, the skirt about her legs gave her a sort of webbed look. She was pretty in spite of the boniness and the dull calico and the barren look; I know now that she couldn't have been over thirty. Her eyes were large and a little vacant, although once I saw them fill with tears; the time I insisted we take the old Victrola over and we played our Japanese records for her. Some of the songs were sad, and I imagined the nostalgia she felt, but my mother said the tears were probably from yawning or from the smoke of her cigarettes. I thought my mother resented her for not being more hospitable; indeed, never a cup of tea appeared before us, and between them the conversation of women was totally absent: the rise and fall of gentle voices, the arched eyebrows, the croon of polite surprise. But more than this, Mrs. Oka was *different*.

Obviously she was shy, but some nights she disappeared altogether. She would see us drive into her yard and then lurch from sight. She was gone all evening. Where could she have hidden in that two-roomed house—where in that silent desert? Some nights she would wait out our visit with enormous forbearance, quietly pushing wisps of stray hair behind her ears and waving gnats away from her great moist eyes, and some nights she moved about with nervous agitation, her khaki canvas shoes slapping loudly as she walked. And sometimes there appeared to be welts and bruises on her usually smooth brown face, and she would sit solemnly, hands on lap, eyes large and intent on us. My mother hurried us home then: "Hurry, Masako, no need to wash well; hurry."

You see, being so poky, I was always last to bathe. I think the Okas bathed after we left because my mother often reminded me to keep the water clean. The routine was to lather outside the tub (there were buckets and pans and a small wooden stool), rinse off the soil and soap, and then soak in the tub of hot hot water and contemplate. Rivulets of perspiration would run down the scalp.

When my mother pushed me like this, I dispensed with ritual, rushed a bar of soap around me and splashed about a pan of water. So hastily toweled, my wet skin strapped the clothes to me, impeding my already clumsy progress. Outside, my mother would be murmuring her many apologies and my father, I knew, would be carrying my brother whose feet were already sandy. We would hurry home.

I thought Mrs. Oka might be insane and I asked my mother about it, but she shook her head and smiled with her mouth drawn down and said that Mrs. Oka loved her sake. This was unusual, yes, but there were other unusual women we knew. Mrs. Nagai was brought by her husband from a geisha house; Mrs. Tani was a militant Christian Scientist; Mrs. Abe, the midwife, was occult. My mother's statement explained much: sometimes Mrs. Oka was drunk and sometimes not. Her taste for liquor and cigarettes was a step in the realm of men; unusual for a Japanese wife, but at that time, in that place, and to me, Mrs. Oka loved her sake in the way my father loved his, in the way of Mr. Oka, and the way I loved my candy. That her psychology may have demanded this anesthetic, that she lived with something unendurable, did not occur to me. Nor did I perceive the violence of emotions that the purple welts indicated—or the masochism that permitted her to display these wounds to us.

In spite of her masculine habits, Mrs. Oka was never less than a woman. She was no lady in the area of social amenities; but the feminine in her was innate and never left her. Even in her disgrace, she was a small broken sparrow, slightly floppy, too slowly enunciating her few words, too carefully rolling her Bull Durham, cocking her small head and moistening the ocher tissue. Her aberration was a protest of the life assigned her; it was obstinate, but unobserved, alas, unheeded. "Strange" was the only concession we granted her.

Toward the end of summer, my mother said we couldn't continue bathing at the Okas'; when winter set in we'd all catch our death from the commuting and she'd always felt dreadful about our imposition on Mrs. Oka. So my father took the corrugated tin sheets he'd found on the highway and had been saving for some other use and built up our bathhouse again. Mr. Oka came to help.

While they raised the quivering tin walls, Mr. Oka began to talk. His voice was sharp and clear above the low thunder of the metal sheets.

He told my father he had been married in Japan previously to the present Mrs. Oka's older sister. He had a child by the marriage, Kiyoko, a girl. He had left the two to come to America intending to send for them soon, but shortly after his departure, his wife passed away from an obscure stomach ailment. At the time, the present Mrs. Oka was young and had foolishly become involved with a man of poor reputation. The family was anxious to part the lovers and conveniently arranged a marriage by proxy and sent him his dead wife's sister. Well that was all right, after all, they were kin, and it would be good for the child when she came to join them. But things didn't work out that way, year after year he postponed calling for his daughter, couldn't get the price of fare together, and the wife—ahhh, the wife, Mr. Oka's groan was lost in the rumble of his hammering.

He cleared his throat. The girl was now fourteen, he said, and begged to come to America to be with her own real family. Those relatives had forgotten the favor he'd done in accepting a slightly used bride, and now tormented his daughter for being forsaken. True, he'd not sent much money, but if they knew, if they only knew how it was here.

"Well," he sighed, "who could be blamed? It's only right she be with me anyway."

"That's right," my father said.

"Well, I sold the horse and some other things and managed to buy a third-class ticket on the Taiyo-Maru. Kiyoko will get here the first week of September." Mr. Oka glanced toward my father, but my father was peering into a bag of nails. "I'd be much obliged to you if your wife and little girl," he rolled his eyes toward me, "would take kindly to her. She'll be lonely."

Kiyoko-san came in September. I was surprised to see so very nearly a woman; short, robust, buxom: the female counterpart of her father; thyroid eyes and protruding teeth, straight black hair banded impudently into two bristly shucks, Cuban heels and white socks. Mr. Oka brought her proudly to us.

"Little Masako here," for the first time to my recollection, he touched me; he put his rough fat hand on the top of my head, "is very smart in school. She will help you with your school work, Kiyoko," he said.

I had so looked forward to Kiyoko-san's arrival. She would be my soul mate; in my mind I had conjured a girl of my own proportion: thin and tall, but with the refinement and beauty I didn't yet possess that would surely someday come to the fore. My disappointment was keen and apparent. Kiyoko-san stepped forward shyly, then retreated with a short bow and small giggle, her fingers pressed to her mouth.

My mother took her away. They talked for a long time—about Japan, about enrollment in American school, the clothes Kiyoko-san would need, and where to look for the best values. As I watched them, it occurred to me that I had been deceived: this was not a child, this was a woman. The smile pressed behind her fingers, the way of her nod, so brief, like my mother when father scolded her: the face was inscrutable, but something—maybe spirit—shrank visibly, like a piece of silk in water. I was disappointed; Kiyoko-san's soul was barricaded in her unenchanting appearance and the smile she fenced behind her fingers.

She started school from third grade, one below me, and as it turned out, she quickly passed me by. There wasn't much I could help her with except to drill her on pronunciation—the "L" and "R" sounds. Every morning walking to our rural school: land, leg, library, loan, lot; every afternoon returning home: ran, rabbit, rim, rinse, roll. That was the extent of our communication; friendly but uninteresting.

One particularly cold November night—the wind outside was icy; I was sitting on my bed, my brother's and mine, oiling the cracks in my chapped hands by lamplight—someone rapped urgently at our door. It was Kiyoko-san; she was hysterical, she wore no wrap, her teeth were chattering, and except for the thin straw zori, her feet were bare. My mother led her to the kitchen, started a pot of tea, and gestured to my brother and me to retire. I lay very still but because of my brother's restless tossing and my father's snoring, was unable to hear much. I was aware, though, that drunken and savage brawling had brought Kiyoko-san to us. Presently they came to the bedroom. I feigned sleep. My mother gave Kiyoko-san a gown and pushed me over to make room for her. My mother spoke firmly: "Tomorrow you will return to them; you must not leave them again. They are your people." I could almost feel Kiyoko-san's short nod.

All night long I lay cramped and still, afraid to intrude into her hulking back. Two or three times her icy feet jabbed into mine and quickly retreated. In the morning I found my mother's gown neatly folded on the spare pillow. Kiyoko-san's place in bed was cold.

She never came to weep at our house again but I know she cried: her eyes were often swollen and red. She stopped much of her giggling and routinely pressed her fingers to her mouth. Our daily pronunciation drill petered off from lack of interest. She walked silently with her shoulders hunched, grasping her books with both arms, and when I spoke to her in my halting Japanese, she absently corrected my prepositions.

Spring comes early in the Valley; in February the skies are clear though the air is still cold. By March, winds are vigorous and warm and wild flowers dot the desert floor, cockleburs are green and not yet tenacious, the sand is crusty underfoot, everywhere there is a smell of things growing and the first tomatoes are showing green and bald.

As the weather changed, Kiyoko-san became noticeably more cheerful. Mr. Oka who hated so to drive could often be seen steering his dusty old Ford over the road that passes our house, and Kiyoko-san sitting in front would sometimes wave gaily to us. Mrs. Oka was never with them. I thought of these trips as the westernizing of Kiyoko-san: with a permanent wave, her straight black hair became tangles of tiny frantic curls; between her textbooks she carried copies of *Modern Screen* and *Photoplay*, her clothes were gay with print and piping, and she bought a pair of brown suede shoes with alligator trim. I can see her now picking her way gingerly over the deceptive white peaks of alkaline crust.

At first my mother watched their coming and going with vicarious pleasure. "Probably off to a picture show; the stores are all closed at this hour," she might say. Later her eyes would get distant and she would muse, "They've left her home again; Mrs. Oka is alone again, the poor woman."

Now when Kiyoko-san passed by or came in with me on her way home, my mother would ask about Mrs. Oka—how is she, how does she occupy herself these rainy days, or these windy or warm or cool days. Often the answers were polite: "Thank you, we are fine," but sometimes Kiyoko-san's upper lip would pull over her teeth, and her voice would become very soft and she would say, "Drink, always drinking and fighting." And those times my mother would invariably say, "Endure, soon you will be marrying and going away."

Once a young truck driver delivered crates at the Oka farm and he dropped back to our place to tell my father that Mrs. Oka had lurched behind his truck while he was backing up, and very nearly let him kill her. Only the daughter pulling her away saved her, he said. Thoroughly unnerved, he stopped by to rest himself and talk about it. Never, never, he said in wide-eyed wonder, had he seen a drunken Japanese woman. My father nodded gravely, "Yes, it's unusual," he said and drummed his knee with his fingers.

Evenings were longer now, and when my mother's migraines drove me from the house in unbearable self-pity, I would take walks in the desert. One night with the warm wind against me, the dune primrose and yellow poppies closed and fluttering, the greasewood swaying in languid orbit, I lay on the white sand beneath a shrub and tried to disappear.

A voice sweet and clear cut through the half-dark of the evening:

> Red lips press against a glass
> Drink the purple wine
>   And the soul shall dance

Mrs. Oka appeared to be gathering flowers. Bending, plucking, standing, searching, she added to a small bouquet she clasped. She held them away; looked at them slyly, lids lowered, demure, then in a sudden and sinuous movement, she broke into a stately dance. She stopped, gathered more flowers, and breathed deeply into them. Tossing her head, she laughed—softly, beautifully, from her dark throat. The picture of her imagined grandeur was lost to me, but the delusion that transformed the bouquet of tattered petals and sandy leaves, and the aloneness of a desert twilight into a fantasy that brought such joy and abandon made me stir with discomfort. The sound broke Mrs. Oka's dance. Her eyes grew large and her neck tense—like a cat on the prowl. She spied me in the bushes. A peculiar chill ran through me. Then abruptly and with childlike delight, she scattered the flowers around her and walked away singing:

Falling, falling, petals on a wind . . .

That was the last time I saw Mrs. Oka. She died before the spring harvest. It was pneumonia. I didn't attend the funeral, but my mother said it was sad. Mrs. Oka looked peaceful, and the minister expressed the irony of the long separation of Mother and Child and the short-lived reunion; hardly a year together, she said. We went to help Kiyoko-san address and stamp those black-bordered acknowledgments.

When harvest was over, Mr. Oka and Kiyoko-san moved out of the Valley. We never heard from them or saw them again and I suppose in a large city, Mr. Oka found some sort of work, perhaps as a janitor or a dishwasher and Kiyoko-san grew up and found someone to marry.

[1974]

Leslie Marmon Silko
(1948–present)

Lullaby

Leslie Marmon Silko was raised on tales told by her great-grand-mother and great-aunts—ranging from Coyote's misadventures to accounts of Apache and Navajo raids on the Pueblo. Such stories became the basis of Silko's sense of identity: They "incorporate you in them. There have to be stories. It's stories that make this a community."

Of Laguna Pueblo, Mexican, and white ancestry, Silko was educated at the Bureau of Indian Affairs schools on the Laguna Pueblo Reservation and at the University of New Mexico. After initially attending law school, she left to do graduate work in English and pursue a writing career.

Native American lives and rituals provide the basis for Silko's fiction. In "Lullaby" she describes the effects of forcing children to choose between tribal traditions and the material, sterile, urban society that is so antithetical to their closely knit culture. But Silko never depicts Indians as morally superior to whites; instead, she implies that both groups positively influence Indian rituals since growth and change "keep ceremonies strong." Overall, Silko's fiction honors the Native American woman who holds her people together by translating song and story across generations.

Silko has taught at Navajo Community College, Many Farms, and the University of New Mexico. The recipient of a MacArthur Foundation fellowship, she is currently writing film scripts.

The sun had gone down but the snow in the wind gave off its own light. It came in thick tufts like new wool—washed before the weaver spins it. Ayah reached out for it like her own babies had, and she smiled when she remembered how she had laughed at them. She was an old woman now, and her life had become memories. She sat down with her back against the wide cottonwood tree, feeling the rough bark on her back bones; she faced east and listened to the wind and snow sing in a high-pitched Yeibechei song. Out of the wind she felt warmer, and she could watch the wide fluffy snow fill in her tracks, steadily, until the direction she had come from was gone. By the light of the snow she could see the dark outline of the big arroyo a few feet away. She was sitting on the edge of Cebolleta Creek, where in the springtime the thin cows would graze on grass already chewed flat to the ground. In the wide deep creek bed where only a trickle of water flowed in the summer, the skinny cows would wander, looking for new grass along winding paths splashed with manure.

Ayah pulled the old Army blanket over her head like a shawl. Jimmie's blanket—the one he had sent to her. That was a long time ago and the green wool was faded, and it was unraveling on the edges. She did not want to think about Jimmie. So she thought about the weaving and the way her mother had done it. On the tall wooden loom set into the sand under a tamarack tree for shade. She could see it clearly. She had been only a little girl when her grandma gave her the wooden combs to pull the twigs and burrs from the raw, freshly washed wool. And while she combed the wool, her grandma sat beside her, spinning a silvery strand of yarn around the smooth cedar spindle. Her mother worked at the loom with yarns dyed bright yellow and red and gold. She watched them dye the yarn in boiling black pots full of beeweed petals, juniper berries, and sage. The blankets her mother made were soft and woven so tight that rain rolled off them like birds' feathers. Ayah remembered sleeping warm on cold windy nights, wrapped in her mother's blankets on the hogan's sandy floor.

The snow drifted now, with the northwest wind hurling it in gusts. It drifted up around her black overshoes—old ones with little metal buckles. She smiled at the snow which was trying to cover her little by little. She could remember when they had no black rubber overshoes; only the high buckskin leggings that they wrapped over their elkhide moccasins. If the snow was dry or frozen, a person could walk all day and not get wet; and in the evenings the beams of the ceiling would hang with lengths of pale buckskin leggings, drying out slowly.

She felt peaceful remembering. She didn't feel cold any more. Jimmie's blanket seemed warmer than it had ever been. And she could remember the morning he was born. She could remember whispering to her mother, who was sleeping on the other side of the hogan, to tell her it was time now. She did not want to wake the others. The second time she called to her, her mother stood up and pulled on her shoes; she knew. They walked to the old stone hogan together, Ayah walking a step behind her mother. She waited alone, learning the rhythms of the pains while her mother went to call the old woman to help them. The morning was already warm even before dawn and Ayah smelled the bee flowers blooming and the young willow growing at the springs. She could remember that so clearly, but his birth merged into the births of the other children and to her it became all the same birth. They named him for the summer morning and in English they called him Jimmie.

It wasn't like Jimmie died. He just never came back, and one day a dark blue sedan with white writing on its doors pulled up in front of the box-car shack where the rancher let the Indians live. A man in a khaki uniform trimmed in gold gave them a yellow piece of paper and told them that Jimmie was dead. He said the Army would try to get the body back and then it would be shipped to them; but it wasn't likely because the helicopter had burned after it crashed. All of this was told to Chato because he could understand English. She stood inside the doorway holding the baby while Chato listened. Chato spoke English like a white man and he spoke Spanish too. He was taller than the white man and he stood straighter too. Chato didn't explain why; he just told the military man they could keep the body if they found it. The white man looked bewildered; he nodded his head and he left. Then Chato looked at her and shook his head, and then he told her, "Jimmie isn't coming home anymore," and when he spoke, he used the words to speak of the dead. She didn't cry then, but she hurt inside with anger. And she mourned him as the years passed, when a horse fell with Chato and broke his leg, and the white rancher told them he wouldn't pay Chato until he could work again. She mourned Jimmie because he would have worked for his father then; he would have saddled the big bay horse and ridden the fence lines each day, with wire cutters and heavy gloves, fixing the breaks in the barbed wire and putting the stray cattle back inside again.

She mourned him after the white doctors came to take Danny and Ella away. She was at the shack alone that day they came. It was back in the days before they hired Navajo women to go with them as interpreters. She recognized one of the doctors. She had seen him at the children's clinic at Cañoncito about a month ago. They were wearing khaki uniforms and they waved papers at her and a black ball-point pen, trying to make her understand their English words. She was frightened by the way they looked at the children, like the lizard watches the fly. Danny was swinging on the tire swing on the elm tree behind the rancher's house, and Ella was toddling around the front door, dragging the broomstick horse Chato made for her. Ayah could see they wanted her to sign the papers, and Chato had taught her to sign her name. It was something she was proud of. She only wanted them to go, and to take their eyes away from her children.

She took the pen from the man without looking at his face and she signed the papers in three different places he pointed to. She stared at the ground by their feet and waited for them to leave. But they stood there and began to point and gesture at the children. Danny stopped swinging. Ayah could see his fear. She moved suddenly and grabbed Ella into her arms; the child squirmed, trying to get back to her toys. Ayah ran with the baby toward Danny; she screamed for him to run and then she grabbed him around his chest and carried him too. She ran south into the foothills of juniper trees and black lava rock. Behind her she heard the doctors running, but they had been taken by surprise, and as the hills became steeper and the cholla cactus were thicker, they stopped. When she reached the top of the hill, she stopped to listen in case they were circling around her. But in a few minutes she heard a car engine start and they drove away. The children had been too surprised to cry while she ran with them. Danny was shaking and Ella's little fingers were gripping Ayah's blouse.

She stayed up in the hills for the rest of the day, sitting on a black lava boulder in the sunshine where she could see for miles all around her. The sky was light blue and cloudless, and it was warm for late April. The sun warmth relaxed her and took the fear and anger away. She lay back on the rock and watched the sky. It seemed to her that she could walk into the sky, stepping through the clouds endlessly. Danny played with little pebbles and stones, pretending they were birds eggs and then little rabbits. Ella sat at her feet and dropped fistfuls of dirt into the breeze, watching the dust and particles of sand intently. Ayah watched a hawk soar high above them, dark wings gliding; hunting or only watching, she did not know. The hawk was patient and he circled all afternoon before he disappeared around the high volcanic peak the Mexicans called Guadalupe.

Late in the afternoon, Ayah looked down at the gray boxcar shack with the paint all peeled from the wood; the stove pipe on the roof was rusted and crooked. The fire she had built that morning in the oil drum stove had burned out. Ella was asleep in her lap now and Danny sat close to her, complaining that he was hungry; he asked when they would go to the house. "We will stay up here until your father comes," she told him, "because those white men were chasing us." The boy remembered then and he nodded at her silently.

If Jimmie had been there he could have read those papers and explained to her what they said. Ayah would have known then, never to sign them. The doctors came back the next day and they brought a BIA policeman with them. They told Chato they had her signature and that was all they needed. Except for the kids. She listened to Chato sullenly; she hated him when he told her it was the old woman who died in the winter, spitting blood; it was her old grandma who had given the children this disease. "They don't spit blood," she said coldly. "The whites lie." She held Ella and Danny close to her, ready to run to the hills again. "I want a medicine man first," she said to Chato, not looking at him. He shook his head. "It's too late now. The policeman is with them. You signed the paper." His voice was gentle.

It was worse than if they had died: to lose the children and to know that somewhere, in a place called Colorado, in a place full of sick and dying strangers, her children were without her. There had been babies that died soon after they were born, and one that died before he could walk. She had carried them herself, up to the boulders and great pieces of the cliff that long ago crashed down from Long Mesa; she laid them in the crevices of sandstone and buried them in fine brown sand with round quartz pebbles that washed down the hills in the rain. She had endured it because they had been with her. But she could not bear this pain. She did not sleep for a long time after they took her children. She stayed on the hill where they had fled the first time, and she slept rolled up in the blanket Jimmie had sent her. She carried the pain in her belly and it was fed by everything she saw: the blue sky of their last day together and the dust and pebbles they played with; the swing in the elm tree and broomstick horse choked life from her. The pain filled her stomach and there was no room for food or for her lungs to fill with air. The air and the food would have been theirs.

She hated Chato, not because he let the policeman and doctors put the screaming children in the government car, but because he had taught her to sign her name. Because it was like the old ones always told her about learning their language or any of their ways: it endangered you. She slept alone on the hill until the middle of November when the first snows came. Then she made a bed for herself where the children had slept. She did not lie down beside Chato again until many years later, when he was sick and shivering and only her body could keep him warm. The illness came after the white rancher told Chato he was too old to work for him anymore, and Chato and his old woman should be out of the shack by the next afternoon because the rancher had hired new people to work there. That had satisfied her. To see how the white man repaid Chato's years of loyalty and work. All of Chato's fine-sounding English talk didn't change things.

It snowed steadily and the luminous light from the snow gradually diminished into the darkness. Somewhere in Cebolleta a dog barked and other village dogs joined with it. Ayah looked in the direction she had come, from the bar where Chato was buying the wine. Sometimes he told her to go on ahead and wait; and then he never came. And when she finally went back looking for him, she would find him passed out at the bottom of the wooden steps to Azzie's Bar. All the wine would be gone and most of the money too, from the pale blue check that came to them once a month in a government envelope. It was then that she would look at his face and his hands, scarred by ropes and the barbed wire of all those years, and she would think, this man is a stranger; for forty years she had smiled at him and cooked his food, but he remained a stranger. She stood up again, with the snow almost to her knees and she walked back to find Chato.

It was hard to walk in the deep snow and she felt the air burn in her lungs. She stopped a short distance from the bar to rest and readjust the blanket. But this time he wasn't waiting for her on the bottom step with his old Stetson hat pulled down and his shoulders hunched up in his long wool overcoat.

She was careful not to slip on the wooden steps. When she pushed the door open, warm air and cigarette smoke hit her face. She

looked around slowly and deliberately, in every corner, in every dark
place that the old man might find to sleep. The bar owner didn't like
Indians in there, especially Navajos, but he let Chato come in because
he could talk Spanish like he was one of them. The men at the bar
stared at her, and the bartender saw that she left the door open wide.
Snowflakes were flying inside like moths and melting into a puddle on
the oiled wood floor. He motioned to her to close the door, but she
did not see him. She held herself straight and walked across the room
slowly, searching the room with every step. The snow in her hair
melted and she could feel it on her forehead. At the far corner of the
room, she saw red flames at the mica window of the old stove door;
she looked behind the stove just to make sure. The bar got quiet
except for the Spanish polka music playing on the jukebox. She stood
by the stove and shook the snow from her blanket and held it near
the stove to dry. The wet wool smell reminded her of new-born goats
in early March, brought inside to warm near the fire. She felt calm.

In past years they would have told her to get out. But her hair was
white now and her face was wrinkled. They looked at her like she was
a spider crawling slowly across the room. They were afraid; she could
feel the fear. She looked at their faces steadily. They reminded her of
the first time the white people brought her children back to her that
winter. Danny had been shy and hid behind the thin white woman
who brought them. And the baby had not known her until Ayah took
her into her arms, and then Ella had nuzzled close to her as she had
when she was nursing. The blonde woman was nervous and kept
looking at a dainty gold watch on her wrist. She sat on the bench near
the small window and watched the dark snow clouds gather around
the mountains; she was worrying about the unpaved road. She was
frightened by what she saw inside too: the strips of venison drying on
a rope across the ceiling and the children jabbering excitedly in a
language she did not know. So they stayed for only a few hours. Ayah
watched the government car disappear down the road and she knew
they were already being weaned from these lava hills and from this sky.
The last time they came was in early June, and Ella stared at her the
way the men in the bar were now staring. Ayah did not try to pick her
up; she smiled at her instead and spoke cheerfully to Danny. When he
tried to answer her, he could not seem to remember and he spoke
English words with the Navajo. But he gave her a scrap of paper that
he had found somewhere and carried in his pocket; it was folded in
half, and he shyly looked up at her and said it was a bird. She asked
Chato if they were home for good this time. He spoke to the white

woman and she shook her head. "How much longer?" he asked, and she said she didn't know; but Chato saw how she stared at the boxcar shack. Ayah turned away then. She did not say good-bye.

She felt satisfied that the men in the bar feared her. Maybe it was her face and the way she held her mouth with teeth clenched tight, like there was nothing anyone could do to her now. She walked north down the road, searching for the old man. She did this because she had the blanket, and there would be no place for him except with her and the blanket in the old adobe barn near the arroyo. They always slept there when they came to Cebolleta. If the money and the wine were gone, she would be relieved because then they could go home again; back to the old hogan with a dirt roof and rock walls where she herself had been born. And the next day the old man could go back to the few sheep they still had, to follow along behind them, guiding them, into dry sandy arroyos where sparse grass grew. She knew he did not like walking behind old ewes when for so many years he rode big quarter horses and worked with cattle. But she wasn't sorry for him; he should have known all along what would happen.

There had not been enough rain for their garden in five years; and that was when Chato finally hitched a ride into the town and brought back brown boxes of rice and sugar and big tin cans of welfare peaches. After that, at the first of the month they went to Cebolleta to ask the postmaster for the check; and then Chato would go to the bar and cash it. They did this as they planted the garden every May, not because anything would survive the summer dust, but because it was time to do this. The journey passed the days that smelled silent and dry like the caves above the canyon with yellow painted buffaloes on their walls.

He was walking along the pavement when she found him. He did not stop or turn around when he heard her behind him. She walked beside him and she noticed how slowly he moved now. He smelled strong of woodsmoke and urine. Lately he had been forgetting. Sometimes he called her by his sister's name and she had been gone for a long time. Once she had found him wandering on the road to the white man's ranch, and she asked him why he was going that way; he laughed at her and said, "You know they can't run that ranch without me," and he walked on determined, limping on the leg that had been crushed many years before. Now he looked at her curiously, as if for the first time, but he kept shuffling along, moving slowly along the side of the highway. His gray hair had grown long and spread out on the shoulders of the long overcoat. He wore the old felt hat pulled down over his ears. His boots were worn out at the toes and he had stuffed pieces of an old red shirt in the holes. The rags made his feet look like little animals up to their ears in snow. She laughed at his feet; the snow muffled the sound of her laugh. He stopped and looked at her again. The wind had quit blowing and the snow was falling straight down; the southeast sky was beginning to clear and Ayah could see a star.

"Let's rest awhile," she said to him. They walked away from the road and up the slope to the giant boulders that had tumbled down from the red sandrock mesa throughout the centuries of rainstorms and earth tremors. In a place where the boulders shut out the wind, they sat down with their backs against the rock. She offered half of the blanket to him and they sat wrapped together.

The storm passed swiftly. The clouds moved east. They were massive and full, crowding together across the sky. She watched them with the feeling of horses—steely blue-gray horses startled across the sky. The powerful haunches pushed into the distances and the tail hairs streamed white mist behind them. The sky cleared. Ayah saw that there was nothing between her and the stars. The light was crystalline. There was no shimmer, no distortion through earth haze. She breathed the clarity of the night sky; she smelled the purity of the half moon and the stars. He was lying on his side with his knees pulled up near his belly for warmth. His eyes were closed now, and in the light from the stars and the moon, he looked young again.

She could see it descend out of the night sky: an icy stillness from the edge of the thin moon. She recognized the freezing. It came gradually, sinking snowflake by snowflake until the crust was heavy and deep. It had the strength of the stars in Orion, and its journey was endless. Ayah knew that with the wine he would sleep. He would not feel it. She tucked the blanket around him, remembering how it was when Ella had been with her; and she felt the rush so big inside her heart for the babies. And she sang the only song she knew to sing for babies. She could not remember if she had ever sung it to her children, but she knew that her grandmother had sung it and her mother had sung it:

> The earth is your mother,
>   she holds you.
> The sky is your father,
>   he protects you.

Sleep,
sleep.
Rainbow is your sister,
          she loves you.
The winds are your brothers,
          they sing to you.
Sleep,
sleep.
We are together always
We are together always
There never was a time
when this
was not so.

[1974]

Anita Desai
(1937–present)

A Devoted Son

Born in North India, Anita Desai studied and wrote in English at an early age. She began publishing stories before marrying in 1958 and having four children. She has published three popular children's books. Her novels include *Cry, the Peacock* (1963), *Bye-bye, Blackbird* (1971), *Clear Light of Day* (1982), and *Baumgartner's Bombay* (1988). Her most widely acclaimed short stories are compiled in *Games at Twilight* (1978), which includes "A Devoted Son."

Desai's heroines struggle silently to retain a sense of dignity, integrity, and honor; her themes are Indian, feminist, and middle-class, laden with psychological implications. Desai encourages Indian women to break their traditionally imposed silence and to become outspoken critics of their culture.

When the results appeared in the morning papers, Rakesh scanned them, barefoot and in his pyjamas, at the garden gate, then went up the steps to the verandah where his father sat sipping his morning tea and bowed down to touch his feet.

"A first division, son?" his father asked, beaming, reaching for the papers.

"At the top of the list, papa," Rakesh murmured, as if awed. "First in the country."

Bedlam broke loose then. The family whooped and danced. The whole day long visitors streamed into the small yellow house at the

196

end of the road, to congratulate the parents of this *Wunderkind,* to slap Rakesh on the back and fill the house and garden with the sounds and colours of a festival. There were garlands and *halwa,* party clothes and gifts (enough fountain pens to last years, even a watch or two), nerves and temper and joy, all in a multicoloured whirl of pride and great shining vistas newly opened: Rakesh was the first son in the family to receive an education, so much had been sacrificed in order to send him to school and then to medical college, and at last the fruits of their sacrifice had arrived, golden and glorious.

To everyone who came to him to say, "*Mubarak,* Varmaji, your son has brought you glory," the father said, "Yes, and do you know what is the first thing he did when he saw the results this morning? He came and touched my feet. He bowed down and touched my feet." This moved many of the women in the crowd so much that they were seen to raise the ends of their saris and dab at their tears while the men reached out for the betel-leaves and sweetmeats that were offered around on trays and shook their heads in wonder and approval of such exemplary filial behaviour. "One does not often see such behaviour in sons any more," they all agreed, a little enviously perhaps. Leaving the house, some of the women said, sniffing, "At least on such an occasion they might have served pure *ghee* sweets," and some of the men said, "Don't you think old Varma was giving himself airs? He needn't think we don't remember that he comes from the vegetable market himself, his father used to sell vegetables, and he has never seen the inside of a school." But there was more envy than rancour in their voices and it was, of course, inevitable—not every son in that shabby little colony at the edge of the city was destined to shine as Rakesh shone, and who knew that better than the parents themselves?

And that was only the beginning, the first step in a great, sweeping ascent to the radiant heights of fame and fortune. The thesis he wrote for his M.D. brought Rakesh still greater glory, if only in select medical circles. He won a scholarship. He went to the USA (that was what his father learnt to call it and taught the whole family to say—not America, which was what the ignorant neighbours called it, but, with a grand familiarity, "the USA") where he pursued his career in the most prestigious of all hospitals and won encomiums from his American colleagues which were relayed to his admiring and glowing family. What was more, he came *back,* he actually returned to that small yellow house in the once-new but increasingly shabby colony, right at the end of the road where the rubbish vans tripped out their stinking contents for pigs to nose in and rag-pickers to build their shacks on, all steaming and smoking just outside the neat wire fences and well-tended gardens. To this Rakesh returned and the first thing he did on entering the house was to slip out of the embraces of his sisters and brothers and bow down and touch his father's feet.

As for his mother, she gloated chiefly over the strange fact that he had not married in America, had not brought home a foreign wife as all her neighbours had warned her he would, for wasn't that what all Indian boys went abroad for? Instead he agreed, almost without argument, to marry a girl she had picked out for him in her own village, the daughter of a childhood friend, a plump and uneducated girl, it was true, but so old-fashioned, so placid, so complaisant that she slipped into the household and settled in like a charm, seemingly too lazy and too good-natured to even try and make Rakesh leave home and set up independently, as any other girl might have done. What was more, she was pretty—really pretty, in a plump, pudding way that only gave way to fat—soft, spreading fat, like warm wax—after the birth of their first baby, a son, and then what did it matter?

For some years Rakesh worked in the city hospital, quickly rising to the top of the administrative organization, and was made a director before he left to set up his own clinic. He took his parents in his car—a new, sky-blue Ambassador with a rear window full of stickers and charms revolving on strings—to see the clinic when it was built, and the large sign-board over the door on which his name was printed in letters of red, with a row of degrees and qualifications to follow it like so many little black slaves of the regent. Thereafter his fame seemed to grow just a little dimmer—or maybe it was only that everyone in town had grown accustomed to it at last—but it was also the beginning of his fortune for he now became known not only as the best but also the richest doctor in town.

However, all this was not accomplished in the wink of an eye. Naturally not. It was the achievement of a lifetime and it took up Rakesh's whole life. At the time he set up his clinic his father had grown into an old man and retired from his post at the kerosene dealer's depot at which he had worked for forty years, and his mother died soon after, giving up the ghost with a sigh that sounded positively happy, for it was her own son who ministered to her in her last illness and who sat pressing her feet at the last moment—such a son as few women had borne.

For it had to be admitted—and the most unsuccessful and most rancorous of neighbours eventually did so—that Rakesh was not only a devoted son and a miraculously good-natured man contrived somehow to obey his parents and humour his wife and show concern equally for his children and his patients, but there was actually a brain inside this beautifully polished and formed body of good manners and kind nature and, in between ministering to his family and playing host to many friends and coaxing them all into feeling happy and grateful and content, he had actually trained his hands as well and emerged an excellent doctor, a really fine surgeon. How one man—and a man born to illiterate parents, his father having worked for a kerosene dealer and his mother having spent her life in a kitchen—had achieved, combined and conducted such a medley of virtues, no one could fathom, but all acknowledged his talent and skill.

It was a strange fact, however, that talent and skill, if displayed for too long, cease to dazzle. It came to pass that the most admiring of all eyes eventually faded and no longer blinked at his glory. Having retired from work and having lost his wife, the old father very quickly went to pieces, as they say. He developed so many complaints and fell ill so frequently and with such mysterious diseases that even his son could no longer make out when it was something of significance and when it was merely a peevish whim. He sat huddled on his string bed most of the day and developed an exasperating habit of stretching out suddenly and lying absolutely still, allowing the whole family to fly around him in a flap, wailing and weeping, and then suddenly sitting up, stiff and gaunt, and spitting out a big gob of betel-juice as if to mock their behaviour.

He did this once too often: there had been a big party in the house, a birthday party for the youngest son, and the celebrations had to be suddenly hushed, covered up and hustled out of the way when the daughter-in-law discovered, or thought she discovered, that the old man, stretched out from end to end of his string bed, had lost his pulse; the party broke up, dissolved, even turned into a band of mourners, when the old man sat up and the distraught daughter-in-law received a gob of red spittle right on the hem of her new organza sari. After that no one much cared if he sat up cross-legged on his bed, hawking and spitting, or lay down flat and turned grey as a corpse. Except, of course, for that pearl amongst pearls, his son Rakesh.

It was Rakesh who brought him his morning tea, not in one of the china cups from which the rest of the family drank, but in the old man's favourite brass tumbler, and sat at the edge of his bed, comfortable and relaxed with the string of his pyjamas dangling out from under his fine lawn night-shirt, and discussed or, rather, read out the morning news to his father. It made no difference to him that his father made no response apart from spitting. It was Rakesh, too, who, on returning from the clinic in the evening, persuaded the old man to come out of his room, as bare and desolate as a cell, and take the evening air out in the garden, beautifully arranging the pillows and bolsters on the *divan* in the corner of the open verandah. On summer nights he saw to it that the servants carried out the old man's bed onto the lawn and himself helped his father down the steps and onto the bed, soothing him and settling him down for a night under the stars.

All this was very gratifying for the old man. What was not so gratifying was that he even undertook to supervise his father's diet. One day when the father was really sick, having ordered his daughter-in-law to make him a dish of *soojie halwa* and eaten it with a saucerful of cream, Rakesh marched into the room, not with his usual respectful step but with the confident and rather contemptuous stride of the famous doctor, and declared, "No more *halwa* for you, papa. We must be sensible, at your age. If you must have something sweet, Veena will cook you a little *kheer*, that's light, just a little rice and milk. But nothing fried, nothing rich. We can't have this happening again."

The old man who had been lying stretched out on his bed, weak and feeble after a day's illness, gave a start at the very sound, the tone of these words. He opened his eyes—rather, they fell open with shock—and he stared at his son with disbelief that darkened quickly to reproach. A son who actually refused his father the food he craved? No, it was unheard of, it was incredible. But Rakesh had turned his back to him and was cleaning up the litter of bottles and packets on the medicine shelf and did not notice while Veena slipped silently out of the room with a little smirk that only the old man saw, and hated.

Halwa was only the first item to be crossed off the old man's diet. One delicacy after the other went—everything fried to begin with, then everything sweet, and eventually everything, everything that the old man enjoyed. The meals that arrived for him on the shining stainless steel tray twice a day were frugal to say the least—dry bread, boiled lentils, boiled vegetables and, if there were a bit of chicken or fish, that was boiled too. If he called for another helping—in a cracked voice that quavered theatrically—Rakesh himself would come to the door, gaze at him sadly and shake his head, saying, "Now, papa, we must be careful, we can't risk another illness, you know," and although the daughter-in-law kept tactfully out of the way, the old man could just see her smirk sliding merrily through the air. He tried to bribe his grand-children into buying him sweets (and how he missed his wife now, that generous, indulgent and illiterate cook), whispering, "Here's fifty paise," as he stuffed the coins into a tight, hot fist. "Run down to the shop at the crossroads and buy me thirty paise worth of *jalebis*, and you can spend the remaining twenty paise on yourself. Eh? Understand? Will you do that?" He got away with it once or twice but then was found out, the conspirator was scolded by his father and smacked by his mother and Rakesh came storming into the room, almost tearing his hair as he shouted through compressed lips, "Now papa, are you trying to turn my little son into a liar? Quite apart from spoiling your own stomach, you are spoiling him as well—you are encouraging him to lie to his own parents. You should have heard the lies he told his mother when she saw him bringing back those *jalebis* wrapped up in filthy newspaper. I don't allow anyone in my house to buy sweets in the bazaar, papa, surely you know that. There's cholera in the city, typhoid, gastroenteritis—I see these cases daily in the hospital, how can I allow my own family to run such risks?" The old man sighed and lay down in the corpse position. But that worried no one any longer.

There was only one pleasure left in the old man now (his son's early morning visits and readings from the newspaper could no longer be called that) and those were visits from elderly neighbours. These were not frequent as his contemporaries were mostly as decrepit and helpless as he and few could walk the length of the road to visit him any more. Old Bhatia, next door, however, who was still spry enough to refuse, adamantly, to bathe in the tiled bathroom indoors and to insist on carrying out his brass mug and towel, in all seasons and usually at impossible hours, into the yard and bathe noisily under the garden tap, would look over the hedge to see if Varma were out on his verandah and would call to him and talk while he wrapped his *dhoti* about him and dried the sparse hair on his head, shivering with enjoyable exaggeration. Of course these conversations, bawled across the hedge by two rather deaf old men conscious of having their entire households overhearing them, were not very satisfactory but Bhatia occasionally came out of his yard, walked down the bit of road and came in at Varma's gate to collapse onto the stone plinth built under the temple tree. If Rakesh was at home he would help his father down the steps into the garden and arrange him on his night bed under the tree and leave the two old men to chew betel-leaves and discuss the ills of their individual bodies with combined passion.

"At least you have a doctor in the house to look after you," sighed Bhatia, having vividly described his martyrdom to piles.

"Look after me?" cried Varma, his voice cracking like an ancient clay jar. "He—he does not even give me enough to eat."

"What?" said Bhatia, the white hairs in his ears twitching. "Doesn't give you enough to eat? Your own son?"

"My own son. If I ask him for one more piece of bread, he says no, papa, I weighed out the *ata* myself and I can't allow you to have more than two hundred grams of cereal a day. He *weighs* the food he gives me, Bhatia—he has scales to weigh it on. That is what it has come to."

"Never," murmured Bhatia in disbelief. "Is it possible, even in this evil age, for a son to refuse his father food?"

"Let me tell you," Varma whispered eagerly. "Today the family was having fried fish—I could smell it. I called to my daughter-in-law to bring me a piece. She came to the door and said no. . . ."

"Said no?" It was Bhatia's voice that cracked. A *drongo* shot out of the tree and sped away. *"No?"*

"No, she said no, Rakesh has ordered her to give me nothing fried. No butter, he says, no oil. . . ."

"No butter? No oil? How does he expect his father to *live?*"

Old Varma nodded with melancholy triumph. "That is how he treats me—after I have brought him up, given him an education, made him a great doctor. Great doctor! This is the way great doctors treat their fathers, Bhatia," for the son's sterling personality and character now underwent a curious sea change. Outwardly all might be the same but the interpretation had altered: his masterly efficiency was nothing but cold heartlessness, his authority was only tyranny in disguise.

There was cold comfort in complaining to neighbours and, on such a miserable diet, Varma found himself slipping, weakening and soon becoming a genuinely sick man. Powders and pills and mixtures were not only brought in when dealing with a crisis like an upset stomach but became a regular part of his diet—became his diet, complained Varma, supplanting the natural foods he craved. There were pills to regulate his bowel movements, pills to bring down his blood pressure, pills to deal with his arthritis and, eventually, pills to keep his heart beating. In between there were panicky rushes to the hospital, some humiliating experiences with the stomach pump and

enema, which left him frightened and helpless. He cried easily,
shrivelling up on his bed, but if he complained of a pain or even a
vague, grey fear in the night, Rakesh would simply open another
bottle of pills and force him to take one. "I have my duty to you
papa," he said when his father begged to be let off.

"Let me be," Varma begged, turning his face away from the pills
on the outstretched hand. "Let me die. It would be better. I do not
want to live only to eat your medicines."

"Papa, be reasonable."

"I leave that to you," the father cried with sudden spirit. "Leave
me alone, let me die now, I cannot live like this."

"Lying all day on his pillows, fed every few hours by his
daughter-in-law's own hands, visited by every member of his family
daily—and then he says he does not want to live 'like this'," Rakesh
was heard to say, laughing, to someone outside the door.

"Deprived of food," screamed the old man on the bed, "his
wishes ignored, taunted by his daughter-in-law, laughed at by his
grand-children—*that* is how I live." But he was very old and weak
and all anyone heard was an incoherent croak, some expressive grunts
and cries of genuine pain. Only once, when old Bhatia had come to
see him and they sat together under the temple tree, they heard him
cry, "God is calling me—and they won't let me go."

The quantities of vitamins and tonics he was made to take were
not altogether useless. They kept him alive and even gave him a kind
of strength that made him hang on long after he ceased to wish to
hang on. It was as though he were straining at a rope, trying to break
it, and it would not break, it was still strong. He only hurt himself,
trying.

In the evening, that summer, the servants would come into his
cell, grip his bed, one at each end, and carry it out to the verandah,
there setting it down with a thump that jarred every tooth in his head.
In answer to his agonized complaints they said the doctor sahib had
told them he must take the evening air and the evening air they would
make him take—thump. Then Veena, that smiling, hypocritical
pudding in a rustling sari, would appear and pile up the pillows under
his head till he was propped up stiffly into a sitting position that made
his head swim and his back ache.

"Let me lie down," he begged. "I can't sit up any more."

"Try, papa, Rakesh said you can if you try," she said, and drifted
away to the other end of the verandah where her transistor radio

vibrated to the lovesick tunes from the cinema that she listened to all day.

So there he sat, like some stiff corpse, terrified, gazing out on the lawn where his grand-sons played cricket, in danger of getting one of their hard-spun balls in his eye, and at the gate that opened onto the dusty and rubbish-heaped lane but still bore, proudly, a newly touched-up signboard that bore his son's name and qualifications, his own name having vanished from the gate long ago.

At last the sky-blue Ambassador arrived, the cricket game broke up in haste, the car drove in smartly and the doctor, the great doctor, all in white, stepped out. Someone ran up to take his bag from him, others to escort him up the steps. "Will you have tea?" his wife called, turning down the transistor set, "Or a Coca-Cola? Shall I fry you some *samosas*?" But he did not reply or even glance in her direction. Ever a devoted son, he went first to the corner where his father sat gazing, stricken, at some undefined spot in the dusty yellow air that swam before him. He did not turn his head to look at his son. But he stopped gobbling air with his uncontrolled lips and set his jaw as hard as a sick and very old man could set it.

"Papa," his son said, tenderly, sitting down on the edge of the bed and reaching out to press his feet.

Old Varma tucked his feet under him, out of the way, and continued to gaze stubbornly into the yellow air of the summer evening.

"Papa, I'm home."

Varma's hand jerked suddenly, in a sharp, derisive movement, but he did not speak.

"How are you feeling, papa?"

Then Varma turned and looked at his son. His face was so out of control, and all in pieces, that the multitude of expressions that crossed it could not make up a whole and convey to the famous man exactly what his father thought of him, his skill, his art.

"I'm dying," he croaked. "Let me die, I tell you."

"Papa, you're joking," his son smiled at him, lovingly. "I've brought you a new tonic to make you feel better. You must take it, it will make you feel stronger again. Here it is. Promise me you will take it regularly, papa."

Varma's mouth worked as hard as though he still had a gob of betel in it (his supply of betel had been cut off years ago). Then he spat out some words, as sharp and bitter as poison, into his son's face. "Keep your tonic—I want none—I want none—I won't take any more of—of your medicines. None. Never," and he swept the bottle out of his son's hand with a wave of his own, suddenly grand, suddenly effective.

His son jumped, for the bottle was smashed and thick brown syrup had splashed up, staining his white trousers. His wife let out a cry and came running. All around the old man was hubbub once again, noise, attention.

He gave one push to the pillows at his back and dislodged them so he could sink down on his back, quite flat again. He closed his eyes and pointed his chin at the ceiling, like some dire prophet, groaning, "God is calling me—now let me go."

[1978]

Angela Carter
(1940–1992)

The Company of Wolves

Born in London, Angela Carter worked as a journalist before taking her degree in medieval literature at the University of Bristol. She then taught creative writing at Sheffield and Brown universities. For two years she lived in Japan, whose culture she described as a "concealed matriarchy" behind a "prostitute society." Carter's experience in Japan inspired her to satirize western patriarchy and capitalism.

Carter's fiction includes *The Magic Toyshop* (1967), *Heroes and Villains* (1969), *The Infernal Desire Machines of Doctor Hoffman* (1972), and *Nights at the Circus* (1984). "The Company of Wolves" appears in *The Bloody Chamber* (1979), a collection of adult fairy tales and short stories. Its theme is the conflict between the artificial and the animal aspects of nature, specifically the struggle between societal repression and women's healthy animal desires. Carter forces us to examine established roles and stereotypes. Her work, which remains counter to the conventional realism of British fiction, is difficult to place in a literary genre.

One beast and only one howls in the woods by night.

The wolf is carnivore incarnate and he's as cunning as he is ferocious; once he's had a taste of flesh then nothing else will do.

At night, the eyes of wolves shine like candle flames, yellowish, reddish, but that is because the pupils of their eyes fatten on darkness and catch the light from your lantern to flash it back to you—red for danger; if a wolf's eyes reflect only moonlight, then they gleam a cold and unnatural green, a mineral, a piercing colour. If the benighted traveller spies those luminous, terrible sequins stitched suddenly on the black thickets, then he knows he must run, if fear has not struck him stock-still.

But those eyes are all you will be able to glimpse of the forest assassins as they cluster invisibly round your smell of meat as you go through the wood unwisely late. They will be like shadows, they will be like wraiths, grey members of a congregation of nightmare; hark! his long, wavering howl . . . an aria of fear made audible.

The wolfsong is the sound of the rending you will suffer, in itself a murdering.

It is winter and cold weather. In this region of mountain and forest, there is now nothing for the wolves to eat. Goats and sheep are locked up in the byre, the deer departed for the remaining pasturage on the southern slopes—wolves grow lean and famished. There is so little flesh on them that you could count the starveling ribs through their pelts, if they gave you time before they pounced. Those slavering jaws; the lolling tongue; the rime of saliva on the grizzled chops—of all the teeming perils of the night and the forest, ghosts, hobgoblins, ogres that grill babies upon gridirons, witches that fatten their captives in cages for cannibal tables, the wolf is worst for he cannot listen to reason.

You are always in danger in the forest, where no people are. Step between the portals of the great pines where the shaggy branches tangle about you, trapping the unwary traveller in nets as if the vegetation itself were in a plot with the wolves who live there, as though the wicked trees go fishing on behalf of their friends—step between the gateposts of the forest with the greatest trepidation and infinite precautions, for if you stray from the path for one instant, the wolves will eat you. They are grey as famine, they are as unkind as plague.

The grave-eyed children of the sparse villages always carry knives with them when they go out to tend the little flocks of goats that provide the homesteads with acrid milk and rank, maggoty cheeses. Their knives are half as big as they are, the blades are sharpened daily.

But the wolves have ways of arriving at your own hearthside. We try and try but sometimes we cannot keep them out. There is no winter's night the cottager does not fear to see a lean, grey, famished snout questing under the door, and there was a woman once bitten in her own kitchen as she was straining the macaroni.

Fear and flee the wolf; for, worst of all, the wolf may be more than he seems.

There was a hunter once, near here, that trapped a wolf in a pit. This wolf had massacred the sheep and goats; eaten up a mad old man who used to live by himself in a hut halfway up the mountain and sing to Jesus all day; pounced on a girl looking after the sheep, but she made such a commotion that men came with rifles and scared him away and tried to track him into the forest but he was cunning and easily gave them the slip. So this hunter dug a pit and put a duck in it, for bait, all alive-oh; and he covered the pit with straw smeared with wolf dung. Quack, quack! went the duck and a wolf came slinking out of the forest, a big one, a heavy one, he weighed as much as a grown man and the straw gave way beneath him—into the pit he tumbled. The hunter jumped down after him, slit his throat, cut off all his paws for a trophy.

And then no wolf at all lay in front of the hunter but the bloody trunk of a man, headless, footless, dying, dead.

A witch from up the valley once turned an entire wedding party into wolves because the groom had settled on another girl. She used to order them to visit her, at night, from spite, and they would sit and howl around her cottage for her, serenading her with their misery.

Not so very long ago, a young woman in our village married a man who vanished clean away on her wedding night. The bed was made with new sheets and the bride lay down in it; the groom said, he was going out to relieve himself, insisted on it, for the sake of decency, and she drew the coverlet up to her chin and she lay there. And she waited and she waited and then she waited again—surely he's been gone a long time? Until she jumps up in bed and shrieks to hear a howling, coming on the wind from the forest.

That long-drawn, wavering howl has, for all its fearful resonance, some inherent sadness in it, as if the beasts would love to be less beastly if only they knew how and never cease to mourn their own condition. There is a vast melancholy in the canticles of the wolves, melancholy infinite as the forest, endless as these long nights of winter and yet that ghastly sadness, that mourning for their own, ir-remediable appetites, can never move the heart for not one phrase in it hints at the possibility of redemption; grace could not come to the wolf from its own despair, only through some external mediator, so that, sometimes, the beast will look as if he half welcomes the knife that despatches him.

The young woman's brothers searched the outhouses and the

haystacks but never found any remains so the sensible girl dried her eyes and found herself another husband not too shy to piss into a pot who spent the nights indoors. She gave him a pair of bonny babies and all went right as a trivet until, one freezing night, the night of the solstice, the hinge of the year when things do not fit together as well as they should, the longest night, her first good man came home again.

A great thump on the door announced him as she was stirring the soup for the father of her children and she knew him the moment she lifted the latch to him although it was years since she'd worn black for him and now he was in rags and his hair hung down his back and never saw a comb, alive with lice.

"Here I am again, missus," he said. "Get me my bowl of cabbage and be quick about it."

Then her second husband came in with wood for the fire and when the first one saw she'd slept with another man and, worse, clapped his red eyes on her little children who'd crept into the kitchen to see what all the din was about, he shouted: "I wish I were a wolf again, to teach this whore a lesson!" So a wolf he instantly became and tore off the eldest boy's left foot before he was chopped up with the hatchet they used for chopping logs. But when the wolf lay bleeding and gasping its last, the pelt peeled off again and he was just as he had been, years ago, when he ran away from his marriage bed, so that she wept and her second husband beat her.

They say there's an ointment the Devil gives you that turns you into a wolf the minute you rub it on. Or, that he was born feet first and had a wolf for his father and his torso is a man's but his legs and genitals are a wolf's. And he has a wolf's heart.

Seven years is a werewolf's natural span but if you burn his human clothing you condemn him to wolfishness for the rest of his life, so old wives hereabouts think it some protection to throw a hat or an apron at the werewolf, as if clothes made the man. Yet by the eyes, those phosphorescent eyes, you know him in all his shapes; the eyes alone unchanged by metamorphosis.

Before he can become a wolf, the lycanthrope strips stark naked. If you spy a naked man among the pines, you must run as if the Devil were after you.

It is midwinter and the robin, the friend of man, sits on the handle of the gardener's spade and sings. It is the worst time in all the year for wolves but this strong-minded child insists she will go off through the wood. She is quite sure the wild beasts cannot harm her although, well-warned, she lays a carving knife in the basket her mother has packed with cheeses. There is a bottle of harsh liquor distilled from brambles; a batch of flat oatcakes baked on the hearthstone; a pot or two of jam. The flaxen-haired girl will take these delicious gifts to a reclusive grandmother so old the burden of her years is crushing her to death. Granny lives two hours' trudge through the winter woods; the child wraps herself up in her thick shawl, draws it over her head. She steps into her stout wooden shoes; she is dressed and ready and it is Christmas Eve. The malign door of the solstice still swings upon its hinges but she has been too much loved ever to feel scared.

Children do not stay young for long in this savage country. There are no toys for them to play with so they work hard and grow wise but this one, so pretty and the youngest of her family, a little late-comer, had been indulged by her mother and the grandmother who'd knitted her the red shawl that, today, has the ominous if brilliant look of blood on snow. Her breasts have just begun to swell; her hair is like lint, so fair it hardly makes a shadow on her pale forehead; her cheeks are an emblematic scarlet and white and she has just started her woman's bleeding, the clock inside her that will strike, henceforward, once a month.

She stands and moves within the invisible pentacle of her own virginity. She is an unbroken egg; she is a sealed vessel; she has inside her a magic space the entrance to which is shut tight with a plug of membrane; she is a closed system; she does not know how to shiver. She has her knife and she is afraid of nothing.

Her father might forbid her, if he were home, but he is away in the forest, gathering wood, and her mother cannot deny her.

The forest closed upon her like a pair of jaws.

There is always something to look at in the forest, even in the middle of winter—the huddled mounds of birds, succumbed to the lethargy of the season, heaped on the creaking boughs and too forlorn to sing; the bright frills of the winter fungi on the blotched trunks of the trees; the cuneiform slots of rabbits and deer, the herringbone tracks of the birds, a hare as lean as a rasher of bacon streaking across the path where the thin sunlight dapples the russet brakes of last year's bracken.

When she heard the freezing howl of a distant wolf, her practised hand sprang to the handle of her knife, but she saw no sign of a wolf at all, nor of a naked man, neither, but then she heard a clattering among the brushwood and there sprang on to the path a fully clothed one, a very handsome young one, in the green coat and wideawake hat of a hunter, laden with carcasses of game birds. She had her hand on her knife at the first rustle of twigs but he laughed with a flash of white teeth when he saw her and made her a comic yet flattering little bow; she'd never seen such a fine fellow before, not among the rustic clowns of her native village. So on they went together, through the thickening light of the afternoon.

Soon they were laughing and joking like old friends. When he offered to carry her basket, she gave it to him although her knife was in it because he told her his rifle would protect them. As the day darkened, it began to snow again; she felt the first flakes settle on her eyelashes but now there was only half a mile to go and there would be a fire, and hot tea, and a welcome, a warm one, surely, for the dashing huntsman as well as for herself.

This young man had a remarkable object in his pocket. It was a compass. She looked at the little round glass face in the palm of his hand and watched the wavering needle with a vague wonder. He assured her this compass had taken him safely through the wood on his hunting trip because the needle always told him with perfect accuracy where the north was. She did not believe it; she knew she should never leave the path on the way through the wood or else she would be lost instantly. He laughed at her again; gleaming trails of spittle clung to his teeth. He said, if he plunged off the path into the forest that surrounded them, he could guarantee to arrive at her grandmother's house a good quarter of an hour before she did, plotting his way through the undergrowth with his compass, while she trudged the long way, along the winding path.

I don't believe you. Besides, aren't you afraid of the wolves?

He only tapped the gleaming butt of his rifle and grinned.

Is it a bet? he asked her. Shall we make a game of it? What will you give me if I get to your grandmother's house before you?

What would you like? she asked disingenuously.

A kiss.

Commonplaces of a rustic seduction; she lowered her eyes and blushed.

He went through the undergrowth and took her basket with him but she forgot to be afraid of the beasts, although now the moon was rising, for she wanted to dawdle on her way to make sure the handsome gentleman would win his wager.

Grandmother's house stood by itself a little way out of the village. The freshly falling snow blew in eddies about the kitchen garden and the young man stepped delicately up the snowy path to the door as if he were reluctant to get his feet wet, swinging his bundle of game and the girl's basket and humming a little tune to himself.

There is a faint trace of blood on his chin; he has been snacking on his catch.

He rapped upon the panels with his knuckles.

Aged and frail, granny is three-quarters succumbed to the mortality the ache in her bones promises her and almost ready to give in entirely. A boy came out from the village to build up her hearth for the night an hour ago and the kitchen crackles with busy firelight. She has her Bible for company, she is a pious old woman. She is propped up on several pillows in the bed set into the wall peasant-fashion, wrapped up in the patchwork quilt she made before she was married, more years ago than she cares to remember. Two china spaniels with liver-coloured blotches on their coats and black noses sit on either side of the fireplace. There is a bright rug of woven rags on the pantiles. The grandfather clock ticks away her eroding time.

We keep the wolves outside by living well.

He rapped upon the panels with his hairy knuckles.

It is your granddaughter, he mimicked in a high soprano.

Lift up the latch and walk in, my darling.

You can tell them by their eyes, eyes of a beast of prey, nocturnal, devastating eyes as red as a wound; you can hurl your Bible at him and your apron after, granny, you thought that was a sure prophylactic against these infernal vermin . . . now call on Christ and his mother and all the angels in heaven to protect you but it won't do you any good.

His feral muzzle is sharp as a knife; he drops his golden burden of gnawed pheasant on the table and puts down your dear girl's basket, too. Oh, my God, what have you done with her?

Off with his disguise, that coat of forest-coloured cloth, the hat with the feather tucked into the ribbon; his matted hair streams down his white shirt and she can see the lice moving in it. The sticks in the hearth shift and hiss; night and the forest has come into the kitchen with darkness tangled in its hair.

He strips off his shirt. His skin is the colour and texture of vellum. A crisp stripe of hair runs down his belly, his nipples are ripe and dark as poison fruit but he's so thin you could count the ribs under his skin if only he gave you the time. He strips off his trousers and she can see how hairy his legs are. His genitals, huge. Ah! huge.

The last thing the old lady saw in all this world was a young man, eyes like cinders, naked as a stone, approaching her bed.

The wolf is carnivore incarnate.

When he had finished with her, he licked his chops and quickly dressed himself again, until he was just as he had been when he came through her door. He burned the inedible hair in the fireplace and wrapped the bones up in a napkin that he hid away under the bed in the wooden chest in which he found a clean pair of sheets. These he carefully put on the bed instead of the tell-tale stained ones he stowed away in the laundry basket. He plumped up the pillows and shook out the patchwork quilt, he picked up the Bible from the floor, closed it and laid it on the table. All was as it had been before except that grandmother was gone. The sticks twitched in the grate, the clock ticked and the young man sat patiently, deceitfully beside the bed in granny's nightcap.

Rat-a-tap-tap.

Who's there, he quavers in granny's antique falsetto.

Only your granddaughter.

So she came in, bringing with her a flurry of snow that melted in tears on the tiles, and perhaps she was a little disappointed to see only her grandmother sitting beside the fire. But then he flung off the blanket and sprang to the door, pressing his back against it so that she could not get out again.

The girl looked round the room and saw there was not even the indentation of a head on the smooth cheek of the pillow and how, for the first time she'd seen it so, the Bible lay closed on the table. The tick of the clock cracked like a whip. She wanted her knife from her basket but she did not dare reach for it because his eyes were fixed upon her—huge eyes that now seemed to shine with a unique, interior light, eyes the size of saucers, saucers full of Greek fire, diabolic phosphorescence.

What big eyes you have.

All the better to see you with.

No trace at all of the old woman except for a tuft of white hair that had caught in the bark of an unburned log. When the girl saw that, she knew she was in danger of death.

Where is my grandmother?

There's nobody here but we two, my darling.

Now a great howling rose up all around them, near, very near, as close as the kitchen garden, the howling of a multitude of wolves; she knew the worst wolves are hairy on the inside and she shivered, in spite of the scarlet shawl she pulled more closely round herself as if it could protect her although it was as red as the blood she must spill.

Who has come to sing us carols, she said.

Those are the voices of my brothers, darling; I love the company of wolves. Look out of the window and you'll see them.

Snow half-caked the lattice and she opened it to look into the garden. It was a white night of moon and snow; the blizzard whirled round the gaunt, grey beasts who squatted on their haunches among the rows of winter cabbage, pointing their sharp snouts to the moon and howling as if their hearts would break. Ten wolves; twenty wolves—so many wolves she could not count them, howling in concert as if demented or deranged. Their eyes reflected the light from the kitchen and shone like a hundred candles.

It is very cold, poor things, she said; no wonder they howl so.

She closed the window on the wolves' threnody and took off her scarlet shawl, the colour of poppies, the colour of sacrifices, the colour of her menses, and, since her fear did her no good, she ceased to be afraid.

What shall I do with my shawl?

Throw it on the fire, dear one. You won't need it again.

She bundled up her shawl and threw it on the blaze, which instantly consumed it. Then she drew her blouse over her head; her small breasts gleamed as if the snow had invaded the room.

What shall I do with my blouse?

Into the fire with it, too, my pet.

The thin muslin went flaring up the chimney like a magic bird and now off came her skirt, her woollen stockings, her shoes, and on to the fire they went, too, and were gone for good. The firelight shone through the edges of her skin; now she was clothed only in her untouched integument of flesh. This dazzling, naked she combed out her hair with her fingers; her hair looked white as the snow outside. Then went directly to the man with red eyes in whose unkempt mane the lice moved; she stood up on tiptoe and unbuttoned the collar of his shirt.

What big arms you have.

All the better to hug you with.

Every wolf in the world now howled a prothalamion outside the window as she freely gave the kiss she owed him.

What big teeth you have!

She saw how his jaw began to slaver and the room was full of the clamour of the forest's Liebestod but the wise child never flinched, even when he answered:

All the better to eat you with.

The girl burst out laughing; she knew she was nobody's meat. She laughed at him full in the face, she ripped off his shirt for him and flung it into the fire, in the fiery wake of her own discarded clothing. The flames danced like dead souls on Walpurgisnacht and the old bones under the bed set up a terrible clattering but she did not pay them any heed.

Carnivore incarnate, only immaculate flesh appeases him.

She will lay his fearful head on her lap and she will pick out the lice from his pelt and perhaps she will put the lice into her mouth and eat them, as he will bid her, as she would do in a savage marriage ceremony.

The blizzard will die down.

The blizzard died down, leaving the mountains as randomly covered with snow as if a blind woman had thrown a sheet over them, the upper branches of the forest pines limed, creaking, swollen with the fall.

Snowlight, moonlight, a confusion of paw-prints.

All silent, all still.

Midnight; and the clock strikes. It is Christmas Day, the werewolves' birthday, the door of the solstice stands wide open; let them all sink through.

See! sweet and sound she sleeps in granny's bed, between the paws of the tender wolf.

[1979]

Alice Walker
(1944–present)

Coming Apart

The eighth child of sharecroppers in Eatonton, Georgia, Alice Walker was given a typewriter by her mother and allowed to write rather than do chores. Her mother expressed her own creativity through her flower garden and through the urgency with which she told her stories. For Walker, the creativity of black women became essential to the emergence of personal and social growth out of horror and waste—a theme that permeates her work.

A poet, novelist, essayist, and writer of short stories, Walker has produced a body of fiction that includes *The Third Life of Grange Copeland* (1970), her first novel; *You Can't Keep a Good Woman Down* (1981); *The Color Purple* (1982); and *The Temple of My Familiar* (1989). *The Color Purple* was the first novel by a black woman to win a Pulitzer Prize; its portrayal of black male oppression of black women provoked controversy. *In Search of Our Mothers' Gardens: Womanist Prose* (1983) is a collection of Walker's autobiographical and literary essays, including her account of discovering the literature of Zora Neale Hurston.

According to Barbara Christian (*Black Woman Novelists*, Greenwood Press, 1980, pp. 237–238), "Walker's quilts reiterate the basic concept that 'the greatest value a person can attain is full humanity which is a state of oneness with all things,' and that until this is possible for all living beings, those of us who seek wholeness must be willing to struggle toward that end."

A middle-aged husband comes home after a long day at the office. His wife greets him at the door with the news that dinner is ready. He is grateful. First, however, he must use the bathroom. In the bathroom, sitting on the commode, he opens up the *Jiveboy* magazine he has brought home in his briefcase. There are a couple of jivemate poses that particularly arouse him. He studies the young women—blond, perhaps (the national craze), with elastic waists and inviting eyes—and strokes his penis. At the same time, his bowels stir with the desire to defecate. He is in the bathroom a luxurious ten minutes. He emerges spent, relaxed—hungry for dinner.

His wife, using the bathroom later, comes upon the slightly damp magazine. She picks it up with mixed emotions. She is a brownskin woman with black hair and eyes. She looks at the white blondes and brunettes. Will he be thinking of them, she wonders, when he is making love to me?

"Why do you need these?" she asks.

"They mean nothing," he says.

"But they hurt me somehow," she says.

"You are being a.) silly, b.) a prude, and c.) ridiculous," he says. "You know I love you."

She cannot say to him: But they are not me, those women. She cannot say she is jealous of pictures on a page. That she feels invisible. Rejected. Overlooked. She says instead, to herself: He is right. I will grow up. Adjust. Swim with the tide.

He thinks he understands her, what she has been trying to say. It is *Jiveboy*, he thinks. The white women.

Next day he brings home *Jivers*, a black magazine, filled with bronze and honey-colored women. He is in the bathroom another luxurious ten minutes.

She stands, holding the magazine: on the cover are the legs and shoes of a well-dressed black man, carrying a briefcase and a rolled *Wall Street Journal* in one hand. At his feet—she turns the magazine cover around and around to figure out how exactly the pose is accomplished—there is a woman, a brownskin woman like herself, twisted and contorted in such a way that her head is not even visible. Only her glistening body—her back and derriere—so that she looks like a human turd at the man's feet.

He is on a business trip to New York. He has brought his wife along. He is eagerly sharing 42nd Street with her. "Look!" he says.

"How *free* everything is. A far cry from Bolton!" (The small town they are from.) He is elated to see the blonde, spaced-out hookers, with their black pimps, trooping down the street. Elated at the shortness of the black hookers' dresses, their long hair, inevitably false and blond. She walks somehow behind him, so that he will encounter these wonders first. He does not notice until he turns a corner that she has stopped in front of a window that has caught her eye. While she is standing alone, looking, two separate pimps ask her what stable she is in or if in fact she is in one. Or simply "You workin'?"

He struts back and takes her elbow. Looks hard for the compliment implied in these questions, then shares it with his wife: "*You* know you're foxy!"

She is immovable. Her face suffering and wondering. "But look," she says, pointing. Four large plastic dolls—one a skinny Farrah Fawcett (or so the doll looks to her) posed for anal inspection; one, an oriental, with her eyes, strangely, closed, but her mouth, a pouting red suction cup, open; an enormous eskimo woman, with fur around her neck and ankles, and vagina; and a black woman dressed entirely in a leopard skin, complete with tail. The dolls are all life-size, and the efficiency of their rubber genitals is explained in detail on a card visible through the plate glass.

For her this is the stuff of nightmares—possibly because all the dolls are smiling. She will see them for the rest of her life. For him the sight is also shocking, but arouses a prurient curiosity. He will return, another time, alone. Meanwhile, he must prevent her from seeing such things, he resolves, whisking her briskly off the street.

Later, in their hotel room, she watches TV as two black women sing their latest hits: the first woman, dressed in a gold dress (because her song is now "solid gold!") is nonetheless wearing a chain around her ankle—the wife imagines she sees a chain—because the woman is singing: "Free me from my freedom, chain me to a tree!"

"What do you think of that?" she asks her husband.

"She's a fool," says he.

But when the second woman sings: "Ready, aim, fire, my name is desire," with guns and rockets going off all around her, he thinks the line "Shoot me with your love!" explains everything.

She is despondent.

She looks in a mirror at her plump brown and black body, crinkly hair and black eyes and decides, foolishly, that she is not beautiful. And that she is not hip, either. Among her other problems is the fact that she does not like the word "nigger" used by anyone at all, and is afraid of marijuana. These restraints, she feels, make her old, too much like her own mother, who loves sex (she has lately learned) but is highly religious and, for example, thinks cardplaying wicked and alcohol deadly. Her husband would not consider her mother sexy, she thinks. Since she herself is aging, this thought frightens her. But, surprisingly, while watching herself become her mother in the mirror, she discovers that *she* considers her mother—who carefully braids her average-length, average-grade, graying hair every night before going to bed; the braids her father still manages to fray during the night—*very* sexy.

At once she feels restored.
Resolves to fight.

"You're the only black woman in the world that worries about any of this stuff," he tells her, unaware of her resolve, and moody at her months of silent studiousness.

She says, "Here, Colored Person, read this essay by Audre Lorde."

He hedges. She insists.

He comes to the line about Lorde "moving into sunlight against the body of a woman I love," and bridles. "Wait a minute," he says, "what kind of a name is 'Audre' for a man? They must have meant 'An*dré.* ' "

"It *is* the name of a woman," she says. "Read the rest of that page."

"No dyke can tell me anything," he says, flinging down the pages.

She has been calmly waiting for this. She brings in the *Jiveboy* and *Jivers*. In both, there are women eating women they don't even know. She takes up the essay and reads:

> This brings me to the last consideration of the erotic. To share the power of each other's feelings is different from using another's feelings as we would use Kleenex. And when we look the other way from our experience, erotic or otherwise, we use rather than share the feelings of those others who participate in the experience with us. And use without consent of the used is abuse.

He looks at her with resentment, because she is reading this passage over again, silently, absorbedly, to herself, holding the pictures of the phony lesbians (a favorite, though unexamined, turn-on) absent-mindedly on her lap. He realizes he can never have her again sexually the way he has had her since the second year of marriage, as though her body belonged to someone else. He sees, down the road, the dissolution of the marriage, a constant search for more perfect bodies, or dumber wives. He feels oppressed by her incipient struggle, and feels somehow as if her struggle to change the pleasure he has enjoyed is a violation of his rights.

Now she is busy pasting Audre Lorde's words on the cabinet over the kitchen sink.

When they make love she tries to look him in the eye, but he refuses to return her gaze.

For the first time he acknowledges the awareness that the pleasure of coming without her is bitter and lonely. He thinks of eating stolen candy alone, behind the barn. And yet, he thinks greedily, it is better than nothing, which he considers her struggle's benefit to him.

The next day, she is reading another essay when he comes home from work. It is called "A Quiet Subversion" and is by Luisah Teish. "Another dyke?" he asks.

"Another one of your sisters," she replies, and begins to read, even before he's had dinner:

> During the "Black Power Movement" much cultural education was focused on the black physique. One of the accomplishments of that period was the popularization of African hairstyles and the Natural. Along with this new hair-do came a new self-image and way of relating. Then the movie industry put out "Superfly," and the Lord Jesus Look, the Konked bead, and an accompanying attitude, ran rampant in the black community. Films like "Shaft" and "Lady Sings the Blues" portray black "heroes" as cocaine-snorting, fast-life fools. In these movies a black woman is always caught in a web of violence . . .
>
> A popular Berkeley theatre featured a porno movie titled "Slaves of Love." Its advertisement portrayed two black women, naked, in chains, and a white man standing over them with a whip! How such *racist* pornographic material escaped the eye of black activists presents a problem . . .

Typically, he doesn't even hear the statement about the women. "What does the bitch know about the Black Power Movement?" he fumes. He is angry at his wife for knowing him so long and so well. She knows, for instance, that because of the Black Power Movement (and really because of the Civil Rights Movement before it), and not because he was at all active in it, he holds the bourgeois job he has. She remembers when his own hair was afroed. Now it is loosely curled. It occurs to him that, because she knows him as he was, he cannot make love to her as she is. Cannot, in fact, *love* her as she is. There is a way in which, in some firmly repressed corner of his mind, he considers his wife to be *still* black, whereas he feels himself to have moved to some other plane.

(This insight, a glimmer of which occurs to him, frightens him so much that he will resist it for several years. Should he accept it at once, however unsettling, it would help him understand the illogic of his acceptance of pornography used against black women: that he has detached himself from his own blackness in attempting to identify black women only by their sex.)

The wife has never considered herself a feminist—though she is, of course, a "womanist."* A womanist is a feminist, only more common. (The author of this piece is a womanist.) So she is surprised when her husband attacks her as a "women's libber," a "white women's lackey," a "pawn" in the hands of Gloria Steinem, an incipient bra-burner! What possible connection could there be, he wants to know, between her and white women—those overprivileged hags now (he's recently read in *Newsweek*) marching and preaching their puritanical horseshit up and down Times Square!

(He remembers only the freedom he felt there, not her long standing before the window of the plastic doll shop.) And if she is going to make a lot of new connections with dykes and whites, where will that leave him, the black man, the most brutalized and oppressed human being on the face of the earth? (*Is it because he can now ogle white women in freedom and she has no similar outlet of expression that he thinks of her as still black and himself as something else?* This thought underlines what he is actually saying, and his wife is unaware of it.) Didn't she know it is over these very same white bodies he has been

---

*"Womanist" approximates "black feminist."

lynched in the past, and is lynched still, by the police and the U.S. prison system, dozens of times a year *even now!?*

The wife has cunningly saved Tracey A. Gardner's essay for just this moment. Because Tracey A. Gardner has thought about it *all,* not just presently but historically, and she is clear about all the abuse being done to herself as a black person, and as a woman, and she is bold and she is cold—she is furious. The wife, given more to depression and self-abnegation than to fury, basks in the fire of Gardner's high-spirited anger.

She begins to read:

> Because from my point of view, racism is everywhere, in-cluding in the women's movement, and the only time I really need to say anything about it is when I *do not* see it . . . and the first time that happens, I will tell you about it.

The husband, surprised, thinks this very funny, not to say pertinent. He slaps his knee and sits up. He is dying to make some sort of positive dyke comment, but nothing comes to mind.

> American slavery relied on the denial of the humanity of Black folks, and the undermining of our sense of nationhood and family, on the stripping away of the Black man's role as protec-tor and provider, and on the structuring of Black women into the American system of *white male* domination . . .

"In other words," she says, "white men think they have to be on top. Other men have been known to savor life from other positions."

> The end of the Civil War brought the end of a certain "form" of slavery for Black folks. It also brought the end of any "job security" and the loss of the protection of their white enslaver. Blacks were now free game, and the terrorization and humilia-tion of Black people, especially black men, began anew. Now the Black man could have his family and prove his worth, but he had no way to support or protect them, or himself. . . .

As she reads, he feels ashamed and senses his wife's wounded embar-rassment, for him and for herself. For their history together. But doggedly, she continues to read:

After the Civil War, popular justice, which meant there usually was no trial and no proof needed, began its reign in the form of the castration, burning at the stakes, beheading, and lynching of Black men. As many as 5,000 white people would turn out to witness these events, as though going to a celebration. [*She pauses, sighs:* beheading?] Over 2,000 Black men were lynched in a 10 year period from 1889–99. There were also a number of Black women lynched. [*She reads this sentence quickly and forgets it.*] Over 50% of the lynched Black males were charged with rape or attempted rape.

He cannot imagine a woman being lynched. He has never even considered the possibility. Perhaps this is why the image of a black woman chained and bruised excites rather than horrifies him? It is the fact that the lynching of her body has never stopped that forces the wife, for the time being, to blot out the historical record. She is not prepared to connect her own husband with the continuation of that past.

She reads:

If a Black man had sex with a consenting white woman, it was rape. [*Why am I always reading about, thinking about, worrying about, my man having sex with white women? she thinks, despairingly, underneath the reading.*] If he insulted a white woman by looking at her, it was attempted rape.

"Yes," he says softly, as if in support of her dogged reading, "I've read Ida B.—what's her last name?"

"By their lynchings, the white man was showing that he hated the Black man carnally, biologically; he hated his color, his features, his genitals. Thus he attacked the Black man's body, and like lover gone mad, maimed his flesh, violated him in the most intimate, pornographic fashion . . ."

I believe that this obscene, inhuman treatment of Black men by white men, has a direct correlation to white men's increasingly obscene and inhuman treatment of women, particularly white women, in pornography and real life. White women, working towards their own strength and identity, their own sexuality, have in a sense become uppity niggers. As the Black man threatens the white man's masculinity and power, so now do women.

"That girl's onto something," says the husband, but thinks, for the first time in his life, that when he is not thinking of fucking white women—fantasizing over *Jiveboy* or clucking at them on the street— he is very often thinking of ways to humiliate them. Then he thinks that, given his history as a black man in America, it is not surprising that he has himself confused fucking them *with* humiliating them. But what does that say about how he sees himself? This thought smothers his inward applause for Gardner, and instead he casts a bewildered, disconcerted look at his wife. He knows that to make love to his wife as she really is, as who she really is—indeed, to make love to any other human being as they really are—will require a soul-rending look into himself, and the thought of this virtually straightens his hair.

His wife continues:

> Some Black men, full of the white man's perspective and values, see the white woman or Blond Goddess as part of the American winning image. Sometimes when he is with the Black woman, he is ashamed of how she has been treated and how he has been powerless, and that they have always had to work together and protect each other. [*Yes, she thinks, we were always all we had, until now. He thinks: We are all we have still, only now we can live without permitting ourselves to know this.*] Frantz Fanon said about white women, "By loving me she proves that I am worthy of white love. I am loved like a white man. I am a white man. I marry the culture, white beauty, white whiteness. When my restless hands caress those white breasts, they grasp white civilization and dignity and make them mine." [*She cannot believe he meant to write "white dignity."*]

She pauses, looks at her husband: "So how does a black woman feel when her black man leaves *Playboy* on the coffee table?"

For the first time he understands fully a line his wife read the day before: "The pornography industry's exploitation of the black woman's body is *qualitatively* different from that of the white woman," because she is holding the cover of *Jivers* out to him and asking: "What does this woman look like?"

What he has refused to see—because to see it would reveal yet another area in which he is unable to protect or defend black women—is that where white women are depicted in pornography as "objects," black women are depicted as animals. Where white women are depicted at least as human bodies if not beings, black women are depicted as shit.

He begins to feel sick. For he realizes that he has bought some if not all of the advertisements about women, black and white. And further, inevitably, he has bought the advertisements about himself. In pornography the black man is portrayed as being capable of fucking anything . . . even a piece of shit. He is defined solely by the size, readiness and unselectivity of his cock.

Still, he does not know how to make love without the fantasies fed to him by movies and magazines. Those movies and magazines (whose characters' pursuits are irrelevant or antithetical to his concerns) that have insinuated themselves between him and his wife, so that the totality of her body, her entire corporeal reality is alien to him. Even to clutch her in lust is automatically to shut his eyes. Shut his eyes, and . . . he chuckles bitterly . . . dream of England.

For years he has been fucking himself.

At first, reading Lorde together, they reject celibacy. Then they discover they need time apart to clear their heads, to search out damage, to heal. In any case, she is unable to fake response; he is unwilling for her to do so. She goes away for a while. Left alone, he soon falls hungrily on the magazines he had thrown out. Strokes himself raw over the beautiful women, spread like so much melon (he begins to see how stereotypes transmute) before him. But he cannot refuse what he knows—or what he knows his wife knows, walking along a beach in some black country where all the women are bleached and straightened and the men never look at themselves; and are ugly, in any case, in their imitation of white men.

Long before she returns he is reading her books and thinking of her—and of her struggles alone and his fear of sharing them—and when she returns, it is sixty percent *her* body that he moves against in the sun, her own black skin affirmed in the brightness of his eyes.

[1980]

Ellen Gilchrist
(1935–present)

There's a Garden of Eden

Growing up at Hopedale Plantation in Grace, Mississippi, Ellen Gilchrist "almost never went to school. That's why I'm a writer," she claims. She read incessantly, put on plays, and edited a high school paper before running away at age nineteen to be married.

Gilchrist wrote steadily from 1975, edited extensively, and adapted Eudora Welty stories for a broadcast play, *A Season of Dreams*. Her first collection of short stories, *In the Land of Dreamy Dreams* (1981), of which "There's a Garden of Eden" is a part, depicts the wealthy class as amoral, "beautiful spoiled crazy." Gilchrist has published several novels, the most recent of which is *Net of Jewels* (1992). Her newest stories appear in *The Blue-Eyed Buddhist* (1991).

Scores of men, including an ex-governor and the owner of a football team, consider Alisha Terrebone to be the most beautiful woman in the state of Louisiana. If she is unhappy what hope is there for ordinary mortals? Yet here is Alisha, cold and bored and lonely, smoking in bed.

Not an ordinary bed either. This bed is eight feet wide and covered with a spread made from Alisha's old fur coats. There are dozens of little pillows piled against the headboard, and the sheets are the color of shells and wild plums and ivory.

Everything else in the room is brown, brown velvet, brown satin, brown leather, brown silk, deep polished woods.

Alisha sleeps alone in the wonderful bed. She has a husband, but he isn't any fun anymore. He went morose on Alisha. Now he has a bed of his own in another part of town.

Alisha has had three husbands. First she married a poor engineer and that didn't work out. Then she married a judge and that didn't work out. Then she married a rich lawyer and that didn't work out.

Now she stays in bed most of the day, reading and drinking coffee, listening to music, cutting pictures out of old magazines, dreaming, arguing with herself.

This morning it is raining, the third straight day of the steady dramatic rains that come in the spring to New Orleans.

"It's on the T.V. a flood is coming," the maid says, bringing in Alisha's breakfast tray. Alisha and the maid adore each other. No matter how many husbands Alisha has she always keeps the same old maid.

"They always say a flood is coming," Alisha says. "It gives them something to talk about on television all day."

"I hope you're right," the maid says. "Anyway, your mother's been calling and calling. And the carpenter's here. He wants to start on the kitchen cabinets."

"Oh," Alisha says, "which carpenter?"

"The new one," the maid says, looking down at her shoes. "The young one." Blue-collar workers, she says to herself. Now it's going to be blue-collar workers.

"All right," Alisha says. "Tell him I'll talk to him as soon as I get dressed. Fix him some coffee."

Alisha gets out of bed, runs a comb through her hair, pulls on a pair of brown velvet pants, and ties a loose white shirt around her waist. I've got to get a haircut, she says, tying back her thick black curls with a pink ribbon. I've really got to do something about this hair.

The carpenter's name is Michael. He used to be a Presbyterian. Now he is a Zen Buddhist carpenter. When he uses wood he remembers the tree. Every day he says to himself. *I am part of the universe. I have a right to be here.*

This is something he learned when he was younger, when he was tripping with his wild friends. Michael is through with tripping now. He wants to go straight and have a car that runs. He wants his parents to call him up and write him letters and lend him money. His parents are busy pediatricians. They kicked him out for tripping. They don't have time for silly shit about the universe.

Alisha found Michael in a classified ad. "Household repairs done by an honest, dedicated craftsman. Call after four."

Alisha called the number and he came right over. As soon as she opened the door she knew something funny was going on. What kind of a carpenter shows up in a handmade white peasant shirt carrying a recorder.

"Can I put this somewhere while you show me what needs fixing," he said, looking at her out of dark blue eyes.

"What is it?" she said, taking it from him, laying it on a sofa.

"It's a musical instrument," he said. "I play with a group on Thursday nights. I was on my way there."

She led him around the house showing him things that were broken, watching his hands as he touched her possessions, watching his shoulders and his long legs and his soft hair and his dark blue eyes.

"This is a nice house," he said, when he had finished his inspection. "It has nice vibrations. I feel good here."

"It's very quiet," she said.

"I know," he said. "It's like a cave."

"You're right," she said. "It is like a cave. I never would have thought of that."

"Do you live here alone?" he said, holding his recorder in his arms. The last rays of the afternoon sun were filtering in through the leaded glass doors in the hallway casting rainbows all over the side of his face. Alisha was watching the blue part of the rainbow slide along the hollows of his cheeks.

"Most of the time," she said. "I have a husband, but he's almost never here anymore."

"It feels like only one person lives here," he said. "Everything seems to belong to you."

"It's very astute of you to see that," she began in a serious voice, then broke into a giggle. "To tell the truth, that's why my husband left. He said only Kierkegaard would believe I loved him. He said the longer he stayed in this house the smaller he became. He said he had gotten to be about the size of an old golf ball in the corner."

"Why did he let you do that to him?" Michael said.

"He did it to himself," she said. "I don't take responsibility for other people's lives. I don't believe in being a scapegoat. That's a thing Jews are historically pretty good at, you know, so I'm always watching out for it in myself. Women are pretty good at it too, for that matter."

"You're a pretty smart lady."

"No, I'm not," she said. "I'm just trying to make it through the days like everybody else."

"I should be leaving," he said. "I'm having a hard time leaving this house."

"Come back, then," she said. "As soon as you have time. I'm looking forward to getting things fixed up around the place."

Now he was back, leaning on a counter in her spotless kitchen, cradling a cup of coffee, listening intently to something the maid was telling him.

"Have you been sick?" Michael asked, looking up from his coffee.

"Not really," she said. "I just stay in bed a lot."

"Do you want me to start on these cabinets?" he said. "I could come back another day."

"Oh, no," she said. "Today is fine. It was nice of you to come out in this weather."

"It says on the television two pumping stations are out," the maid said. "It says it's going to flood and your mother's been calling and calling."

"Maybe you should go home then," Alisha said. "Just in case."

"I think I will," the maid said. "They might let the schools out early and I'm taking care of my grandchild this week."

"Go on then," Alisha said. "I can manage here."

"What about the cabinets?" the maid said. "I was going to put in shelf paper when he finished."

"It doesn't matter," Alisha said. "I'll do it. Look out there. The sky is black as it can be. You better call a cab."

Michael finished his coffee, rinsed out the cup in the sink, set it neatly upside down to dry and began to work on the hardware of the cabinet doors, aligning them so they stayed closed when they were shut.

"They go out of tune," he said, "like a piano. I wonder who installed these to begin with. He must have been an impatient man. See how he drove these screws in. I should take the hardware off and start all over."

"Will that take a long time?" she said.

"Well," he laughed, "you'd probably have to refinish the cabinets if I did that."

"Then do it," she said. "Go on. Fix them right while you're here."

"I'll see," he said. "Perhaps I will change the worst ones, like the ones over the stove."

He went back to work. Outside torrents of rain beat against the windows and the sky was black as evening. Alisha moved around the kitchen straightening things inside the cabinets. She had not looked inside these cabinets in ages. She had forgotten all the interesting and beautiful things she owned. There were shelves of fine Limoges china and silver serving pieces wrapped carelessly in cellophane bags from the dry cleaners. There were copper pans and casserole dishes. There were stainless-steel mixing bowls and porcelain soufflé dishes and shelves and shelves of every sort of wineglass from the time when she gave dinner parties. There was one cabinet full of cookbooks and recipe folders and flower vases and candles and candleholders.

She took down a cookbook called *The Joy of Cooking*. Her first mother-in-law had given it to her. On the flyleaf was an inscription, "Much love for good cooking and a few fancy dishes." Underneath the inscription the maid had written TAKE FROM THE LEFT, SERVE FROM THE RIGHT, in large letters.

Alisha laughed out loud.

"What's so funny," the carpenter said.

"I found a book I used to use when I gave dinner parties," she said. "I wasn't very good at dinner parties. I was too ambitious. I used to make things with *curry*. And the maid and I used to get drunk while we were waiting for the guests to arrive. We never could remember which side to serve the vegetables from. No matter how many dinner parties we had we never could remember."

"Why did you get drunk?" Michael said. "Were you unhappy?"

"No," she said. "I don't think so. To tell the truth I think I was hungry. I used to take diet pills so I wouldn't eat any of the good things I was always cooking. I would be so hungry by nighttime I would get drunk if I only had a glass of wine."

"Why did you do all that?" he said, wondering if she always said anything that came into her head.

"I did it so I would look like Audrey Hepburn," she said. "At that time most of the women in the United States wanted to look like Audrey Hepburn."

"Really?" he said.

"Well, all of my friends did at least. I spent most of my waking hours trying not to eat anything. It was a lot of trouble, being hungry all the time."

"It sounds terrible," Michael said. "Do you still do it?"

"No," she said. "I quit giving a damn about Audrey Hepburn. Then I quit taking diet pills, and then I quit drinking, and then I quit giving dinner parties. Then I quit doing anything I didn't like to do."

"What do you like to do?" he asked.

"I don't know," she said. "I haven't found out yet."

"Your phone is ringing," he said. "Aren't you going to answer it?"

"No," she said. "I don't like to talk on the telephone."

"The maid said your mother had been trying to call you."

"I know. That's probably her on the phone now."

"You aren't going to answer it?"

"No. Because I already know what she's going to say. She's going to tell me a flood is coming. Don't pay any attention to the phone. It'll stop in a minute."

He put down his tools and turned around to face her. "There's a whole lot going on in this room right now," he said. "Are you aware of that?" He looked very serious, wiping his hands across his sleeves.

"How old are you?" Alisha said.

"What difference does that make?" he said and crossed the room and put his arms around her. She felt very nice in his arms, soft and brave and sad, like an old actress.

"Oh, my," she said. "I was afraid this was going to happen." Then they laid down their weapons and walked awkwardly down the hall to the bedroom, walking slowly as though they were going to do something embarrassing and awkward and absurd.

At the door to the bedroom he picked her up and carried her to the bed, hoping that was the romantic thing to do. Then he saw it. "What in the name of God is this?" he said, meaning the fur bedspread.

"Something my mother gave me," she said. "Isn't it the tackiest thing you've ever seen in your life."

"Your body is very beautiful," she said when he had taken off his clothes and was standing before her, shy and human. "You *look* like a grown man. That's a relief."

"Do you always say whatever comes into your head?" he said.

"Oh, yes," she said. "I think everyone knows what everyone else is thinking all the time anyway. Do you mind? Do you think I talk too much?"

"Oh, no," he said. "I like it. It keeps surprising me."

"Do you like my body," she said, for now she had taken off her clothes and had struck a pose, sitting cross-legged on the bed.

"Of course I do," he said. "I've been wanting to touch your tits ever since the first moment I saw you. The whole time we were walking around your house I was wanting to touch your tits."

"Oh, my," she said. "Not my tits again. For years I believed men liked me for my mind. Imagine that! I read hundreds of books so they would like me better. All the time they were only wanting to touch my tits. Think of that!"

"Now you're talking too much," he said.

Then Alisha closed her eyes and pretended she was an Indian princess lying in a tent deep in a forest, dressed in a long white deerskin robe, waiting for Jeff Chandler to come and claim her for his bride. Outside the wind and rain beat down upon the forest.

Then Michael closed his eyes and pretended he was a millionaire going to bed with a beautiful, sad old actress.

The phone woke them with its ringing. Alisha was startled for a moment. Then she settled back down, remembering where she was. Michael's legs were smooth and warm beside her. She was safe.

"You really ought to answer that," he said. "This is quite a storm we're having."

She picked his shirt up off the floor, put it on for a bathrobe, and went into the other room to talk.

"That was my mother," she reported. "She's crying. She's almost got her companion crying. I think they're both crying. He's this real sensitive young man we found in the drama department at Tulane. They watch T.V. together. He's learning to be an actor watching T.V."

"Why is she crying?" Michael said, sitting up in bed, pulling the plum-colored sheets around his waist.

"She's crying because the basement of her house is flooding. It always does that in heavy rains. She lives on Jefferson Avenue, around the corner. Anyway, she can't find one of her cats and she thinks he's getting wet."

"Her cats?"

"She has six or seven cats. At least six cats. Anyway, she thinks the water is going to keep on rising and drown her cats."

"You'd better go and see about her then. We'd better go and help her."

"Help her? How can we help her? It's a flash flood on Jefferson Avenue. It'll go away as soon as the pumping stations start working. I told her to sell that goddamn house the last time this happened."

"It's flooding your mother's house and you don't want to go and help her?"

"It's only flooding the basement."

"How old is she?"

"My mother. She's seventy-eight. She has a companion. Besides, she does anything she wants to do. Last year she went to *China*. She's perfectly all right."

"Then why is she crying?"

"Because she thinks her silly goddamn cats are getting wet."

"Then we'll have to go and help her."

"How can we. It's *flooded* all the way down Jefferson Avenue."

"Does that canoe in the garage work?"

"I think so. No one's ever used it. Stanley ordered it last year when he got interested in the Sierra Club. But no one's ever *used* it."

"Then we'll go in that. Every time I see a flood on television and people going to get other people in boats I want to be one of them. This is my chance. We can take the canoe in my truck to where the water starts. Go on. Call your mother back and tell her we're coming to save her. Tell her we'll be right there. And, Alisha."

"Yes."

"Tell her to stop crying. After all, she is your mother."

"This is a great canoe," he said, maneuvering it down from the floored platform of the garage. "Your husband never uses it?"

"He never uses anything," she said. "He just likes to have things. To tell the truth he's almost never here."

"Then why are you married?" he asked.

"That's a good question," Alisha said. "But I don't know the answer to it."

"Well, look, let's go on over there. I can't wait to put this in the water. I'm afraid the water will go down before we get there."

"It's really nice of you to do this," Alisha said, standing close to him, smelling the warm smell of his clothes, taking everything that she could get while she could get it.

"Everybody loves to be a hero," Michael said, putting his arms around her again, running his hands up and down her strange soft body.

"Say I'm not your mother," she said.

"You're not my mother," he said. "Besides, it doesn't matter. We're probably only dreaming."

They drove down Freret Street with the city spread out before them, clean and shining after the rain. The sun was lighting up the red tile roofs of the houses, and Tulane students were on the porches with glasses in their hands, starting their flood parties.

The inside of Michael's truck was very cosy. He used it for a business office. File folders stuffed with bills and invoices were piled in one corner, and an accounting book was on the dashboard.

"Will I make love to you again?" Alisha said, for she was too old to play hard to get.

"Whenever you want to," he said. "As soon as we finish saving your mother."

They could see the flood now. They took the canoe out of the back of the truck and carried it to where the water began at the foot of Skippy Nevelson's front yard. Alisha sat in the bow and Michael waded out pushing her until it was deep enough for him to climb in.

"I don't believe I'm doing this," she said. "You're the craziest man I ever met in my life."

"Which way is the house," he said.

"It's the second house off Willow," Alisha said. "I guess we'll just go down Jefferson and take a right at Willow."

They floated along with Michael paddling. The water was three feet deep, thick and brown and slow-moving. An envelope floated by, then an orange barrette, then a purple Frisbee.

Alisha was feeling wonderful. If Skippy Nevelson was leaning out of her front window with her eyes the size of plates, if the WDSU Minicam crew was filming her for the evening news, if the levee broke and carried them all out to sea, what was that to Alisha, who had been delivered of an angel.

"What will happen next?" she asked, pushing her luck.

"Whatever we want to happen," he said, lifting the paddle and throwing the muddy water up into the air.

"Oh, my," she said to no one in particular. "This was the year I was going to stop dying my hair."

Now they were only a block away from their destination. Alisha kept her face to the front wishing she had a hat so Michael couldn't see her wrinkles. I have to remember this a long time, she told herself. I have to watch everything and hear everything and smell everything and remember everything. This may have to last me a long, long time.

Then Alisha did a stupid thing. She wrote a little script for herself. This is the very last time I will ever love anyone she told herself. I will love this boy until he leaves me. And then I will never love another human being.

And he will leave me, because no man has ever left me in my whole life and sooner or later it has to be my turn. After a while he will stop loving me and nothing will bring him back, not all the money or love or passion in the world will hold him. So he will leave me and go into the future and I will stay here and remember love. *And that is what I get for devoting my life to love instead of wisdom.*

So Alisha sat in the bow and wrote a script for herself and then she went to work to make it all come true.

"There it is," she said, spotting the house. "The one with the green awnings. See the balconies on the top. When I was a child I always dreamed of walking out there and waving to people, but the windows were always locked so I wouldn't fall to my death on Willow Street."

"That's terrible," he said. "You had a fancy place like that and you couldn't even walk out on the balconies."

"I couldn't do anything," she said. "They were too afraid I'd get hurt. That's how wealthy Jews used to raise their children. They didn't let me ride a bicycle or roller skate or swim or anything."

"You don't know how to *swim!*" he said.

"No," she said. "Isn't that dreadful?"

"Then what are you doing in this boat?"

"Hoping it won't turn over," she said, smiling a wonderful mysterious French smile, holding on lightly to the gunwales while he rowed her to her mother's doorstep.

[1981]

Fay Weldon
(1933–present)

Angel, All Innocence

Fay Weldon has written over eighteen novels, several collections of stories, and dozens of plays, in addition to writing for radio and television. She has become famous for her acerbic and deadly humor; she delivers telling blows with an effortlessly light touch. Most often, her wit reveals the sexual and social injustices of society. A feminist, Weldon exposes the absurdities of the status quo and the artificiality of social constructs. She revels in intimate connections with her readers, whispering in their ears her truths about women and men, relationships, and families.

Weldon says about writing: "Fiction, of course, is much more powerful, and more believable, than fact. You may not believe fact unless it is fictionally presented: and there are facts which it is perhaps necessary for you to know." These facts are related in novels like *Remember Me* (1976), *Letters to Alice* (1977), *The Life and Loves of a She-Devil* (1983), *Down among the Women* (1984), and *Darcy's Utopia* (1990).

A graduate of St. Andrew's University, Weldon holds degrees in economics and psychology. She is the mother of four sons and currently lives in London.

There is a certain kind of unhappiness, experienced by a certain kind of woman married to a certain kind of man, which is timeless: outrunning centuries, interweaving generations, perpetuating itself from mother to daughter, feeding off the wet eyes of the puzzled girl, gaining fresh strength from the dry eyes of the old woman she will become—who, looking back on her past, remembers nothing of love except tears and the pain in the heart which must be endured, in silence, in case the heart stops altogether.

Better for it to stop, now.

Angel, waking in the night, hears sharp footsteps in the empty attic above and wants to wake Edward. She moves her hand to do so, but then stills it for fear of making him angry. Easier to endure in the night the nightmare terror of ghosts than the day-long silence of Edward's anger.

The footsteps, little and sharp, run from a point above the double bed in which Angel and Edward lie, she awake, he sleeping, to a point somewhere above the chest of drawers by the door; they pause briefly, then run back again, tap-tap, clickety-click. There comes another pause and the sound of pulling and shuffling across the floor; and then the sequence repeats itself, once, twice. Silence. The proper unbroken silence of the night.

Too real, too clear, for ghosts. The universe is not magic. Everything has an explanation. Rain, perhaps? Hardly. Angel can see the moon shine through the drawn blind, and rain does not fall on moonlit nights. Perhaps, then, the rain of past days collected in some blocked gutter, to finally splash through on to the rolls of wallpaper and pots of paint on the attic floor, sounding like footsteps through some trick of domestic acoustics. Surely! Angel and Edward have not been living in the house for long. The attic is still unpainted, and old plaster drops from disintegrating laths. Edward will get round to it sooner or later. He prides himself on his craftsman's skills, and Angel, a year married, has learned to wait and admire, subduing impatience in herself. Edward is a painter—of pictures, not houses—and not long out of art school, where he won many prizes. Angel is the lucky girl he has loved and married. Angel's father paid for the remote country house, where now they live in solitude and where Edward can develop his talents, undisturbed by the ugliness of the city, with Angel, his inspiration, at his side. Edward, as it happened, consented to the gift unwillingly, and for Angel's sake rather than his own. Angel's father Terry writes thrillers and settled a large sum upon his daughter in her childhood, thus avoiding death duties and the anticipated gift tax. Angel kept the fact hidden from Edward until after they were married. He'd thought her an ordinary girl about Chelsea, sometime secretary, sometime barmaid, sometime artist's model.

Angel, between jobs, did indeed take work as an artist's model. That was how Edward first clapped eyes upon her; Angel, all innocence, sitting nude upon her plinth, fair curly hair glinting under strong lights, large eyes closed beneath stretched blue-veined lids, strong breasts pointed upwards, stubby pale bush irritatingly and coyly hidden behind an angle of thigh that both gave Angel cramps and spoiled the pose for the students. So they said.

"If you're going to be an exhibitionist," as Edward complained to her later in the coffee bar, "at least don't be coy about it." He took her home to his pad, that handsome, dark-eyed, smiling young man, and wooed her with a nostalgic Sinatra record left behind by its previous occupant; half mocking, half sincere, he sang love words into her pearly ear, his warm breath therein stirring her imagination, and the gentle occasional nip of his strong teeth in her flesh promising passion and pain beyond belief. Angel would not take off her clothes for him: he became angry and sent her home in a taxi without her fare. She borrowed from her flatmate at the other end. She cried all night, and the next day, sitting naked on her plinth, had such swollen eyelids as to set a student or two scratching away to amend the previous day's work. But she lowered her thigh, as a gesture of submission, and felt a change in the studio ambience from chilly spite to warm approval, and she knew Edward had forgiven her. Though she offered herself to multitudes, Edward had forgiven her.

"I don't mind you being an exhibitionist," Edward said to her in the coffee bar, "in fact that rather turns me on, but I do mind you being coy. You have a lot to learn, Angel." By that time Angel's senses were so aroused, her limbs so languid with desire, her mind so besotted with his image, that she would have done whatever Edward wished, in public or in private. But he rose and left the coffee bar, leaving her to pay the bill.

Angel cried a little, and was comforted by and went home with Edward's friend Tom, and even went to bed with him, which made her feel temporarily better, but which she was to regret for ever.

"I don't mind you being a whore," Edward said before the next studio session, "but can't you leave my friends alone?"

It was a whole seven days of erotic torment for Angel before Edward finally spent the night with her: by that time her thigh hung loosely open in the studio. Let anyone see. Anyone. She did not care.

The job was coming to an end anyway. Her new one as secretary in a solicitor's office began on the following Monday. In the nick of time, just as she began to think that life and love were over, Edward brought her back to their remembrance. "I love you," he murmured in Angel's ear. "Exhibitionist slut, typist, I don't care. I still love you."

Tap-tap, go the footsteps above, starting off again: clickety-click. Realer than real. No, water never sounded like that. What then? Rats? No. Rats scutter and scamper and scrape. There were rats in the barn in which Angel and Edward spent a camping holiday together. Their tent had blown away: they'd been forced to take refuge in the barn. All four of them. Edward, Angel, Tom and his new girlfriend Ray. Angel missed Edward one night after they all stumbled back from the pub to the barn, and searching for him in the long grass beneath an oak tree, found him in tight embrace with Ray.

"Don't tell me you're hysterical as well as everything else," complained Edward. "You're certainly irrational. You went to bed with Tom, after all."

"But that was before."

Ah, before, so much before. Before the declarations of love, the abandoning of all defence, all prudence, the surrendering of common sense to faith, the parcelling up and handing over of the soul into apparent safe-keeping. And if the receiving hands part, the trusted fingers lose their grip, by accident or by design, why then, one's better dead.

Edward tossed his Angel's soul into the air and caught it with his casual hands.

"But if it makes you jealous," he said, "why I won't . . . Do you want to marry me? Is that it? Would it make you happier?"

What would it look like when they came to write his biography? Edward Holst, the famous painter, married at the age of twenty-four—to what? Artist's model, barmaid, secretary, crime-writer's daughter? Or exhibitionist, whore, hysteric? Take your choice. Whatever makes the reader happiest, explains the artist in the simplest terms, makes the most successful version of a life. Crude strokes and all.

"Edward likes to keep his options open," said Tom, but would not explain his remark any further. He and Ray were witnesses at the secular wedding ceremony. Angel thought she saw Edward nip Ray's ear as they all formally kissed afterwards, then thought she must have imagined it.

This was his overture of love: turning to Angel in the dark warmth of the marriage bed, Edward's teeth would seek her ear and nibble the tender flesh, while his hand travelled down to open her thighs. Angel never initiated their lovemaking. No. Angel waited, patiently. She had tried once or twice, in the early days, letting her hand roam over his sleeping body, but Edward not only failed to respond, but was thereafter cold to her for days on end, sleeping carefully on his side of the bed, until her penance was paid and he lay warm against her again.

Edward's love made flowers bloom, made the house rich and warm, made water taste like wine. Edward, happy, surrounded Angel with smiles and soft encouragement. He held her soul with steady hands. Edward's anger came unexpectedly, out of nowhere, or nowhere that Angel could see. Yesterday's permitted remark, forgiven fault, was today's outrage. To remark on the weather to break an uneasy silence, might be seen as evidence of a complaining nature: to be reduced to tears by his first unexpected biting remark, further fuel for his grievance.

Edward, in such moods, would go to his studio and lock the door, and though Angel (soon learning that to weep outside the door or beat against it, moaning and crying and protesting, would merely prolong his anger and her torment) would go out to the garden and weed or dig or plant as if nothing were happening, would feel Edward's anger seeping out from under the door, darkening the sun, poisoning the earth; or at any rate spoiling her fingers in relation to the earth, so that they trembled and made mistakes and nothing grew.

The blind shakes. The moon goes behind a cloud. Tap, tap, overhead. Back and forth. The wind? No. Don't delude yourself. Nothing of this world. A ghost. A haunting. A woman. A small, desperate, busy woman, here and not here, back and forth, out of her time, back from the grave, ill-omened, bringing grief and ruin: a message that nothing is what it seems, that God is dead and the forces of evil abroad and unstoppable. Does Angel hear, or not hear?

Angel, through her fear, wants to go to the bathroom. She is three months' pregnant. Her bladder is weak. It wakes her in the night, crying out its need, and Angel, obeying, will slip cautiously out of bed, trying not to wake Edward. Edward needs unbroken sleep if he is to paint well the next day. Edward, even at the best of times, suspects that Angel tossing and turning, and moaning in her sleep, as she will, wakes him on purpose to annoy.

Angel has not yet told Edward that she is pregnant. She keeps putting it off. She has no real reason to believe he does not want

babies: but he has not said he does want them, and to assume that
Edward wants what other people want is dangerous.

Angel moans aloud: afraid to move, afraid not to move, afraid to
hear, afraid not to hear. So the child Angel lay awake in her little white
bed, listening to her mother moaning, afraid to move, afraid not to
move, to hear or not to hear. Angel's mother was a shoe-shop girl
who married the new assistant manager after a six-week courtship.
That her husband went on to make a fortune, writing thrillers that
sold by the million, was both Dora's good fortune and tragedy. She
lived comfortably enough on alimony, after all, in a way she could
never have expected, until dying by mistake from an overdose of
sleeping pills. After that Angel was brought up by a succession of her
father's mistresses and au-pairs. Her father Terry liked Edward, that
was something, or at any rate he had been relieved at his appearance
on the scene. He had feared an element of caution in Angel's soul:
that she might end up married to a solicitor or stockbroker. And
artists were at least creative, and an artist such as Edward Holst might
well end up rich and famous. Terry had six Holst canvases on his walls
to hasten the process. Two were of his daughter, nude, thigh slackly
falling away from her stubby fair bush. Angel, defeated—as her
mother had been defeated. "I love you, Dora, but you must
understand. I am not *in* love with you." As I'm in love with Helen,
Audrey, Rita, whoever it was: off to meetings, parties, off on his
literary travels, looking for fresh copy and new backgrounds,
encountering always someone more exciting, more interesting, than
an ageing ex shoe-shop assistant. Why couldn't Dora understand?
Unreasonable of her to suffer, clutching the wretched Angel to her
alarmingly slack bosom. Could he, Terry, really be the only animation
of her flesh? There was a sickness in her love, clearly; unaccompanied
as it was by the beauty which lends grace to importunity.

Angel had her mother's large, sad eyes. The reproach in them was
in-built. Better Dora's heart had stopped (she'd thought it would: six
months' pregnant, she found Terry in the housemaid's bed. She,
Dora, mistress of servants! What bliss!) and the embryo Angel never
emerged to the light of day.

The noise above Angel stops. Ghosts! What nonsense! A fallen
lath grating and rattling in the wind. What else? Angel regains her
courage, slips her hand out from beneath Edward's thigh preparatory
to leaving the bed for the bathroom. She will turn on all the lights and
run. Edward wakes; sits up.

"What's that? What in God's name's that?"

"I can't hear anything," says Angel, all innocence. Nor can she, not now. Edward's displeasure to contend with now; worse than the universe rattling its chains.

"Footsteps, in the attic. Are you deaf? Why didn't you wake me?"

"I thought I imagined it."

But she can hear them, once again, as if with his ears. The same pattern across the floor and back. Footsteps or heartbeats. Quicker and quicker now, hastening with the terror and tension of escape.

Edward, unimaginably brave, puts on his slippers, grabs a broken banister (five of these on the landing—one day soon, some day, he'll get round to mending them—he doesn't want some builder, paid by Angel, bungling the job) and goes on up to the attic. Angel follows behind. He will not let her cower in bed. Her bladder aches. She says nothing about that. How can she? Not yet. Not quite yet. Soon. "Edward, I'm pregnant." She can't believe it's true, herself. She feels a child, not a woman.

"Is there someone there?"

Edward's voice echoes through the three dark attic rooms. Silence. He gropes for and switches on the light. Empty, derelict rooms: plaster falling, laths hanging, wallpaper peeling. Floorboards broken. A few cans of paint, a pile of wallpaper rolls, old newspapers. Nothing else.

"It could have been mice," says Edward, doubtfully.

"Can't you hear it?" asks Angel, terrified. The sound echoes in her ears: footsteps clattering over a pounding heart. But Edward can't, not any more.

"Don't start playing games," he murmurs, turning back to warmth and bed. Angel scuttles down before him, into the bathroom; the noise in her head fades. A few drops of urine tinkle into the bowl.

Edward lies awake in bed: Angel can feel his wakefulness, his increasing hostility towards her, before she is so much as back in the bedroom.

"Your bladder's very weak, Angel," he complains. "Something else you inherited from your mother?"

Something else, along with what? Suicidal tendencies, alcoholism, a drooping bosom, a capacity for being betrayed, deserted and forgotten?

Not forgotten by me, Mother. I don't forget, I love you. Even when my body cries out beneath the embraces of this man, this lover, this husband, and my mouth forms words of love, promises of eternity, still I don't forget. I love you, Mother.

"I don't know about my mother's bladder," murmurs Angel rashly.

"Now you're going to keep me awake all night," says Edward. "I can feel it coming. You know I've nearly finished a picture."

"I'm not going to say a word," she says, and then, fulfilling his prophesy, sees fit to add, "I'm pregnant."

Silence. Stillness. Sleep?

No, a slap across nostrils, eyes, mouth. Edward has never hit Angel before. It is not a hard slap: it contains the elements of a caress.

"Don't even joke about it," says Edward, softly.

"But I am pregnant."

Silence. He believes her. Her voice made doubt impossible.

"How far?" Edward seldom asks for information. It is an act which infers ignorance, and Edward likes to know more than anyone else in the entire world.

"Three and a half months."

He repeats the words, incredulous.

"Too far gone to do anything," says Angel, knowing now why she did not tell Edward earlier, and the knowledge making her voice cold and hard. Too far gone for the abortion he will most certainly want her to have. So much for the fruits of love. Love? What's love? Sex, ah, that's another thing. Love has babies: sex has abortions.

But Angel will turn sex into love—yes, she will—seizing it by the neck, throttling it till it gives up and takes the weaker path. Love! Edward is right to be frightened, right to hate her.

"I hate you," he says, and means it. "You mean to destroy me."

"I'll make sure it doesn't disturb your nights," says Angel. Angel of the bristly fair bush, "if that's what you're worrying about. And you won't have to support it. I do that, anyway. Or my father does."

Well, how dare she! Angel, not nearly as nice as she thought. Soft-eyed, vicious Angel.

Slap, comes the hand again, harder. Angel screams, he shouts; she collapses, crawls about the floor—he spurns her, she begs forgiveness; he spits his hatred, fear, and she her misery. If the noise above continues, certainly no one hears it, there is so much going on below. The rustlings of the night erupting into madness. Angel is suddenly quiet, whimpering, lying on the floor; she squirms. At first Edward thinks she is acting, but her white lips and taloned fingers convince him that something is wrong with her body and not just her mind. He gets her back on the bed and rings the doctor. Within an hour Angel finds herself in a hospital with a suspected ectopic pregnancy.

They delay the operation and the pain subsides; just one of those things, they shrug. Edward has to interrupt his painting the next afternoon to collect her from the hospital.

"What was it? Hysteria?" he enquires.

"I dare say!"

"Well, you had a bad beginning, what with your mother and all," he concedes, kissing her nose, nibbling her earlobe. It is forgiveness; but Angel's eyes remain unusually cold. She stays in bed, after Edward has left it and gone back to his studio, although the floors remain unswept and the dishes unwashed.

Angel does not say what is in her mind, what she knows to be true. That he is disappointed to see both her and the baby back, safe and sound. He had hoped the baby would die, or failing that, the mother would die and the baby with her. He is pretending forgiveness, while he works out what to do next.

In the evening the doctor comes to see Angel. He is a slight man with a sad face: his eyes, she thinks, are kind behind his pebble glasses. His voice is slow and gentle. I expect his wife is happy, thinks Angel, and actually envies her. Some middle-aged, dowdy, provincial doctor's wife, envied by Angel! Rich, sweet, young and pretty Angel. The efficient secretary, lovable barmaid, and now the famous artist's wife! Once, for two rash weeks, even an art school model.

The doctor examines her, then discreetly pulls down her nightie to cover her breasts and moves the sheet up to cover her crotch. If he were my father, thinks Angel, he would not hang my naked portrait on his wall for the entertainment of his friends. Angel had not known until this moment that she minded.

"Everything's doing nicely inside there," says the doctor. "Sorry to rush you off like that, but we can't take chances."

Ah, to be looked after. Love. That's love. The doctor shows no inclination to go.

"Perhaps I should have a word with your husband," he suggests. He stands at the window gazing over daffodils and green fields. "Or is he very busy?"

"He's painting," says Angel. "Better not disturb him now. He's had so many interruptions lately, poor man."

"I read about him in the Sunday supplement," says the doctor.

"Well, don't tell him so. He thought it vulgarised his work."

"Did you think that?"

Me? Does what I think have anything to do with anything?

"I thought it was quite perceptive, actually," says Angel, and feels a surge of good humour. She sits up in bed.

"Lie down," he says. "Take things easy. This is a large house. Do you have any help? Can't afford it?"

"It's not that. It's just why should I expect some other woman to do my dirty work?"

"Because she might like doing it and you're pregnant, and if you can afford it, why not?"

"Because Edward doesn't like strangers in the house. And what else have I got to do with my life? I might as well clean as anything else."

"It's isolated out here," he goes on. "Do you drive?"

"Edward needs peace to paint," says Angel. "I do drive but Edward has a thing about women drivers."

"You don't miss your friends?"

"After you're married," says Angel, "you seem to lose contact. It's the same for everyone, isn't it?"

"Um," says the doctor. And then, "I haven't been in this house for fifteen years. It's in a better state now than it was then. The house was divided into flats, in those days. I used to visit a nice young woman who had the attic floor. Just above this. Four children, and the roof leaked; a husband who spent his time drinking cider in the local pub and only came home to beat her."

"Why did she stay?"

"How can such women leave? How do they afford it? Where do they go? What happens to the children?" His voice is sad.

"I suppose it's money that makes the difference. With money, a woman's free," says Angel, trying to believe it.

"Of course," says the doctor. "But she loved her husband. She couldn't bring herself to see him for what he was. Well, it's hard. For a certain kind of woman, at any rate."

Hard, indeed, if he has your soul in his safe-keeping, to be left behind at the bar, in the pub, or in some other woman's bed, or in a seat in the train on his literary travels. Careless!

"But it's not like that for you, is it?" says the doctor calmly. "You have money of your own, after all."

Now how does he know that? Of course, the Sunday supplement article.

"No one will read it," wept Angel, when Edward looked up, stony-faced from his first perusal of the fashionable columns. "No one will notice. It's tucked away at the very bottom."

So it was. "Edward's angelic wife Angel, daughter of best-selling crime-writer Terry Toms, has smoothed the path upwards, not just with the soft smiles our cameraman has recorded, but by enabling the emergent genius to forswear the cramped and inconvenient, if traditional, artist's garret for a sixteenth-century farmhouse in greenest Gloucestershire. It is interesting, moreover, to ponder whether a poor man would have been able to develop the white-on-white techniques which have made Holst's work so noticeable: or whether the sheer price of paint these days would not have deterred him."

"Edward, I didn't say a word to that reporter, not a word," she said, when the ice showed signs of cracking, days later.

"What are you talking about?" he asked, turning slow, unfriendly eyes upon her.

"The article. I know it's upset you. But it wasn't my fault."

"Why should a vulgar article in a vulgar newspaper upset me?"

And the ice formed over again, thicker than ever. But he went to London for two days, presumably to arrange his next show, and on his return casually mentioned that he'd seen Ray while he was there.

Angel had cleaned, baked, and sewed curtains in his absence, hoping to soften his heart towards her on his return: and lay awake all the night he was away, the fear of his infidelity so agonising as to make her contemplate suicide, if only to put an end to it. She could not ask for reassurance. He would throw the fears so neatly back at her. "Why do you think I should want to sleep with anyone else? Why are you so guilty? Because that's what you'd do if you were away from me?"

Ask for bread and be given stones. Learn self-sufficiency: never show need. Little, tough Angel of the soft smiles, hearing some other woman's footsteps in the night, crying for another's grief. Well, who wants a soul, tossed here and there by teasing hands, over-bruised and over-handled. Do without it!

Edward came home from London in a worse mood than he'd left, shook his head in wondering stupefaction at his wife's baking—"I thought you said we were cutting down on carbohydrates"—and shut himself into his studio for twelve hours, emerging just once to say—"Only a mad woman would hang curtains in an artist's studio, or else a silly rich girl playing at artist's wife, and in public at that"—and thrusting the new curtains back into her arms, vanished inside again.

Angel felt that her mind was slowing up, and puzzled over the last remark for some time before realising that Edward was still harking back to the Sunday supplement article.

"I'll give away the money if you like," she pleaded through the keyhole. "If you'd rather. And if you want not to be married to me I don't mind." That was before she was pregnant.

Silence.

Then Edward emerged laughing, telling her not to be so ridiculous, bearing her off to bed, and the good times were restored. Angel sang about the house, forgot her pill, and got pregnant.

"You have money of your own, after all," says the doctor. "You're perfectly free to come and go."

"I'm pregnant," says Angel. "The baby has to have a father."

"And your husband's happy about the baby?"

"Oh yes!" says Angel. "Isn't it a wonderful day!"

And indeed today the daffodils nod brightly under a clear sky. So far, since first they budded and bloomed, they have been obliged to droop beneath the weight of rain and mist. A disappointing spring. Angel had hoped to see the countryside leap into energy and colour, but life returned only slowly, it seemed, struggling to surmount the damage of the past: cold winds and hard frosts, unseasonably late. "Or at any rate," adds Angel, softly, unheard, as the doctor goes, "he *will* be happy about the baby."

Angel hears no more noises in the night for a week or so. There had been misery in the attic rooms, and the misery had ceased. Good times can wipe out bad. Surely!

Edward sleeps soundly and serenely: she creeps from bed to bathroom without waking him. He is kind to her and even talkative, on any subject, that is, except that of her pregnancy. If it were not for the doctor and her stay in the hospital, she might almost think she was imagining the whole thing. Edward complains that Angel is getting fat, as if he could imagine no other cause for it but greed. She wants to talk to someone about hospitals, confinements, layettes, names—but to whom?

She tells her father on the telephone—"I'm pregnant."

"What does Edward say?" asks Terry, cautiously.

"Nothing much," admits Angel.

"I don't suppose he does."

"There's no reason *not* to have a baby," ventures Angel.

"I expect he rather likes to be the centre of attention." It is the nearest Terry has ever got to a criticism of Edward.

Angel laughs. She is beyond believing that Edward could ever be jealous of her, ever be dependent upon her.

"Nice to hear you happy, at any rate," says her father wistfully. His twenty-year-old girlfriend has become engaged to a salesman of agricultural machinery, and although she has offered to continue the relationship the other side of marriage, Terry feels debased and used, and was obliged to break off the liaison. He has come to regard his daughter's marriage to Edward in a romantic light. The young bohemians!

"My daughter was an art school model before she married Edward Holst . . . you've heard of him? It's a real Rembrandt and Saskia affair." He even thinks lovingly of Dora: if only she'd understood, waited for youth to wear itself out. Now he's feeling old and perfectly capable of being faithful to an ex shoe-shop assistant. If only she weren't dead and gone!

An art school model. Those two weeks! Why had she done it? What devil wound up her works and set poor Angel walking in the wrong direction? It was in her nature, surely, as it was in her mother's to follow the paths to righteousness, fully clothed.

Nightly, Edward studied her naked body, kissing her here, kissing her there, parting her legs. Well, marriage! But now I'm pregnant, now I'm pregnant. Oh, be careful. That hard lump where my soft belly used to be. Be careful! Silence, Angel. Don't speak of it. It will be the worse for you and your baby if you do.

Angel knows it.

Now Angel hears the sound of lovemaking up in the empty attic, as she might hear it in hotels in foreign lands. The couplings of strangers in an unknown tongue—only the cries and breathings universal, recognisable anywhere.

The sounds chill her: they do not excite her. She thinks of the mother of four who lived in this house with her drunken, violent husband. Was that what kept you by his side? The chains of fleshly desire? Was it the thought of the night that got you through the perils of the day?

What indignity, if it were so.

Oh, I imagine it. I, Angel, half-mad in my unacknowledged pregnancy, my mind feverish, and the doctor's anecdotes feeding the fever—I imagine it! I must!

Edward wakes.

"What's that noise?"

"What noise?"

"Upstairs."

"I don't hear anything."

"You're deaf."

"What sort of noise?"

But Edward sleeps again. The noise fades, dimly. Angel hears the sound of children's voices. Let it be a girl, dear Lord, let it be a girl.

"Why do you want a girl?" asks the doctor, on Angel's fourth monthly visit to the clinic.

"I'd love to dress a girl," says Angel vaguely, but what she means is, if it's a girl, Edward will not be so—what is the word?—hardly jealous, difficult perhaps. Dreadful. Yes, dreadful.

Bright-eyed Edward: he walks with Angel now—long walks up and over stiles, jumping streams, leaping stones. Young Edward. She has begun to feel rather old, herself.

"I am a bit tired," she says, as they set off one night for their moon-lit walk.

He stops, puzzled.

"Why are you tired?"

"Because I'm pregnant," she says, in spite of herself.

"Don't start that again," he says, as if it were hysteria on her part. Perhaps it is.

That night, he opens her legs so wide she thinks she will burst. "I love you," he murmurs in her nibbled ear, "Angel, I love you. I do love you." Angel feels the familiar surge of response, the holy gratitude, the willingness to die, to be torn apart if that's what's required. And then it stops. It's gone. Evaporated! And in its place, a new strength. A chilly icicle of non-response, wonderful, cheerful. No. It isn't right; it isn't what's required: on the contrary. "I love you," she says in return, as usual; but crossing her fingers in her mind, forgiveness for a lie. Please God, dear God, save me, help me save my baby. It is not me he loves, but my baby he hates: not me he delights in, but the pain he causes me, and knows he does. He does not wish to take root in me: all he wants to do is root my baby out. I don't love him. I never have. It is sickness. I must get well. Quickly.

"Not like that," says Angel, struggling free—bold, unkind, prudish Angel—rescuing her legs. "I'm pregnant. I'm sorry, but I am pregnant."

Edward rolls off her, withdraws.

"Christ, you can be a monster. A real ball-breaker."

"Where are you going?" asks Angel, calm and curious. Edward is dressing. Clean shirt; cologne. Cologne!

"To London."

"Why?"

"Where I'm appreciated."

"Don't leave me alone. Please." But she doesn't mean it.

"Why not?"

"I'm frightened. Here alone at night."

"Nothing ever frightened you." Perhaps he is right.

Off he goes; the car breaking open the silence of the night. It closes again. Angel is alone.

Tap, tap, tap, up above. Starting up as if on signal. Back and forward. To the attic bed which used to be, to the wardrobe which once was; the scuffle of the suitcase on the floor. Goodbye. I'm going. I'm frightened here. The house is haunted. Someone upstairs, downstairs. Oh, women everywhere, don't think your misery doesn't seep into walls, creep downstairs, and then upstairs again. Don't think it will ever be done with, or that the good times wipe it out. They don't.

Angel feels her heart stop and start again. A neurotic symptom, her father's doctor had once said. It will get better, he said, when she's married and has babies. Everything gets better for women when they're married with babies. It's their natural state. Angel's heart stops all the same, and starts again, for good or bad.

Angel gets out of bed, slips on her mules with their sharp little heels, and goes up the attic stairs. Where does she find the courage? The light, reflected up from the hallway, is dim. The noise from the attic stops. Angel hears only—what?—the rustling noise of old newspapers in a fresh wind. That stops, too. As if a film were now running without sound. And coming down towards Angel, a small, tired woman in a nightie, slippers silent on the stairs, stopping to stare at Angel as Angel stares at her. Her face marked by bruises.

"How can I see that," wonders Angel, now unafraid, "since there isn't any light?"

She turns on the switch, hand trembling, and in the light, as she'd known, there is nothing to be seen except the empty stairs and the unmarked dust upon them.

Angel goes back to the bedroom and sits on the bed.

"I saw a ghost," she tells herself, calmly enough. Then fear reasserts itself: panic at the way the universe plays tricks. Quick, quick! Angel pulls her suitcase out from under the bed—there are still traces of wedding confetti within—and tap-tap she goes, with sharp little footsteps, from the wardrobe to the bed, from the chest of drawers and back again, not so much packing as retrieving, salvaging. Something out of nothing!

Angel and her predecessor, rescuing each other, since each was incapable of rescuing herself, and rescue always comes, somehow. Or else death.

Tap, tap, back and forth, into the suitcase, out of the house.

The garden gate swings behind her.

Angel, bearing love to a safer place.

[1981]

Anne Tyler
(1941–present)

Teenage Wasteland

Born in an experimental Quaker community in the wilderness outside of Raleigh, North Carolina, Anne Tyler spent her childhood "sitting behind a book waiting for childhood to arrive." She studied at Duke, won awards for creative writing, and published her first story in 1959. After receiving her degree in Russian, she did graduate work at Columbia and worked as a Russian biographer.

Tyler has written eight novels in sixteen years and several short stories, which have appeared in magazines including *McCalls* and *The New Yorker.* Her novels, which show an influence by Eudora Welty, include *If Morning Ever Comes* (1964), *Searching for Caleb* (1975), *The Accidental Tourist* (1985), and *Breathing Lessons* (1988). *The Accidental Tourist* was made into a film in 1988. "Teenage Wasteland" was chosen to be included in *Editor's Choice: New American Stories, Volume 1.* Here, as in all her fiction, Tyler addresses serious and often tragic situations without sacrificing the comic element.

He used to have very blond hair—almost white—cut shorter than other children's so that on his crown a little cowlick always stood up to catch the light. But this was when he was small. As he grew older, his hair grew darker, and he wore it longer—past his collar even. It hung in lank, taffy-colored ropes around his face, which was still an endearing face, fine-featured, the eyes an unusual aqua blue. But his cheeks, of course, were no longer round, and a sharp new Adam's apple jogged in his throat when he talked.

In October, they called from the private school he attended to request a conference with his parents. Daisy went alone; her husband was at work. Clutching her purse, she sat on the principal's couch and learned that Donny was noisy, lazy, and disruptive; always fooling around with his friends, and he wouldn't respond in class.

In the past, before her children were born, Daisy had been a fourth-grade teacher. It shamed her now to sit before this principal as a parent, a delinquent parent, a parent who struck Mr. Lanham, no doubt, as unseeing or uncaring. "It isn't that we're not concerned," she said. "Both of us are. And we've done what we could, whatever we could think of. We don't let him watch TV on school nights. We don't let him talk on the phone till he's finished his homework. But he tells us he doesn't *have* any homework or he did it all in study hall. How are we to know what to believe?"

From early October through November, at Mr. Lanham's suggestion, Daisy checked Donny's assignments every day. She sat next to him as he worked, trying to be encouraging, sagging inwardly as she saw the poor quality of everything he did—the sloppy mistakes in math, the illogical leaps in his English themes, the history questions left blank if they required any research.

Daisy was often late starting supper, and she couldn't give as much attention to Donny's younger sister. "You'll never guess what happened at . . ." Amanda would begin, and Daisy would have to tell her, "Not now, honey."

By the time her husband, Matt, came home, she'd be snappish. She would recite the day's hardships—the fuzzy instructions in English, the botched history map, the morass of unsolvable algebra equations. Matt would look surprised and confused, and Daisy would gradually wind down. There was no way, really, to convey how exhausting all this was.

In December, the school called again. This time, they wanted Matt to come as well. She and Matt had to sit on Mr. Lanham's couch like two bad children and listen to the news: Donny had improved only slightly, raising a D in history to a C, and a C in algebra to a B-minus. What was worse, he had developed new problems. He had cut classes on at least three occasions. Smoked in the furnace room. Helped Sonny Barnett break into a freshman's locker. And last week, during athletics, he and three friends had been seen off the school grounds; when they returned, the coach had smelled beer on their breath.

Daisy and Matt sat silent, shocked. Matt rubbed his forehead with his fingertips. Imagine, Daisy thought, how they must look to Mr. Lanham: an overweight housewife in a cotton dress and a too-tall, too-thin insurance agent in a baggy, frayed suit. Failures, both of them—the kind of people who are always hurrying to catch up, missing the point of things that everyone else grasps at once. She wished she'd worn nylons instead of knee socks.

It was arranged that Donny would visit a psychologist for testing. Mr. Lanham knew just the person. He would set this boy straight, he said.

When they stood to leave, Daisy held her stomach in and gave Mr. Lanham a firm, responsible handshake.

Donny said the psychologist was a jackass and the tests were really dumb; but he kept all three of his appointments, and when it was time for the follow-up conference with the psychologist and both parents, Donny combed his hair and seemed unusually sober and subdued. The psychologist said Donny had no serious emotional problems. He was merely going through a difficult period in his life. He required some academic help and a better sense of self-worth. For this reason, he was suggesting a man named Calvin Beadle, a tutor with considerable psychological training.

In the car going home, Donny said he'd be damned if he'd let them drag him to some stupid fairy tutor. His father told him to watch his language in front of his mother.

That night, Daisy lay awake pondering the term "self-worth." She had always been free with her praise. She had always told Donny he had talent, was smart, was good with his hands. She had made a big to-do over every little gift he gave her. In fact, maybe she had gone too far, although, Lord knows, she had meant every word. Was that his trouble?

She remembered when Amanda was born. Donny had acted lost and bewildered. Daisy had been alert to that, of course, but still, a new baby keeps you so busy. Had she really done all she could have? She longed—she ached—for a time machine. Given one more chance, she'd do it perfectly—hug him more, praise him more, or perhaps praise him less. Oh, who can say . . .

The tutor told Donny to call him Cal. All his kids did, he said. Daisy thought for a second that he meant his own children, then realized her mistake. He seemed too young, anyhow, to be a family man. He wore a heavy brown handlebar mustache. His hair was as long and stringy as Donny's and his jeans as faded. Wire-rimmed spectacles slid down his nose. He lounged in a canvas director's chair with his fingers laced across his chest, and he casually, amiably questioned Donny, who sat upright and glaring in an armchair.

"So they're getting on your back at school," said Cal. "Making a big deal about anything you do wrong."

"Right," said Donny.

"Any idea why that would be?"

"Oh, well, you know, stuff like homework and all," Donny said.

"You don't do your homework?"

"Oh, well, I might do it sometimes but not just exactly like they want it." Donny sat forward and said, "It's like a prison there, you know? You've got to go to every class, you can never step off the school grounds."

"You cut classes sometimes?"

"Sometimes," Donny said, with a glance at his parents.

Cal didn't seem perturbed. "Well," he said, "I'll tell you what. Let's you and me try working together three nights a week. Think you could handle that? We'll see if we can show that school of yours a thing or two. Give it a month; then if you don't like it, we'll stop. If *I* don't like it, we'll stop. I mean, sometimes people just don't get along, right? What do you say to that?"

"Okay," Donny said. He seemed pleased.

"Make it seven o'clock till eight, Monday, Wednesday, and Friday," Cal told Matt and Daisy. They nodded. Cal shambled to his feet, gave them a little salute, and showed them to the door.

This was where he lived as well as worked, evidently. The interview had taken place in the dining room, which had been transformed into a kind of office. Passing the living room, Daisy winced at the rock music she had been hearing, without registering it, ever since she had entered the house. She looked in and saw a boy about Donny's age lying on a sofa with a book. Another boy and a girl were playing Ping-Pong in front of the fireplace. "You have several here together?" Daisy asked Cal.

"Oh, sometimes they stay on after their sessions, just to rap. They're a pretty sociable group, all in all. Plenty of goof-offs like young Donny here."

He cuffed Donny's shoulder playfully. Donny flushed and grinned.

Climbing into the car, Daisy asked Donny, "Well? What did you think?"

But Donny had returned to his old evasive self. He jerked his chin toward the garage. "Look," he said. "He's got a basketball net."

Now on Mondays, Wednesdays, and Fridays, they had supper early—the instant Matt came home. Sometimes, they had to leave before they were really finished. Amanda would still be eating her dessert. "Bye, honey. Sorry," Daisy would tell her.

Cal's first bill sent a flutter of panic through Daisy's chest, but it was worth it, of course. Just look at Donny's face when they picked him up: alight and full of interest. The principal telephoned Daisy to tell her how Donny had improved. "Of course, it hasn't shown up in his grades yet, but several of the teachers have noticed how his attitude's changed. Yes, sir, I think we're onto something here."

At home, Donny didn't act much different. He still seemed to have a low opinion of his parents. But Daisy supposed that was unavoidable—part of being fifteen. He said his parents were too "controlling"—a word that made Daisy give him a sudden look. He said they acted like wardens. On weekends, they enforced a curfew. And any time he went to a party, they always telephoned first to see if adults would be supervising. "For God's sake!" he said. "Don't you trust me?"

"It isn't a matter of trust, honey . . ." But there was no explaining to him.

His tutor called one afternoon. "I get the sense," he said, "that this kid's feeling . . . underestimated, you know? Like you folks expect the worst of him. I'm thinking we ought to give him more rope."

"But see, he's still so suggestible," Daisy said. "When his friends suggest some mischief—smoking or drinking or such—why, he just finds it very hard not to go along with them."

"Mrs. Coble," the tutor said, "I think this kid is hurting. You know? Here's a serious, sensitive kid, telling you he'd like to take on some grown-up challenges, and you're giving him the message that he can't be trusted. Don't you understand how that hurts?"

"Oh," said Daisy.

"It undermines his self-esteem—don't you realize that?"

"Well, I guess you're right," said Daisy. She saw Donny suddenly from a whole new angle: his pathetically poor posture, that slouch so forlorn that his shoulders seemed about to meet his chin . . . oh, wasn't it awful being young? She'd had a miserable adolescence herself and had always sworn no child of hers would ever be that unhappy.

They let Donny stay out later, they didn't call ahead to see if the parties were supervised, and they were careful not to grill him about his evening. The tutor had set down so many rules! They were not allowed any questions at all about any aspect of school, nor were they to speak with his teachers. If a teacher had some complaint, she should phone Cal. Only one teacher disobeyed—the history teacher, Miss Evans. She called one morning in February. "I'm a little concerned about Donny, Mrs. Coble."

"Oh, I'm sorry, Miss Evans, but Donny's tutor handles these things now . . ."

"I always deal directly with the parents. You are the parent," Miss Evans said, speaking very slowly and distinctly. "Now, here is the problem. Back when you were helping Donny with his homework, his grades rose from a D to a C, but now they've slipped back, and they're closer to an F."

"They are?"

"I think you should start overseeing his homework again."

"But Donny's tutor says . . ."

"It's nice that Donny has a tutor, but you should still be in charge of his homework. With you, he learned it. Then he passed his tests. With the tutor, well, it seems the tutor is more of a crutch. 'Donny,' I say, 'a quiz is coming up on Friday. Hadn't you better be listening instead of talking?' 'That's okay, Miss Evans,' he says. 'I have a tutor now.' Like a talisman! I really think you ought to take over, Mrs. Coble."

"I see," said Daisy. "Well, I'll think about that. Thank you for calling."

Hanging up, she felt a rush of anger at Donny. A talisman! For a talisman, she'd given up all luxuries, all that time with her daughter, her evenings at home!

She dialed Cal's number. He sounded muzzy. "I'm sorry if I woke you," she told him, "but Donny's history teacher just called. She says he isn't doing well."

"She should have dealt with me."

"She wants me to start supervising his homework again. His grades are slipping."

"Yes," said the tutor, "but you and I both know there's more to it than mere grades, don't we? I care about the *whole* child—his happiness, his self-esteem. The grades will come. Just give them time."

When she hung up, it was Miss Evans she was angry at. What a narrow woman!

It was Cal this, Cal that, Cal says this, Cal and I did that. Cal lent Donny an album by the Who. He took Donny and two other pupils to a rock concert. In March, when Donny began to talk endlessly on the phone with a girl named Miriam, Cal even let Miriam come to one of the tutoring sessions. Daisy was touched that Cal would grow so involved in Donny's life, but she was also a little hurt, because she had offered to have Miriam to dinner and Donny had refused. Now he asked them to drive her to Cal's house without a qualm.

This Miriam was an unappealing girl with blurry lipstick and masses of rough red hair. She wore a short, bulky jacket that would not have been out of place on a motorcycle. During the trip to Cal's she was silent, but coming back, she was more talkative. "What a neat guy, and what a house! All those kids hanging out, like a club. And the stereo playing rock . . . gosh, he's not like a grown-up at all! Married and divorced and everything, but you'd think he was our own age."

"Mr. Beadle was married?" Daisy asked.

"Yeah, to this really controlling lady. She didn't understand him a bit."

"No, I guess not," Daisy said.

Spring came, and the students who hung around at Cal's drifted out to the basketball net above the garage. Sometimes, when Daisy and Matt arrived to pick up Donny, they'd find him there with the others—spiky and excited, jittering on his toes beneath the backboard. It was staying light much longer now, and the neighboring fence cast narrow bars across the bright grass. Loud music would be spilling from Cal's windows. Once it was the Who, which Daisy recognized from the time that Donny had borrowed the album. *"Teenage Wasteland,"* she said aloud, identifying the song, and Matt gave a short, dry laugh. "It certainly is," he said. He'd misunderstood; he thought she was commenting on the scene spread before them. In fact, she might have been. The players looked like hoodlums, even her son. Why, one of Cal's students had recently been knifed in a tavern. One had been shipped off to boarding school in midterm; two had been withdrawn by their parents. On the other hand, Donny had mentioned someone who'd been studying with Cal for five years. "Five years!" said Daisy. "Doesn't anyone ever stop needing him?"

Donny looked at her. Lately, whatever she said about Cal was read as criticism. "You're just feeling competitive," he said. "And controlling."

She bit her lip and said no more.

In April, the principal called to tell her that Donny had been expelled. There had been a locker check, and in Donny's locker they found five cans of beer and half a pack of cigarettes. With Donny's previous record, this offense meant expulsion.

Daisy gripped the receiver tightly and said, "Well, where is he now?"

"We've sent him home," said Mr. Lanham. "He's packed up all his belongings, and he's coming home on foot."

Daisy wondered what she would say to him. She felt him looming closer and closer, bringing this brand-new situation that no one had prepared her to handle. What other place would take him? Could they enter him in a public school? What were the rules? She stood at the living room window, waiting for him to show up. Gradually, she realized that he was taking too long. She checked the clock. She stared up the street again.

When an hour had passed, she phoned the school. Mr. Lanham's secretary answered and told her in a grave, sympathetic voice that yes, Donny Coble had most definitely gone home. Daisy called her husband. He was out of the office. She went back to the window and thought awhile, and then she called Donny's tutor.

"Donny's been expelled from school," she said, "and now I don't know where he's gone. I wonder if you've heard from him?"

There was a long silence. "Donny's with me, Mrs. Coble," he finally said.

"With you? How'd he get there?"

"He hailed a cab, and I paid the driver."

"Could I speak to him, please?"

There was another silence. "Maybe it'd be better if we had a conference," Cal said.

"I don't *want* a conference. I've been standing at the window picturing him dead or kidnapped or something, and now you tell me you want a—"

"Donny is very, very upset. Understandably so," said Cal. "Believe me, Mrs. Coble, this is not what it seems. Have you asked Donny's side of the story?"

"Well, of course not, how could I? He went running off to you instead."

"Because he didn't feel he'd be listened to."

"But I haven't even—"

"Why don't you come out and talk? The three of us," said Cal, "will try to get this thing in perspective."

"Well, all right," Daisy said. But she wasn't as reluctant as she sounded. Already, she felt soothed by the calm way Cal was taking this.

Cal answered the doorbell at once. He said, "Hi, there," and led her into the dining room. Donny sat slumped in a chair, chewing the knuckle of one thumb. "Hello, Donny," Daisy said. He flicked his eyes in her direction.

"Sit here, Mrs. Coble," said Cal, placing her opposite Donny. He himself remained standing, restlessly pacing. "So," he said.

Daisy stole a look at Donny. His lips were swollen, as if he'd been crying.

"You know," Cal told Daisy, "I kind of expected something like this. That's a very punitive school you've got him in—you realize that. And any half-decent lawyer will tell you they've violated his civil rights. Locker checks! Where's their search warrant?"

"But if the rule is—" Daisy said.

"Well, anyhow, let him tell you his side."

She looked at Donny. He said, "It wasn't my fault. I promise."

"They said your locker was full of beer."

"It was a put-up job! See, there's this guy that doesn't like me. He put all these beers in my locker and started a rumor going, so Mr. Lanham ordered a locker check."

"What was the boy's name?" Daisy asked.

"Huh?"

"Mrs. Coble, take my word, the situation is not so unusual," Cal said. "You can't imagine how vindictive kids can be sometimes."

"What was the boy's *name*," said Daisy, "so that I can ask Mr. Lanham if that's who suggested he run a locker check."

"You don't believe me," Donny said.

"And how'd this boy get your combination in the first place?"

"Frankly," said Cal, "I wouldn't be surprised to learn the school was in on it. Any kid that marches to a different drummer, why, they'd just love an excuse to get rid of him. The school is where I lay the blame."

"Doesn't *Donny* ever get blamed?"

"Now, Mrs. Coble, you heard what he—"

"Forget it," Donny told Cal. "You can see she doesn't trust me."

Daisy drew in a breath to say that of course she trusted him—a reflex. But she knew that bold-faced, wide-eyed look of Donny's. He had worn that look when he was small, denying some petty misdeed with the evidence plain as day all around him. Still, it was hard for her to accuse him outright. She temporized and said, "The only thing I'm sure of is that they've kicked you out of school, and now I don't know what we're going to do."

"We'll fight it," said Cal.

"We can't. Even you must see we can't."

"I could apply to Brantly," Donny said.

Cal stopped his pacing to beam down at him. "Brantly! Yes. They're really onto where a kid is coming from, at Brantly. Why, *I* could get you into Brantly. I work with a lot of their students."

Daisy had never heard of Brantly, but already she didn't like it. And she didn't like Cal's smile, which struck her now as feverish and avid—a smile of hunger.

On the fifteenth of April, they entered Donny in a public school, and they stopped his tutoring sessions. Donny fought both decisions bitterly. Cal, surprisingly enough, did not object. He admitted he'd made no headway with Donny and said it was because Donny was emotionally disturbed.

Donny went to his new school every morning, plodding off alone with his head down. He did his assignments, and he earned average grades, but he gathered no friends, joined no clubs. There was something exhausted and defeated about him.

The first week in June, during final exams, Donny vanished. He simply didn't come home one afternoon, and no one at school remembered seeing him. The police were reassuring, and for the first few days, they worked hard. They combed Donny's sad, messy room for clues; they visited Miriam and Cal. But then they started talking about the number of kids who ran away every year. Hundreds, just in this city. "He'll show up, if he wants to," they said. "If he doesn't, he won't."

Evidently, Donny didn't want to.

It's been three months now and still no word. Matt and Daisy still look for him in every crowd of awkward, heartbreaking teenage boys. Every time the phone rings, they imagine it might be Donny. Both parents have aged. Donny's sister seems to be staying away from home as much as possible.

At night, Daisy lies awake and goes over Donny's life. She is trying to figure out what went wrong, where they made their first mistake. Often, she finds herself blaming Cal, although she knows he didn't begin it. Then at other times she excuses him, for without him, Donny might have left earlier. Who really knows? In the end, she can only sigh and search for a cooler spot on the pillow. As she falls asleep, she occasionally glimpses something in the corner of her vision. It's something fleet and round, a ball—a basketball. It flies up, it sinks through the hoop, descends, lands in a yard littered with last year's leaves and striped with bars of sunlight as white as bones, bleached and parched and cleanly picked.

[1983]

Ruth Rendell
(1930–present)

The Convolvulus Clock

Born in London, Ruth Rendell worked as a newspaper reporter and subeditor at a young age; she then established herself as a major crime writer through her often-macabre style. She writes detective novels, which are centered on her character Chief Inspector Reginald Wexford, as well as other novels. Her Wexford series includes *From Doon to Death* (1964), *No More Dying, Then* (1971), and *A Sleeping Life* (1978). Her other fiction includes *An Unkindness of Ravens* (1985), *Live Flesh* (1986), *Heartstones* (1987), and *Talking to Strange Men* (1987).

Rendell, who has won enormous acclaim and many awards in the mystery genre, has also written under the name "Barbara Vine." Her collected stories, of which "The Convolvulus Clock" is one, appeared in 1987 in *The New Girlfriend and Other Stories*.

"Is that your own hair, dear?"

Sibyl only laughed. She made a roguish face.

"I didn't think it could be," said Trixie. "It looks so thick."

"A woman came up to me in the street the other day," said Sibyl, "and asked me where I had my hair set. I just looked at her. I gave a tiny little tip to my wig like this. You should have seen her face."

She gave another roar of laughter. Trixie smiled austerely. She had come to stay with Sibyl for a week and this was her first evening. Sibyl had bought a cottage in Devonshire. It was two years since Trixie had seen Sibyl and she could detect signs of deterioration. What a pity that was! Sibyl enquired after the welfare of the friends they had in common. How was Mivvy? Did Trixie see anything of the Fishers? How was Poppy?

"Poppy is beginning to go a bit funny," said Trixie.

"How do you mean, 'funny'?"

"You know. Funny. Not quite *compos mentis* any more."

Sibyl of all people ought to know what going funny meant, thought Trixie.

"We're none of us getting any younger," said Sibyl, laughing.

Trixie didn't sleep very well. She got up at five and had her bath so as to leave the bathroom clear for Sibyl. At seven she took Sibyl a cup of tea. She gave a little scream and nearly dropped the tray.

"Oh my conscience! I'm sorry, dear, but I thought that was a squirrel on your chest of drawers. I thought it must have come in through the window."

"What on earth was that noise in the middle of the night?" When Sibyl wasn't laughing she could be downright peevish. She looked a hundred without her wig. "It woke me up, I thought the tank was overflowing."

"The middle of the night! I like that. The sun had been up a good hour, I'm sure. I was just having my bath so as not to be a nuisance."

They went out in Sibyl's car. They had lunch in Dawlish and tea in Exmouth. The following day they went out early and drove across Dartmoor. When they got back there was a letter on the mat for Trixie from Mivvy, though Trixie had only been away two days. On Friday Sibyl said they would stay at home and have a potter about the village. The church was famous, the Manor House gardens were open to the public and there was an interesting small gallery where an exhibition was on. She started to get the car out but Trixie said why couldn't they walk. It could hardly be more than a mile. Sibyl said it was just under two miles but she agreed to walk if Trixie really wanted to. Her knee hadn't been troubling her quite so much lately.

"The gallery is called Artifacts," said Sibyl. "It's run by a very nice young couple."

"A husband and wife team?" asked Trixie, very modern.

"Jimmy and Judy they're called. I don't think they are actually married."

"Oh my conscience, Sibyl, how can one be 'actually' married? Surely one is either married or not?" Trixie herself had been married once, long ago, for a short time. Sibyl had never been married and neither had Mivvy or Poppy. Trixie thought that might have something to do with their going funny. "Thankfully, I'm broad-minded. I shan't say anything. I think I can see a seat ahead in that bus shelter. Would you like a little sit-down before we go on?"

Sibyl got her breath back and they walked on more slowly. The road passed between high hedges on high banks dense with wild flowers. It crossed a stream by a hump-backed bridge where the clear brown shallow water rippled over a bed of stones. The church appeared with granite nave and tower, standing on an eminence and approached, Sibyl said, by fifty-three steps. Perhaps they should go to Artifacts first?

The gallery was housed in an ancient building with bow windows and a front door set under a Georgian portico. When the door was pushed open a bell tinkled to summon Jimmy or Judy. This morning, however, they needed no summoning for both were in the first room, Judy dusting the dolls' house and Jimmy doing something to the ceiling spotlights. Sibyl introduced Trixie to them and Trixie was very gracious towards Judy, making no difference in her manner than she would have if the young woman had been properly married and worn a wedding ring.

Trixie was agreeably surprised by the objects in the exhibition and by the items Jimmy and Judy had for sale. She had not expected such a high standard. What she admired most particularly were the small pictures of domestic interiors done in embroidery, the patchwork quilts and the blown glass vases in colours of mother-of-pearl and butterfly wings. What she liked best of all and wanted to have was a clock.

There were four of these clocks, all different. The cases were ceramic, plain and smooth or made in a trellis work, glazed in blues and greens, painted with flowers or the moon and stars, each incorporating a gilt-rimmed face and quartz movement. Trixie's favourite was blue with a green trellis over the blue, a convolvulus plant with green leaves and pale pink trumpet flowers climbing the trellis and a gilt rim round the face of the clock which had hands of gilt and blue. The convolvulus reminded her of the pattern on her best china tea service. All the clocks had price cards beside them and red discs stuck to the cards.

"I should like to buy this clock," Trixie said to Judy.

"I'm terribly sorry but it's sold."

"Sold?"

"All the clocks were sold at the private view. Roland Elm's work is tremendously popular. He can't make enough of these clocks and he refuses to take orders."

"I still don't understand why I can't buy this one," said Trixie. "This is a shop, isn't it?"

Sibyl had put on her peevish look. "You can see the red sticker, can't you? You know what that means."

"I know what it means at the Royal Academy but hardly here surely."

"I really do wish I could sell it to you," said Judy, "but I can't."

Trixie lifted her shoulders. She was very disappointed and wished she hadn't come. She had been going to buy Sibyl a pear carved from polished pear wood but now she thought better of it. The church also was a let-down, dark, poky and smelling of mould.

"Things have come to a pretty pass when shopkeepers won't sell their goods to you because they're upset by your manner."

"Judy wasn't upset by your manner," said Sibyl, puffing. "It's more than her reputation is worth to sell you something she's already sold."

"Reputation! I like that."

"I mean reputation as a gallery owner. Artifacts is quite highly regarded round here."

"You would have thought she and her—well, partner, would be glad of £62. I don't suppose they have two half-pennies to bless themselves with."

What Sibyl would have thought was never known for she was too out of breath to utter and when they got home had to lie down. Next morning another letter came from Mivvy.

"Nothing to say for herself, of course," said Trixie at breakfast. "Practically a carbon copy of Thursday's. She's going very funny. Do you know she told me sometimes she writes fifty letters in a week? God bless your pocket, I said. It's fortunate you can afford it."

They went to Princetown in Sibyl's car and Widecombe-in-the-Moor. Trixie sent postcards to Mivvy, Poppy, the Fishers and the woman who came in to clean and water the plants in the greenhouse. She would have to buy some sort of present for Sibyl before she left. A plant would have done, only Sibyl didn't like gardening. They went to a bird sanctuary and looked at some standing stones of great antiquity. Trixie was going home on Tuesday afternoon. On Tuesday morning another letter arrived from Mivvy all about the Fishers going to see the Queen Mother open a new arts centre in Leighton Buzzard. The Fishers were crazy about the Queen

Mother, watched for her engagements in advance and went wherever she went within a radius of 150 miles in order just to catch a glimpse of her. Once they had been at the front of the crowd and the Queen Mother had shaken hands with Dorothy Fisher.

"We're none of us getting any younger," said Sibyl, giggling.

"Well, my conscience, I know one thing," said Trixie. "The days have simply flown past while I've been here."

"I'm glad you've enjoyed yourself."

"Oh, I have, dear, only it would please me to see you a little less frail."

Trixie walked to the village on her own. Since she couldn't think of anything else she was going to have to buy the pear-wood pear for Sibyl. It was a warm sunny morning, one of the best days she'd had, and the front door of Artifacts stood open to the street. The exhibition was still on and the clocks (and their red "sold" discs) still there. A shaft of sunlight streamed across the patchwork quilts on to the Georgian dolls' house. There was no sign of Jimmy and Judy. The gallery was empty but for herself.

Trixie closed the door and opened it to make the bell ring. She picked up one of the pear-wood pears and held it out in front of her on the palm of her hand. She held it at arm's length the way she did when she had helped herself to an item in the supermarket just so that there couldn't be the slightest question of anyone suspecting her of shoplifting. No one came. Trixie climbed the stairs, holding the pear-wood pear out in front of her and clearing her throat to attract attention. There was no one upstairs. A blue Persian cat lay sleeping on a shelf between a ginger jar and a mug with an owl on it. Trixie descended. She closed the front door and opened it to make the bell ring. Jimmy and Judy must be a heedless pair, she thought. Anyone could walk in here and steal the lot.

Of course she could just take the pear-wood pear and leave a £5 note to pay for it. It cost £4.75. Why should she make Jimmy and Judy a present of 25p just because they were too idle to serve her? Then she remembered that when she had been here with Sibyl a door at the end of the passage had been open and through that door one could see the garden where there was a display of terracotta pots. It was probable Jimmy and Judy were out there, showing the pots to a customer.

Trixie went through the second room and down the passage. The door to the garden was just ajar and she pushed it open. On the lawn, in a cane chair, Judy lay fast asleep. A ledger had fallen off her lap and lay on the grass alongside a heap of books. Guides to the management of tax they were and some which looked like the gallery account books. It reminded Trixie of Poppy who was always falling asleep in the daytime, most embarrassingly sometimes, at the table or even while waiting for a bus. Judy had fallen asleep over her book-keeping. Trixie coughed. She said "Excuse me" very loudly and repeated it but Judy didn't stir.

What a way to run a business! It would serve them right if someone walked in and cleared their shop. It would teach them a lesson. Trixie pulled the door closed behind her. She found herself tiptoeing as she walked back along the passage and through the second room. In the first room she took the ceramic clock with the convolvulus on it off the shelf and put it into her bag and she took the card too with the red sticker on it so as not to attract attention to the clock's absence. The pear-wood pear she replaced among the other carved fruit.

The street outside seemed deserted. Trixie's heart was beating rather fast. She went across the road into the little newsagent's and gift shop and bought Sibyl a teacloth with a map of Devonshire on it. At the door, as she was coming out again, she saw Jimmy coming along the street towards the gallery with a bag of groceries under one arm and two pints of milk in the other. Trixie stayed where she was until he had gone into Artifacts.

She didn't much fancy the walk back but there was no help for it. When she got to the bridge over the stream she heard hooves behind her and for a second or two had a feeling she was pursued by men on horseback but it was only a girl who passed her, riding a fat white pony. Sibyl laughed when she saw the teacloth and said it was a funny thing to give someone who *lived* in Devonshire. Trixie felt nervous and couldn't eat her lunch. Jimmy and Judy would have missed the clock by now and the newsagent would have remembered a furtive-looking woman skulking in his doorway and described her to them and soon the police would come. If only Sibyl would hurry with the car! She moved so slowly, time had no meaning for her. At this rate Trixie wouldn't even catch her train at Exeter.

She did catch it—just. Sibyl's car had been followed for several miles of the way by police in a Rover with a blue lamp on top and Trixie's heart had been in her mouth. Why had she done it? What had possessed her to take something she hadn't paid for, she who when shopping in supermarkets held 17p pots of yogurt at arm's length?

Now she was safely in the train rushing towards Paddington she began to see things in a different light. She would have paid for that clock if they had let her. What did they expect if they refused to sell things they had on sale? And what *could* they expect if they went to sleep leaving their shop unattended? For a few moments she had a nasty little qualm that the police might be waiting for her outside her own door but they weren't. Inside all was as it should be, all was as she had left it except that Poppy had put a pint of milk in the fridge and someone had arranged dahlias in a vase—not Poppy, she wouldn't know a dahlia from a runner bean.

That would be just the place for the clock, on the wall bracket where at present stood a photograph of herself and Dorothy Fisher at Broadstairs in 1949. Trixie put the photograph away in a drawer and the clock where the photograph had been. It looked nice. It transformed a rather dull corner of the room. Trixie put one of the cups from her tea service beside it and it was amazing how well they matched.

Mivvy came round first thing in the morning. Before letting her in Trixie quickly snatched the clock off the shelf and thrust it inside the drawer with the photograph. It seemed so *exposed* up there, it seemed to tell its history in every tiny tick.

"How did you find Sibyl?"

Trixie wanted to say, I went in the train to Exeter and got out at the station and there was Sibyl waiting for me in her car . . . Only if you started mocking poor Mivvy where would you end? "Very frail, dear. I thought she was going a bit funny."

"I must drop her a line."

Mivvy always spoke as if her letters held curative properties. Receiving one of them would set you up for the winter. After she had gone Trixie considered replacing the clock on the shelf but thought better of it. Let it stay in the drawer for a bit. She had read of South American millionaires who have Old Masters stolen for them which they can never show but are obliged, for fear of discovery, to keep hidden away for ever in dark vaults.

Just before Christmas a letter came from Sibyl. They always sent each other Christmas letters. As Trixie said, if you can't get around to writing the rest of the year, at least you can at Christmas. Mivvy wrote hundreds. Sibyl didn't mention the theft of the clock or indeed mention the gallery at all. Trixie wondered why not. The clock was still in the drawer. Sometimes she lay awake in the night thinking about it, fancying she could hear its tick through the solid mahogany of the drawer, through the ceiling and the bedroom floorboards.

It was curious how she had taken a dislike to the convolvulus tea service. One day she found herself wrapping it in tissue paper and putting it away in the cupboard under the stairs. She took down all the trellis work round the front door and put up wires for the clematis instead. In March she wrote to Sibyl to enquire if there was a new exhibition on at Artifacts. Sibyl didn't answer for weeks. When she did she told Trixie that months and months back one of those ceramic clocks had been stolen from the gallery and a few days later an embroidered picture had also gone and furniture out of the dolls' house. Hadn't Sibyl mentioned it before? She thought she had but she was getting so forgetful these days.

Trixie took the clock out of the drawer and put it on the shelf. Because she knew she couldn't be found out she began to feel she hadn't done anything wrong. The Fishers were bringing Poppy round for a cup of tea. Trixie started unpacking the convolvulus tea service. She lost her nerve when she heard Gordon Fisher's car door slam and she put the clock away again. If she were caught now she might get blamed for the theft of the picture and the dolls' house furniture as well. They would say she had sold those things and how could she prove she hadn't?

Poppy fell asleep halfway through her second buttered scone.

"She gets funnier every time I see her," Trixie said. "Sad, really. Sibyl's breaking up too. She'll forget her own name next. You should see her letters. I'll just show you the last one." She remembered she couldn't do that, it wouldn't be wise, so she had to pretend she'd mislaid it.

"Will you be going down there again this year, dear?" said Dorothy.

"Oh, I expect so. You know how it is, you get to the stage of thinking it may be the last time."

Poppy woke up with a snort, said she hadn't been asleep and finished her scone.

Gordon asked Trixie, "Would you like to come with us and see Her Majesty open the new leisure complex in Rayleigh on Monday?"

Trixie declined. The Fishers went off to do their shopping, leaving Poppy behind. She was asleep again. She slept till six and, waking, asked Trixie if she had put something in her tea. It was most unusual, she said, for her to nod off like that. Trixie walked her back to the bus stop because the traffic whipped along there so fast you had to have your wits about you and drivers didn't respect zebra crossings the way they used to. Trixie marched across on the stripes, confident as a lollipop lady but without the lollipop, taking her life in her hands instead.

She wrote to Sibyl that she would come to Devonshire at the end of July, thinking that while there it might be best to make some excuse to avoid going near Artifacts. The clock was still in the drawer but wrapped up now in a piece of old flannel. Trixie had taken a dislike to seeing the colour of it each time she opened the drawer. She had a summer dress that colour and she wondered why she had ever bought it, it didn't flatter her, whatever it might do for the Queen Mother. Dorothy could have it for her next jumble sale.

Walking back from posting a letter, Mivvy fell over and broke her ankle. It was weeks getting back to normal. Well, you had to face it, it was never going to be *normal*. You wouldn't be exaggerating, Trixie wrote to Sibyl, if you said that obsession of hers for writing letters had crippled her for life. Sibyl wrote back to say she was looking forward to the last week of July and what did Trixie think had happened? They had caught the thief of the pieces from Artifacts trying to sell the picture to a dealer in Plymouth. He had said in court he hadn't taken the clock but you could imagine how much credence the magistrate placed on that!

Trixie unwrapped the clock and put it on the shelf. Next day she got the china out. She wondered why she had been so precipitate in pulling all that trellis off the wall, it looked a lot better than strands of wire on metal hooks. Mivvy came round in a taxi, hobbling up the path on two sticks, refusing the offer of the taxi driver's arm.

"You'll be off to Sibyl's in a day or two, will you, dear?"

Trixie didn't know how many times she had told her not till Monday week. She was waiting for Mivvy to notice the clock but at this rate she was going to have to wait till Christmas.

"What do you think of my clock?"

"What, up there? Isn't that your Wedgwood coffee pot, dear?"

Trixie had to get it down. She thrust it under Mivvy's nose and started explaining what it was.

But Mivvy knew already. "Of course I know it's a clock, dear. It's not the first time I've seen one of these. Oh my goodness, no. The young man who makes these, he's a friend of my nephew Tony, they were at art school together. Let me see, what's his name? It will come to me in a minute. A tree, isn't it? Oak? Ash? Peter Oak? No, Elm is his name. Something Elm. Roland Elm."

Trixie said nothing. The glazed surface of the clock felt very cold against the skin of her hands.

"He never makes them to order, you know. He just makes a limited number for a few selected galleries. Tony told me that. Where did you get yours, I wonder?"

Trixie said nothing. There was worse coming and she waited for it.

"Not around here, I'm sure. I know there are only two or three places in the country they go to. It will come to me in a minute. I shall be writing to Tony tomorrow and I'll mention about you having one of Richard's—no, I mean Raymond's, that is, Roland's, clocks. I always write to him on Tuesdays. Tuesday is his day. I'll mention you've got one with bindweed on it. They're all different, you know. He never makes two alike."

"It's convolvulus, not bindweed," said Trixie. "I'd rather you didn't write to Tony about it if you don't mind."

"Oh, but I'd like to mention it, dear. Why ever not? I won't mention your name if you don't want me to. I'll just say that lady who goes down to stay with Auntie Sibyl in Devonshire."

Trixie said she would walk with Mivvy up to the High Street. It was hopeless trying to get a taxi outside here. She fetched Mivvy's two sticks.

"You take my arm and I'll hold your other stick."

The traffic whipped along over the zebra crossing. You were at the mercy of those drivers, Trixie said, it was a matter of waiting till they condescended to stop.

"Don't you set foot on those stripes till they stop," she said to Mivvy.

Mivvy didn't, so the cars didn't stop. A container lorry, a juggernaut, came thundering along, but a good way off still. Trixie thought it was going much too fast.

"Now if we're quick," she said. "Run for it!"

Startled by the urgency in her voice, Mivvy obeyed, or tried to obey as Trixie dropped her arm and gave her a little push forward. The lorry's brakes screamed like people being tortured and Trixie jumped back, screaming herself, covering her face with her hands so as not to see Mivvy under those giant wheels.

Dorothy Fisher said she quite understood Trixie would still want to go to Sibyl's for her holiday. It was the best thing in the world for her, a rest, a complete change, a chance to forget. Trixie went down by train on the day after the funeral. She had the clock in her bag with her, wrapped first in tissue paper and then in her sky-blue dress. The first opportunity that offered itself she would take the clock back to Artifacts and replace it on the shelf she had taken it from. This shouldn't be too difficult. The clock was a dangerous possession, she could see that, like one of those notorious diamonds that carry a curse with them. Pretty though it was, it was an *unlucky* clock that had involved her in trouble from the time she had first taken it.

There was no question of walking to Artifacts this time. Sibyl was too frail for that. She had gone downhill a lot since last year and symptomatic of her deterioration was her exchange of the grey wig for a lilac-blue one. They went in the car though Trixie was by no means sure Sibyl was safe at the wheel.

As soon as they walked into the gallery Trixie saw that she had no hope of replacing the clock without being spotted. There was a desk in the first room now with a plump smiling lady sitting at it who Sibyl said was Judy's mother. Trixie thought that amazing—a mother not minding her daughter cohabiting with a man she wasn't married to. Living with a daughter living in sin, you might put it. Jimmy was in the second room, up on a ladder doing something to the window catch.

"They're having upstairs remodelled," said Sibyl. "You can't go up there." And when Trixie tried to make her way towards the garden door, "You don't want to be had up for trespassing, do you?" She winked at Judy's mother. "We're none of us getting any younger when all's said and done, are we?"

They went back to Sibyl's, the clock still in Trixie's bag. It seemed to have grown heavier. She could hear it ticking through the leather and the folds of the sky-blue dress. In the afternoon when Sibyl lay down on the sofa for her rest, the lilac wig stuck on top of a Poole pottery vase, Trixie went out for a walk, taking the clock with her. She came to the hump-backed bridge over the stream where the water was very low, for it had been a dry summer. She unwrapped the clock and dropped it over the low parapet into the water. It cracked but the trellis work and the convolvulus remained intact and the movement continued to move and to tick as well for all Trixie knew. The blue and green, the pink flowers and the gilt, gleamed through the water like some exotic iridescent shell.

Trixie went down the bank. She took off her shoes and waded into the water. It was surprisingly cold. She picked up a large flat stone and beat at the face of the clock with it. She beat with unrestrained fury, gasping and grunting at each blow. The green trellis and the blue sky, the glass face and the pink flowers, all shattered. But they were still there, bright jewel-like shards, for all to see who came this way across the bridge.

Squatting down, Trixie scooped up handfuls of pebbles and buried the pieces of clock under them. With her nails she dug a pit in the bed of the stream and pushed the coloured fragments into it, covering them with pebbles. Her hands were bleeding, her knees were bruised and her dress was wet. In spite of her efforts the bed of the stream was still spread with ceramic chips and broken glass and pieces of gilt metal. Trixie began to sob and crawl from side to side of the stream, ploughing her hands through the blue and green and gold gravel, and it was there that one of Sibyl's neighbours found her as he was driving home over the bridge.

He lifted her up and carried her to his car.

"Tick-tock," said Trixie. "Tick-tock. Convolvulus clock."

[1987]

Sandra Cisneros
(1954–present)

Geraldo No Last Name

Born in Chicago to a Mexican father and a Mexican-American mother, Sandra Cisneros never did well in school as a child. Out of class, however, she read voraciously: "Books transformed my surroundings into something wonderful." Her mother often took her and her brother to the public library; now Cisneros speaks regularly at public libraries and advocates their government and community support.

Her reading inspired her to write, so Cisneros joined the staff of her high school literary magazine, took a writing workshop in her junior year in college, and has since dedicated herself to writing. Integral to her writing process is communal inspiration and editing with others, an aspect that is important to a writer whose roots are firmly based in the Hispanic-American community.

Cisneros has received a National Endowment for the Arts fellowship for fiction writing. She has published *House on Mango Street,* an acclaimed collection of stories, and *Woman Howling Creek and Other Stories* (1991), a collection that was chosen as one of the "Best Books of 1991." *Woman Howling Creek* defines in biting language what it is like to be a Hispanic-American woman in a world dominated by white men.

She met him at a dance. Pretty too, and young. Said he worked in a restaurant, but she can't remember which one. Geraldo. That's all. Green pants and Saturday shirt. Geraldo. That's what he told her.

And how was she to know she'd be the last one to see him alive. An accident, don't you know, Hit and run. Marin, she goes to all those dances. Uptown. Logan. Embassy. Palmer. Aragon. Fontana. The Manor. She likes to dance. She knows how to do cumbias and salsas and rancheras even. And he was just someone she danced with. Somebody she met that night. That's right.

That's the story. That's what she said again and again. Once to the hospital people and twice to the police. No address. No name. Nothing in his pockets. Ain't it a shame.

Only Marin can't explain why it mattered, the hours and hours, for somebody she didn't even know. The hospital emergency room. Nobody but an intern working all alone. And maybe if the surgeon would've come, maybe if he hadn't lost so much blood, if the surgeon had only come, they would know who to notify and where. But what difference does it make? He wasn't anything to her. He wasn't her boyfriend or anything like that. Just another *brazer* who didn't speak English. Just another wetback. You know the kind. The ones who always look ashamed. And what was she doing out at three a.m. anyway? Marin who was sent home with her coat and some aspirin. How does she explain it?

She met him at a dance. Geraldo in his shiny shirt and green pants. Geraldo going to a dance.

What does it matter?

They never saw the kitchenettes. They never knew about the two-room flats and sleeping rooms he rented, the weekly money orders sent home, the currency exchange. How could they?

His name was Geraldo. And his home is in another country. The ones he left behind are far away. They will wonder. Shrug. Remember. Geraldo. He went north . . . we never heard from him again.

[1985]

Helena Maria Viramontes
(1954–present)

Snapshots

Born in East Los Angeles, Helena Maria Viramontes received her B.A. in English literature from Immaculate Heart College and went on to study at the University of California at Irvine. After winning a number of literary awards, she published her first story, "The Long Reconciliation towards the Heartland," in 1981. Her other published fiction— including "The Moths" (1982), "Snapshots" (1983), and "Growing" (1983)—addresses Latin American issues.

Viramontes reads and lectures extensively on issues concerning women of color, especially Chicanas, and self-awareness through writing. She edits a number of publications and continues to write.

It was the small things in life, I admit, that made me happy: ironing straight arrow creases on Dave's work khakis, cashing in enough coupons to actually save some money, or having my bus halt just right, so that I don't have to jump off the curb and crack my knee cap like that poor shoe salesman I read about in Utah. Now, it's no wonder that I wake mornings and try my damndest not to mimic the movements of ironing or cutting those stupid, dotted lines or slipping into my house shoes, groping for my robe, going to Marge's room to check if she's sufficiently covered, scruffling to the kitchen, dumping out the soggy coffee grounds, refilling the pot and only later realizing that the breakfast nook has been set for three, the iron is plugged in, the bargain page is open in front of me and I don't remember, I mean I really don't remember doing any of it because I've done it for thirty years now and Marge is already married. It kills me, the small things.

Like those balls of wool on the couch. They're small and senseless and yet, every time I see them, I want to scream. Since the divorce, Marge brings me balls and balls and balls of wool thread because she insists that I "take up a hobby," "keep as busy as a bee," or "make the best of things" and all that other goodnatured advice she probably hears from old folks who answer in such a way when asked how they've managed to live so long. Honestly, I wouldn't be surprised if she walked in one day with bushels of straw for me to weave baskets. My only response to her endeavors is to give her the hardest stares I know how when she enters the living room, opens up her plastic shopping bag and brings out another ball of bright colored wool thread. I never move. Just sit and stare.

"Mother."

She pronounces the words not as a truth but as an accusation.

"Please, Mother. Knit. Do something." And then she places the new ball on top of the others on the couch, turns toward the kitchen and leaves. I give her a minute before I look out the window to see her standing on the sidewalk. I stick out my tongue, even make a face, but all she does is stand there with that horrible yellow and black plastic bag against her fat leg, and wave good-bye.

Do something, she says. If I had a penny for all the things I have done, all the little details I was responsible for but which amounted to nonsense, I would be rich. But I haven't a thing to show for it. The human spider gets on prime time television for climbing a building because it's there. Me? How can people believe that I've fought against motes of dust for years or dirt attracting floors or perfected bleached white sheets when a few hours later the motes, the dirt, the stains return to remind me of the uselessness of it all? I missed the sound of swans slicing the lake water or the fluttering wings of wild geese flying south for a warm winter or the heartbeat I could have heard if I had just held Marge a little closer.

I realize all that time is lost now, and I find myself searching for it frantically under the bed where the balls of dust collect undisturbed and untouched, as it should be.

To be quite frank, the fact of the matter is I wish to do nothing, but allow indulgence to rush through my veins with frightening speed. I do so because I have never been able to tolerate it in anyone, including myself.

I watch television to my heart's content now, a thing I rarely did in my younger days. While I was growing up, television had not been invented. Once it was and became a must for every home, Dave saved and saved until we were able to get one. But who had the time? Most of mine was spent working part time as a clerk for Grants, then returning to create a happy home for Dave. This is the way I pictured it:

> His wife in the kitchen wearing a freshly ironed apron, stirring a pot of soup, whistling a whistle-while-you-work tune, and preparing frosting for some cupcakes so that when he drove home from work, tired and sweaty, he would enter his castle to find his cherub baby in a pink day suit with newly starched ribbons crawling to him and his wife looking at him with pleasing eyes and offering him a cupcake.

It was a good image I wanted him to have and every day I almost expected him to stop, put down his lunch pail and cry at the whole scene. If it wasn't for the burnt cupcakes, my damn varicose veins, and Marge blubbering all over her day suit, it would have made a perfect snapshot.

Snapshots are ghosts. I am told that shortly after women are married, they become addicted to one thing or another. In *Reader's Digest* I read stories of closet alcoholic wives who gambled away grocery money or broke into their children's piggy banks in order to quench their thirst and fill their souls. Unfortunately I did not become addicted to alcohol because my only encounter with it had left me senseless and with my face in the toilet bowl. After that, I never had the desire to repeat the performance of a senior in high school whose prom date never showed. I did consider my addiction a lot more incurable. I had acquired a habit much more deadly: nostalgia.

I acquired the habit after Marge was born, and I had to stay in bed for months because of my varicose veins. I began flipping through my family's photo albums (my father threw them away after mom's death) to pass the time and pain away. However I soon became haunted by the frozen moments and the meaning of memories. Looking at the old photos, I'd get real depressed over my second grade teacher's smile or my father's can of beer or the butt naked smile of me as a young teen, because every detail, as minute as it may seem, made me feel that so much had passed unnoticed. As a result, I began to convince myself that my best years were up and that I had nothing to look forward to in the future. I was too young and too ignorant to realize that that section of my life relied wholly on those crumbling photographs and my memory and I probably wasted more time longing for a past that never really existed. Dave eventually packed them up in a wooden crate to keep me from hurting myself. He was good in that way. Like when he clipped roses for me. He made sure the thorns were cut off so I didn't have to prick myself while putting them in a vase. And it was the same thing with the albums. They stood in the attic for years until I brought them down a day after he remarried.

The photo albums are unraveling and stained with spills and fingerprints and filled with crinkled faded gray snapshots of people I can't remember anymore, and I turn the pages over and over again to see if somehow, some old dream will come into my blank mind. Like the black and white television box does when I turn it on. It warms up then flashes instant pictures, instant lives, instant people.

Parents. That I know for sure. The woman is tall and long, her plain, black dress is over her knees, and she wears thick spongelike shoes. She's over to the right of the photo, looks straight ahead at the camera. The man wears white, baggy pants that go past his waist, thick suspenders. He smiles while holding a dull-faced baby. He points to the camera. His sleeves pulled up, his tie undone, his hair is messy, as if some wild woman has driven his head between her breasts and run her fingers into his perfect greased ducktail.

My mother always smelled of smoke and vanilla and that is why I stayed away from her. I suppose that is why my father stayed away from her as well. I don't even remember a time when I saw them show any sign of affection. Not like today. No sooner do I turn off the soaps when I turn around and catch two youngsters on a porch swing, their mouths open, their lips chewing and chewing as if they were sharing a piece of three day old liver. My mom was always one to believe that such passion be restricted to the privacy of one's house and then, there too, be demonstrated with efficiency and not this urgency I witness almost every day. Dave and I were good about that.

Whenever I saw the vaseline jar on top of Dave's bedstand, I made sure the door was locked and the blinds down. This anticipation was more exciting to me than him lifting up my flannel gown over my head, pressing against me, slipping off my underwear then slipping in me. The vaseline came next, then he came right afterwards. In the morning, Dave looked into my eyes and I could never figure out what he expected to find. Eventually, there came a point in our relationship when passion passed to Marge's generation, and I was somewhat relieved. And yet, I could never imagine Marge doing those types of things that these youngsters do today, though I'm sure she did them on those Sunday afternoons when she carried a blanket and a book, and told me she was going to the park to do some reading and returned hours later with the bookmark in the same place. She must have done them, or else how could she have gotten engaged, married, had three children all under my nose, and me still going to check if she's sufficiently covered?

"Mother?" Marge's voice from the kitchen. It must be evening. Every morning it's the ball of wool, every evening it's dinner. Honestly, she treats me as if I have an incurable heart ailment. She stands under the doorway.

"Mother?" Picture it: She stands under the doorway looking befuddled, as if a movie director instructs her to stand there and look confused and upset; stand there as if you have seen your mother sitting in the same position for the last nine hours.

"What are you doing to yourself?" Marge is definitely not one for originality and she repeats the same lines every day. I'm beginning to think our conversation is coming from discarded scripts. I know the lines by heart, too. She'll say: "Why do you continue to do this to us?" and I'll answer: "Do what?" and she'll say: "This"—waving her plump, coarse hands over the albums scattered at my feet—and I'll say: "Why don't you go home and leave me alone?" This is the extent of our conversation and usually there is an optional line like: "I brought you something to eat," or "Let's have dinner," or "Come look what I have for you," or even "I brought you your favorite dish."

I think of the times, so many times, so many Mother's Days that passed without so much as a thank you or how sweet you are for giving us thirty years of your life. I know I am to blame. When Marge first started school, she had made a ceramic handprint for me to hang in the kitchen. My hands were so greasy from cutting the fat off some porkchops, I dropped it before I could even unwrap my first Mother's Day gift. I tried gluing it back together again with flour and water paste, but she never forgave me and I never received another gift until after the divorce. I wonder what happened to the ceramic handprint I gave to my mother?

In the kitchen I see that today my favorite dish is Chinese food getting cold in those little coffin-like containers. Yesterday my favorite dish was a salami sandwich, and before that a half eaten rib, no doubt left over from Marge's half hour lunch. Last week she brought me some Sunday soup that had fish heads floating around in some greenish broth. When I threw it down the sink, all she could think of to say was: "Oh, Mother."

We eat in silence. Or rather, she eats. I don't understand how she can take my indifference. I wish that she would break out of her frozen look, jump out of any snapshot and slap me in the face. Do something. Do something. I begin to cry.

"Oh, Mother," she says, picking up the plates and putting them in the sink.

"Mother, please."

There's fingerprints all over this one, my favorite. Both woman and child are clones: same bathing suit, same ponytails, same ribbons. The woman is looking directly at the camera, but the man is busy making a sand castle for his daughter. He doesn't see the camera or the woman. On the back of this one, in vague pencil scratching, it says: San Juan Capistrano.

This is a bad night. On good nights I avoid familiar spots. On bad nights I am pulled towards them so much so that if I sit on the chair next to Dave's I begin to cry. On bad nights I can't sleep and on bad nights I don't know who the couples in the snapshots are. My mother and me? Me and Marge? I don't remember San Juan Capistrano and I don't remember the woman. She faded into thirty years of trivia. I don't even remember what I had for dinner, or rather, what Marge had for dinner, just a few hours before. I wrap a blanket around myself and go into the kitchen to search for some evidence, but except for a few crumbs on the table, there is no indication that Marge was here. Suddenly, I am relieved when I see the box containers in the trash under the sink. I can't sleep the rest of the night wondering what happened to my ceramic handprint, or what was in the boxes. Why can't I remember? My mind thinks of nothing but those boxes in all shapes and sizes. I wash my face with warm water, put cold cream on, go back to bed, get up and wash my face again. Finally, I decide to call Marge at 3:30 in the morning. The voice is faint and there is static in the distance.

"Yes?" Marge asks automatically.

"Hello," Marge says. I almost expected her to answer her usual "Dave's Hardware."

"Who is this?" Marge is fully awake now.

"What did we . . ." I ask, wondering why it was suddenly so important for me to know what we had for dinner. "What did you

have for dinner?" I am confident that she'll remember every movement I made or how much salt I put on whatever we ate, or rather,
she ate. Marge is good about details.

"Mother?"

"Are you angry that I woke you up?"

"Mother. No. Of course not."

I could hear some muffled sounds, vague voices, static. I can tell
she is covering the mouthpiece with her hand. Finally George's voice.

"Mrs. Ruiz," he says, restraining his words so that they almost
come out slurred, "Mrs. Ruiz, why don't you leave us alone?" and
then there is a long, buzzing sound. Right next to the vaseline jar are
Dave's cigarettes. I light one though I don't smoke. I unscrew the jar
and use the lid for an ashtray. I wait, staring at the phone until it rings.

"Dave's Hardware," I answer. "Don't you know what time it
is?"

"Yes." It isn't Marge's voice. "Why don't you leave the kids
alone?" Dave's voice is not angry. Groggy, but not angry. After a
pause I say:

"I don't know if I should be hungry or not."

"You're a sad case." Dave says it as coolly as a doctor would say,
you have terminal cancer. He says it to convince me that it is totally
out of his hands. I panic. I picture him sitting on his side of the bed
in his shorts, smoking under a dull circle of light. I know his bifocals
are down to the tip of his nose.

"Oh, Dave," I say. "Oh, Dave." The static gets worse.

"Let me call you tomorrow."

"No. It's just a bad night."

"Olga," Dave says so softly that I can almost feel his warm breath
on my face.

"Olga, why don't you get some sleep?"

The first camera I ever saw belonged to my grandfather. He won
it in a cock fight. Unfortunately he didn't know two bits about it, but
he somehow managed to load the film. Then he brought it over to
our house. He sat me on the lawn. I was only five or six years old,
but I remember the excitement of everybody coming around to get
into the picture. I can see my grandfather clearly now. I can picture
him handling the camera slowly, touching the knobs and buttons to
find out how the camera worked while the men began milling around
him expressing their limited knowledge of the invention. I remember
it all so clearly. Finally he was able to manage the camera, and he took
pictures of me standing near my mother with the wives behind us.

My grandmother was very upset. She kept pulling me out of the picture, yelling to my grandfather that he should know better, that snapshots steal the souls of the people and that she would not allow my soul to be taken. He pushed her aside and clicked the picture.

The picture, of course, never came out. My grandfather, not knowing better, thought that all he had to do to develop the film was unroll it and expose it to the sun. After we all waited for an hour, we realized it didn't work. My grandmother was very upset and cut a piece of my hair, probably to save me from a bad omen.

It scares me to think that my grandmother may have been right. It scares me even more to think I don't have a snapshot of her. If I find one, I'll tear it up for sure.

[1985]

Nicholasa Mohr

(?–present)

A Time with a Future

(Carmela)

Puerto Rican and born in New York City, Nicholasa Mohr has developed a style of fiction rooted in her cultural identity that universalizes the condition of characters who share her background. Her books include *Nilda* (1974); *El Bronx Remembered* (1975); *In Nueva York* (1977); *Felita* (1979); *Rituals of Survival* (1985), a collection of which "A Time with a Future" is a part; and *Going Home* (1986).

Mohr's many books have received a number of coveted literary awards, and she has lectured extensively throughout the country. She has been described in the *New York Times Book Review* as "an old-fashioned writer whose stories stick to your ribs. No complicated symbolism here, no trendy obscurity of meaning, no hopeless despair or militant ethnicity. Her people endure because they are people."

Rituals of Survival is a testimonial to poor urban women who persevere despite their suppression by men.

"A whole lifetime together, imagine! And now it's over." Edna spoke, holding back tears. "I don't know what I would do if I were Mama, honest."

"Poor Mama," murmured Mary, "she's had such a hard time of it. I'm glad that in these last few years they had each other. Papa was her whole life . . ." Mary stopped and began to sob quietly. Edna put her arms around Mary, who buried her head in her sister's bosom.

285

"Oh Edna, it's so sad to see it all come to an end. The end of something so special."

"Come on, Mary." Edna very gently pushed Mary away from her. "Let's not get like this. Think of Ma. If she sees us crying, it'll be worse for her. We all have to figure this thing out calmly and rationally."

"I know." Mary wiped her eyes and swallowed. "It's . . . the finality of it that's so hard for me to bear, you know? But you're right, we're all Mom's got now, so it's up to us to decide what's best. At her age, it's like you say, she can't be left alone."

"That's more like it, and we can't stay here day after day indefinitely like this. I don't know how long Joe's mother is going to hold out with my kids. How about you? Exactly how long do you think Mark's gonna come home from work to take care of your three and do housework? That's why, when Roberto gets here, I'll discuss what Joe and I have agreed to. Then all three of us have to sit down and decide Mama's future."

Carmela had left her daughters seated in the kitchen, entered the small bedroom of her four-room flat and closed the door, shutting out their voices. She was sick of her daughters' tear-stained faces, their wailing, crying and self-pity. Grown women, with families, acting like children. Carmela shook her head; it was all too much. Her whole body was tired; every bone, every muscle ached. She pulled back the bedspread, kicked off her shoes and lay down.

They had buried Benjamin two days ago, but her daughters had insisted on remaining with her both nights. And that meant Carmela had to make the daybed in the other room, share her own bed with one of her daughters, find more sheets, towels, dishes and all the extra work that was part of caring for others. She had not been able to rest; not as she should, by herself, alone with her private grief and deep sense of relief. There had been too many people at the funeral. Benjamin's friends from the union, neighbors and people she had not seen in years. Carmela felt her eyelids closing with a heaviness from lack of sleep. She had not really slept peacefully in over a week and, before that, for what had seemed like a timeless battle, she had hardly known sleep at all.

Her mind was still filled with him, with Benjamin. When they had laid Benjamin out in the casket, they had pinned a bright scarlet carnation on the lapel of his best suit. The rich red color of the flower contrasted sharply with the dry greyness of his skin and accentuated the dark purple lines of pain that the long illness had etched in his face.

Carmela had asked the morticians to replace the red carnation with a white one; this change had made it easier to look at him.

She remembered her Freddie all too vividly. There are things one never forgets, always feels. Like my Freddie, Carmela nodded. His small casket had been laden with flowers. They had placed a bright red rose in his hands which were cupped together as if in prayer. For him, this had been the right color, matching his full red mouth which was fixed in a serene smile. He appeared to be sleeping and, for one long moment, Carmela had actually believed that Freddie would look up, his dark eyes smiling, and question her. "Where am I, Mami? What am I doing here?" And she would respond, "A bad dream, my baby. Freddie, you and me, we are both having a bad dream."

But it was no dream. Freddie's illness had been unexpected, swift and real. In a matter of days she had lost him. Not like Benjamin; more than a year of waiting patiently for him to die.

At first it had seemed no more than a bad cold. Freddie had a low fever and a sore throat. But he got sicker and his breathing became difficult, then unbearable. With each intake of air, he emitted a rasping, honking sound, and his small chest caved in, then extended until it seemed about to burst. Carmela was frightened and alone. Benjamin was on the night shift again. While the others slept soundly, Carmela dressed Freddie warmly. She went to a neighbor and asked her to look after the children until she returned from the clinic with Freddie. The bus was not there, and Carmela decided it would be quicker to walk the many long blocks to the emergency clinic. Even through the blankets she could feel Freddie struggling to breathe as she carried him as fast as her feet could take her. At the emergency clinic she explained with great effort in her halting English why she was there, and then waited for her name to be called.

The young doctor spoke gently to her. "You have a very sick baby. He must stay here, in the hospital. Understand . . . mother? Usted comprende? Si, very good." Carmela's head was spinning. She asked "But how? Why? He all right yesterday. He play with the brother and sisters. Por favor, doctor, give to me the medicina, and I take care of my baby in home. Mi casa is much better for him, yes?" The young doctor shook his head, "No! He's too sick to leave hospital." Lifting his hands, he covered his head and face, gesturing to her. "We have to put him in an oxygen tent so he can breathe. He has pneumonia, understand? Muy enfermo niño . . . comprende, madre?" She felt the fear deep inside, shivering as if someone had replaced her blood with ice water. "Por favor, doctor, he never go away from me, he no talk good English too much . . . pero Freddie understands good everything. He no go in school . . . only cuatro, four years." The young doctor nodded reassuringly, "He'll be all right in hospital, Mrs. Puig, you go home to your casa. Take care of your other children. Then you can come back later and stay with Freddie. The nurse will give you all the information. Don't worry, no apures, we are going to take good care of your baby. Make him well. Go home, get some rest." As they took him away, Freddie had turned to her, wide-eyed and scared, fighting for breath.

As soon as Benjamin came home from work, Carmela returned, staying by Freddie's side for the better part of two days. Freddie was not improving, but he had not gotten worse. When he was awake, he smiled at her from under the oxygen tent and she smiled back, telling him all about the things she would get for him after he got well again.

When on the third day she had made her brief visit home to check on the others, Benjamin complained.

"Two days! Two days! I can't stay out another day. Woman, what am I gonna do for money to buy food, pay rent . . . when they dock me? I must get back to work. Freddie's all right now. He's in the best place, in the hospital with the doctors who know better than you what to do." This time Carmela fought back. "But if something should happen to him, I want to be there at his side. Freddie mustn't be alone." Benjamin was unshaken. "I can't be here with the kids, cooking, washing and doing your housework . . . just in case something happens! There's plenty men out there looking for jobs. I'll lose my job . . . woman! If you want to go when I'm not here, call in a neighbor or get a friend. How about Sara, you've done her plenty of favors, eh?" Carmela resisted. "What friends? When do I have time to make friends? Neighbors can't be staying here all day with our kids, and neither can Sara. Besides, she's alone with her own children and worse off than us. There's only you; nobody else can stay here except you. Ben . . . maybe you can ask for part-time work just a few more days until Freddie is over the crisis . . . maybe . . ." Benjamin shouted, "Stop it!" Full of his own fears, his mind raced with memories of his childhood in a time where death and starvation had dictated his existence. And for two days now, the words to a song he had not heard since he was a small boy would not leave his mind; they played on his lips over and over.

First the tremors,
then the typhoid

follows hunger with every breath
we pray for joy, for better times
but the only relief is the promise of death!

The peasants of his tiny rural village would sing this song during the typhoid epidemic. Benjamin had lost his father, two older brothers and baby sister, leaving only his mother, older sister and younger brother. He was nine when he became head of the household. Sometimes he would get work at the fields or at the sugar refinery, working from sun-up to sundown, bringing home twenty-five, maybe thirty cents a day, depending on the work to be done. Other days he would work chopping wood, running errands and cleaning the hog pens, to be paid in food; usually leftovers, but enough so that they wouldn't starve at home. At thirteen, when his mother died, his sister found work as a domestic and he and his younger brother set out on their own.

"Absolutely not, woman! There's a goddam depression out there. Do you think I'm gonna let us all starve? I ain't selling apples or shoelaces in the street, not when I got a job to go to. And we don't take charity in this family. I go back to work tomorrow and you . . . you can do what the hell you want!" Carmela kept silent. Benjamin had a strong will and his fears justified his reasoning. She understood she could not persuade him.

Carmela had not wanted Freddie to die alone in the hospital, but that's how it had happened. For the next three days, she had only been able to be with him for a few hours, and always with the thought of the others that she left at home, unattended for the most part. That evening when Mr. Cooper, owner of the candy store, sent a message that the hospital had called on the public phone asking her to come right away, Carmela guessed what it was they would tell her.

"Too late. We did everything we possibly could." The young doctor was compassionate and visibly upset. "Double pneumonia . . . there was nothing we could give him. All of us did the best we could. We are all very, very sorry. Mrs. Puig, Freddie was a wonderful little boy."

That was in another lifetime, the time of the Great Depression, before the Second World War, before penicillin, antibiotics and miracle drugs. Today it would have been different; children don't have to die from that illness anymore. Medicine, in this lifetime, knows no limits. Look at an old man like Benjamin, eh? Kept alive, full of disease and tortured by pain beyond human endurance. And for what? No future, no hope, only the knowledge that each day he remained alive would be a torment for both of them.

Carmela opened her eyes and yawned, stretching her body. There was no sense in expecting sleep to come, take over and soothe away her weariness. Too much was still happening inside, repeating itself. The past was still the present and the present was not yet real.

When the doctor told her about Benjamin, she had insisted he be told as well. It was too much for her at this time; no longer did she have that kind of strength for others. Besides, Benjamin was a proud man, and it was only right. He had already suspected what the doctors confirmed; he was frightened, but not shocked. Calmly, Benjamin had told her he was resigned to the inevitable, but wanted to ask her for one last favor. And that request stirred and brought to the surface those deep and private feelings of hatred and revenge that can only be felt by one human being for another when they have been as close as Benjamin and Carmela. Then, as he spoke, Carmela felt herself spinning with rage.

"Carmela, no matter how sick I get, don't send me away. Let me die here in my own bed, Carmelita, here with you, by your side."

A tirade of words she had been nurturing, rehearsing and storing away for that day when she would leave him, walk out, walk out for good, choked Carmela. "Remember Freddie? Remember our son, Benjamin? How he died alone? In a strange place, in a strange bed. Without me by his side. I owed him at least as much as you ask of me. A baby, four years old with no one to comfort him from the fear of death, to guide him gently into the unknown. It all happened thirty-eight years ago, but I remember. And now, today, now . . . you want the right to die here, safe and secure in my arms. I didn't give birth to you! You selfish, hateful man, how well I know you!"

They had looked at each other silently. He, waiting for her to answer. She, unable to speak, afraid of that explosion of terrible words that would vent her rage. Now it was so easy to hurt him, to make him suffer as she had suffered the death and loss of her child. She couldn't speak, not one word left her lips. Carmela saw him old and tired, bracing himself against death, preparing himself and seeking her help. He spoke again, this time pleading.

"Promise, Carmela, that's all I ask of you. Just this favor and never will I ask you for another thing; I give you my word . . . just don't, don't send me away; no matter what, let me die at home."

Carmela had hidden her resentment and put aside her hatred.

Instead, she responded as always, to the unspoken bond that existed between them, that dependency on each other.

And she had promised, "It'll be all right, Benjamin, you can remain at home. No matter how sick you get. Don't worry, I won't let them take you away. You can stay here with me . . . until it's over."

This pact, built on survival, was what held them together; it was what had cemented them to a lifetime of sharing without so much as a day's voluntary separation. That security, that dependency, was the foundation of their marriage; solid and tough, like a boulder of impenetrable granite.

For a full year she had nursed him, giving him medicine, caring for him as he got weaker, almost every minute of the day and night. In time, she had to bathe him, give him the bedpan and finally spoon-feed him. His body, at first, was still strong and straight. They had not slept together for many years and so Carmela had been amazed by his supple body, the muscular limbs and tightness of skin that was unusual for a man as old as Benjamin. But, as he got sicker and lost weight, his body became frail and bent; his skin hung loosely as if lightly tacked onto his bones.

The sleepless nights, when he called out to her for comfort not once, but constantly . . . the three flights she had to climb, loaded with bundles, began to rip Carmela apart. The burden of his illness gave her no time to rest. Completely exhausted, she decided to speak to him about her promise.

"Benjamin, maybe it's better for you in the hospital. Listen, think about it, please. They can care for you better there, give you stronger medicine, maybe, eh? Look, Benjamin, I'm so tired, because there's nothing more I can do for you. Please, I don't know how long I can hold out . . . please think about it. I promise, I'll be out to see you every day; every single day I'll be by your side at the hospital, I swear . . ."

"No, you promised me! And now you talk about sending me out! You said I could stay. Carmela, you've become hard-hearted to say this to me. No!" His eyes had filled with tears. Like a child, he clung desperately to her, grabbing her hands, groping at her body. "Please, in the name of God . . . please don't send me away. Let me die here, with you . . . you promised!" Carmela had pushed him away, tearing at his fingers, shoving and struggling, unable to free herself from his fierce grip. "You promised! Now that I'm dying, I don't matter anymore . . . you can't send me away . . . you can't . . ."

"Selfish man, you deserve to die alone, just like my dead baby! It would be justice to send you away . . . away from me."

Again the words remained unspoken; instead, she said "All right, stop it! Stop! For God's sake, you can stay, I promise you. But I'm getting some help. I can't do it all alone. All right, I said you can stay!" Only then, after she had reassured him, had Benjamin released her.

Carmela had run away to the other side of the apartment and had put her hands over her ears to shut out his crying. But she still heard his loud sobbing and screaming.

"Carmela, Carmelita, you are a good woman!"

Carmela was able to get some help; a practical nurse came three times a week and later, every day. Benjamin journeyed each day on a long painful road that would lead to death. The kind of merciless journey that comes with cancer. The cancer had started in his lower intestines and finally ran rampant through his body, leaving him helpless, barely able to move. But still he clung to life, determined to put up a battle; fighting to survive was all he knew.

He would call out "Carmela . . . get me some water, Carmela, I don't want the nurse, tell her to leave. Do something for this pain! Carmela, give me something. Don't leave me, Carmela." And she would hope and pray that before he could utter her name once more, he would stop breathing.

Then, at last, he lapsed into a coma, feebly clinging to life. He would utter sounds and sentences which were, for the most part, unintelligible. Sometimes he screamed out the names of his own parents, brothers and sisters. Events of his childhood, memories of back home filled his mind and escaped from his lips. He spoke mostly in Spanish, laughing, crying and asking questions. No one knew what he wanted and, after two days, no one listened except Carmela. Maybe at this time, Carmela hoped, he would say something about their dead child; but in all his tangled words and gibberish, Freddie's name was never mentioned.

Her children had been at the apartment since their father's latest turn for the worse. That day, they all sat in the kitchen, drinking coffee and hot chocolate, waiting for him to die. They shared the vigil, taking turns at Benjamin's bedside. Late that evening, Roberto called his mother and when she returned, they found Benjamin staring blankly, not breathing. A look of peace spread over his face, as if the pain had finally disappeared. Gently, Carmela closed his eyes and mouth, kissed his dry lips and covered his face with the sheet.

Again, thoughts about the funeral, the people, the flowers and Freddie crowded Carmela's thoughts. It was as if her thinking pattern were following a cycle, winding up always with Benjamin's death. Perhaps she was avoiding this latest part of the whole business? Carmela knew she had to deal with her children, grown-ups who still insisted on that relationship of mother and child. Now they felt themselves to be in charge. Carmela sighed, almost out of patience. She heard the front door and voices. That would be Roberto, and now her children would begin another discussion about her future.

She had been through their weddings, the birth of their children, marital disputes from time to time; always she had listened and given her support. What they wanted now, and what they might ask of her, created an anxiety that drained Carmela's energy. In a few minutes she would get up and speak to them. Sooner or later they had to talk.

"Mama can come home with me, we'll find the room; Suzie and Gigi can double up . . ." Mary looked at her brother and sister nervously, then continued, "Mark won't mind, honest."

"No," Edna responded, "I think it's better if she comes with me; after all, we have the big house. Nobody will be put out for space."

"I wish I could say it's all right at my house, but the way things are with me and Gloria, well . . ." Roberto hesitated.

"We understand, don't worry," Edna said. "Besides, it's better for Mama to be with her own daughter."

"Financially, I can always help out, you know that," Roberto smiled.

"She's got Papa's pension and some savings; she's all right as far as that goes," Edna said, "but if we need anything more, I'll let you know."

"There's only one thing about her going with you," Mary said. "She's not gonna want to go way out to Long Island. Port Jefferson is too far away from everything for her."

"She'll get used to it. It'll take a little time, that's all. Anyway, you're far away yourself, Mary. Mount Vernon isn't around the corner! And your apartment isn't big enough for another person. Where are you gonna put her?"

"You know what I think? I don't think we are gonna get Mama out of this old apartment, period." Roberto nodded emphatically. "She's too attached to it. Remember the time they took a trip to Puerto Rico, back to Papa's town, to see about retiring there? Ma said she couldn't stand it. She missed the city, her friends, everything.

How long have they been living here in this place? Twenty-six years or something like that, right?"

"It'll be better for her to leave here. Personally, I don't know how anybody can live here, in this city, if they can get out . . ." Edna shook her head, "The noise, the pollution, the crime! Oh, I know I wouldn't want my kids here. When we were kids, maybe it was different . . . it just seems worse today . . ."

"Mama said it's not too bad since they put up all the new middle-income buildings. She says it's better than ever with new shops and all kinds of interesting people around. Ma says she can go right to Broadway and buy anything she wants at any time of the day or . . ."

"Stop being so naive . . ." Edna interrupted. "Mary, how long can Mama stay by herself? She's sixty-six. In a few years, when she can't cope, then what? It'll be a lot worse to get her out of here. I'm not going to be commuting back and forth. And I know you, Mary . . . you too, Roberto, especially the way your marriage is going, who knows where you'll be, eh? No, we have to make a decision between us and stick to it. Now, listen to what Joe and I have planned . . ." Edna paused, making sure her brother and sister were listening. "Mama has a fairly good income from Papa's pension, so she won't be a financial burden to anyone. She's in good health, except for some arthritis now and then, but nobody ever hears her complain. And, she has some savings . . . all right, then. With a little more than half her savings we can convert the playroom area on the lower level of my house into living quarters for Mama. Like a kind of efficiency apartment, with her own kitchenette and half-bath. She won't need much more because she will have the rest of the house as well. This is necessary because we all know how independent Mama is. After that initial investment, I won't charge her rent or anything. She can live there as long as she wants . . . I mean, for the rest of her days."

Roberto opened his mouth to speak, but thought better of it. Instead, he shrugged and smiled, looking at Mary. She smiled back. After a long silence, Mary said, "It sounds pretty good . . . what do you think, Roberto?" "Well, so far it's the best plan, and also the only plan. There's only one thing, like I said, Ma's gotta go for it." "She will," Edna said, "but it's up to us to convince her. The two of you better back me on this. Understand? We have to be united in this thing? Well?" Mary and Robert nodded in agreement. "Good," Edna continued, "now, what to do with this place? Mama's got all kinds of pots and pans . . . look at all of this furniture and junk. I suppose she'll want to take some of this with her . . . let's see . . ."

Carmela sat up, put on her shoes and placed the bedspread neatly back on her bed. She heard the voices of her children. Well, she might as well get it over with. Carmela opened a bureau drawer, removed a small grey metal box and opened it. She searched among her valuable papers; the will she and Benjamin had made, the life insurance policy she had taken out on herself many years ago and still faithfully paid every month, some very old photographs, letters from her children as youngsters and from her grandchildren. Finally, she found the large manilla envelope with all the material she was looking for. She closed the box and put it back. Then she walked into the kitchen where her children were waiting.

"Ma, how you feeling?" Roberto kissed his mother lightly on the forehead.

"How about something to eat, Ma?" Edna asked. "Some tea? Or a little hot broth?"

"No," Carmela sat, holding the envelope in her hands. "I'm fine; I'm not hungry."

"Mama, you should eat more, you're getting too thin . . . it's not good for you. You should eat regularly, it could affect your . . ."

"Ma . . ." interrupted Edna, ignoring Mary, "we have to have a serious talk."

"I wasn't finished," snapped Mary.

"Mama's not hungry!" Edna looked directly at Mary. "All right?"

"Listen . . ." Roberto spoke. "Why don't I go out and get us all something to eat. Chinese or Cuban . . . so nobody has to cook."

"Sit down, Roberto." Edna then continued in a quiet, calm voice, "We have all the food we need here . . ." Turning to Carmela, she went on, "Mama, now that Papa isn't here anymore . . . we want you to know that you have us and you don't have to be alone. You are our responsibility now, just as if you had Papa. We all know this . . . don't we?" She turned to Mary and Roberto.

"Yes."

"Oh yes, Mama."

"We've all discussed this a great deal, just between ourselves. And, we've decided on a plan that we know you'll like. Of course, we want to talk it over with you first, so that we have your approval. But, I'm certain that when you hear what it is, you'll be pleased."

"Oh yes, Mama, wait until you hear what Edna . . . what we . . . oh, go ahead, Edna, tell her . . ." Mary smiled.

"Joe and I agreed and thought this out carefully. You . . . are coming to live with us, Mama. With me, Joe and the kids. We are the ones with a big house. Mary's in an apartment and Roberto doesn't exactly know where he's gonna settle; not the way things are right now. I know how proud you are and how independent, so you'll want to contribute something. Here's what we think . . . you know my house is a split level and there's room for expansion, right?"

Carmela felt an urge to open the envelope at that moment and tell them, so that Edna could stop talking nonsense. But instead, she listened, trying to hide her impatience.

". . . so that your savings, or part anyway, can pay for your private apartment. Of course, as I said, you don't need such a big area, because you can share the house with the rest of us. Outside, you can take a section of the lot, Mama, if you want to have a vegetable garden or flowers. The kids would love it, and of course Joe and I won't take a cent, you can live the rest of your days rent free. You know Joe's pleased, he wants you to feel welcome in our home." Edna was almost out of breath. "Well, there, I've said my piece . . . now what do you think, Mama?"

All three waited for Carmela to respond. She held out the envelope.

"I've got something to show all of you." Carefully she removed its contents and spread several sheets of paper out on the kitchen table. "I suppose I should have said something before this, but with your father's illness and everything else . . ." Carmela gestured that they come closer. "Here we are . . . take a look. It's a co-op. The building's only been up about three years. Everything is brand new. My apartment is on the sixteenth floor, on the northwest corner, just like I wanted, with lots of windows and it's got a terrace! Imagine, a terrace . . . I'm gonna feel rich . . . that's what. Look . . . kids, here are the floor plans, see? I got one bedroom, a living room–dining room, a brand-new kitchen. Oh, and here's an incinerator for garbage. They've got one on every floor and a community room with all kinds of activities. I heard from some of the people who live there, that there are some well-known experts, lecturers, coming in to speak about all kinds of subjects. The best part is that it's right here, around the corner, on Amsterdam Avenue. On the premises we have a drugstore, stationery and delicatessen. You know, I put my name down for this with a deposit right after Papa got sick. He hadn't wanted us to move, but once I knew how things would be, I went ahead. They called me just before Benjamin died, when he was almost in a coma, and asked if I could move in around the first of the month. I took a chance . . . I knew he couldn't last much longer, and said yes. That's in two weeks!" Carmela was busy tracing the floor plans with her fingers showing them the closets and cabinet space. "Here? See, I've paid the purchase, my savings covered the amount. You are all welcome to come and sit on the terrace . . . wait until you see how beautiful it is . . ."

"Mama . . ." Edna's voice was sharp, "what about what I just said? I finished explaining to you . . . a very important plan concerning your future. What about it?"

"I'm moving the first of the month, Edna," Carmela continued to look at floor plans. "But, I thank you and your husband for thinking of me."

"Is that it, Mama?"

"Yes, Edna."

"You already signed the lease, paid the money and everything?"

"Yes, all I have to do is move in, Edna."

"Well . . . I'm glad to see you figured it all out, Mama." Edna looked at Mary and Roberto; they avoided her eyes. "There's just one thing, eh? Who is gonna look after you when you can't . . . ? You are sixty-six, ma! Sixty-six!"

"Not you, Edna." Carmela looked at her children. "Or you, Mary, or you, Roberto."

"Mama, I don't think you are being practical. Now, I'm too far away to be here if anything happens! If you get sick . . . and so is Mary. And as far as Roberto is concerned . . ."

"I'll manage."

"Manage? Please, Mama. Mary, Roberto, what do you have to say? Don't you think Mama should have asked us first about this? Mama, you should have spoken to us! After all, we are your children."

"I didn't ask any of you to come here when Papa was so sick, did I? I never called or bothered you. I took care of all of you once, and I took care of him . . . now, I want the privilege of taking care of myself!" There was a long silence and Carmela continued. "Thank you Edna, Mary, Roberto; you are all good children. But I can take care of myself; I've done it all my life."

"If that's the way you see it, Mama, I'm with you." Roberto said. "Right, Mary?"

"Okay . . . I guess . . ." Mary smiled weakly at Edna.

"All right, Mama." Edna stood up. "Go ahead . . . but remember, I tried my best to work something out for you. When something happens, you won't have anybody near you."

"I appreciate your good intentions, Edna, but it's all settled."

"When are you moving in, Mama?" asked Mary.

"I hope on the first, but since the landlord here knows me so well after twenty-six years, and we always paid our rent, I might be able to stay a few days extra, if things are not ready at the new place. I've already arranged everything with the movers and with the super of the new building and . . ."

They spoke for a while and Carmela talked excitedly about her new apartment.

"I feel better now that you all know . . . in fact," a feeling of drowziness overcame her, "I think I might take a nap."

"Mama," Edna said, "we are all gonna have to leave soon, you know, get back to our families. But if you need us, please call."

"Good," Carmela smiled, "we should all get back to our own business of living, eh? The dead are at peace, after all. You were all a great help. Your husbands and children need you, and you too, Roberto . . . Gloria and the kids would like to see you, I'm sure."

"Go on, Mama, take your nap. Edna and I will cook something light, and then I think I'll call Mark to pick me up."

Carmela put everything back into her envelope and left. She closed her door and lay down, a sweet twilight state embraced her; it seemed to promise a deep sleep.

"Papa isn't even buried more than two days and she's acting like he's been dead forever." Edna was on the verge of tears. "She looks so happy . . . I don't understand it. You would think . . . Oh, I don't know anymore!"

"I'm sure she feels bad," Mary said, "it's just that she's also happy about her new apartment."

"She feels bad, all right. Mama doesn't want to show it, so that we don't feel worse than we already do," Roberto said.

"Well then, why is it that when Papa died she hardly cried. A few tears and moist eyes, but you can't call that crying!"

"Well, what do you want from her?" Roberto snapped.

"I don't know! She should be sorry . . . yes, that's what; I want her to be sorry!"

"What do you mean, sorry?!" Roberto whispered angrily.

"He was her husband of a lifetime, and my father, I . . ." Edna's voice became louder "want her to feel it!"

"Shh . . ." Mary snapped, "stop it!"

"How do you know what she feels inside? Leave her alone! It's always what you want? What about what she wants?"

"Go on, defend her. You've always been her favorite; mama's boy!"

"Quit that shit!" Roberto went towards Edna.

"For God's sake," Mary whimpered, "we're acting like kids . . . what's happening?"

"That's right, whimper like a baby, Mary." Edna began to cry, "that's all you know how to do. Everybody else has to make your decisions . . ."

"This is ridiculous," Roberto said, "I'm leaving."

"Go on . . . walk out, that's what you always do, you've done it to your own family now."

"Screw you . . . bitch!" Roberto called out, then slammed the front door.

"Come on, Edna, please stop it. What's the use of fighting? Mama's made up her mind. Let's make supper and forget about all of this. Roberto will come back after he cools off. You better call Joe; I think it's time we went home."

The two sisters began to open the refrigerator and pantry to prepare the evening meal. Mary turned to Edna, who was still sobbing quietly.

"What's the matter now?"

"I . . . wish she would be sorry . . ."

Carmela stood on the small terrace of her new apartment. She looked down at the city laid out before her. In between and over some of the buildings she could see the Hudson River and part of the George Washington Bridge. The river was dotted with sailboats and small craft that slipped in and out of sight. Overhead she had a view of a wide blue sky, changing clouds competing with the bright sun. Flocks of birds were returning home now that winter was over. Carmela took a deep breath. There was a warmth in the air; spring was almost here. In a couple of weeks she could bring out her new folding chair, lounger and snack table. Soon she would bring out her plants. New buds would begin to sprout, growing strong and healthy with the abundant sunlight and fresh air.

Carmela missed no one in particular. From time to time her children and grandchildren visited. She was pleased to see them for a short while and then was even happier when they left. In a few days it would be a whole year since Benjamin's death. It seemed like yesterday sometimes, and sometimes it was like it never happened.

She rarely thought about Benjamin. Memories of her days as a young girl became frequent, clear and at times quite vivid. Before Carmela had married at sixteen, she had dreamed of traveling to all the many places she had seen in her geography book. After school she would often go with her brothers to the docks of San Juan just to watch the freighters and big ships.

"When I grow up I'm going to work and travel on those ships."

"Carmelita, don't be silly, you can't. Girls can't join the navy or the merchant marine."

How she had wished she had been born a boy, to be able to travel anywhere, to be part of that world. Carmela loved the water; ocean, sea, river, all gave her a feeling of freedom.

She looked out from her terrace at the river, and a sense of peace filled her whole being. Carmela recognized it was the same exhilarating happiness she had experienced as a young girl, when each day would be a day for her to reckon with, all her own, a time with a future.

[1986]

Louise Erdrich
(1954–present)

Fleur

Born in Little Falls, Minnesota, the daughter of a Chippewa Indian and a German-born teacher working with the Bureau of Indian Affairs, Louise Erdrich grew up influenced by her Indian roots and by cross-cultural pressures. After earning degrees from Dartmouth and Johns Hopkins universities, she began to write extensively. In 1982 she won literary awards for her stories "The World's Greatest Fisherman," "Scales," and "Saint Marie." *Love Medicine* (1984) includes fourteen interwoven stories told by people of different cultures; *The Beet Queen* (1986) presents the tales of a number of characters of Native-American descent who survive despite the odds. *Tracks* (1988), from which "Fleur" is taken, also deals with issues of Native Americans and survival. Erdrich has co-authored her most recent novel, *The Crown of Columbus* (1992), with her husband, Michael Dorris. She publishes in various journals and continues to write.

The first time she drowned in the cold and glassy waters of Lake Turcot, Fleur Pillager was only a girl. Two men saw the boat tip, saw her struggle in the waves. They rowed over to the place she went down, and jumped in. When they dragged her over the gunwales, she was cold to the touch and stiff, so they slapped her face, shook her by the heels, worked her arms back and forth, and pounded her back until she coughed up lake water. She shivered all over like a dog, then took a breath. But it wasn't long afterward that those two men disappeared. The first wandered off, and the other, Jean Hat, got himself run over by a cart.

It went to show, my grandma said. It figured to her, all right. By saving Fleur Pillager, those two men had lost themselves.

The next time she fell in the lake, Fleur Pillager was twenty years old and no one touched her. She washed onshore, her skin a dull dead gray, but when George Many Women bent to look closer, he saw her chest move. Then her eyes spun open, sharp black riprock, and she looked at him. "You'll take my place," she hissed. Everybody scattered and left her there, so no one knows how she dragged herself home. Soon after that we noticed Many Women changed, grew afraid, wouldn't leave his house, and would not be forced to go near water. For his caution, he lived until the day that his sons brought him a new tin bathtub. Then the first time he used the tub he slipped, got knocked out, and breathed water while his wife stood in the other room frying breakfast.

Men stayed clear of Fleur Pillager after the second drowning. Even though she was good-looking, nobody dared to court her because it was clear that Misshepeshu, the waterman, the monster, wanted her for himself. He's a devil, that one, love-hungry with desire and maddened for the touch of young girls, the strong and daring especially, the ones like Fleur.

Our mothers warn us that we'll think he's handsome, for he appears with green eyes, copper skin, a mouth tender as a child's. But if you fall into his arms, he sprouts horns, fangs, claws, fins. His feet are joined as one and his skin, brass scales, rings to the touch. You're fascinated, cannot move. He casts a shell necklace at your feet, weeps gleaming chips that harden into mica on your breasts. He holds you under. Then he takes the body of a lion or a fat brown worm. He's made of gold. He's made of beach moss. He's a thing of dry foam, a thing of death by drowning, the death a Chippewa cannot survive.

Unless you are Fleur Pillager. We all knew she couldn't swim. After the first time, we thought she'd never go back to Lake Turcot. We thought she'd keep to herself, live quiet, stop killing men off by drowning in the lake. After the first time, we thought she'd keep the good ways. But then, after the second drowning, we knew that we were dealing with something much more serious. She was haywire, out of control. She messed with evil, laughed at the old women's advice, and dressed like a man. She got herself into some half-forgotten medicine, studied ways we shouldn't talk about. Some say she kept the finger of a child in her pocket and a powder of unborn rabbits in a leather thong around her neck. She laid the heart of an owl on her tongue so she could see at night, and went out, hunting, not even in her own body. We know for sure because the next morning, in the snow or dust, we followed the tracks of her bare feet and saw where they changed, where the claws sprang out, the pad broadened and pressed into the dirt. By night we heard her chuffing cough, the bear cough. By day her silence and the wide grin she threw to bring down our guard made us frightened. Some thought that Fleur Pillager should be driven off the reservation, but not a single person who spoke like this had the nerve. And finally, when people were just about to get together and throw her out, she left on her own and didn't come back all summer. That's what this story is about.

During that summer, when she lived a few miles south in Argus, things happened. She almost destroyed that town.

When she got down to Argus in the year of 1920, it was just a small grid of six streets on either side of the railroad depot. There were two elevators, one central, the other a few miles west. Two stores competed for the trade of the three hundred citizens, and three churches quarreled with one another for their souls. There was a frame building for Lutherans, a heavy brick one for Episcopalians, and a long narrow shingled Catholic church. This last had a tall slender steeple, twice as high as any building or tree.

No doubt, across the low, flat wheat, watching from the road as she came near Argus on foot, Fleur saw that steeple rise, a shadow thin as a needle. Maybe in that raw space it drew her the way a lone tree draws lightning. Maybe, in the end, the Catholics are to blame. For if she hadn't seen that sign of pride, that slim prayer, that marker, maybe she would have kept walking.

But Fleur Pillager turned, and the first place she went once she came into town was to the back door of the priest's residence attached to the landmark church. She didn't go there for a handout, although she got that, but to ask for work. She got that too, or the town got her. It's hard to tell which came out worse, her or the men or the town, although the upshot of it all was that Fleur lived.

The four men who worked at the butcher's had carved up about a thousand carcasses between them, maybe half of that steers and the other half pigs, sheep, and game animals like deer, elk, and bear. That's not even mentioning the chickens, which were beyond counting. Pete Kozka owned the place, and employed Lily Veddar, Tor Grunewald, and my stepfather, Dutch James, who had brought my mother down from the reservation the year before she disappointed him by dying. Dutch took me out of school to take her place. I kept house half the time and worked the other in the butcher shop, sweeping floors, putting sawdust down, running a hambone across the street to a customer's bean pot or a package of sausage to the corner. I was a good one to have around because until they needed me, I was invisible. I blended into the stained brown walls, a skinny, big-nosed girl with staring eyes. Because I could fade into a corner or squeeze beneath a shelf, I knew everything, what the men said when no one was around, and what they did to Fleur.

Kozka's Meats served farmers for a fifty-mile area, both to slaughter, for it had a stock pen and chute, and to cure the meat by smoking it or spicing it in sausage. The storage locker was a marvel, made of many thicknesses of brick, earth insulation, and Minnesota timber, lined inside with sawdust and vast blocks of ice cut from Lake Turcot, hauled down from home each winter by horse and sledge.

A ramshackle board building, part slaughterhouse, part store, was fixed to the low, thick square of the lockers. That's where Fleur worked. Kozka hired her for her strength. She could lift a haunch or carry a pole of sausages without stumbling, and she soon learned cutting from Pete's wife, a string-thin blonde who chain-smoked and handled the razor-sharp knives with nerveless precision, slicing close to her stained fingers. Fleur and Fritzie Kozka worked afternoons, wrapping their cuts in paper, and Fleur hauled the packages to the lockers. The meat was left outside the heavy oak doors that were only opened at 5:00 each afternoon, before the men ate supper.

Sometimes Dutch, Tor, and Lily ate at the lockers, and when they did I stayed too, cleaned floors, restoked the fires in the front smokehouses, while the men sat around the squat cast-iron stove spearing slats of herring onto hardtack bread. They played long games of poker or cribbage on a board made from the planed end of a slat crate. They talked and I listened, although there wasn't much to hear since almost nothing ever happened in Argus. Tory was married, Dutch had lost my mother, and Lily read circulars. They mainly discussed about the auctions to come, equipment, or women.

Every so often, Pete Kozka came out front to make a whist, leaving Fritzie to smoke cigarettes and fry raised doughnuts in the back room. He sat and played a few rounds but kept his thoughts to himself. Fritzie did not tolerate him talking behind her back, and the one book he read was the New Testament. If he said something, it concerned weather or a surplus of sheep stomachs, a ham that smoked green or the markets for corn and wheat. He had a good-luck talisman, the opal-white lens of a cow's eye. Playing cards, he rubbed it between his fingers. That soft sound and the slap of cards was about the only conversation.

Fleur finally gave them a subject.

Her cheeks were wide and flat, her hands large, chapped, muscular. Fleur's shoulders were broad as beams, her hips fishlike, slippery, narrow. An old green dress clung to her waist, worn thin where she sat. Her braids were thick like the tails of animals, and swung against her when she moved, deliberately, slowly in her work, held in and half-tamed, but only half. I could tell, but the others never saw. They never looked into her sly brown eyes or noticed her teeth, strong and curved and very white. Her legs were bare, and since she padded around in beadwork moccasins they never saw that her fifth toes were missing. They never knew she'd drowned. They were blinded, they were stupid, they only saw her in the flesh.

And yet it wasn't just that she was a Chippewa, or even that she was a woman, it wasn't that she was good-looking or even that she was alone that made their brains hum. It was how she played cards.

Women didn't usually play with men, so the evening that Fleur drew a chair up to the men's table without being so much as asked, there was a shock of surprise.

"What's this," said Lily. He was fat, with a snake's cold pale eyes and precious skin, smooth and lily-white, which is how he got his name. Lily had a dog, a stumpy mean little bull of a thing with a belly drum-tight from eating pork rinds. The dog liked to play cards just like Lily, and straddled his barrel thighs through games of stud, rum poker, vingt-un. The dog snapped at Fleur's arm that first night, but cringed back, its snarl frozen, when she took her place.

"I thought," she said, her voice soft and stroking, "you might deal me in."

There was a space between the heavy bin of spiced flour and the wall where I just fit. I hunkered down there, kept my eyes open, saw her black hair swing over the chair, her feet solid on the wood floor. I couldn't see up on the table where the cards slapped down, so after they were deep in their game I raised myself up in the shadows, and crouched on a sill of wood.

I watched Fleur's hands stack and ruffle, divide the cards, spill them to each player in a blur, rake them up and shuffle again. Tor, short and scrappy, shut one eye and squinted the other at Fleur. Dutch screwed his lips around a wet cigar.

"Gotta see a man," he mumbled, getting up to go out back to the privy. The others broke, put their cards down, and Fleur sat alone in the lamplight that glowed in a sheen across the push of her breasts. I watched her closely, then she paid me a beam of notice for the first time. She turned, looked straight at me, and grinned the white wolf grin a Pillager turns on its victims, except that she wasn't after me.

"Pauline there," she said, "how much money you got?"

We'd all been paid for the week that day. Eight cents was in my pocket.

"Stake me," she said, holding out her long fingers. I put the coins in her palm and then I melted back to nothing, part of the walls and tables. It was a long time before I understood that the men would not have seen me no matter what I did, how I moved. I wasn't anything like Fleur. My dress hung loose and my back was already curved, an old woman's. Work had roughened me, reading made my eyes sore, caring for my mother before she died had hardened my face. I was not much to look at, so they never saw me.

When the men came back and sat around the table, they had drawn together. They shot each other small glances, stuck their tongues in their cheeks, burst out laughing at odd moments, to rattle Fleur. But she never minded. They played their vingt-un, staying even as Fleur slowly gained. Those pennies I had given her drew nickels and attracted dimes until there was a small pile in front of her.

Then she hooked them with five-card draw, nothing wild. She dealt, discarded, drew, and then she sighed and her cards gave a little shiver. Tor's eye gleamed, and Dutch straightened in his seat.

"I'll pay to see that hand," said Lily Veddar.

Fleur showed, and she had nothing there, nothing at all.

Tor's thin smile cracked open, and he threw his hand in too.

"Well, we know one thing," he said, leaning back in his chair, "the squaw can't bluff."

With that I lowered myself into a mound of swept sawdust and slept. I woke up during the night, but none of them had moved yet, so I couldn't either. Still later, the men must have gone out again, or Fritzie come out to break the game, because I was lifted, soothed, cradled in a woman's arms and rocked so quiet that I kept my eyes shut while Fleur rolled me into a closet of grimy ledgers, oiled papers, balls of string, and thick files that fit beneath me like a mattress.

The game went on after work the next evening. I got my eight cents back five times over, and Fleur kept the rest of the dollar she'd won for a stake. This time they didn't play so late, but they played regular, and then kept going at it night after night. They played poker now, or variations, for one week straight, and each time Fleur won exactly one dollar, no more and no less, too consistent for luck.

By this time, Lily and the other men were so lit with suspense that they got Pete to join the game with them. They concentrated, the fat dog sitting tense in Lily Veddar's lap, Tor suspicious, Dutch stroking his huge square brow, Pete steady. It wasn't that Fleur won that hooked them in so, because she lost hands too. It was rather that she never had a freak hand or even anything above a straight. She only took on her low cards, which didn't sit right. By chance, Fleur should have gotten a full or flush by now. The irritating thing was she beat with pairs and never bluffed, because she couldn't, and still she ended up each night with exactly one dollar. Lily couldn't believe, first of all, that a woman could be smart enough to play cards, but even if she was, that she would then be stupid enough to cheat for a dollar a night. By day I watched him turn the problem over, his hard white face dull, small fingers probing at his knuckles, until he finally thought he had Fleur figured out as a bit-time player, caution her game. Raising the stakes would throw her.

More than anything now, he wanted Fleur to come away with something but a dollar. Two bits less or ten more, the sum didn't matter, just so he broke her streak.

Night after night she played, won her dollar, and left to stay in a place that just Fritzie and I knew about. Fleur bathed in the slaughtering tub, then slept in the unused brick smokehouse behind the lockers, a windowless place tarred on the inside with scorched fats. When I brushed against her skin I noticed that she smelled of the walls, rich and woody, slightly burnt. Since that night she put me in the closet I was no longer afraid of her, but followed her close, stayed with her, became her moving shadow that the men never noticed, the shadow that could have saved her.

August, the month that bears fruit, closed around the shop, and Pete and Fritzie left for Minnesota to escape the heat. Night by night, running, Fleur had won thirty dollars, and only Pete's presence had kept Lily at bay. But Pete was gone now, and one payday, with the heat so bad no one could move but Fleur, the men sat and played and waited while she finished work. The cards sweat, limp in their fingers, the table was slick with grease, and even the walls were warm to the touch. The air was motionless. Fleur was in the next room boiling heads.

Her green dress, drenched, wrapped her like a transparent sheet. A skin of lakeweed. Black snarls of veining clung to her arms. Her braids were loose, half-unraveled, tied behind her neck in a thick loop. She stood in steam, turning skulls through a vat with a wooden paddle. When scraps boiled to the surface, she bent with a round tin sieve and scooped them out. She'd filled two dishpans.

"Ain't that enough now?" called Lily. "We're waiting." The stump of a dog trembled in his lap, alive with rage. It never smelled me or noticed me above Fleur's smoky skin. The air was heavy in my corner, and pressed me down. Fleur sat with them.

"Now what do you say?" Lily asked the dog. It barked. That was the signal for the real game to start.

"Let's up the ante," said Lily, who had been stalking this night all month. He had a roll of money in his pocket. Fleur had five bills in her dress. The men had each saved their full pay.

"Ante a dollar then," said Fleur, and pitched hers in. She lost, but they let her scrape along, cent by cent. And then she won some. She played unevenly, as if chance was all she had. She reeled them in. The game went on. The dog was stiff now, poised on Lily's knees, a ball of vicious muscle with its yellow eyes slit in concentration. It gave advice, seemed to sniff the lay of Fleur's cards, twitched and nudged. Fleur was up, then down, saved by a scratch. Tor dealt seven cards, three down. The pot grew, round by round, until it held all the money. Nobody folded. Then it all rode on one last card and they went silent. Fleur picked hers up and blew a long breath. The heat lowered like a bell. Her card shook, but she stayed in.

Lily smiled and took the dog's head tenderly between his palms.

"Say, Fatso," he said, crooning the words, "you reckon that girl's bluffing?"

The dog whined and Lily laughed. "Me too," he said, "let's show." He swept his bills and coins into the pot and then they turned their cards over.

Lily looked once, looked again, then he squeezed the dog up like a fist of dough and slammed it on the table.

Fleur threw her arms out and drew the money over, grinning that same wolf grin that she'd used on me, the grin that had them. She jammed the bills in her dress, scooped the coins up in waxed white paper that she tied with string.

"Let's go another round," said Lily, his voice choked with burrs. But Fleur opened her mouth and yawned, then walked out back to gather slops for the one big hog that was waiting in the stock pen to be killed.

The men sat still as rocks, their hands spread on the oiled wood table. Dutch had chewed his cigar to damp shreds, Tor's eye was dull. Lily's gaze was the only one to follow Fleur. I didn't move. I felt them gathering, saw my stepfather's veins, the ones in his forehead that stood out in anger. The dog had rolled off the table and curled in a knot below the counter, where none of the men could touch it.

Lily rose and stepped out back to the closet of ledgers where Pete kept his private stock. He brought back a bottle, uncorked and tipped it between his fingers. The lump in his throat moved, then he passed it on. They drank, quickly felt the whiskey's fire, and planned with their eyes things they couldn't say out loud.

When they left, I followed. I hid out back in the clutter of broken boards and chicken crates beside the stock pen, where they waited. Fleur could not be seen at first, and then the moon broke and showed her, slipping cautiously along the rough board chute with a bucket in her hand. Her hair fell, wild and coarse, to her waist, and her dress was a floating patch in the dark. She made a pig-calling sound, rang the tin pail lightly against the wood, froze suspiciously. But too late. In the sound of the ring Lily moved, fat and nimble, stepped right behind Fleur and put out his creamy hands. At his first touch, she whirled and doused him with the bucket of sour slops. He pushed her against the big fence and the package of coins split, went clinking and jumping, winked against the wood. Fleur rolled over once and vanished in the yard.

The moon fell behind a curtain of ragged clouds, and Lily followed into the dark muck. But he tripped, pitched over the huge flank of the pig, who lay mired to the snout, heavily snoring. I sprang out of the weeds and climbed the side of the pen, stuck like glue. I saw the sow rise to her neat, knobby knees, gain her balance, and sway, curious, as Lily stumbled forward. Fleur had backed into the angle of rough wood just beyond, and when Lily tried to jostle past, the sow tipped up on her hind legs and struck, quick and hard as a snake. She plunged her head into Lily's thick side and snatched a mouthful of his shirt. She grunted in pained surprise. He seemed to ponder, breathing deep. Then he launched his huge body in a swimmer's dive.

The sow screamed as his body smacked over hers. She rolled, striking out with her knife-sharp hooves, and Lily gathered himself upon her, took her foot-long face by the ears and scraped her snout and cheeks against the trestles of the pen. He hurled the sow's tight skull against an iron post, but instead of knocking her dead, he merely woke her from her dream.

She reared, shrieked, drew him with her so that they posed standing upright. They bowed jerkily to each other, as if to begin. Then his arms swung and flailed. She sank her black fangs into his shoulder, clasping him, dancing him forward and backward through the pen. Their steps picked up pace, went wild. The two dipped as one, box-stepped, tripped each other. She ran her split foot through his hair. He grabbed her kinked tail. They went down and came up, the same shape and then the same color, until the men couldn't tell one from the other in that light and Fleur was able to launch herself over the gates, swing down, hit gravel.

The men saw, yelled, and chased her at a dead run to the smokehouse. And Lily too, once the sow gave up in disgust and freed him. That is where I should have gone to Fleur, saved her, thrown myself on Dutch. But I went stiff with fear and couldn't unlatch myself from the trestles or move at all. I closed my eyes and put my head in my arms, tried to hide, so there is nothing to describe but what I couldn't block out, Fleur's hoarse breath, so loud it filled me, her cry in the old language, and my name repeated over and over among the words.

The heat was still dense the next morning when I came back to work. Fleur was gone but the men were there, slack-faced, hung over. Lily was paler and softer than ever, as if his flesh had steamed on his bones. They smoked, took pulls off a bottle. It wasn't noon yet. I worked awhile, waiting shop and sharpening steel. But I was sick, I was smothered, I was sweating so hard that my hands slipped on the knives, and I wiped my fingers clean of the greasy touch of the customers' coins. Lily opened his mouth and roared once, not in anger. There was no meaning to the sound. His boxer dog, sprawled limp beside his foot, never lifted its head. Nor did the other men.

They didn't notice when I stepped outside, hoping for a clear breath. And then I forgot them because I knew that we were all balanced, ready to tip, to fly, to be crushed as soon as the weather broke. The sky was so low that I felt the weight of it like a yoke. Clouds hung down, witch teats, a tornado's green-brown cones, and as I watched one flicked out and became a delicate probing thumb. Even as I picked up my heels and ran back inside, the wind blew suddenly, cold, and then came rain.

Inside, the men had disappeared already and the whole place was trembling as if a huge hand was pinched at the rafters, shaking it. I ran straight through, screaming for Dutch or for any of them, and then I stopped at the heavy doors of the lockers, where they had surely taken shelter. I stood there a moment. Everything went still. Then I heard a cry building in the wind, faint at first, a whistle and then a shrill scream that tore through the walls and gathered around me, spoke plain so I understood that I should move, put my arms out, and slam down the great iron bar that fit across the hasp and lock.

Outside, the wind was stronger, like a hand held against me. I struggled forward. The bushes tossed, the awnings flapped off storefronts, the rails of porches rattled. The odd cloud became a fat snout that nosed along the earth and sniffled, jabbed, picked at things, sucked them up, blew them apart, rooted around as if it was following a certain scent, then stopped behind me at the butcher shop and bored down like a drill.

I went flying, landed somewhere in a ball. When I opened my eyes and looked, stranger things were happening.

A herd of cattle flew through the air like giant birds, dropping dung, their mouths opened in stunned bellows. A candle, still lighted, blew past, and tables, napkins, garden tools, a whole school of drifting eyeglasses, jackets on hangers, hams, a checkerboard, a lampshade, and at last the sow from behind the lockers, on the run, her hooves a blur, set free, swooping, diving, screaming as everything in Argus fell apart and got turned upside down, smashed and thoroughly wrecked.

Days passed before the town went looking for the men. They were bachelors, after all, except for Tor, whose wife had suffered a blow to the head that made her forgetful. Everyone was occupied with digging out, in high relief because even though the Catholic steeple had been torn off like a peaked cap and sent across five fields, those huddled in the cellar were unhurt. Walls had fallen, windows were demolished, but the stores were intact and so were the bankers and shop owners who had taken refuge in their safes or beneath their cash registers. It was a fair-minded disaster, no one could be said to have suffered much more than the next, at least not until Fritzie and Pete came home.

Of all the businesses in Argus, Kozka's Meats had suffered worst. The boards of the front building had been split to kindling, piled in a huge pyramid, and the shop equipment was blasted far and wide. Pete paced off the distance the iron bathtub had been flung—a hundred feet. The glass candy case went fifty, and landed without so much as a cracked pane. There were other surprises as well, for the back rooms where Fritzie and Pete lived were undisturbed. Fritzie said the dust still coated her china figures, and upon her kitchen table, in the ashtray, perched the last cigarette she'd put out in haste. She lit it up and finished it, looking through the window. From there, she could see the old smokehouse Fleur had slept in was crushed to a reddish sand and the stock pens were completely torn apart, the rails stacked helter-skelter. Fritzie asked for Fleur. People shrugged. Then she asked about the others and suddenly, the town understood that three men were missing.

There was a rally of help, a gathering of shovels and volunteers. We passed boards from hand to hand, stacked them, uncovered what lay beneath the pile of jagged splinters. The lockers, full of the meat that was Pete and Fritzie's investment, slowly came into sight, still intact. When enough room was made for a man to stand on the roof, there were calls, a general urge to hack through and see what lay below. But Fritzie shouted that she wouldn't allow it because the meat would spoil. And so the work continued, board by board, until at last the heavy oak doors of the freezer were revealed and people pressed to the entry. Everyone wanted to be the first, but since it was my stepfather lost, I was let go in when Pete and Fritzie wedged through into the sudden icy air.

Pete scraped a match on his boot, lit the lamp Fritzie held, and then the three of us stood still in its circle. Light glared off the skinned and hanging carcasses, the crates of wrapped sausages, the bright and cloudy blocks of lake ice, pure as winter. The cold bit into us, pleasant at first, then numbing. We must have stood there a couple of minutes before we saw the men, or more rightly, the humps of fur, the iced and shaggy hides they wore, the bearskins they had taken down and wrapped around themselves. We stepped closer and tilted the lantern beneath the flaps of fur into their faces. The dog was there, perched among them, heavy as a doorstop. The three had hunched around a barrel where the game was still laid out, and a dead lantern and an empty bottle, too. But they had thrown down their last hands and hunkered tight, clutching one another, knuckles raw from beating at the door they had also attacked with hooks. Frost stars gleamed off their eyelashes and the stubble of their beards. Their faces were set in concentration, mouths open as if to speak some careful thought, some agreement they'd come to in each other's arms.

Power travels in the bloodlines, handed out before birth. It comes down through the hands, which in the Pillagers are strong and knotted, big, spidery, and rough, with sensitive fingertips good at dealing cards. It comes through the eyes, too, belligerent, darkest brown, the eyes of those in the bear clan, impolite as they gaze directly at a person.

In my dreams, I look straight back at Fleur, at the men. I am no longer the watcher on the dark sill, the skinny girl.

The blood draws us back, as if it runs through a vein of earth. I've come home and, except for talking to my cousins, live a quiet life. Fleur lives quiet too, down on Lake Turcot with her boat. Some say she's married to the waterman, Misshepeshu, or that she's living in shame with white men or windigos, or that she's killed them all. I'm about the only one here who ever goes to visit her. Last winter, I went to help out in her cabin when she bore the child, whose green eyes and skin the color of an old penny made more talk, as no one could decide if the child was mixed blood or what, fathered in a smokehouse, or by a man with brass scales, or by the lake. The girl is bold, smiling in her sleep, as if she knows what people wonder, as if she hears the old men talk, turning the story over. It comes up different every time and has no ending, no beginning. They get the middle wrong too. They only know that they don't know anything.

[1986]

Gish Jen
(1956–present)

In the American Society

Born to Chinese immigrant parents and raised in Scarsdale, New York, Gish Jen dutifully studied pre-med at Harvard and then business at Stanford. When neither field appealed to her, her parents suggested law school. But Jen (whose real name is Lillian) wanted to be a writer. When she chose the Iowa Writers Workshop for her graduate work, her parents refused to pay her tuition. She survived on grants, prizes, and the encouragement of her professors, developing a medium through which to describe the cultural gap she had struggled with since childhood.

Jen's novel, *Typical Americans* (1991), explores this culture gap, as do her stories. "In the American Society" is a part of the anthology *The New Generation: Fiction for Our Time from America's Writing Programs* (1987).

I. His Own Society

When my father took over the pancake house, it was to send my little sister Mona and me to college. We were only in junior high at the time, but my father believed in getting a jump on things. "Those Americans always saying it," he told us. "Smart guys thinking in advance." My mother elaborated, explaining that businesses took bringing up, like children. They could take years to get going, she said, years.

In this case, though, we got rich right away. At two months we were breaking even, and at four, those same hotcakes that could barely withstand the weight of butter and syrup were supporting our family with ease. My mother bought a station wagon with air conditioning, my father an oversized, red vinyl recliner for the back room; and as time went on and the business continued to thrive, my father started to talk about his grandfather and the village he had reigned over in China—things my father had never talked about when he worked for other people. He told us about the bags of rice his family would give out to the poor at New Year's, and about the people who came to beg, on their hands and knees, for his grandfather to intercede for the more wayward of their relatives. "Like that Godfather in the movie," he would tell us as, his feet up, he distributed paychecks. Sometimes an employee would get two green envelopes instead of one, which meant that Jimmy needed a tooth pulled, say, or that Tiffany's husband was in the clinker again.

"It's nothing, nothing," he would insist, sinking back into his chair. "Who else is going to take care of you people?"

My mother would mostly just sigh about it. "Your father thinks this is China," she would say, and then she would go back to her mending. Once in a while, though, when my father had given away a particularly large sum, she would exclaim, outraged, "But this here is the U—S—of—A!"—this apparently having been what she used to tell immigrant stock boys when they came in late.

She didn't work at the supermarket anymore; but she had made it to the rank of manager before she left, and this had given her not only new words and phrases, but new ideas about herself, and about America, and about what was what in general. She had opinions, now, on how downtown should be zoned; she could pump her own gas and check her own oil; and for all she used to chide Mona and me for being "copycats," she herself was now interested in espadrilles, and wallpaper, and most recently, the town country club.

"So join already," said Mona, flicking a fly off her knee.

My mother enumerated the problems as she sliced up a quarter round of watermelon: There was the cost. There was the waiting list. There was the fact that no one in our family played either tennis or golf.

"So what?" said Mona.

"It would be waste," said my mother.

"Me and Callie can swim in the pool."

"Plus you need that recommendation letter from a member."

"Come *on*," said Mona. "Annie's mom'd write you a letter in a *sec*."

My mother's knife glinted in the early summer sun. I spread some more newspaper on the picnic table.

"*Plus* you have to eat there twice a month. You know what that means." My mother cut another enormous slice of fruit.

"No, I *don't* know what that means," said Mona.

"It means Dad would have to wear a jacket, dummy," I said.

"Oh! Oh! Oh!" said Mona, clasping her hand to her breast. "Oh! Oh! Oh! Oh! Oh!"

We all laughed: my father had no use for nice clothes, and would wear only ten-year-old shirts, with grease-spotted pants, to show how little he cared what anyone thought.

"Your father doesn't believe in joining the American society," said my mother. "He wants to have his own society."

"So go to dinner without him." Mona shot her seeds out in long arcs over the lawn. "Who cares what he thinks?"

But of course we all did care, and knew my mother could not simply up and do as she pleased. For in my father's mind, a family owed its head a degree of loyalty that left no room for dissent. To embrace what he embraced was to love; and to embrace something else was to betray him.

He demanded a similar sort of loyalty of his workers, whom he treated more like servants than employees. Not in the beginning, of course. In the beginning all he wanted was for them to keep on doing what they used to do, and to that end he concentrated mostly on leaving them alone. As the months passed, though, he expected more and more of them, with the result that for all his largesse, he began to have trouble keeping help. The cooks and busboys complained that he asked them to fix radiators and trim hedges, not only at the restaurant, but at our house; the waitresses that he sent them on errands and made them chauffeur him around. Our head waitress, Gertrude, claimed that he once even asked her to scratch his back.

"It's not just the blacks don't believe in slavery," she said when she quit.

My father never quite registered her complaint, though, nor those of the others who left. Even after Eleanor quit, then Tiffany, then Gerald, and Jimmy, and even his best cook, Eureka Andy, for whom he had bought new glasses, he remained mostly convinced that the fault lay with them.

"All they understand is that assembly line," he lamented. "Robots, they are. They want to be robots."

There *were* occasions when the clear running truth seemed to eddy, when he would pinch the vinyl of his chair up into little peaks and wonder if he was doing things right. But with time he would always smooth the peaks back down; and when business started to slide in the spring, he kept on like a horse in his ways.

By the summer our dishboy was overwhelmed with scraping. It was no longer just the hashbrowns that people were leaving for trash, and the service was as bad as the food. The waitresses served up French pancakes instead of German, apple juice instead of orange, spilt things on laps, on coats. On the Fourth of July some greenhorn sent an entire side of fries slaloming down a lady's *massif centrale*. Meanwhile in the back room, my father labored through articles on the economy.

"What is housing starts?" he puzzled. "What is GNP?"

Mona and I did what we could, filling in as busgirls and bookkeepers and, one afternoon, stuffing the comments box that hung by the cashier's desk. That was Mona's idea. We rustled up a variety of pens and pencils, checked boxes for an hour, smeared the cards up with coffee and grease, and waited. It took a few days for my father to notice that the box was full, and he didn't say anything about it for a few days more. Finally, though, he started to complain of fatigue; and then he began to complain that the staff was not what it could be. We encouraged him in this—pointing out, for instance, how many dishes got chipped—but in the end all that happened was that, for the first time since we took over the restaurant, my father got it into his head to fire someone. Skip, a skinny busboy who was saving up for a sportscar, said nothing as my father mumbled on about the price of dishes. My father's hands shook as he wrote out the severance check; and he spent the rest of the day napping in his chair once it was over.

As it was going on midsummer, Skip wasn't easy to replace. We hung a sign in the window and advertised in the paper, but no one called the first week, and the person who called the second didn't show up for his interview. The third week, my father phoned Skip to see if he would come back, but a friend of his had already sold him a Corvette for cheap.

Finally a Chinese guy named Booker turned up. He couldn't have been more than thirty, and was wearing a lighthearted seersucker suit, but he looked as though life had him pinned: his eyes were bloodshot and his chest sunken, and the muscles of his neck seemed to strain with the effort of holding his head up. In a single dry breath he told us that he had never bussed tables but was willing to learn, and that he was on the lam from the deportation authorities.

"I do not want to lie to you," he kept saying. He had come to the United States on a student visa, had run out of money, and was now in a bind. He was loath to go back to Taiwan, as it happened—he looked up at this point, to be sure my father wasn't pro-KMT—but all he had was a phony social security card and a willingness to absorb all blame, should anything untoward come to pass.

"I do not think, anyway, that it is against law to hire me, only to be me," he said, smiling faintly.

Anyone else would have examined him on this, but my father conceived of laws as speed bumps rather than curbs. He wiped the counter with his sleeve, and told Booker to report the next morning.

"I will be good worker," said Booker.

"Good," said my father.

"Anything you want me to do, I will do."

My father nodded.

Booker seemed to sink into himself for a moment. "Thank you," he said finally. "I am appreciate your help. I am very, very appreciate for everything." He reached out to shake my father's hand.

My father looked at him. "Did you eat today?" he asked in Mandarin.

Booker pulled at the hem of his jacket.

"Sit down," said my father. "Please, have a seat."

My father didn't tell my mother about Booker, and my mother didn't tell my father about the country club. She would never have applied, except that Mona, while over at Annie's, had let it drop that our mother wanted to join. Mrs. Lardner came by the very next day.

"Why, I'd be honored and delighted to write you people a letter," she said. Her skirt billowed around her.

"Thank you so much," said my mother. "But it's too much trouble for you, and also my husband is . . ."

"Oh, it's no trouble at all, no trouble at all. I tell you." She leaned forward so that her chest freckles showed. "I know just how it is. It's a secret of course, but you know, my natural father was Jewish. Can you see it? Just look at my skin."

"My husband," said my mother.

"I'd be honored and delighted," said Mrs. Lardner with a little wave of her hands. "Just honored and delighted."

Mona was triumphant. "See, Mom," she said, waltzing around the kitchen when Mrs. Lardner left. "What did I tell you? 'I'm just honored and delighted, just honored and delighted.' " She waved her hands in the air.

"You know, the Chinese have a saying," said my mother. "To do nothing is better than to overdo. You mean well, but you tell me now what will happen."

"I'll talk Dad into it," said Mona, still waltzing. "Or I bet Callie can. He'll do anything Callie says."

"I can try, anyway," I said.

"Did you hear what I said?" said my mother. Mona bumped into the broom closet door. "You're not going to talk anything; you've already made enough trouble." She started on the dishes with a clatter.

Mona poked diffidently at a mop.

I sponged off the counter. "Anyway," I ventured, "I bet our name'll never even come up."

"That's if we're lucky," said my mother.

"There's all these people waiting," I said.

"Good," she said. She started on a pot.

I looked over at Mona, who was still cowering in the broom closet. "In fact, there's some black family's been waiting so long, they're going to sue," I said.

My mother turned off the water. "Where'd you hear that?"

"Patty told me."

She turned the water back on, started to wash a dish, then put it back down and shut the faucet.

"I'm sorry," said Mona.

"Forget it," said my mother. "Just forget it."

*   *   *

Booker turned out to be a model worker, whose boundless gratitude translated into a willingness to do anything. As he also learned quickly, he soon knew not only how to bus, but how to cook, and how to wait table, and how to keep the books. He fixed the walk-in door so that it stayed shut, reupholstered the torn seats in the dining room, and devised a system for tracking inventory. The only stone in the rice was that he tended to be sickly; but, reliable even in illness, he would always send a friend to take his place. In this way we got to know Ronald, Lynn, Dirk, and Cedric, all of whom, like Booker, had problems with their legal status and were anxious to please. They weren't all as capable as Booker, though, with the exception of Cedric, whom my father often hired even when Booker was well. A round wag of a man who called Mona and me *shou hou*—skinny monkeys—he was a professed nonsmoker who was nevertheless always begging drags off of other people's cigarettes. This last habit drove our head cook, Fernando, crazy, especially since, when refused a hit, Cedric would occasionally snitch one. Winking impishly at Mona and me, he would steal up to an ashtray, take a quick puff, and then break out laughing so that the smoke came rolling out of his mouth in a great incriminatory cloud. Fernando accused him of stealing fresh cigarettes too, even whole packs.

"Why else do you think he's weaseling around in the back of the store all the time," he said. His face was blotchy with anger. "The man is a frigging thief."

Other members of the staff supported him in this contention and joined in on an "Operation Identification," which involved numbering and initialing their cigarettes—even though what they seemed to fear for wasn't so much their cigarettes as their jobs. Then one of the cooks quit; and rather than promote someone, my father hired Cedric for the position. Rumors flew that he was taking only half the normal salary, that Alex had been pressured to resign, and that my father was looking for a position with which to placate Booker, who had been bypassed because of his health.

The result was that Fernando categorically refused to work with Cedric.

"The only way I'll cook with that piece of slime," he said, shaking his huge tattooed fist, "is if it's his ass frying on the grill."

My father cajoled and cajoled, to no avail, and in the end was simply forced to put them on different schedules.

The next week Fernando got caught stealing a carton of minute steaks. My father would not tell even Mona and me how he knew to be standing by the back door when Fernando was on his way out, but everyone suspected Booker. Everyone but Fernando, that is, who was sure Cedric had been the tip-off. My father held a staff meeting in which he tried to reassure everyone that Alex had left on his own, and that he had no intention of firing anyone. But though he was careful not to mention Fernando, everyone was so amazed that he was being allowed to stay that Fernando was incensed nonetheless.

"Don't you all be putting your bug eyes on me," he said. "*He's* the frigging crook." He grabbed Cedric by the collar.

Cedric raised an eyebrow. "Cook, you mean," he said.

At this Fernando punched Cedric in the mouth; and the words he had just uttered notwithstanding, my father fired him on the spot.

With everything that was happening, Mona and I were ready to be getting out of the restaurant. It was almost time: the days were still stuffy with summer, but our window shade had started flapping in the evening as if gearing up to go out. That year the breezes were full of salt, as they sometimes were when they came in from the East, and they blew anchors and docks through my mind like so many tumbleweeds, filling my dreams with wherries and lobsters and grainy-faced men who squinted, day in and day out, at the sky.

It was time for a change, you could feel it; and yet the pancake house was the same as ever. The day before school started my father came home with bad news.

"Fernando called police," he said, wiping his hand on his pant leg.

My mother naturally wanted to know what police; and so with much coughing and hawing, the long story began, the latest installment of which had the police calling immigration, and immigration sending an investigator. My mother sat stiff as whalebone as my father described how the man summarily refused lunch on the house and how my father had admitted, under pressure, that he knew there were "things" about his workers.

"So now what happens?"

My father didn't know. "Booker and Cedric went with him to the jail," he said. "But me, here I am." He laughed uncomfortably.

The next day my father posted bail for "his boys" and waited apprehensively for something to happen. The day after that he waited again, and the day after that he called our neighbor's law student son, who suggested my father call the immigration department under an alias. My father took his advice; and it was thus that he discovered that Booker was right: it was illegal for aliens to work, but it wasn't to hire them.

In the happy interval that ensued, my father apologized to my mother, who in turn confessed about the country club, for which my father had no choice but to forgive her. Then he turned his attention back to "his boys."

My mother didn't see that there was anything to do.

"I like to talking to the judge," said my father.

"This is not China," said my mother.

"I'm only talking to him. I'm not give him money unless he wants it."

"You're going to land up in jail."

"So what else I should do?" My father threw up his hands. "Those are my boys."

"Your boys!" exploded my mother. "What about your family? What about your wife?"

My father took a long sip of tea. "You know," he said finally, "in the war my father sent our cook to the soldiers to use. He always said it—the province comes before the town, the town comes before the family."

"A restaurant is not a town," said my mother.

My father sipped at his tea again. "You know, when I first come to the United States, I also had to hide-and-seek with those deportation guys. If people did not help me, I'm not here today."

My mother scrutinized her hem.

After a minute I volunteered that before seeing a judge, he might try a lawyer.

He turned. "Since when did you become so afraid like your mother?"

I started to say that it wasn't a matter of fear, but he cut me off.

"What I need today," he said, "is a son."

My father and I spent the better part of the next day standing in lines at the immigration office. He did not get to speak to a judge, but with much persistence he managed to speak to a judge's clerk, who tried to persuade him that it was not her place to extend him advice. My father, though, shamelessly plied her with compliments and offers of free pancakes until she finally conceded that she personally doubted anything would happen to either Cedric or Booker.

"Especially if they're 'needed workers,' " she said, rubbing at the red marks her glasses left on her nose. She yawned. "Have you thought about sponsoring them to become permanent residents?"

Could he do that? My father was overjoyed. And what if he saw to it right away? Would she perhaps put in a good word with the judge?

She yawned again, her nostrils flaring. "Don't worry," she said. "They'll get a fair hearing."

My father returned jubilant. Booker and Cedric hailed him as their savior, their Buddha incarnate. He was like a father to them, they said; and laughing and clapping, they made him tell the story over and over, sorting over the details like jewels. And how old was the assistant judge? And what did she say?

That evening my father tipped the paperboy a dollar and bought a pot of mums for my mother, who suffered them to be placed on the dining room table. The next night he took us all out to dinner. Then on Saturday, Mona found a letter on my father's chair at the restaurant.

> Dear Mr. Chang,
> You are the grat boss. But, we do not like to trial, so will runing away now. Plese to excus us. People saying the law in America is fears like dragon. Here is only $140. We hope some day we can pay back the rest bale. You will getting intrest, as you diserving, so grat a boss you are. Thank you for every thing. In next life you will be burn in rich family, with no more pancaks.
> > Yours truley,
> > Booker + Cedric

In the weeks that followed my father went to the pancake house for crises, but otherwise hung around our house, fiddling idly with the sump pump and boiler in an effort, he said, to get ready for winter. It was as though he had gone into retirement, except that instead of moving South, he had moved to the basement. He even took to showering my mother with little attentions, and to calling her "old girl," and when we finally heard that the club had entertained all the applications it could for the year, he was so sympathetic that he seemed more disappointed than my mother.

II. In the American Society

Mrs. Lardner tempered the bad news with an invitation to a bon voyage "bash" she was throwing for a friend of hers who was going to Greece for six months.

"Do come," she urged. "You'll meet everyone, and then, you know, if things open up in the spring . . ." She waved her hands.

My mother wondered if it would be appropriate to show up at a party for someone they didn't know, but "the honest truth" was that this was an annual affair. "If it's not Greece, it's Antibes," sighed Mrs. Lardner. "We really just do it because his wife left him and his daughter doesn't speak to him, and poor Jeremy just feels so *unloved*."

She also invited Mona and me to the goings on, as "*demi*-guests" to keep Annie out of the champagne. I wasn't too keen on the idea, but before I could say anything, she had already thanked us for so generously agreeing to honor her with our presence.

"A pair of little princesses, you are!" she told us. "A pair of princesses!"

The party was that Sunday. On Saturday, my mother took my father out shopping for a suit. As it was the end of September, she insisted that he buy a worsted rather than a seersucker, even though it was only ten, rather than fifty percent off. My father protested that it was as hot out as ever, which was true—a thick Indian summer had cozied murderously up to us—but to no avail. Summer clothes, said my mother, were not properly worn after Labor Day.

The suit was unfortunately as extravagant in length as it was in price, which posed an additional quandary, since the tailor wouldn't be in until Monday. The salesgirl, though, found a way of tacking it up temporarily.

"Maybe this suit not fit me," fretted my father.

"Just don't take your jacket off," said the salesgirl.

He gave her a tip before they left, but when he got home refused to remove the price tag.

"I like to asking the tailor about the size," he insisted.

"You mean you're going to *wear* it and then return it?" Mona rolled her eyes.

"I didn't say I'm return it," said my father stiffly. "I like to asking the tailor, that's all."

The party started off swimmingly, except that most people were wearing bermudas or wrap skirts. Still, my parents carried on, sharing with great feeling the complaints about the heat. Of course my father tried to eat a cracker full of shallots and burnt himself in an attempt to help Mr. Lardner turn the coals of the barbecue; but on the whole he seemed to be doing all right. Not nearly so well as my mother, though, who had accepted an entire cupful of Mrs. Lardner's magic punch, and seemed indeed to be under some spell. As Mona and Annie skirmished over whether some boy in their class inhaled when he smoked, I watched my mother take off her shoes, laughing and laughing as a man with a beard regaled her with navy stories by the pool. Apparently he had been stationed in the Orient and remembered a few words of Chinese, which made my mother laugh still more. My father excused himself to go to the men's room, then drifted back and "dropped" anchor at the hors d'oeuvre table, while my mother sailed on to a group of women, who tinkled at length over the clarity of her complexion. I dug out a book I had brought.

Just when I'd cracked the spine, though, Mrs. Lardner came by to bewail her shortage of servers. Her caterers were criminals, I agreed; and the next thing I knew I was handing out bits of marine life, making the rounds as amicably as I could.

"Here you go, Dad," I said when I got to the hors d'oeuvre table.

"Everything is fine," he said.

I hesitated to leave him alone; but then the man with the beard zeroed in on him, and though he talked of nothing but my mother, I thought it would be okay to get back to work. Just that moment, though, Jeremy Brothers lurched our way, an empty, albeit corked, wine bottle in hand. He was a slim, well-proportioned man, with a Roman nose and small eyes and a nice manly jaw that he allowed to hang agape.

"Hello," he said drunkenly. "Pleased to meet you."

"Pleased to meeting you," said my father.

"Right," said Jeremy. "Right. Listen. I have this bottle here, this most recalcitrant bottle. You see that it refuses to do my bidding. I bid it open sesame, please, and it does nothing." He pulled the cork out with his teeth, then turned the bottle upside down.

My father nodded.

"Would you have a word with it please?" said Jeremy. The man with the beard excused himself. "Would you please have a god-damned word with it?"

My father laughed uncomfortably.

"Ah!" Jeremy bowed a little. "Excuse me, excuse me, excuse me. You are not my man, not my man at all." He bowed again and started to leave, but then circled back. "Viticulture is not your forte, yes I can see that, see that plainly. But may I trouble you on another matter? Forget the damned bottle." He threw it into the pool, and winked at the people he splashed. "I have another matter. Do you speak Chinese?"

My father said he did not, but Jeremy pulled out a handkerchief with some characters on it anyway, saying that his daughter had sent it from Hong Kong and that he thought the characters might be some secret message.

"Long life," said my father.

"But you haven't looked at it yet."

"I know what it says without looking." My father winked at me.
"You do?"

"Yes, I do."

"You're making fun of me, aren't you?"

"No, no, no," said my father, winking again.

"Who are you anyway?" said Jeremy.

His smile fading, my father shrugged.

"Who are you?"

My father shrugged again.

Jeremy began to roar. "This is my party, *my party*, and I've never
seen you before in my life." My father backed up as Jeremy came
toward him. *"Who are you? WHO ARE YOU?"*

Just as my father was going to step back into the pool, Mrs.
Lardner came running up. Jeremy informed her that there was a man
crashing his party.

"Nonsense," said Mrs. Lardner. "This is Ralph Chang, who I
invited extra especially so he could meet you." She straightened the
collar of Jeremy's peach-colored polo shirt for him.

"Yes, well we've had a chance to chat," said Jeremy.

She whispered in his ear; he mumbled something; she whispered
something more.

"I do apologize," he said finally.

My father didn't say anything.

"I do." Jeremy seemed genuinely contrite. "Doubtless you've
seen drunks before, haven't you? You must have them in China."

"Okay," said my father.

As Mrs. Lardner glided off, Jeremy clapped his arm over my
father's shoulders. "You know, I really am quite sorry, quite sorry."

My father nodded.

"What can I do, how can I make it up to you?"

"No thank you."

"No, tell me, tell me," wheedled Jeremy. "Tickets to Casino
night?" My father shook his head. "You don't gamble. Dinner at
Bartholomew's?" My father shook his head again. "You don't eat."
Jeremy scratched his chin. "You know, my wife was like you. Old
Annabelle could never let me make things up—never, never, never,
never, never."

My father wriggled out from under his arm.

"How about sport clothes? You are rather overdressed, you
know, excuse me for saying so. But here." He took off his polo shirt

and folded it up. "You can have this with my most profound apologies." He ruffled his chest hairs with his free hand.

"No thank you," said my father.

"No, take it, take it. Accept my apologies." He thrust the shirt into my father's arms. "I'm so very sorry, so very sorry. Please, try it on."

Helplessly holding the shirt, my father searched the crowd for my mother.

"Here, I'll help you off with your coat."

My father froze.

Jeremy reached over and took his jacket off. "Milton's, one hundred twenty-five dollars reduced to one hundred twelve-fifty," he read. "What a bargain, what a bargain!"

"Please give it back," pleaded my father. "Please."

"Now for your shirt," ordered Jeremy.

Heads began to turn.

"Take off your shirt."

"I do not take orders like a servant," announced my father.

"Take off your shirt, or I'm going to throw this jacket right into the pool, just right into this little pool here." Jeremy held it over the water.

"Go ahead."

"One hundred twelve-fifty," taunted Jeremy. "One hundred twelve . . ."

My father flung the polo shirt into the water with such force that part of it bounced back up into the air like a fluorescent fountain. Then it settled into a soft heap on top of the water. My mother hurried up.

"You're a sport!" said Jeremy, suddenly breaking into a smile and slapping my father on the back. "You're a sport! I like that. A man with spirit, that's what you are. A man with panache. Allow me to return to you your jacket." He handed it back to my father. "Good value you got on that, good value."

My father hurled the coat into the pool too. "We're leaving," he said grimly. "Leaving!"

"Now, Ralphie," said Mrs. Lardner, bustling up; but my father was already stomping off.

"Get your sister," he told me. To my mother: "Get your shoes."

"That was *great*, Dad," said Mona as we walked down to the car. "You were *stupendous*."

"Way to show 'em," I said.

"What?'" said my father offhandedly.

Although it was only just dusk, we were in a gulch, which made it hard to see anything except the gleam of his white shirt moving up the hill ahead of us.

"It was all my fault," began my mother.

"Forget it," said my father grandly. Then he said, "The only trouble is I left those keys in my jacket pocket."

"Oh *no*," said Mona.

"Oh no is right," said my mother.

"So we'll walk home," I said.

"But how're we going to get into the *house*," said Mona.

The noise of the party churned through the silence.

"Someone has to going back," said my father.

"Let's go to the pancake house first," suggested my mother. "We can wait there until the party is finished, and then call Mrs. Lardner."

Having all agreed that that was a good plan, we started walking again.

"God, just think," said Mona. "We're going to have to *dive* for them."

My father stopped a moment. We waited.

"You girls are good swimmers," he said finally. "Not like me."

Then his shirt started moving again, and we trooped up the hill after it, into the dark.

[1987]

Tina McElroy Ansa
(1949–present)

Sarah

When Tina McElroy was a young girl in Macon, Georgia, her father took her to a fountain in the town park and told her that the site was the exact center of Georgia. She grew up with that image, feeling enveloped by her community, her state, and her Southern heritage. Her fiction, which is set mainly in the mythical Georgia town of Mulberry, is drawn from that heritage and explores the lives of women, small communities, and the folklore that holds a culture together.

Ansa graduated from Spelman College in 1971 and then worked at the *Atlanta Constitution* in a variety of editing and writing positions. Since 1982 she has been a freelance journalist, newspaper columnist, and writing workshop instructor. She writes articles and book reviews and is currently completing her second novel and a screenplay adaptation of *Baby of the Family* (1989), from which "Sarah" is excerpted. She lives on St. Simons Island, Georgia, where she and her husband have directed and produced the Georgia Sea Island Festival, a grassroots festival that seeks to preserve the crafts, music, slave chants, games, food, and spirit of the local people and their ancestors who worked as slaves on the area's rice and cotton plantations.

When Lena ran onto the side screen porch she was too excited about her new friend Sarah to remember not to let the screen door slam. But her grandmother only smiled absentmindedly when she ran into the sewing room chattering away about the little girl across the street.

"Lena, baby, be careful 'round that hot iron," she said as Lena nearly collided with the ironing board that was always set up in the room while her grandmother and mother sewed. Then she made the girl stand straight and still while she held a green-and-red plaid pleated skirt with matching suspenders up to the child's waist. The entire woolen skirt was only about half a foot long.

"Hmmm-huh," the old lady muttered with a few straight pins still in her mouth as Lena wove the story about magic fruit made out of red jewels and a little girl named Puddin'.

Her mother, when Lena found her sitting in the living room in her favorite rose-colored chair reading a thick book without any pictures in it, was no more receptive.

"Lena, baby, sit still for just a minute so Mama can finish this one last page. You've been such a good girl all afternoon. As soon as I finish this one last page, I'll put on some music for you. Some Billie Holiday or some Sarah Vaughan, how about that? Then you can help me bake a cake. What kind do you want? A chocolate or a coconut?"

Nellie's voice was as seductive as the thought of a homemade cake.

"Chocolate, chocolate, chocolate," Lena screamed as she jumped down from the arm of her mother's chair and ran over to the sofa to sit quietly until her mother finished her reading. The thought of a moist yellow cake covered with warm smooth brown icing pushed the image of Sarah right out of her head.

But the next morning, with the sun barely breaking through the trees and the boys still stumbling into each other half-asleep in the bathroom as they got ready for school, the household seemed to rock with the sound of banging at the front door.

At first everyone but Nellie, who knew she had left him snoring in the bed next to her, thought it was Jonah again firing off shots from the pistol he always carried with him—*bam, bam, bam, bam, bam*—the way he had done late one night when he came home and found that Nellie had locked and barred all the doors against him. Weary from a long night of poker and carousing, he hadn't yelled and he hadn't cussed. He had just pulled the gun out of his back pocket and fired into the roof of the side porch, and the doors of the house had magically opened to him.

The five small holes that the gunshots made were still in the porch's forest-green ceiling. Lena giggled whenever she looked up and saw them. Her father's brashness frightened most people, but it didn't scare her one bit. She knew she was immune.

The gunshots had not only opened the locked door for her father, they also had held in check all the talk Nellie had said she had for him about him staying out as late as he wanted and not expecting anybody to say anything about it. About what did he think she was, anyway? About how sick and tired she was of him and his whores.

Overhearing Nellie's mutterings, Lena, sitting on the toilet, had wondered what a whore was, since it didn't exactly sound like the thing her grandma used to turn the dirt over in her garden. A simple garden tool couldn't have made her mother as mad as this whore seemed to. And Lena didn't think anything that sounded as bad as her mama made the word sound could be so harmless. The way her mama said it, "whore" sounded like it was covered with spikes and prickly barbs.

So, as she pulled up her panties, she asked her mother for a definition. Nellie just snapped, "Go back to bed, Lena."

The early-morning banging at the door was loud and insistent. Lena's grandmother strode down the stairs with Lena beside her. Lena was walking so close to her grandmother that she almost got tangled up in the length of chenille robe flapping between the old lady's legs and tumbled down the steps head over heels. Grandmama scratched the side of her nose again and marched down the downstairs hall on her way to the front door muttering to herself, "Who the hell is this come to our door this time of morning banging like the goddamn police? If it's one of Jonah's half-witted flunkies, they'll be sorry they were ever born. Yes, if it's one of those fanatical fools from The Place come here this time of morning to borrow a couple of dollars to throw away on some foolishness, they'll be sorry they ever learned how to count pennies when I finish with 'em. Knocking on this door like they the damn police or something."

Lena had to walk fast to keep up with her grandmother. Despite the threatening banging at the door, she wasn't a bit afraid. She thought nothing could befall her as long as the older lady stood between her and the world.

Grandmama was out of breath and still cussing out "that fool out there" when they reached the door. She didn't even peep out of one of the panes of glass that edged the big door first. She just flung it open and stood there with her arms folded over her flat breasts as Lena peered around her legs.

At first all Grandmama and Lena could see in the breaking

morning light was a wide smile and a pink blouse. Then Lena recognized her friend.

"Sarah!" Lena screamed as she dashed past her grandmother's legs and ran up to the door, pressing her face against the screen.

Grandmama still annoyed at the early-morning visit, looked down at Lena with a confused expression.

"It's Sarah, Grandmama, Puddin' Tame. I told you all 'bout her yesterday. She's my friend. Don't you remember?"

Grandmama was still puzzled. It had never occurred to her that Lena could have anything to do with this early-morning commotion at their front door. On top of that she was having a hard time believing that Lena, her baby, had made a friend without her grandmama knowing about it. And what a friend!

The dark little girl who stood on the front porch smiling for all she was worth looked to Grandmama like a little piece of street trash who had tried to doll herself up.

Grandmama was halfway right. Sarah had stayed up nearly all night preparing for her first visit to Lena's big house. It felt like the most important event of her short life, and she knew if she didn't prepare for it, nobody would.

Everyone in Sarah's family was used to her doing things on her own. So the night before, when her mother had heard her bumping around in the nearly darkened house, the woman had just smacked her lips a couple of times sleepily, turned over against the warm body of her husband, and gone back to sleep.

Sarah had stopped rummaging through a cluttered drawer and stood perfectly still when she heard her mother stir. She knew she had her work cut out for her, and she didn't need anybody asking a lot of questions and getting in the way while she tried her best to piece together some kind of outfit.

Sarah wanted so much to look nice when she met Lena's people. But she had so little to work with. When she thought she couldn't find a decent pair of matching socks in the whole house, Sarah sat in the middle of the cold bathroom floor and wept.

The only matching set was the tiny pair of faded lacy pink baby socks she found stuck in the back of a drawer, which her mother had bought for one of the children but had never had a fancy enough occasion to use. Sarah brightened when she found a dark blue sock and a dark brown one that belonged to her younger brother. If she didn't fold down the cuffs of the socks, they almost looked like they were bought for her. And in the light thrown off by the lone lamp with the broken shade in the front room, the brown and blue socks looked like a perfect match. Sarah didn't realize until she was standing in Lena's mama's big bright kitchen that she was wearing mismatched socks. By then she was too happy to care.

There was no shoe polish of any color in the house, so Sarah just took a damp rag and wiped the red dust from her lace-up brown oxfords. They looked fine as long as the leather remained wet, but as soon as the shoes began to dry, they reverted to the smoky hue they had been for months.

At least, Sarah thought, I don't have to worry that much about my underwear. If I keep my dress down and don't flounce around too much, it won't matter if I got holes in my drawers or not. As luck would have it, she found a pair of her own panties that were still white and didn't even have a pin hole in them in a pile of clean laundry someone had taken off the line and left on the swayback chair in the kitchen.

Then her main concern became finding a dress without a hole in it. Because she was usually as raggedy or neat as anyone else in her house, Sarah rarely gave any thought to her attire. She woke in the morning, put on something to cover her body, and went on with her day. But the way Lena had been dressed that day, and the size of the house Lena lived in, had made Sarah look at herself for a long time in the wavy mirror of the old hall dresser and decide she wanted to wear something special to her new friend's house.

With tiny lines of concentration creasing her forehead, she picked up and discarded nearly every piece of clothing she found in two chests of drawers, stuck down between the frayed cushions of the couch, or lying under the cot where she and two of her sisters slept. She had long ago outgrown the only "nice" Easter dress she had ever owned. It had been passed down to her next sister, who despoiled it right away by putting it on and playing in the mud.

The search seemed hopeless. Then she remembered the cardboard box full of old clothes that a white woman her mother had once worked for had dropped off at their house the Christmas before instead of coming up with the five dollars she owed for almost a week's work. Her mother was so disgusted that she had thrown the box into a corner of the porch and dared anybody to go near it.

At the time, Sarah had shared her mother's anger and disappointment and wouldn't touch the box of old clothes for anything in the world. She had even stopped her sisters and brothers from messing with it. But that was then. Now Sarah needed something that wasn't ripped and torn and soiled beyond repair, so she broke down and dragged the box into the kitchen from the back porch.

She pulled out dozens of old men's shirts and plaid housedresses and faded pastel dusters before she came to anything that looked like it might fit her. At the bottom of the box, under a piece of a yellowed sheet, she found a layer of children's clothes. She lifted them all out and laid them on the kitchen table. Then she threw everything else back into the box.

The bare light bulb hanging from the cord in the ceiling was one of the brightest ones in the house, so Sarah stayed in the kitchen to examine her discovery.

"Too little, too little, too big, too little, too big," Sarah muttered to herself as she held up each piece to examine it briefly and then dropped it into one of two piles on the table. When she had gone through all the children's clothes on the table, she realized she hadn't once said "My size." So she picked up the small pile of "too little" clothes, dropped them back into the cardboard box, and pushed it back onto the porch. Then she returned to the "too big" pile on the table to see what she could use.

First Sarah went through the pile to check for pants and dresses and blouses that had no holes or rips in them. Earlier, while Lena had been engrossed in the piles of rocks and sand they had been building to dam up the flow of the stream cascading beside the street, Sarah had examined her new friend close up. She had been struck with the vivid red of Lena's frock, which was unlike anything she owned.

But later, going over the afternoon meeting in her mind, the thing that stood out about Lena's dress was not only its bright color but also its neatness. No rips or tears at the seams, no threads hanging down—none of the hem of the wide skirt dipping like a shelf below the rest of the dress. Sarah was sharp enough to see that the collar was hand sewn and the sleeves were eased into the armholes so they didn't pucker. And she just somehow felt that the hem of the skirt had been turned under, ironed flat, and stitched before the final edge was expertly measured and hemmed. That's the kind of dress she was looking for in the pile of "too big" items on the kitchen table.

In what was left of her childish hopes, Sarah fully expected to find it there. But there was no hand-made red dress to fit her in the pile of children's apparel on the kitchen table. The closest she came to it was a long-sleeved pink blouse with stitching on the cuff and around the buttonholes that was only slightly frayed at the collar, and a navy-blue pleated skirt with elastic at the waist that some little girl had worn as part of her school uniform.

The blouse's long sleeves hung below her knuckles and the armholes sagged beneath her shoulders, but when she tucked the hem of the blouse down into the elastic waistband of the blue skirt, it settled into neat little pleats all around her rib cage and looked kind of cute, Sarah thought. The skirt was longer than she would have liked, but it made a pretty umbrella-like display when she twirled around, and since she had a clean white pair of panties to wear that weren't holey, she figured she could twirl around a few times and remind everyone who thought the skirt was a sad little sack that it was really quite attractive on her.

She planned to hit the skirt and blouse a few times with the ancient iron her mama kept on a kitchen shelf under the sink. But when she plugged it in, the iron shot golden sparks from the raw copper coils exposed beneath the ragged black covering on the cord. Sarah jumped back and yanked the plug from the wall socket for fear of going up in flames before she got the chance to see inside Lena's house. She spread the outfit on the kitchen table and tried to press out the wrinkles by running the palm of her hand over and over the material. But she gave up after a few tries.

"I'll just walk fast and whip them wrinkles out, like Mama say to do," Sarah told herself as she went into the bathroom and started running warm water into the sink.

It was much too cold in the small bathroom for Sarah to think about stripping naked and getting into a tub full of tepid water—the only kind that came out of their hot-water faucets. And besides, if she had run water into the tub, everybody in the house would have awakened to find out what was going on that deserved a full bath. Instead, Sarah took the bar of rough gray soap from the wire dish above the sink, held it under the warm running water, and rubbed up enough suds on a rag she took from hanging on the side of the tub to run over the trunk of her body and leave a light trail of suds behind on her skin. It was the type of bath her mother took when she was late running out to work or going downtown to a juke joint. "I don't have time to bathe," she'd mutter to herself as she undressed. "I'll just take a wipe-off."

The toilette was what most women in Pleasant Hill, regardless of where they lived, called a "whore's bath," but Sarah didn't know what a whore was any more than Lena did.

After she rinsed the suds off with the wet rag, she dried off with a stiff towel hanging on a nail behind the door and quickly slipped into the pair of panties and undershirt she had found in the laundry. As she walked around the house in her bare feet turning off lights, she shivered a bit as the air seeping through gaps in the thin walls hit her damp skin. When she finally settled in for the night, she was grateful for the warm spots her sisters, asleep in their narrow cot, made for her to snuggle into.

The walls of her house were so thin and holey that in winter the wind whistled through the small rooms like a prairie storm through a log cabin. The floors, buckled and rough in unexpected places, creaked each time someone in the house shifted, let alone walked across them. And the whole place smelled of dried and fresh urine that seemed to have soaked into the very wood of the structure so long ago that its residents no longer even noticed the scent.

When Sarah awoke the next morning, she didn't feel as if she had slept a bit that night. She had dozed off a little, but the excitement of her visit to her new friend's house woke her before daylight and before anyone else got up. She put on her socks and shoes in the dark room, turned on the light in the bathroom only long enough to find the hair brush and rake it over her head one time, then switched the light off and headed for the kitchen.

Her new pink blouse and blue skirt were still lying on the table, wrinkled as they had been the night before, but Sarah didn't pay the wrinkles any attention as she quickly buttoned up the blouse and pulled the skirt over her head.

She twirled one time to make sure the skirt still ballooned prettily the way it had the night before and headed out the door to Lena's house without waking anyone—not even her father who woke early to get a spot on the day-worker's truck that drove through the neighborhood. By the time she got halfway down the driveway leading to Lena's house, she couldn't keep from grinning.

Before Sarah knew anything, she and Lena were standing on opposite sides of the screen door beaming at each other in the glow of their new friendship. But Lena soon grew impatient with her grandmama's dazed gaping from one to the other of the two little girls and pulled a handful of chenille robe.

"Grandmama, open the door. Let Sarah in. She came to visit me."

"Okay, baby," her grandmother answered vaguely as she flipped the metal hook from its eye and pushed the door just wide enough for Sarah to squeeze through.

Sarah bounded into the hall and stood beneath the overhead light, excitement and awe written all over her ashy face. It was like a palace to Sarah: the highly polished hardwood floors, the pictures hanging on the wall near the door, the simple chandelier over the dining-room table in the next room, the dining room itself with its big oval table and six high-backed matching chairs pulled up to it, the mouth-watering bowl of fruit sitting in the middle of the table were like something in her dreams.

Grandmama thought just what Lena knew she would when she got a good look at Sarah: I sure would like to scrub that little rusty neck and grease her down with Vaseline. And when the old woman got a whiff of Sarah's mildewed clothes, she thought, I bet she hasn't ever had a real good hot soapy bath in a tub in her life.

"So you're our baby's new friend?" Grandmama said out loud.

"Yeah," Sarah answered, her voice gravelly from getting up so early but so respectful that her short answer didn't imply rudeness, even to Grandmama.

"Say, 'yes, ma'am,' " Grandmama instructed Sarah gently.

"Yes, ma'am," Sarah said carefully, repeating Grandmama's gentle inflection.

"Well, next time wait till the sun has come up good before you come visiting," Grandmama said pointedly. Then, "I guess ya'll want something to eat. You had breakfast yet, Sarah?"

"Bre'fast?" Sarah was puzzled.

"Have you eaten this morning?" the old lady rephrased her question as she headed for the kitchen.

"Oh, no," Sarah answered with her eyes caressing the fruit on the dining-room table as they passed by.

All three of them had to blink a few times as they entered the black-and-white kitchen situated at the eastern corner of the house. The early-morning sun flooded the spacious room with shafts of startlingly bright light that hadn't reached the other parts of the house yet. Sarah felt as though she were walking out onto a stage: it didn't seem real. She had seen kitchens similar to Lena's when she accompanied her mother to her occasional day-work jobs in the white neighborhood behind their house. But those kitchens didn't smell like Lena's. In fact there had been no smell at all except the ones she and her mother brought there.

But even first thing in the morning, Lena's kitchen smelled wonderful. And it wasn't just the fresh aroma of coffee brewing on the stove and buttery grits and sausage grease and cinnamon and sugar dusted lightly on buttered slices of toast. It was the layers of smells that had settled on the walls and floor and worked their way into the fiber of the room that made Sarah come to a halt near the threshold. Sarah could smell the vegetable soup Nellie had made the week before when the weather first turned chilly. She smelled the fish dinner they had had that Friday. She smelled the chocolate layer cake even before she saw it sitting in a glass-covered cake dish on the top of the refrigerator. She came close to bursting into tears with the yearning that the room called up in her swelling heart.

Lena grabbed her friend's dry hand and pulled her into the kitchen and over to the white enamel table to sit down.

"Nellie," Grandmama said to Lena's mother who stood by the sink looking out the window in the direction of the woods. "Look who was making all that noise at our front door this time of morning."

Nellie turned around with her thin eyebrows raised. They shot up even higher when she saw Sarah.

"Well, I be damned," she said. "Now, who is this?"

Lena giggled and so did Sarah.

"This is a new friend of Lena's," Grandmama said with a strange lilt to her voice on the word "friend" that made both little girls stop laughing and look into the old woman's face.

Lena kicked Sarah under the table to encourage her to speak.

"Girl, what you kicked me for?" Sarah asked in her gruff, raspy voice.

"This my mama, Sarah," Lena said as she reached under the table and patted the spot on Sarah's leg that she had kicked.

"Where do you live?" Grandmama asked Sarah as she placed a small glass decorated with circus animals and filled full with orange juice in front of each girl.

"She lives across the street in those houses next to Mrs. Willback's house. Next to that big tree. What kind of tree is that?" Lena asked Sarah.

Sarah couldn't answer at first because she had picked up her glass of juice and was drinking down the fresh tart drink in small continuous swallows, allowing the citrus tang to coat the inside of her mouth and throat. With one last gulp and a loud smack of her lips, she put the glass back on the table and answered.

"Chinaberry."

"And just how did the two of you get together?" Grandmama asked as she walked over to the table with more orange juice and

poured another stream into Sarah's glass that made the child's eyes
light up even more.

But before Sarah had a chance to answer, Nellie jumped in and
said nervously, "Oh, with our little girl, it's no telling, but I assume
that you didn't cross that street out there, Lena."

"No, Mama, Sarah did. You ought to see her dodge those cars,"
Lena said proudly.

Nellie laughed softly. "I bet she can."

After that, Sarah would show up on their doorstep regularly to
join Lena and the boys for breakfast. Some days she had to run home
after eating to "do something." Other times she stayed all day until
Grandmama made her go home. When anyone asked her why she
didn't go to school, she'd say, "We going up there any day now, soon
as Mama gets a chance to 'roll me." But for more than a year she
never attended any school other than the one she found in her own
backyard.

"Lena, what are you and old Rough-and-Ready doing today?"
Grandmama would ask as the two girls came into the kitchen and took
seats next to where she sat making peach puffs or carefully cutting the
seams away from a pile of pole beans covering the table. Lena's father
said he had gagged and nearly choked on strings Nellie had left on the
beans soon after they got married. From that time on, Grandmama
always prepared the pole beans in their house.

"Don't know yet," Sarah would answer for both of them, not
minding the old lady's all too appropriate nickname for her.
Grandmama made a point of always having something healthful for
Sarah whenever she came into the kitchen—a piece of fruit, a
sandwich with extra slices of tomato, a pile of raisins—and she always
gave the bigger portion to Sarah.

But whatever their plans were, everyone knew that they would
involve pretend. It was their favorite game. Everything they played
hinged on the basic unit of Let's Pretend. These games sometimes
involved props and background and sometimes they didn't, and that
was fine, too. At Lena's house, where her attic, filled to bursting,
yielded all kinds of costumes and paraphernalia to fill in the chinks of
the stories, their games were elaborate and staged. But Grandmama
or Nellie or one of the boys always had to go up the steps and drag
down boxes or armloads of stuff because Lena still refused to go into
the attic as long as she knew the portrait of her dead infant aunt was
stored up there.

For the few days each winter when it was too cold to play

out-of-doors, Sarah came to Lena's house and they played and danced in the big upstairs hall in front of the wide floor-length mirror so they could see every movement they made. In the daytime, with her friend by her side, Lena was never frightened of the big mirror, as she was during the nights on her bathroom runs.

At Sarah's it was bare-bones pretending under the chinaberry tree, which was the only place they were allowed to play at her house year-round, but that didn't bother the girls. Despite the house's deficiencies—glaringly obvious to the adults in the neighborhood—Sarah had two things in her yard that Lena and every other child in Pleasant Hill envied her for: a mature and flourishing pomegranate tree and the ancient chinaberry whose broad sturdy limbs swooped down to the ground and back to the sky to form natural nooks and dens. Lena and Sarah called it their "house."

The year Sarah and Lena discovered each other, the two of them planned all winter that, when the warm weather came, they would both move into the chinaberry tree by themselves and live off the fruits of the pomegranate.

"You'll have a room, and I'll have a room," Lena assured Sarah. Sarah's two sisters still wet the cot she shared with them in the front room of her house. "We'll make two beds out of pine straw and Grandmama's flowers, and it'll smell so good in our house, we won't never have to clean up." It was hard for Lena to believe, considering the number of babies and toddlers that roamed the house and yard all day long, but Sarah was the eldest child in the Stanley household. She had responsibilities that Lena never knew about.

They were best friends, sharing games and secrets, special words and questions. But the first time Lena remembered seeing Sarah's world clearly, it was winter and raining very hard, too hard for Lena to head out the door into the cold sheets of water. Lena was stuck at Sarah's for dinner, even though her mother had told her not to accept dinner invitations because Sarah's family had enough trouble feeding their own members without having guests' mouths as well.

"Just say, 'No thank you, I already ate' or 'I'm going to eat when I get home,' " Nellie instructed Lena.

By the time Raymond came running up on the porch with her yellow raincoat and an umbrella, Lena had seen Sarah's family at home for dinner. It was a revelation.

Sarah's mother stood in the tiny kitchen, moving quickly from the sink to the tiny white stove, opening cans, stirring, and chopping. She worked quietly, not saying a word to Lena and the other children assembled on the floor and sitting in the room's one swaybacked chair. When she was finished, Sarah's mother laid down the big metal spoon with holes in it, turned to the children, and announced, "Catch as catch can." Then she walked out onto the lean-to porch to light up a cigarette, blowing long furls of white smoke out into the driving rain.

The other children rose quickly and lined up behind Sarah with small plates and bowls in their hands. Lena could tell what was cooking in the big blue pot even before Sarah lifted the lid off and steam roiled up to the cracking ceiling.

It was neckbones. The distinctive pork scent mixed with tomatoes from the two big yellow-labeled cans sitting on the kitchen table had wrapped itself around the very hairs in Lena's nose. She didn't dare look in the pot for fear of going against her mother's orders and succumbing to the temptation to share the meal, but she guessed that Sarah's mother had put in lots of onions and pungent bell peppers and fistfuls of spaghetti that she broke in half first. Neckbones was one of Lena's favorite dinners. They had them two ways at her house. If her mother cooked, they were made the way Sarah's mother did, with tomatoes and spaghetti. If her grandmother was in charge of cooking the meal, the bony meat was always prepared with potatoes and thick brown gravy.

Although Lena knew both her mother and grandmama wanted her to lean one way or the other in her preference for neckbones, prepared red or brown, she never made a choice. She could never bear the thought of life without neckbones both ways.

When Sarah had filled all the children's bowls and plates, she filled her own plate, broke off a piece of bread from the charred hoecake in the black skillet, and sat on the floor with the others who were already wolfing down their food. Not a word was said until every plate was clean. When Lena asked why everybody was so quiet while they ate, Sarah looked at her as if she had just pointed out the holes in her sisters' drawers, and Lena was sorry she had said anything.

One warm murky day in their second summer, Lena found her friend sitting beneath the protected wings of the chinaberry tree, playing with mounds of dirt between her opened legs. Sarah's house seemed strangely quiet, free of the noises and traffic that usually encircled the house.

The dirt in Sarah's yard was gray and dusty and didn't look as tempting to Lena as the rich brown loam under the pine trees in her own yard. But she had to fight the urge to reach down and put a handful of it into her mouth anyway. Lena understood perfectly why Estelle, who came from time to time to help clean the house, kept chunks of stark white laundry starch in her apron pockets and munched on it throughout the day.

But Lena had promised her mother that she would stop eating dirt. And it seemed no matter how hard she wiped her mouth, Nellie could always tell when she had been eating the stuff. So, instead of picking up a palmful, holding her head back, and letting the grains of dirt trickle into her open mouth from the fist of her hand, she just sat down next to Sarah and started building her own pile of earth into a hill.

"What's your name?" Lena asked playfully, in their customary greeting.

Sarah looked up from the sandhill of earth at her knees and smiled at Lena. "Puddin' Tame," she answered.

"What do you want to play?" she asked Sarah after a while.

"Let's play like we married," Sarah said without hesitation.

"Okay," Lena agreed.

"I'll be the man and you be the woman," Sarah said as she pushed aside the top of the pile of dirt.

"You sit at the table and I'll cook us some breakfast," suggested Lena as she looked around the yard for the few pieces of plastic and china plates and cups they used for serving pieces of sticks for bread; rocks for meat; mounds of dirt for rice, mashed potatoes, and grits; and dark green leaves from the trees around them for collard and turnip greens.

It was a careful game of pretend eating they played. Lena treated it with as much reverence as the real thing was accorded in her own household. She always got a pan of water and washed the rock of "meat" well before putting it in an old dented pot or shoebox "oven" to cook. And she washed and fingered the chinaberry leaves carefully and tenderly, just the way her mother and grandmother did before shredding them and putting them in a pot with a rock for seasoning.

She had been in the kitchen once and seen her grandmother stand at the sink for the longest time examining each leaf in a pile of collards she had just picked from her garden, where they grew year-round. Lena had thought at first that the old lady was looking for worms until she beckoned her over to stand on a chair at the drain beside her.

"Look at this, baby, all these little roads in a single leaf," Grandmama said softly as she traced the separate pale veins in the dark verdant leaf with her wrinkled index finger. "And listen, just listen to this music." Then she had run the soft pad of her thumb over the dark green surface of a leaf, and the thing let out a little baby squeak. They both just smiled in wonder.

Sarah sat near her pile of dirt and thought a while. Then she shook her head as she watched Lena begin to gather the plates. "No, not like that. You want me to show you how to really play house? I know. I seen it plenty of times."

"Okay," Lena agreed easily, even though she knew she had watched her family all her life and knew how to play house just as well as Sarah. But she figured she and her friend enjoyed each other too much to waste time disagreeing over something that didn't matter all that much.

"We just need one thing," Sarah said. "I'll go get it."

And she hurried off to the empty front porch of her house and returned right away with a copy of the *Mulberry Clarion* in her hand. It looked so stiff and clean, Lena knew it had to be that day's copy of the newspaper. Besides, it was Friday and Lena knew that most people in Pleasant Hill, even those who didn't read the newspaper every day, took the *Clarion* on Fridays because that was the day the paper included the page that Rowana Jordan wrote and edited. Stretched across the top of that inside page, just before the want ads, was the standard heading "News of Our Colored Community."

When Mulberry's one colored newspaper had gone out of business at the beginning of the fifties, Miss Rowana, as everyone called her, persuaded the *Clarion* to insert black folks' news once a week by promising to sell ads, take photographs, and write all the stories herself. And she was true to her word, rushing all over town in her too-fancy dresses and outrageous hats collecting news, church notices, wedding and birth announcements, and gossip, along with receipts and ads from funeral homes, barbershops, grocery stores, and the Burghart Theatre. She already had a tiny storefront office on Cherry Street, far enough away from the newspaper's building to please both her and her employers. So she just changed the sign from the *Mulberry Crier* to the *Mulberry Clarion* and continued working.

The newspaper Sarah carried was still rolled up the way it had been thrown. And the little girl held it out in front of her like a magic wand. As soon as she got back to their spot under the tree, she plopped down in the dust and began unrolling the paper.

"Sarah," Lena said, "your daddy read that paper yet?"

"Uh-uh," Sarah answered as she continued to spread the paper out in her hands.

"Then you better leave it alone till they do read it. Nothing makes my daddy madder than for somebody to come and tear up the paper before he gets a chance to read it. He says it shows a goddamn lack of consideration."

Sarah sucked her teeth derisively as she separated one big broadsheet from the others and laid it up on the elbow of a limb of the chinaberry tree they sat under. "Shoot, nobody'll even notice it's gone. If I didn't move it, it woulda sat there forever."

Lena still wasn't convinced, but she was too intrigued with what Sarah was going to do with the paper to press her argument.

When Sarah had all the sheets separated from one another, she divided them evenly, giving Lena four double wide sheets and keeping the others for herself.

"What we gonna do with these?" Lena wanted to know.

Sarah looked around the base of the tree that was their "house" and picked a corner where the limbs touched the ground.

"We need to go over to our bedroom. It's nighttime," Sarah said as she picked up her sheets of newsprint and stepped into another part of the "house."

Lena followed her.

Sarah sat down and pointed to the spot next to her for Lena to join her in the dust. Lena sat down. She was beginning to realize that this was a private, ritualized game they were about to play. And when Sarah said, "Our children 'sleep so we gotta be quiet," Lena knew she had been right, and she was excited. As many times as she had been frightened by some apparition or discovery, she couldn't keep herself from loving a mystery, especially when she was with someone in her family or Sarah and felt safe.

"This what you got to do," Sarah explained as she crumpled a sheet of the newspaper up into a ball, lifted up her skirts, and stuck the paper down into the front of her panties. She leaned back against the stump of the tree and looked down at her crotch, appraising the difference the addition made. Lena sat next to her staring at it, too.

Lena couldn't take her eyes off Sarah's dingy panties, now bulging at the crotch as Sarah added another ball of newspaper, then another. The newspaper balled up like it was and nestled inside Sarah's drawers didn't look like anything other than what it was. But Sarah continued to fool with it, arranging the rounded part against her body and making one end of the clump of paper into a pointed edge, which she aimed at the pad of her panties.

Lena knew she was supposed to keep quiet because the ritual had begun, but she just had to ask. "Sarah," she whispered, "what's that supposed to be?"

"I'm the man," Sarah said authoritatively. "That's my thing, my johnson. I'm supposed to have it."

She patted her newspaper growth one last time, then grabbed one of Lena's sheets of paper and scooted over to her spot in the dust.

"Here," Sarah said as she handed Lena a ball of newspaper. "You do the same thing. That'll be your thing, you a grown 'oman, so that'll be your pussy."

"I already got one," Lena said as she started to pull down her panties to show Sarah. "We call it a matchbox at our house. It just ain't as big as a grown woman."

"I know you got a thing," Sarah said, with a touch of exasperation creeping into her voice. "All girls do, but you right, it ain't big enough. So, go on, put the paper down in your panties like me."

And Lena complied, shoving the stiff paper into the front of her white panties, now rapidly turning gray in the dust. "Ouch, that's scratchy," she complained as she moved the paper around trying to find a more comfortable place against her skin.

"That's okay," Sarah said as she scooted over to Lena to sit facing her between her opened legs. "I think it's supposed to hurt some. That's what my daddy make it sound like. He say, 'Oooo, baby, yeah, that hurt so good, do it some more, uh, yeah, that hurt just right.' "

Sarah had moved in so close to Lena that their two panty fronts, both bulging out in front of them, were now touching. Without any further explanation, she started moving her body around, rubbing her paper penis against Lena's panties and making short sucking sounds as she pulled air between her clenched teeth. She threw her head back and closed her eyes, imitating her father, the whole time repeating, "Uh, yeah, uh, yeah, right there, uh-huh."

Lena watched in fascination as her friend continued to rub up against her in the dust and to suck her teeth as if she were in pain.

Sarah's face was a picture of pleasure glazed over with a thin icing of pain, like the faces of women at The Place who danced and ground their hips to the beat of a saxophone solo played on the jukebox. She seemed to pay Lena no attention, so Lena figured she was supposed to imitate her friend.

She threw her own head back and closed her eyes like Sarah and began rotating the bottom of her body, the part in her panties stuffed with stiff newspaper, up against Sarah. Lena felt a little silly at first and couldn't stop thinking about how dirty the seat of her panties was getting from being ground into the fine gray dust under the big chinaberry tree. But since Sarah, with her eyes still closed and her raspy voice still spitting out the litany of "Yeah, ooh, yeah, ooh, yeah, do it," seemed intent on playing this game, she closed her eyes and gave herself over to the pretending.

"Oh, baby," Lena mimicked her friend in earnest and scooted her bottom a little closer to Sarah's. The movement forward suddenly pressed an edge of the newspaper in her panties into the split of her vagina and across her clitoris. "Uh," she yiped in surprise, and the prick of pleasure shot through her pelvis and slowly melted in her stomach.

Her elbows, resting on the crook of a low limb of the chinaberry behind her to prop her back up off the ground, suddenly lost their gristle and slipped off the edge. Her shoulders landed on the ground with a dull plop, raising a dry dust storm around her ears. But Lena didn't stop to give the fall a thought. She was lost in the exquisite wet feeling that was spreading through her hips and rolling down her thighs. Letting the ball of newspaper lead her, she rose up on her elbows and pushed her bottom back toward Sarah, brushing her stuffed panties back up against her friend in search of more of that quick warm feeling.

She opened her eyes briefly to stare into Sarah's face to see if it mirrored what she imagined her own must look like. Satisfied that it did, she closed her eyes again and continued gyrating her little body against her friend's, sucking air between her teeth the way she had done automatically when the quick warm thing inside her had melted before.

Suddenly she felt the large strong grasp of a fist clutch her upper arm just below the sleeve of her dress and pull her roughly away from Sarah. At first Lena thought it was the strong arms of the chinaberry tree come to life to grab her. Her eyes flew open.

Sarah's mama's face was a mask of rage. She had just been weary when she came looking for Sarah, calling her name over and over to ask what had happened to the newspaper, but when she found her with Lena pressed together, rubbing against each other in the dust, their panties protruding with the turgescence of her Friday newspaper, she turned furious.

"What are ya'll doing!" she screamed as she loomed over the two girls. "What are ya'll doing over here?"

But she didn't wait for an answer. She just screamed at Lena. "Don't be trying to hide from me. I see you. I see what you doing. You little nasty girl. I shoulda known better than to let Sarah play with you."

Sarah and Lena didn't know what to say. Sarah's mama still had Lena's arm in her grasp and lifted her away from her daughter like a rag doll. "Think you so damn fine with your little red dresses and your hair ribbons and your big house. Well, you ain't so fine, is you? Just another dirty little girl, trying to do nasty when you think ain't nobody looking."

Sarah, seeing the attack on her friend, tried to jump in with an explanation.

"It was me, Mama, it wasn't Lena. It was my game."

But the woman didn't want to hear any of that. "Shut up, Sarah. I know what I see with my own eyes. You go on up to the house. I'll deal with your butt later. You know better than this." But Sarah didn't move.

Then, turning back to Lena, who was trying to wrench herself away from the woman's grasp, "I got a good mind to go across the street and tell your fine-ass ma just what I caught her precious baby doing. Yeah, I oughta go tell her what her precious daughter was doing with my little girl."

Then she turned on Sarah again. "Sarah, if you don't get your ass in that house, you better, girl."

With her attention wandering from Lena, her grasp on the child loosened, too, and Lena, suddenly free, started to dash away from the screaming woman. But Sarah's mama looked back in time and caught Lena's skirt tail in her fist.

"Yeah, but she probably wouldn't believe me. Yeah, probably put it off on Sarah. That's right, little girl, you better run on home, get on out my yard. You don't own everything, you know." Sarah's mother was about to release her grip on Lena's skirt. Then she had a thought. She flipped the girl's skirt tail and grabbed the elastic band of Lena's panties and reached inside.

"And gimme back my newspaper," she said with a snarl as she yanked the crumpled paper from Lena's drawers. "I ain't read it yet."

Lena ran all the way home and sat quietly on the side porch steps getting her breath until her mama called her in to dinner.

The last thing Lena thought before she fell into a dreamless sleep

that night was that she and Sarah would be friends forever, no matter
how her mama had acted earlier that day. Nothing could change that.

Sarah had always been there when Lena called her. Usually, when
Lena's household got busy midmorning, she would just go to the end
of her driveway and yell for Sarah, and Sarah would emerge from her
house or the chinaberry tree and lead Lena safely across the street or
just come over to Lena's house to play. Lena could count on Sarah's
consistency. Consistency of any kind pleased and reassured Lena in
her world of apparitions and uncertainties.

So she couldn't understand it when, late in the afternoon, three
days after Sarah's mother had found them rubbing their bodies
together, she went to the end of her driveway as usual and shouted
for her friend and no one appeared in the yard across the street. No
one. Lena didn't think she had ever seen Sarah's house when there
wasn't someone playing in the yard or sitting on the porch or standing
in the doorway. Whenever she and her family drove past, she always
threw up her hand in greeting before she even looked over that way
good, as her grandmother said, because she was so sure there would
be someone there to return her greeting.

Lena called for Sarah a couple more times, and when she still
didn't get a response, she looked both ways up and down Forest
Avenue then dashed across the street by herself. She giggled with
pride at having made it safely across the street, but as soon as she
stepped into Sarah's yard she felt something was different. It was so
quiet and still.

Not only was no member of Sarah's family visible, there was no
sign that any of them were even there. The front door, usually
standing wide open except on the few bitterly cold winter days, was
shut tight. No light burned in the front room or the kitchen window
on the side. The radio that was turned on every time Lena had ever
been there was gone from its spot on the front-room windowsill and
the window itself was tightly shut.

"Sarah! Sarah!" She called as she headed around the side of the
house past the low limbs of the chinaberry tree that looked as deserted
as the house did. But there was no answer. When Lena got around
to the back of the house she saw that even the raggedy curtains that
had hung at the kitchen window in back were no longer there.

Maybe they're doing spring cleaning like at my house, Lena said
to herself. She headed up the plank steps leading to the back porch
with the idea in mind of looking through the low kitchen window and

rapping on it to stir someone inside. With each step she took, the tiny porch made a mournful squeak that sent small shivers up her legs. But even before she made it to the window, Lena had a strong feeling that she wouldn't like what she saw. So the kitchen with its dirty linoleum floor bare of its few pieces of furniture and the hall without its old dresser and mirror and what she could see of the empty front room didn't surprise her. It just left her very sad. As if she had lost the delicate pearl necklace her grandmama had given her.

At first Lena tried to tell herself that Sarah would probably show up soon, laughing in her familiar raspy way, her brother and sisters in tow. But even as she thought of her friend, Lena realized with a start that she couldn't even remember what her friend's voice sounded like, and her sadness turned to fear.

A sudden cool breeze raised goose bumps on her arms and she looked up and noticed that dark clouds were gathering in the western sky. When the smell of rain blew in on the next gust of wind, Lena knew it was time to go back home. There didn't seem to be anything else to do. She couldn't wait any longer.

As she hurried back through the empty yard in front of Sarah's house, big drops of rain began hitting the ground, raising tiny clouds of gray dust like puffs of smoke. Suddenly, going through Sarah's yard felt like a walk through a graveyard. As a sense of loss enveloped her, Lena began to feel as if her friend Sarah were dead.

Not bothering to look either way, Lena dashed across the street toward her house as the rain started coming down in pellets. She didn't stop running until she had reached the kitchen, where she found her mama and grandmama cleaning out the pantry.

"Mama, Mama," she cried as she ran into the first pair of arms she came to, knocking her mother to the floor. "Sarah's gone, Sarah's gone!"

"What, baby? What in God's name is wrong?" Nellie asked, becoming frantic at the sight of Lena's tears.

"Sarah, she's gone—nothing there. I think she's dead!" Lena sobbed.

"Oh, sugar," Grandmama said as she stopped beside Lena and Nellie sitting on the floor. "I forgot all about it. I shoulda told you, baby."

"Told her what, Miss Lizzie?" Nellie demanded.

"It's Rough-and-Ready, Lena's little friend Sarah. She and her family moved away. Moved on the other side of town, to East Mulberry. You know, Nellie, Yamacraw, you know that neighborhood. Miss Willback 'cross the street told me. Sarah and her people got put out over there. Miss Willback saw their pitiful little few sticks of furniture out in the yard yesterday."

"Sarah's gone, Sarah's gone," was all Lena could say.

"Oh, don't worry, baby, you and your friend can still visit each other," Grandmama tried to reassure her. She would say anything to make Lena feel better.

"Oh no she won't, not in that neighborhood she won't," Nellie said.

"See, I told you Sarah was gone, she's gone for good," Lena cried, her sobs turning into hiccups.

"Lord," Nellie said to Miss Lizzie as she kissed the top of Lena's head and rocked her in the salty, sweaty valley between her breasts. "My baby is getting to be so high-strung. Just like I was when I was her age."

Nellie's ministration finally calmed Lena down, but it did nothing to ease the knot of pain Lena felt at the loss of her friend. The following fall when she went to grade school for the first time, she stood around in the yard searching for a little girl who looked like Sarah. There was none. All these girls were shined, polished, and pressed, their hair neatly snatched back into braids and barrettes. None had Sarah's rusty beauty. Then one of her first-grade classmates, a chubby girl who stood alone with her blouse already creeping out of her skirt first thing in the morning, caught Lena's attention. Her eyes didn't sparkle like Sarah's, but they did seem to be full of as much mischief. And when Lena sidled up to her, she smiled and slipped her hand into Lena's.

The gesture reminded Lena of Sarah.

When the first bell clanged, Lena and her new friend Gwen marched bravely into the strange schoolhouse side by side.

Still, on her way home from school that day, Lena felt a tug at her heart when she passed Sarah's house and missed her all over again. From time to time down at The Place, Lena saw Sarah's mother, but when the girl tried to speak and ask about Sarah, the woman pretended she hadn't heard and kept walking from the back door on out the front.

[1989]

Margaret Atwood
(1939–present)

True Trash

Born in Nova Scotia, Margaret Atwood spent summers with her family in northern Ontario. Her entymologist father influenced her preoccupation with metamorphosis and the wilderness. At Victoria College, University of Toronto, she was influenced by the critic Northrop Frye and by Jay Macpherson and examined the dualities in the poetry of William Blake. As a Woodrow Fellow at Radcliffe, she developed a dissertation on the English metaphysical gothic romance, a genre whose conventions her own fiction often parodies.

Editor of the first comprehensive thematic guide to Canadian literature and author of five novels, two children's books, and numerous short stories, Atwood is Canada's most public literary personality. Her books include *Double Persephone* (1961); *The Circle Game* (1966), a collection of poetry; *The Edible Woman* (1969); *Surfacing* (1973); *Life before Man* (1980); *Bluebeard's Egg* (1983); and *The Handmaid's Tale* (1986).

Atwood's work attempts to define identities and defend values in a world in which, in her own words, there is "almost nothing you can write about which has not been outdone in absurdity and ghastliness by real events."

The waitresses are basking in the sun like a herd of skinned seals, their pinky-brown bodies shining with oil. They have their bathing suits on because it's the afternoon. In the early dawn and the dusk they sometimes go skinny-dipping, which makes this itchy crouching in the mosquito-infested bushes across from their small private dock a great deal more worthwhile.

Donny has the binoculars, which are not his own but Monty's. Monty's dad gave them to him for bird-watching but Monty isn't interested in birds. He's found a better use for the binoculars: he rents them out to the other boys, five minutes maximum, a nickel a look or else a chocolate bar from the tuck shop, though he prefers the money. He doesn't eat the chocolate bars; he resells them, black market, for twice their original price; but the total supply on the island is limited, so he can get away with it.

Donny has already seen everything worth seeing, but he lingers on with the binoculars anyway, despite the hoarse whispers and the proddings from those next in line. He wants to get his money's worth.

"Would you look at that," he says, in what he hopes is a tantalizing voice. "Slobber, slobber." There's a stick poking into his stomach, right on a fresh mosquito bite, but he can't move it without taking one hand off the binoculars. He knows about flank attacks.

"Lessee," says Ritchie, tugging at his elbow.

"Piss off," says Donny. He shifts the binoculars, taking in a slippery bared haunch, a red-polka-dotted breast, a long falling strand of bleach-blond hair: Ronette the tartiest, Ronette the most forbidden. When there are lectures from the masters at St. Jude's during the winter about the dangers of consorting with the town girls, it's those like Ronette they have in mind: the ones who stand in line at the town's only movie theater, chewing gum and wearing their boyfriends' leather jackets, their ruminating mouths glistening and deep red like mushed-up raspberries. If you whistle at them or even look, they stare right through you.

Ronette has everything but the stare. Unlike the others, she has been known to smile. Every day Donny and his friends make bets over whether they will get her at their table. When she leans over to clear the plates, they try to look down the front of her sedate but V-necked uniform. They angle towards her, breathing her in: she smells of hair spray, nail polish, something artificial and too sweet. Cheap, Donny's mother would say. It's an enticing word. Most of the things in his life are expensive, and not very interesting.

Ronette changes position on the dock. Now she's lying on her stomach, chin propped on her hands, her breasts pulled down by gravity. She has a real cleavage, not like some of them. But he can see her collar-bone and some chest ribs, above the top of her suit. Despite the breasts, she's skinny, scrawny; she has little stick arms and a thin, sucked-in face. She has a missing side tooth, you can see it when she smiles, and this bothers him. He knows he's supposed to feel lust for her, but this is not what he feels.

The waitresses know they're being looked at: they can see the bushes jiggling. The boys are only twelve or thirteen, fourteen at most, small fry. If it was counselors, the waitresses would giggle more, preen more, arch their backs. Or some of them would. As it is, they go on with their afternoon break as if no one is there. They rub oil on one another's backs, toast themselves evenly, turning lazily this way and that and causing Ritchie, who now has the binoculars, to groan in a way that is supposed to madden the other boys, and does. Small punches are dealt out, mutterings of "Jerk" and "Asshole." "Drool, drool," says Ritchie, grinning from ear to ear.

The waitresses are reading out loud. They are taking turns: their voices float across the water, punctuated by occasional snorts and barks of laughter. Donny would like to know what they're reading with such absorption, such relish, but it would be dangerous for him to admit it. It's their bodies that count. Who cares what they read?

"Time's up, shitface," he whispers to Ritchie.

"Shitface yourself," says Ritchie. The bushes thrash.

What the waitresses are reading is a *True Romance* magazine. Tricia has a whole stash of them, stowed under her mattress, and Sandy and Pat have each contributed a couple of others. Every one of these magazines has a woman on the cover, with her dress pulled down over one shoulder or a cigarette in her mouth or some other evidence of a messy life. Usually these women are in tears. Their colors are odd: sleazy, dirt-permeated, like the hand-tinted photos in the five-and-ten. Knee-between-the-legs colors. They have none of the cheerful primaries and clean, toothy smiles of the movie magazines: these are not success stories. True Trash, Hilary calls them. Joanne calls them Moan-o-dramas.

Right now it's Joanne reading. She reads in a serious, histrionic voice, like someone on the radio; she'd been in a play, at school. *Our Town.* She's got her sunglasses perched on the end of her nose, like a teacher. For extra hilarity she's thrown in a fake English accent.

The story is about a girl who lives with her divorced mother in a cramped, run-down apartment above a shoe store. Her name is Marleen. She has a part-time job in the store, after school and on Saturdays, and two of the shoe clerks are chasing around after her. One is dependable and boring and wants them to get married. The other one, whose name is Dirk, rides a motorcycle and has a knowing, audacious grin that turns Marleen's knees to jelly. The mother slaves over Marleen's wardrobe, on her sewing machine—she makes a meager living doing dressmaking for rich ladies who sneer at her, so the wardrobe comes out all right—and she nags Marleen about choosing the right man and not making a terrible mistake, the way she did. The girl herself has planned to go to trade school and learn hospital management, but lack of money makes this impossible. She is in her last year of high school and her grades are slipping, because she is discouraged and also she can't decide between the two shoe clerks. Now the mother is on her case about the slipping grades as well.

"Oh God," says Hilary. She is doing her nails, with a metal file rather than an emery board. She disapproves of emery boards. "Someone please give her a double Scotch."

"Maybe she should murder the mother, collect the insurance, and get the hell out of there," says Sandy.

"Have you heard one word about any insurance?" says Joanne, peering over the tops of her glasses.

"You could put some in," says Pat.

"Maybe she should try out both of them, to see which one's the best," says Liz brazenly.

"We know which one's the best," says Tricia. "Listen, with a name like *Dirk*! How can you miss?"

"They're both creeps," says Stephanie.

"If she does that, she'll be a Fallen Woman, capital F, capital W," says Joanne. "She'd have to Repent, capital R."

The others hoot. Repentance! The girls in the stories make such fools of themselves. They are so weak. They fall helplessly in love with the wrong men, they give in, they are jilted. Then they cry.

"Wait," says Joanne. "Here comes the big night." She reads on, breathily. *"My mother had gone out to deliver a cocktail dress to one of her customers. I was all alone in our shabby apartment."*

"Pant, pant," says Liz.

"No, that comes later. *I was all alone in our shabby apartment. The evening was hot and stifling. I knew I should be studying, but I could not concentrate. I took a shower to cool off. Then, on impulse, I decided to try on the graduation formal my mother had spent so many late-night hours making for me."*

"That's right, pour on the guilt," says Hilary with satisfaction. "If it was me I'd axe the mother."

"It was a dream of pink—"

"A dream of pink what?" says Tricia.

"A dream of pink, period, and shut up. *I looked at myself in the full-length mirror in my mother's tiny bedroom. The dress was just right for me. It fitted my ripe but slender body to perfection. I looked different in it, older, beautiful, like a girl used to every luxury. Like a princess. I smiled at myself. I was transformed.*

"I had just undone the hooks at the back, meaning to take the dress off and hang it up again, when I heard footsteps on the stairs. Too late I remembered that I'd forgotten to lock the door on the inside, after my mother's departure. I rushed to the door, holding up my dress—it could be a burglar, or worse! But instead it was Dirk."

"Dirk the jerk," says Alex, from underneath her towel.

"Go back to sleep," says Liz.

Joanne drops her voice, does a drawl. *" 'Thought I'd come up and keep you company,' he said mischievously. 'I saw your mom go out.' He knew I was alone! I was blushing and shivering. I could hear the blood pounding in my veins. I couldn't speak. Every instinct warned me against him—every instinct but those of my body, and my heart."*

"So what else is there?" says Sandy. "You can't have a mental instinct."

"You want to read this?" says Joanne. "Then shush. *I held the frothy pink lace in front of me like a shield. 'Hey, you look great in that,' Dirk said. His voice was rough and tender. 'But you'd look even greater out of it.' I was frightened of him. His eyes were burning, determined. He looked like an animal stalking its prey."*

"Pretty steamy," says Hilary.

"What kind of animal?" says Sandy.

"A weasel," says Stephanie.

"A skunk," says Tricia.

"Shh," says Liz.

"I backed away from him," Joanne reads. *"I had never seen him look that way before. Now I was pressed against the wall and he was crushing me in his arms. I felt the dress slipping down . . ."*

"So much for all that sewing," says Pat.

". . . and his hand was on my breast, his hard mouth was seeking

mine. I knew he was the wrong man for me but I could no longer resist. My whole body was crying out to his."

"What did it say?"

"It said, *Hey, body, over here!*"

"Shh."

"*I felt myself lifted. He was carrying me to the sofa. Then I felt the length of his hard, sinewy body pressing against mine. Feebly I tried to push his hands away, but I didn't really want to. And then*—dot dot dot—*we were One,* capital O, exclamation mark."

There is a moment of silence. Then the waitresses laugh. Their laughter is outraged, disbelieving. *One.* Just like that. There has to be more to it.

"The dress is a wreck," says Joanne in her ordinary voice. "Now the mother comes home."

"Not today, she doesn't," says Hilary briskly. "We've only got ten more minutes. I'm going for a swim, get some of this oil off me." She stands up, clips back her honey-blond hair, stretches her tanned athlete's body, and does a perfect swan-dive off the end of the dock.

"Who's got the soap?" says Stephanie.

Ronette has not said anything during the story. When the others have laughed, she has only smiled. She's smiling now. Hers is an off-center smile, puzzled, a little apologetic.

"Yeah, but," she says to Joanne, "why is it funny?"

The waitresses stand at their stations around the dining hall, hands clasped in front of them, heads bowed. Their royal-blue uniforms come down almost to the tops of their white socks, worn with white bucks or white-and-black saddle shoes or white sneakers. Over their uniforms they wear plain white aprons. The rustic log sleeping cabins at Camp Adanaqui don't have electric lights, the toilets are outhouses, the boys wash their own clothes, not even in sinks but in the lake; but there are waitresses, with uniforms and aprons. Roughing it builds a boy's character, but only certain kinds of roughing it.

Mr. B. is saying grace. He owns the camp, and is a master at St. Jude's as well, during the winters. He has a leathery, handsome face, the gray, tailored hair of a Bay Street lawyer, and the eyes of a hawk: he sees all, but pounces only sometimes. Today he's wearing a white V-necked tennis sweater. He could be drinking a gin and tonic, but is not.

Behind him on the wall, above his head, there's a weathered plank with a motto painted on it in black Gothic lettering: *As the Twig Is Bent*. A piece of bleached driftwood ornaments each end of the plank, and beneath it are two crossed paddles and a gigantic pike's head in profile, its mouth open to show its needle teeth, its one glass eye fixed in a ferocious maniac's glare.

To Mr. B.'s left is the end window, and beyond it is Georgian Bay, blue as amnesia, stretching to infinity. Rising out of it like the backs of whales, like rounded knees, like the calves and thighs of enormous floating women, are several islands of pink rock, scraped and rounded and fissured by glaciers and lapping water and endless weather, a few jack pines clinging to the larger ones, their twisted roots digging into the cracks. It was through these archipelagos that the waitresses were ferried here, twenty miles out from shore, by the same cumbersome mahogany inboard launch that brings the mail and the groceries and everything else to the island. Brings, and takes away. But the waitresses will not be shipped back to the mainland until the end of summer: it's too far for a day off, and they would never be allowed to stay away overnight. So here they are, for the duration. They are the only women on the island, except for Mrs. B. and Miss Fisk, the dietitian. But those two are old and don't count.

There are nine waitresses. There are always nine. Only the names and faces change, thinks Donny, who has been going to this camp ever since he was eight. When he was eight he paid no attention to the waitresses except when he felt homesick. Then he would think of excuses to go past the kitchen window when they were washing the dishes. There they would be, safely aproned, safely behind glass: nine mothers. He does not think of them as mothers anymore.

Ronette is doing his table tonight. From between his half-closed eyelids Donny watches her thin averted face. He can see one earring, a little gold hoop. It goes right through her ear. Only Italians and cheap girls have pierced ears, says his mother. It would hurt to have a hole put through your ear. It would take bravery. He wonders what the inside of Ronette's room looks like, what other cheap, intriguing things she's got in there. About someone like Hilary he doesn't have to wonder, because he already knows: the clean bedspread, the rows of shoes in their shoe-trees, the comb and brush and manicure set laid out on the dresser like implements in a surgery.

Behind Ronette's bowed head there's the skin of a rattlesnake, a big one, nailed to the wall. That's what you have to watch out for around here: rattlesnakes. Also poison ivy, thunderstorms, and drowning. A whole war canoe full of kids drowned last year, but they were from another camp. There's been some talk of making everyone wear sissy life-jackets; the mothers want it. Donny would like a rattlesnake skin of his own, to nail up over his bed; but even if he caught the snake himself, strangled it with his bare hands, bit its head off, he'd never be allowed to keep the skin.

Mr. B. winds up the grace and sits down, and the campers begin again their three-times-daily ritual of bread-grabbing, face-stuffing, under-the-table kicking, whispered cursing. Ronette comes from the kitchen with a platter: macaroni and cheese. "There you go, boys," she says, with her good-natured, lopsided smile.

"Thank you kindly, ma'am," says Darce the counselor, with fraudulent charm. Darce has a reputation as a make-out artist; Donny knows he's after Ronette. This makes him feel sad. Sad, and too young. He would like to get out of his own body for a while; he'd like to be somebody else.

The waitresses are doing the dishes. Two to scrape, one to wash, one to rinse in the scalding-hot rinsing sink, three to dry. The other two sweep the floors and wipe off the tables. Later, the number of dryers will vary because of days off—they'll choose to take their days off in twos, so they can double-date with the counselors—but today all are here. It's early in the season, things are still fluid, the territories are not yet staked out.

While they work they sing. They're missing the ocean of music in which they float during the winter. Pat and Liz have both brought their portables, though you can't pick up much radio out here, it's too far from shore. There's a record player in the counselors' rec hall, but the records are out of date. Patti Page, The Singing Rage. "How Much Is That Doggie in the Window." "The Tennessee Waltz." Who waltzes anymore?

" 'Wake up, little Susie,' " trills Sandy. The Everly Brothers are popular this summer; or they were, on the mainland, when they left.

" 'What're we gonna tell your mama, what're we gonna tell your pa,' " sing the others. Joanne can improvise the alto harmony, which makes everything sound less screechy.

Hilary, Stephanie, and Alex don't sing this one. They go to a private school, all girls, and are better at rounds, like "Fire's Burning" and "White Coral Bells." They are good at tennis though, and sailing, skills that have passed the others by.

It's odd that Hilary and the other two are here at all, waitressing at Camp Adanaqui; it's not as if they need the money. (Not like me, thinks Joanne, who haunts the mail desk every noon to see if she got her scholarship.) But it's the doing of their mothers. According to Alex, the three mothers banded together and jumped Mrs. B. at a charity function, and twisted her arm. Naturally Mrs. B. would attend the same functions as the mothers: they've seen her, sunglasses pushed up on her forehead, a tall drink in her hand, entertaining on the veranda of Mr. B.'s white hilltop house, which is well away from the camp proper. They've seen the guests, in their spotless, well-pressed sailing clothes. They've heard the laughter, the voices, husky and casual. *Oh, God don't tell me.* Like Hilary.

"We were kidnapped," says Alex. "They thought it was time we met some boys."

Joanne can see it for Alex, who is chubby and awkward, and for Stephanie, who is built like a boy and walks like one; but Hilary? Hilary is classic. Hilary is like a shampoo ad. Hilary is perfect. She ought to be sought after. Oddly, here she is not.

Ronette is scraping, and drops a plate. "Shoot," she says. "What a stunned broad." Nobody bawls her out or even teases her as they would anyone else. She is a favorite with them, though it's hard to put your finger on why. It isn't just that she's easygoing: so is Liz, so is Pat. She has some mysterious, extra status. For instance, everyone else has a nickname: Hilary is Hil, Stephanie is Steph, Alex is Al, Joanne is Jo, Tricia is Trish, Sandy is San. Pat and Liz, who cannot be contracted any further, have become Pet and Lizard. Only Ronette has been accorded the dignity of her full, improbable name.

In some ways she is more grown-up than the rest of them. But it isn't because she knows more things. She knows fewer things; she often has trouble making her way through the vocabularies of the others, especially the offhand slang of the private-school trio. "I don't get that" is what she says, and the others take a delight in explaining, as if she's a foreigner, a cherished visitor from some other country. She goes to movies and watches television like the rest of them but she has few opinions about what she has seen. The most she will say is "Crap" or "He's not bad." Though friendly, she is cautious about expressing approval in words. "Fair" is her best compliment. When the others talk about what they've read or what subjects they will take next year at university, she is silent.

But she knows other things, hidden things. Secrets. And these other things are older, and on some level more important. More fundamental. Closer to the bone.

Or so thinks Joanne, who has a bad habit of novelizing.

Outside the window Darce and Perry stroll by, herding a group of campers. Joanne recognizes a few of them: Donny, Monty. It's hard to remember the campers by name. They're just a crowd of indistinguishable, usually grimy young boys who have to be fed three times a day, whose crusts and crumbs and rinds have to be cleaned up afterwards. The counselors call them Grubbies.

But some stand out. Donny is tall for his age, all elbows and spindly knees, with huge deep-blue eyes; even when he's swearing—they all swear during meals, furtively but also loudly enough so that the waitresses can hear them—it's more like a meditation, or more like a question, as if he's trying the words out, tasting them. Monty on the other hand is like a miniature forty-five-year-old: his shoulders already have a businessman's slump, his paunch is fully formed. He walks with a pompous little strut. Joanne thinks he's hilarious.

Right now he's carrying a broom with five rolls of toilet paper threaded onto the handle. All the boys are: they're on Bog Duty, sweeping out the outhouses, replacing the paper. Joanne wonders what they do with the used sanitary napkins in the brown paper bag in the waitresses' private outhouse. She can imagine the remarks.

"Company . . . halt!" shouts Darce. The group shambles to a stop in front of the window. "Present . . . arms!" The brooms are raised, the ends of the toilet-paper rolls fluttering in the breeze like flags. The girls laugh and wave.

Monty's salute is half-hearted: this is well beneath his dignity. He may rent out his binoculars—that story is all over camp, by now—but he has no interest in using them himself. He has made that known. *Not on these girls,* he says, implying higher tastes.

Darce himself gives a comic salute, then marches his bunch away. The singing in the kitchen has stopped; the topic among the waitresses is now the counselors. Darce is the best, the most admired, the most desirable. His teeth are the whitest, his hair the blondest, his grin the sexiest. In the counselors' rec hall, where they go every night after the dishes are done, after they've changed out of their blue uniforms into their jeans and pullovers, after the campers have been inserted into their beds for the night, he has flirted with each one of them in turn. So who was he really saluting?

"It was me," says Pat, joking. "Don't I wish."

"Dream on," says Liz.

"It was Hil," says Stephanie loyally. But Joanne knows it wasn't. It wasn't her, either. It was Ronette. They all suspect it. None of them says it.

"Perry likes Jo," says Sandy.

"Does not," says Joanne. She has given out that she has a boyfriend already and is therefore exempt from these contests. Half of this is true: she has a boyfriend. This summer he has a job as a salad chef on the Canadian National, running back and forth across the continent. She pictures him standing at the back of the train, on the caboose, smoking a cigarette between bouts of salad-making, watching the country slide away behind him. He writes her letters, in blue ball-point pen, on lined paper. *My first night on the Prairies,* he writes. *It's magnificent—all that land and sky. The sunsets are unbelievable.* Then there's a line across the page and a new date, and he gets to the Rockies. Joanne resents it a little that he raves on about places she's never been. It seems to her a kind of male showing-off: he's footloose. He closes with *Wish you were here* and several X's and O's. This seems too formal, like a letter to your mother. Like a peck on the cheek.

She put the first letter under her pillow, but woke up with blue smears on her face and the pillowcase both. Now she keeps the letters in her suitcase under the bed. She's having trouble remembering what he looks like. An image flits past, his face close up, at night, in the front seat of his father's car. The rustle of cloth. The smell of smoke.

Miss Fisk bumbles into the kitchen. She's short, plump, flustered; what she wears, always, is a hairnet over her gray bun, worn wool slippers—there's something wrong with her toes—and a faded blue knee-length sweater-coat, no matter how hot it is. She thinks of this summer job as her vacation. Occasionally she can be seen bobbing in the water in a droopy-chested bathing suit and a white rubber cap with the earflaps up. She never gets her head wet, so why she wears the cap is anyone's guess.

"Well, girls. Almost done?" She never calls the waitresses by name. To their faces they are *girls,* behind their backs *My girls.* They are her excuse for everything that goes wrong: *One of the girls must have done it.* She also functions as a sort of chaperon: her cabin is on the pathway that leads to theirs, and she has radar ears, like a bat.

I will never be that old, thinks Joanne. I will die before I'm thirty.

She knows this absolutely. It's a tragic but satisfactory thought. If necessary, if some wasting disease refuses to carry her off, she'll do it herself, with pills. She is not at all unhappy but she intends to be, later. It seems required.

This is no country for old men, she recites to herself. One of the poems she memorized, though it wasn't on the final exam. Change that to old women.

When they're all in their pajamas, ready for bed, Joanne offers to read them the rest of the True Trash story. But everyone is too tired, so she reads it herself, with her flashlight, after the one feeble bulb has been switched off. She has a compulsion about getting to the ends of things. Sometimes she reads books backwards.

Needless to say, Marleen gets knocked up and Dirk takes off on his motorcycle when he finds out. *I'm not the settling-down type, baby. See ya round.* Vroom. The mother practically has a nervous breakdown, because she made the same mistake when young and blew her chances and now look at her. Marleen cries and regrets, and even prays. But luckily the other shoe clerk, the boring one, still wants to marry her. So that's what happens. The mother forgives her, and Marleen herself learns the true value of quiet devotion. Her life isn't exciting maybe, but it's a good life, in the trailer park, the three of them. The baby is adorable. They buy a dog. It's an Irish setter, and chases sticks in the twilight while the baby laughs. This is how the story ends, with the dog.

Joanne stuffs the magazine down between her narrow little bed and the wall. She's almost crying. She will never have a dog like that, or a baby either. She doesn't want them, and anyway how would she have time, considering everything she has to get done? She has a long, though vague, agenda. Nevertheless she feels deprived.

Between two oval hills of pink granite there's a small crescent of beach. The boys, wearing their bathing suits (as they never do on canoe trips but only around the camp where they might be seen by girls), are doing their laundry, standing up to their knees and swabbing their wet T-shirts and underpants with yellow bars of Sunlight soap. This only happens when they run out of clothes, or when the stench of dirty socks in the cabin becomes too overpowering. Darce the counselor is supervising, stretched out on a rock, taking the sun on his already tanned torso and smoking a fag. It's forbidden to smoke in front of the campers but he knows this bunch won't tell. To be on the safe side he's furtive about it, holding the cigarette down close to the rock and sneaking quick puffs.

Something hits Donny in the side of the head. It's Ritchie's wet underpants, squashed into a ball. Donny throws them back and soon there's an underpants war. Monty refuses to join in, so he becomes the common target. "Sod off!" he yells.

"Cut it out, you pinheads," Darce says. But he isn't really paying attention: he's seen something else, a flash of blue uniform, up among the trees. The waitresses aren't supposed to be over here on this side of the island. They're supposed to be on their own dock, having their afternoon break.

Darce is up among the trees now, one arm braced against a trunk. A conversation is going on; there are murmurs. Donny knows it's Ronette, he can tell by the shape, by the color of the hair. And here he is, with his wash-board ribs exposed, his hairless chest, throwing underpants around like a kid. He's disgusted with himself.

Monty, outnumbered but not wanting to admit defeat, says he needs to take a crap and disappears along the path to the outhouse. By now Darce is nowhere in sight. Donny captures Monty's laundry, which is already finished and wrung out and spread neatly on the hot rock to dry. He starts tossing it up into a jack pine, piece by piece. The others, delighted, help him. By the time Monty gets back, the tree is festooned with Monty's underpants and the other boys are innocently rinsing.

They're on one of the pink granite islands, the four of them: Joanne and Ronette, Perry and Darce. It's a double date. The two canoes have been pulled half out of the water and roped to the obligatory jack pines, the fire has done its main burning and is dying down to coals. The western sky is still peach-toned and luminous, the soft ripe juicy moon is rising, the evening air is warm and sweet, the waves wash gently against the rocks. It's the Summer Issue, thinks Joanne. *Lazy Daze. Tanning Tips. Shipboard Romance.*

Joanne is toasting a marshmallow. She has a special way of doing it: she holds it close to the coals but not so close that it catches fire, just close enough so that it swells up like a pillow and browns gently. Then she pulls off the toasted skin and eats it, and toasts the white inside part the same way, and peeling it down to the core. She licks marshmallow goo off her fingers and stares pensively into the shifting red glow of the coal bed. All of this is a way of ignoring or pretending to ignore what is really going on.

There ought to be a teardrop, painted and static, on her cheek. There ought to be a caption: *Heartbreak.* On the spread-out groundsheet right behind her, his knee touching her back, is Perry, cheesed off with her because she won't neck with him. Off behind the rocks, out of the dim circle of firelight, are Ronette and Darce. It's the third week in July and by now they're a couple, everyone knows it. In the rec hall she wears his sweatshirt with the St. Jude's crest; she smiles more these days, and even laughs when the other girls tease her about him. During this teasing Hilary does not join in. Ronette's face seems rounder, healthier, its angles smoothed out as if by a hand. She is less watchful, less diffident. She ought to have a caption too, thinks Joanne. *Was I Too Easy?*

There are rustlings from the darkness, small murmurings, breathing noises. It's like a movie theater on Saturday night. Group grope. *The young in one another's arms.* Possibly, thinks Joanne, they will disturb a rattlesnake.

Perry puts a hand, tentatively, on her shoulder. "Want me to toast you a marshmallow?" she says to him politely. The frosty freeze. Perry is no consolation prize. He merely irritates her, with his peeling sunburnt skin and begging spaniel's eyes. Her so-called real boyfriend is no help either, whizzing on his train tracks back and forth across the prairies, writing his by-now infrequent inky letters, the image of his face all but obliterated, as if it's been soaked in water.

Nor is it Darce she wants, not really. What she wants is what Ronette has: the power to give herself up, without reservation and without commentary. It's that languor, that leaning back. Voluptuous mindlessness. Everything Joanne herself does is surrounded by quotation marks.

"Marshmallows. Geez," says Perry, in a doleful, cheated voice. All that paddling, and what for? Why the hell did she come along, if not to make out?

Joanne feels guilty of a lapse of manners. Would it hurt so much to kiss him?

Yes. It would.

Donny and Monty are on a canoe trip, somewhere within the tangled bush of the mainland. Camp Adanaqui is known for its tripping. For five days they and the others, twelve boys in all, have been paddling across lake after lake, hauling the gear over wave-rounded boulders or through the suck and stench of the moose-meadows at the portage entrances, grunting uphill with the packs and canoes, slapping the mosquitoes off their legs. Monty has blisters, on both his feet and his hands. Donny isn't too sad about that. He himself has a festering sliver. Maybe he will get blood-poisoning, become delirious, collapse and die on a portage, among the rocks and pine needles. That will serve someone right. Someone ought to be made to pay for the pain he's feeling.

The counselors are Darce and Perry. During the days they crack the whip; at night they relax, backs against a rock or tree, smoking and supervising while the boys light the fire, carry the water, cook the Kraft Dinners. They both have smooth large muscles which ripple under their tans, they both—by now—have stubbly beards. When everyone goes swimming Donny sneaks covert, envious looks at their groins. They make him feel spindly, and infantile in his own desires.

Right now it's night. Perry and Darce are still up, talking in low voices, poking the embers of the dying fire. The boys are supposed to be asleep. There are tents in case of rain, but nobody's suggested putting them up since the day before yesterday. The smell of grime and sweaty feet and wood smoke is getting too potent at close quarters; the sleeping bags are high as cheese. It's better to be outside, rolled up in the bag, a groundsheet handy in case of a deluge, head under a turned-over canoe.

Monty is the only one who has voted for a tent. The bugs are getting to him; he says he's allergic. He hates canoe trips and makes no secret of it. When he's older, he says, and can finally get his hands on the family boodle, he's going to buy the place from Mr. B. and close it down. "Generations of boys unborn will thank me," he says. "They'll give me a medal." Sometimes Donny almost likes him. He's so blatant about wanting to be filthy rich. No hypocrisy about him, not like some of the other millionaire offshoots, who pretend they want to be scientists or something else that's not paid much.

Now Monty is twisting around, scratching his bites. "Hey Finley," he whispers.

"Go to sleep," says Donny.

"I bet they've got a flask."

"What?"

"I bet they're drinking. I smelled it on Perry's breath yesterday."

"So?" says Donny.

"So," says Monty. "It's against the rules. Maybe we can get something out of them."

Donny has to hand it to him. He certainly knows the angles. At the very least they might be able to share the wealth.

The two of them inch out of their sleeping bags and circle around behind the fire, keeping low. Their practice while spying on the waitresses stands them in good stead. They crouch behind a bushy spruce, watching for lifted elbows or the outlines of bottles, their ears straining.

But what they hear isn't about booze. Instead it's about Ronette. Darce is talking about her as if she's a piece of meat. From what he's implying, she lets him do anything he wants. "Summer sausage" is what he calls her. This is an expression Donny has never heard before, and ordinarily he would think it was hilarious.

Monty sniggers under his breath and pokes Donny in the ribs with his elbow. Does he know how much it hurts, is he rubbing it in? *Donny loves Ronette.* The ultimate grade six insult, to be accused of loving someone. Donny feels as if it's he himself who's been smeared with words, who's had his face rubbed in them. He knows Monty will repeat this conversation to the other boys. He will say Darce has been porking Ronette. Right now Donny detests this word, with its conjuring of two heaving pigs, or two dead but animate uncooked Sunday roasts; although just yesterday he used it himself, and found it funny enough.

He can hardly charge out of the bushes and punch Darce in the nose. Not only would he look ridiculous, he'd get flattened.

He does the only thing he can think of. Next morning, when they're breaking camp, he pinches Monty's binoculars and sinks them in the lake.

Monty guesses, and accuses him. Some sort of pride keeps Donny from denying it. Neither can he say why he did it. When they get back to the island there's an unpleasant conversation with Mr. B. in the dining hall. Or not a conversation: Mr. B. talks, Donny is silent. He does not look at Mr. B. but at the pike's head on the wall, with its goggling voyeur's eye.

The next time the mahogany inboard goes back into town, Donny is in it. His parents are not pleased.

It's the end of summer. The campers have already left, though some of the counselors and all of the waitresses are still here. Tomorrow they'll go down to the main dock, climb into the slow launch, thread their way among the pink islands, heading towards winter.

It's Joanne's half-day off so she isn't in the dining hall, washing the dishes with the others. She's in the cabin, packing up. Her duffle bag is finished, propped like an enormous canvas wiener against her bed; now she's doing her small suitcase. Her paycheck is already tucked inside: two hundred dollars, which is a lot of money.

Ronette comes into the cabin, still in her uniform, shutting the screen door quietly behind her. She sits down on Joanne's bed and lights a cigarette. Joanne is standing there with her folded-up flannelette pajamas, alert: something's going on. Lately, Ronette has returned to her previous taciturn self; her smiles have become rare. In the counselors' rec hall, Darce is again playing the field. He's been circling around Hilary, who's pretending—out of consideration for Ronette—not to notice. Maybe, now, Joanne will get to hear what caused the big split. So far Ronette has not said anything about it.

Ronette looks up at Joanne, through her long yellow bangs. Looking up like that makes her seem younger, despite the red lipstick. "I'm in trouble," she says.

"What sort of trouble?" says Joanne.

Ronette smiles sadly, blows out smoke. Now she looks old. "You know. Trouble."

"Oh," says Joanne. She sits down beside Ronette, hugging the flannelette pajamas. She feels cold. It must be Darce. *Caught in that sensual music.* Now he will have to marry her. Or something. "What're you going to do?"

"I don't know," says Ronette. "Don't tell, okay? Don't tell the others."

"Aren't you going to tell *him?*" says Joanne. She can't imagine doing that, herself. She can't imagine any of it.

"Tell who?" Ronette says.

"Darce."

Ronette blows out more smoke. "Darce," she says. "Mr. Chickenshit. It's not *his.*"

Joanne is astounded, and relieved. But also annoyed with herself: what's gone past her, what has she missed? "It's not? Then whose is it?"

But Ronette has apparently changed her mind about confiding. "That's for me to know and you to find out," she says, with a small attempt at a laugh.

"Well," says Joanne. Her hands are clammy, as if it's her that's in trouble. She wants to be helpful, but has no idea how. "Maybe you could—I don't know." She doesn't know. An abortion? That is a dark and mysterious word, connected with the States. You have to go away. It costs a lot of money. A home for unwed mothers, followed by adoption? Loss washes through her. She foresees Ronette, bloated beyond recognition, as if she's drowned—a sacrifice, captured by her own body, offered up to it. Truncated in some way, disgraced. Unfree. There is something nun-like about this condition. She is in awe. "I guess you could get rid of it, one way or another," she says; which is not at all what she feels. *Whatever is begotten, born, and dies.*

"Are you kidding?" says Ronette, with something like contempt. "Hell, not me." She throws her cigarette on the floor, grinds it out with her heel. "I'm keeping it. Don't worry, my mom will help me out."

"Yeah," says Joanne. Now she has caught her breath; now she's beginning to wonder why Ronette has dumped all this on her, especially since she isn't willing to tell the whole thing. She's beginning to feel cheated, imposed upon. So who's the guy, so which one of them? She shuffles through the faces of the counselors, trying to remember hints, traces of guilt, but finds nothing.

"Anyways," says Ronette, "I won't have to go back to school. Thank the Lord for small mercies, like they say."

Joanne hears bravado, and desolation. She reaches out a hand, gives Ronette's arm a small squeeze. "Good luck," she says. It comes out sounding like something you'd say before a race or an exam, or a war. It sounds stupid.

Ronette grins. The gap in her teeth shows, at the side. "Same to you," she says.

* * *

Eleven years later Donny is walking along Yorkville Avenue, in Toronto, in the summer heat. He's no longer Donny. At some point, which even he can't remember exactly, he has changed into Don. He's wearing sandals, and a white Indian-style shirt over his cut-off jeans. He has longish hair and a beard. The beard has come out yellow, whereas the hair is brown. He likes the effect: WASP Jesus or Hollywood Viking, depending on his mood. He has a string of wooden beads around his neck.

This is how he dresses on Saturdays, to go to Yorkville; to go there and just hang around, with the crowds of others who are doing the same. Sometimes he gets high, on the pot that circulates as freely as cigarettes did once. He thinks he should be enjoying this experience more than he actually does.

During the rest of the week he has a job in his father's law office. He can get away with the beard there, just barely, as long as he balances it with a suit. (But even the older guys are growing their sideburns and wearing colored shirts, and using words like "creative" more than they used to.) He doesn't tell the people he meets in Yorkville about this job, just as he doesn't tell the law office about his friends' acid trips. He's leading a double life. It feels precarious, and brave.

Suddenly, across the street, he sees Joanne. He hasn't even thought about her for a long time, but it's her all right. She isn't wearing the tie-dyed or flowing-shift uniform of the Yorkville girls; instead she's dressed in a brisk, businesslike white mini-skirt, with matching suit-jacket top. She's swinging a briefcase, striding along as if she has a purpose. This makes her stand out: the accepted walk here is a saunter.

Donny wonders whether he should run across the street, intercept her, reveal what he thinks of as his true but secret identity. Now all he can see is her back. In a minute she'll be gone.

"Joanne," he calls. She doesn't hear him. He dodges between cars, catches up to her, touches her elbow. "Don Finley," he says. He's conscious of himself standing there, grinning like a fool. Luckily and a little disappointingly, she recognizes him at once.

"Donny!" she says. "My God, you've grown!"

"I'm taller than you," he says, like a kid, an idiot.

"You were then," she says, smiling. "I mean you've grown *up*."

"So have you," says Donny, and they find themselves laughing, almost like equals. Three years, four years between them. It was a large difference, then. Now it's nothing.

So, thinks Joanne, Donny is no longer Donny. That must mean Ritchie is now Richard. As for Monty, he has become initials only, and a millionaire. True, he inherited some of it, but he's used it to advantage; Joanne has tuned in on his exploits now and then, in the business papers. And he got married to Hilary, three years ago. Imagine that. She saw that in the paper too.

They go for coffee and sit drinking it at one of the new, daring, outside tables, under a large, brightly painted wooden parrot. There's an intimacy between them, as if they are old friends. Donny asks Joanne what she's doing. "I live by my wits," she says. "I freelance." At the moment she's writing ad copy. Her face is thinner, she's lost that adolescent roundness; her once nondescript hair has been shaped into a stylish cap. Good enough legs too. You have to have good legs to wear a mini. So many women look stumpy in them, hams in cloth, their legs bulging out the bottom like loaves of white bread. Joanne's legs are out of sight under the table, but Donny finds himself dwelling on them as he never did when they were clearly visible, all the way up, on the waitresses' dock. He'd skimmed over those legs then, skimmed over Joanne altogether. It was Ronette who had held his attention. He is more of a connoisseur, by now.

"We used to spy on you," he says. "We used to watch you skinny-dipping." In fact they'd never managed to see much. The girls had held their towels around their bodies until the last minute, and anyway it was dusk. There would be a blur of white, some shrieking and splashing. The great thing would have been pubic hair. Several boys claimed sightings, but Donny had felt they were lying. Or was that just envy?

"Did you?" says Joanne absently. Then, "I know. We could see the bushes waving around. We thought it was so cute."

Donny feels himself blushing. He's glad he has the beard; it conceals things. "It wasn't cute," he says. "Actually we were pretty vicious." He's remembering the word *pork*. "Do you ever see the others?"

"Not anymore," says Joanne. "I used to see a few of them, at university. Hilary and Alex. Pat sometimes."

"What about Ronette?" he says, which is the only thing he really wants to ask.

"I used to see Darce," says Joanne, as if she hasn't heard him.

Used to see is an exaggeration. She saw him once.

It was in the winter, a February. He phoned her, at *The Varsity* office: that was how he knew where to find her, he'd seen her name in the campus paper. By that time Joanne scarcely remembered him. The summer she'd been a waitress was three years, light-years, away. The railroad-chef boyfriend was long gone; nobody so innocent had replaced him. She no longer wore white bucks, no longer sang songs. She wore turtlenecks and drank beer and a lot of coffee, and wrote cynical exposés of such things as the campus dining facilities. She'd given up the idea of dying young, however. By this time it seemed overly romantic.

What Darce wanted was to go out with her. Specifically, he wanted her to go to a fraternity party with him. Joanne was so taken aback that she said yes, even though fraternities were in political disfavor among the people she traveled with now. It was something she would have to do on the sly, and she did. She had to borrow a dress from her roommate, however. The thing was a semi-formal, and she had not deigned to go to a semi-formal since high school.

She had last seen Darce with sun-bleached hair and a deep glowing tan. Now, in his winter skin, he looked wan and malnourished. Also, he no longer flirted with everyone. He didn't even flirt with Joanne. Instead he introduced her to a few other couples, danced her perfunctorily around the floor, and proceeded to get very drunk on a mixture of grape juice and straight alcohol that the fraternity brothers called Purple Jesus. He told her he'd been engaged to Hilary for over six months, but she'd just ditched him. She wouldn't even say why. He said he'd asked Joanne out because she was the kind of girl you could talk to, he knew she would understand. After that he threw up a lot of Purple Jesus, first onto her dress, then—when she'd led him outside, to the veranda—onto a snowdrift. The color scheme was amazing.

Joanne got some coffee into him and hitched a lift back to the residence, where she had to climb up the icy fire escape and in at a window because it was after hours.

Joanne was hurt. All she was for him was a big flapping ear. Also she was irritated. The dress she'd borrowed was pale blue, and the Purple Jesus would not come out with just water. Darce called the next day to apologize—St. Jude's at least taught manners, of a sort—and Joanne stuck him with the cleaning bill. Even so there was a faint residual stain.

While they were dancing, before he started to slur and reel, she said, "Do you ever hear from Ronette?" She still had the narrative habit, she still wanted to know the ends of stories. But he'd looked at her in complete bewilderment.

"Who?" he said. It wasn't a put-down, he really didn't remember. She found this blank in his memory offensive. She herself might forget a name, a face even. But a body? A body that had been so close to your own, that had generated those murmurings, those rustlings in the darkness, that aching pain—it was an affront to bodies, her own included.

After the interview with Mr. B. and the stuffed pike's head, Donny walks down to the small beach where they do their laundry. The rest of his cabin is out sailing, but he's free now of camp routine, he's been discharged. A dishonorable discharge. After seven summers of being under orders here he can do what he wants. He has no idea what this might be.

He sits on a bulge of pink rock, feet on the sand. A lizard goes across the rock, near his hand, not fast. It hasn't spotted him. Its tail is blue and will come off if grabbed. Skinks, they're called. Once he would have taken joy from this knowledge. The waves wash in, wash out, the familiar heartbeat. He closes his eyes and hears only a machine. Possibly he is very angry, or sad. He hardly knows.

Ronette is there without warning. She must have come down the path behind him, through the trees. She's still in her uniform, although it isn't close to dinner. It's only late afternoon, when the waitresses usually leave their dock to go and change.

Ronette sits down beside him, takes out her cigarettes from some hidden pocket under her apron. "Want a cig?" she says.

Donny takes one and says "Thank you." Not *thanks*, not wordlessly like leather-jacketed men in movies, but "Thank you," like a good boy from St. Jude's, like a suck. He lets her light it. What else can he do? She's got the matches. Gingerly he inhales. He doesn't smoke much really, and is afraid of coughing.

"I heard they kicked you out," Ronette says. "That's really tough."

"It's okay," says Donny. "I don't care." He can't tell her why, how noble he's been. He hopes he won't cry.

"I heard you tossed Monty's binoculars," she says. "In the lake."

Donny can only nod. He glances at her. She's smiling; he can see the heartbreaking space at the side of her mouth: the missing tooth. She thinks he's funny.

"Well, I'm with you," she says. "He's a little creep."

"It wasn't because of him," says Donny, overcome by the need to confess, or to be taken seriously. "It was because of Darce." He turns, and for the first time looks her straight in the eyes. They are so green. Now his hands are shaking. He drops the cigarette into the sand. They'll find the butt tomorrow, after he's gone. After he's gone, leaving Ronette behind, at the mercy of other people's words. "It was because of you. What they were saying about you. Darce was."

Ronette isn't smiling anymore. "Such as what?" she says.

"Never mind," says Donny. "You don't want to know."

"I know anyhow," Ronette says. "That shit." She sounds resigned rather than angry. She stands up, puts both her hands behind her back. It takes Donny a moment to realize she's untying her apron.

When she's got it off she takes him by the hand, pulls gently. He allows himself to be led around the hill of rock, out of sight of anything but the water. She sits down, lies down, smiles as she reaches up, arranges his hands. Her blue uniform unbuttons down the front. Donny can't believe this is happening, to him, in full daylight. It's like sleepwalking, it's like running too fast, it's like nothing else.

"Want another coffee?" Joanne says. She nods to the waitress. Donny hasn't heard her.

"She was really nice to me," he is saying. "Ronette. You know, when Mr. B. turfed me out. That meant a lot to me at the time." He's feeling guilty, because he never wrote her. He didn't know where she lived, but he didn't take any steps to find out. Also, he couldn't keep himself from thinking: *They're right. She's a slut.* Part of him had been profoundly shocked by what she'd done. He hadn't been ready for it.

Joanne is looking at him with her mouth slightly open, as if he's a talking dog, a talking stone. He fingers his beard nervously, wondering what he's said wrong, or given away.

Joanne has just seen the end of the story, or one end of one story. Or at least a missing piece. So that's why Ronette wouldn't tell: it was Donny. She'd been protecting him; or maybe she'd been protecting herself. A fourteen-year-old boy. Ludicrous.

Ludicrous then, possible now. You can do anything now and it won't cause a shock. Just a shrug. Everything is *cool*. A line has been drawn and on the other side of it is the past, both darker and more brightly intense than the present.

She looks across the line and sees the nine waitresses in their bathing suits, in the clear blazing sunlight, laughing on the dock, herself among them; and off in the shadowy rustling bushes of the shoreline, sex lurking dangerously. It had been dangerous, then. It had been sin. Forbidden, secret, sullying. *Sick with desire.* Three dots had expressed it perfectly, because there had been no ordinary words for it.

On the other hand there had been marriage, which meant wifely checked aprons, play-pens, a sugary safety.

But nothing has turned out that way. Sex has been domesticated, stripped of the promised mystery, added to the category of the merely expected. It's just what is done, mundane as hockey. It's celibacy these days that would raise eyebrows.

And what has become of Ronette, after all, left behind in the past, dappled by its chiaroscuro, stained and haloed by it, stuck with other people's adjectives? What is she doing, now that everyone else is following in her footsteps? More practically: did she have the baby, or not? Keep it or not? Donny, sitting sweetly across the table from her, is in all probability the father of a ten-year-old child, and he knows nothing about it at all.

Should she tell him? The melodrama tempts her, the idea of a revelation, a sensation, a neat ending.

But it would not be an ending, it would only be the beginning of something else. In any case, the story itself seems to her outmoded. It's an archaic story, a folk-tale, a mosaic artifact. It's a story that would never happen now.

[1991]

Dorothy Parker. Used by permission of Viking Penguin, a division of Penguin Books U.S.A., Inc.

Ruth Rendell, "The Convolvulus Clock." From *The New Girlfriend and Other Stories* by Ruth Rendell. Copyright © 1985 by Kingsmarkham Enterprises, Ltd. Reprinted by permission of Pantheon Books, a division of Random House, Inc.

Leslie Marmon Silko, "Lullaby." Copyright © 1981 by Leslie Marmon Silko. Reprinted from *Storyteller* by Leslie Marmon Silko, published by Seaver Books, New York, N.Y.

Muriel Spark, "The House of the Famous Poet." From *The Stories of Muriel Spark.* Copyright © 1985 by Copyright Administration Limited.

Anne Tyler, "Teenage Wasteland." Reprinted by permission of Russell & Volkening as agents for the author. Copyright © 1983 by Anne Tyler.

Helena Maria Viramontes, "Snapshots." © 1985 by Helena Maria Viramontes. Reprinted by permission of Arte Publico Press, Houston.

Alice Walker, "Coming Apart." From *You Can't Keep a Good Woman Down.* Copyright © 1980 by Alice Walker. Reprinted by permission of Harcourt Brace Jovanovich, Inc.

Fay Weldon, "Angel, All Innocence." Copyright © Fay Weldon 1977. This story first appeared in *The Thirteenth Ghost Book* published by Barrie & Jenkins, 1977, and was first published in Great Britain in anthology form by Hodder & Stoughton, 1981, in a collection of stories entitled *Watching Me, Watching You.*

Edith Wharton, "The Other Two." From *Roman Fever and Other Stories* by Edith Wharton (New York: Charles Scribner's Sons, 1964), first published in *Collier's,* February 13, 1904.

Virginia Woolf, "Lappin and Lapinova." From *A Haunted House and Other Stories* by Virginia Woolf. Copyright 1944 and renewed 1972 by Harcourt Brace Jovanovich, Inc. Reprinted by permission of the publisher. Used also with permission of the Estate of Virginia Woolf and The Hogarth Press.

Wakako Yamauchi, "And the Soul Shall Dance." Reprinted by permission of the author.